MR. JOAB'S WILL

SONNY CLANTON

To Omar,
my Vardaman, Ms. friend!!
Best wishes!!!

[signature]
1/12/19

SP

Sabougla Press

Library of Congress Cataloging-in-Publication Data applied for

ISBN 978-1-7322644-0-3
Copyright© 2018 by Sonny Clanton
All Rights Reserved
First Edition

Cover Design by Brandi Doane McCann

SP

Sabougla Press

SONNY CLANTON

MR. JOAB'S WILL

ACKNOWLEDGEMENTS

To: My office staff, Amy Harmon and Alicia Havens for their support in getting the book to print.

And to Carol Easley and Sandra Hamilton who wisely and tactfully critiqued my work.

MR. JOAB'S WILL

CHAPTER 1
REGRETS

The snowstorm moved in before daylight and dropped five inches of heavy, wet snow by sunrise. The weatherman predicted the snow would continue to fall steadily for the rest of the day and all through the night. Before the storm ended, the overnight temperatures would plunge to zero or below. This weather was unusual for Mississippi.

The substitute mail carrier, Pete Sellers, struggled to see through the falling snow to where the loop road split off from the county highway on this Friday, December 31. The post office would be closed until Monday because of the holiday. He had been notified by the postmaster the night before that the regular carrier had chosen to take personal leave on Friday. Pete mused, as he fought the steering wheel of the pickup to stay in the center of the icy road, that Frank Odom always took off from work on days when he suspected the mail would be heavy or that weather conditions would be adverse. Pete had picked up the part-time job to supplement his work as a title abstracter for a local finance company. He had considered leaving the postal service because of the irregularity of the work. But then his wife had lost her job when her company shifted its operations to Mexico. The family needed all the income he could produce.

Pete had been monitoring the weather reports throughout the morning. The overhead thermometer on the pickup cab showed 20°. Pete turned the heater vents upward to keep the snow from freezing on the windshield. He only had three more mail boxes to serve on this leg of the rural route. The loop road for which he was searching split from the paved road, circled by Mr. Joab McMath's house, and then came back out on top of the hill a half mile ahead. The other two boxes were on the opposite side of the county road about a mile further away. Then the mail route would be finished for the day.

The falling snow slowed, and Pete saw his turn. The snow was not disturbed; so he knew no one had been in or out from Mr. Joab's house since the storm had begun. The pickup slid as he left the paved road. He turned into the slide without tapping his brakes, and the vehicle gained traction as it climbed the hill. As Pete started up the hill, he noticed that a large limb had broken off an oak tree snapping the telephone line going to Mr. Joab's house. He would report the break when he got to the mail drop at Four Points.

Joab McMath lived alone in a rambling two-story white house over the hill and around a curve. The house, with a front porch across the entire front, was set back about thirty yards from the road. A tall magnolia sat in the corner of the yard, partially shielding the front door of the house from the mailbox. An open pasture was directly across the road from the house, and between the back side of the pasture and the county highway was a stand of hardwood trees.

Mr. Joab lost Georgianne, his wife of fifty years, to cancer twelve summers earlier. He still felt the sting of the loss. They had been very close all the years of their marriage. To the disappointment of both, no children had been born to them. As they grew older, that fact drew them even closer; they had no one but each other.

Mr. Joab was eighty-five years old, a tall slender man, with slightly stooped shoulders and in reasonably good health. He was a retired timber buyer and had worked for himself ever since the age of twenty-five. He had joined the U. S. Marine Corps during World War II and had seen action on Saipan. Mr. Joab had been wounded on Okinawa about a week before hostilities ended. His unit had been involved in a mopping-up operation in an area that was behind the front line. A Japanese sniper had shot him through his left forearm, with the bullet striking a tattoo of a partially naked mermaid. The medics snickered when they saw how the bullet centered the navel of the sea nymph. Joe Tibbs, Mr. Joab's corporal, had exclaimed, "Joab, you'll get two Purple Hearts! One for you and one for your girlfriend."

After Joab came home from the war and settled into the routine of civilian life, the fact that he had a visible tattoo bothered him. He regretted ever having gone to the tattoo parlor in San Diego with his Marine buddies. To hide the tattoo he wore shirts with long sleeves, even in hot weather, until he got to the age that it didn't matter anymore.

The postmaster had instructed Pete to watch the rate of accumulation of the falling snow and make his own decision of whether or not to cut the route short. Pete was to run the route backwards so he could at least pick up the mail at Four Points where the postal service had a drop box. The village of Four Points was two miles west of where Mr. Joab lived. Pete, after listening to the weather reports on his radio and watching how the snowfall had increased, decided that the roads would be impassible before he could run the full mail route.

He was driving up the loop road two hours early.

Mr. Joab got up at his usual time on this Friday morning. He prepared a breakfast of oatmeal, pancakes with berries and cream, and his favorite coffee. After placing the dishes in the sink, he mixed a can of sunflower seed and cracked corn to put in the bird feeders outside the kitchen door in the back yard. As he was scraping the snow off the feeder, song birds filled the limbs on the nearby trees and bushes, chirping with joy. They sensed the severity of the approaching snowstorm knowing that the whole landscape would soon be iced over, and their survival would depend on the feed put out by Mr. Joab.

After filling the feeders, Mr. Joab started up the back steps. He was trying to be careful. At that moment a red-tailed hawk swooped down out of the gray sky toward the birds sitting on the tree limbs. The songbirds created a sudden, loud racket at the sight of the airborne danger, startling Mr. Joab in a mid-step. His planted foot on the icy top step twisted out, causing him to fall sideways on top of a large rock that was a border for a flower bed. He felt his hip snap with a sharp crack. The feeling in his right leg was lost.

Mr. Joab passed out from the pain of his injury. When he came to, he was covered in an inch of frosty snow; and the clothes on his underside were damp. He grimly thought, "I'm in bad trouble. I need to get to the telephone."

Mr. Joab realized that all his resolve would be needed to drag himself, through all his pain, into his house. He was able to grasp the icy steps and pull upwards to the kitchen door. It took a while, for he would sometimes slip and lose ground. The door had been left ajar; he was able to push it open with his head. He grabbed the corner of the counter and pulled himself into the kitchen. The effort left him exhausted. He lay on his back staring at the ceiling, gasping deep breaths of air into his lungs. As he lay there, he began to assess his situation. He had to get to the local hospital as soon as possible.

He would have to crawl from the kitchen, through the small dining room, and into the front room to the telephone. After resting, he began the journey across the floor which was made of four-inch wide heart pine planks. He noticed how the varnish was more worn than he had remembered. When winter broke, he would have Earl Ray Fowler, his carpenter friend, strip the floors and put down a new coat of varnish.

By the time he made it to the small wooden stand upon which sat the old, rotary dial telephone, he was fatigued, his hands were raw, and his nails were broken and bleeding. He grasped the cord to the telephone, and it crashed onto the floor. He began to dial 911. When he put the receiver to his ear, he panicked. There was no dial tone. The phone was dead. Mr. Joab jiggled the button, but to no avail. As he lay there on his side with his chest heaving, he slowly managed to control the rising panic. Mr. Joab had been very resourceful all his life and, as a result, had been able to get out of some jams in which a lesser man would have failed. Mr. Joab realized he was in the most trouble of anytime in his life, but he had to be calm and figure out a plan of action.

He could hear the Seth Thomas clock on the fireplace mantle ticking as the pendulum swung slowly and regularly. Then the clock began to strike the hour. Mr. Joab noted that Frank Odom would be by on his mail route in two hours. Mr. Joab had observed how Frank was a creature of habit and had been coming by his box at the same time for years. He lay there thinking if he could get to the front door before Frank gets here and have it open, he could flag him. Frank always looks toward the house as he goes by.

It took a great deal of mental effort to make his limbs respond to move his body toward the front door. Just as he made it to the door and was reaching upward to grasp the doorknob, he heard a vehicle, making a muffled sound in the snow, go by the house. He pulled himself up to the windows on the top half of the door in time to see the back of Pete Sellers' truck disappear around the curve in the road.

"No!" he moaned.

He fell heavily to the floor. Tears began to stream down his rugged face. A lifetime of regret came to his thoughts: things he should have done but hadn't and the things he did but shouldn't have. Memories, old and new, began to flood his mind. He remembered his childhood and how hard his mother had struggled through the Great Depression just to provide him with shoes and a few clothes to wear to school; the days at school one year when he had no lunch at all; how he would hide at the back of the schoolhouse away from where the other students gathered to eat from their pails so nobody would notice that he had no food; how his father had been lazy and no good, more interested in hunting and fishing, rather than working for money or barter to support the family; how his mother had cried her pillow wet at night, worrying how she was going to feed him the next day; how sad his wife had been for never having children; how, in his youth, he had failed to visit his old grandmother more often; the tattoo.

———————

Mr. Joab was shivering. The fire in the wood heater had gone out. He had been passed out again for a while. He lay there listening to the wind gusting through the barren tops of the oak trees across the road in front of the house. Then to the mournful sound of the wind whistling around the corner of the house as it had during every winter storm of years past. For the first time in his life, he was deeply afraid. There was no more time in the bottle.

Mr. Joab realized he had to make one long, last crawl. He had left a matter undone.

———————

He completed his task and relaxed. For a while his smoky breaths matched the ticks of the clock on the mantle. As he listened, the thought came to Mr. Joab that he would never wind the clock again. Slowly, the rhythm of his breathing began to lag. Then to stop. Forever. The pendulum continued its swing, back and forth, paying a tribute to its keeper.

CHAPTER 2
THE SHOWSHOES

The snowstorm ended early Saturday afternoon. The winds had blown straight east from Texas, intercepting the moist air from the Gulf causing the snow to fall furiously. A total of fifteen inches rested over the countryside. The old-timers called the covering an "ice cream" snow. The trees, buildings, and all else were covered completely, giving the whole world the appearance of one large bowl of white, fluffy ice cream. The wind was still howling, now coming at a steady gale from the north. The temperature had dropped to five degrees on Friday night and to minus nine degrees on Sunday morning, which was near the record low of Chicago. No one was surprised: there was really nothing between Mississippi and the North Pole except an occasional, four-strand barbed wire fence.

Dark gray, heavy clouds stayed overhead all day Sunday scurrying about as directed by the winds. The wind chill was measured by the local weather recorder at minus twenty-five degrees. No wildlife moved all day Saturday and Sunday. The birds and 4-legged animals had anticipated the storm and were deep inside their respective covers.

The only people who stirred outside their homes were those who had to, such as law enforcement officers and utility crews. Power lines were down all around the county, and the repairmen struggled to get the lines to the hospitals in Baxter and Central City back in operation. The icy roads were too treacherous for unnecessary traffic. The few souls who had the foresight to buy tire chains were able to move about easily. And not surprisingly, there was only one pair of snowshoes in the entire county, owned by the respectable high school history teacher, Sherman Tims. On a lark he had ordered the shoes from L. L. Bean a month earlier while drinking red wine by his fireside. He was trying to forget Rita Arnwine, who had dropped him after months of steady dating.

On that cold rainy night, Sherman sat by the fire and reflected on how his relationship with Rita had begun. Rita had moved into the county to work as the school counselor at the Cade County Education Central Office in Poston just after she graduated from Ole Miss. She was from Vicksburg, but Sherman had grown up in Cade County, coming from an old and respected family. Both were in their early twenties. Sherman had not dated much through high school and college but had been smitten by Rita from the first day he saw her. She was a pretty, slender red head. Her hair color was the perfect red and her body was such, that in Sherman's mind, if one could make female bodies, hers would be the pattern. Even though Sherman could hardly take his eyes from her, he had been reluctant to ask her out. He had gotten word from a college friend of his that Rita had been considered "fast" while she pursued her twin degrees in sociology and psychology. Sherman and Rita were the only single people in the school system except for the old maid librarian, Miss Maude Phillips. Sherman's fascination with Rita had not gone unnoticed by the faculty. Mr. Phil Mayo, the seventy-year old principal, cornered Sherman one day outside the school store at recess. He sensed the reason for Sherman's shyness toward asking Rita for a date.

Mr. Mayo said, "Sherman, it's time you quit looking for the perfect woman. You need to get real with your standards and also hope that Rita will lower hers! Ask the woman out!"

With those instructions, Sherman worked up enough courage at 5:30 one Friday evening to call Rita. The only idea for a date that he could come up with was to ask her if she would like to ride with him to Sleazey's, a joint just across the county line in Gallatin County, to get some beer. One of Sherman's favorite pastimes was to ice down a cooler full of beer and ride around with a couple of his buddies on back roads at night. That was party time! Drinking cold beer, smoking, and listening to the radio.

To his surprise, Rita said, "That sounds like a great idea. Would you give me thirty minutes to clean up?"

Sherman consented. He could hardly believe his luck! He had just known that she would turn him down. Exactly thirty minutes later he knocked on the door of Rita's half of a duplex on the north side of town. Sherman nearly fell off the steps when the door opened. Rita was wearing a low-cut blouse and the tightest pair of jeans he had ever seen on a woman. And the perfume she had on smelled so nice! On a later date, after they had become comfortable with each other, Rita confided to Sherman that when she tried on her jeans at the local dress shop, she had to lie on her back on the floor to get the waist snapped. Sherman listened in awe.

Sherman opened the car door for her, and she sweetly thanked him. As he walked around the vehicle, he saw from the corner of his eye a window curtain flip closed on the adjoining end of Rita's duplex. He groaned inwardly. Mrs. Burson, an elderly widow and the town's biggest gossip, lived there. In fact, she owned the building and had been glad to rent the other end to Rita. Sherman knew that before they got back from Gallatin County everyone in town would know he had picked Rita up.

They talked easily during the ride to Sleazy's. The conversation became pleasant, and Sherman found himself relaxing. Rita stayed in the car while he went inside Sleazy's to buy the beer. He decided to get a whole case in the event the night went well or in the event the night became a weekend. Back in the car, he opened a Coors Lite for Rita and wrapped a paper napkin around the bottle for her. They left riding down a favorite road of his which also was the longest route back to town. To him this was a good way to spend time with Rita since he was a little unsure about what to do when they got back to her duplex. Sherman drove slowly. There was no traffic on the isolated road after dark; few people lived in this part of the county.

They were on their third beer when Rita asked, "How far is it to the nearest restroom?"

Sherman was crestfallen. He had not thought about that! He had never ridden around drinking beer with a woman.

He stammered, "Back at town which is about ten miles."

"Okay."

Sherman said, "I'll drive fast. We can be there in ten minutes."

When they arrived at her place he was invited in. He followed her with the cooler, smiling at his good fortune. She came out of the bathroom, put on a Reba McEntire CD, and they listened to the music, talked, and drank beer. Sherman left about midnight. Rita gave him a small kiss on his cheek and said, "I enjoyed your company!" As he backed out of the driveway, he saw the curtains on Mrs. Burson's window flip down again in the glare of his headlights. He wasn't aware that old women stayed up this late.

Early Saturday morning he called Rita to see if she wanted to come to his place that night for steaks. She agreed. He was on cloud nine as he made rounds shopping for food and candles for the table.

The teenage clerk at the register, who was one of his students, remarked, "Mr. Tims, I've never seen you this happy. What's going on?"

Caught off guard, Sherman replied, "Oh, nothing and everything!"

So on the second date, Rita and Sherman stayed the night together. And the next night. He took her home at daylight on Monday morning so she could get ready for school. Sherman knew he should have taken her home Sunday night, but he didn't want her to go, and she didn't want to leave. To his chagrin, the only person they saw on the short trip to her duplex was Mr. Mayo, who was out walking his dog, Precious. Mr. Mayo smiled broadly and gave them a huge wave!

Sherman quickly and deeply fell in love with Rita. When his friend reminded him that Rita had been around the block at Ole Miss and that he was being set up for a fool, Sherman cockily replied, "If that's so, all I can say is that I'm putting on track shoes and keeping up with her!" At this point in the romance, he didn't care if Rita had been around the town limits, for that matter!

They dated regularly for nearly a year. Sherman was known to be frugal, and, to the surprise of his fellow teachers, he spent large sums of money on Rita. He regularly took her to the restaurants in Tupelo that were recommended by a college friend who was an architect in the premier firm in town; beach trips to Destin; and shopping sprees to Nashville. The local flower shop became accustomed to delivering peach roses to Rita's duplex each Monday that followed a trip. The town kept track of their relationship. Mrs. Burson, her landlady, was heard to remark to her friends at the beauty shop, "I'll have to give Rita a refund at the end of the month. She is not home most nights."

In October, Sherman took an allowed vacation and went to South Dakota with a group of local hunters for their annual pheasant hunt. He called or texted Rita daily. Because of her, his attention was diverted from hunting, and his usual good shooting was mediocre. He wasn't even interested in going out with the guys at night to the local strip clubs. Sherman was so heartsick from being away from Rita that he decided to fly back to Memphis two days early. He had a buddy pick him up from the airport; they got back to Central City about 4 a.m. Sherman was so exhausted that he slept till noon. Getting out of bed, he eagerly dressed, jumped into his pickup, and drove over to Rita's to surprise her on her lunch hour. As he turned the curve, he saw a yellow Corvette sitting in her drive. He stopped on the side of the road and sat there frozen. Wild thoughts sped through his brain. Who? What's this? He eased by the duplex and noticed a Kentucky license plate on the Corvette with an Ole Miss Alumni sticker on the back window. Sherman quickly jotted down the tag number and drove home. His mind was racing. Maybe it's one of her girl friends from college. He sat on his sofa for most of an hour trying to figure out this situation. Then he decided to call Mrs. Burson. Maybe she knows something. She's probably pulled that curtain off the window keeping an eye on Rita.

He knew Mrs. Burson didn't really like him because of the time in high school when he had loaned his pickup to a classmate, Ronnie, whose vehicle was in the shop for repairs. Sherman found out later that Ronnie and some of his pals, before he returned the pickup, rolled Mrs. Burson's yard with toilet paper late one night. The next morning, Mrs. Burson irately surveyed her now white lawn, shrubs, and trees. Being stingy and not wanting the paper to waste, she got busy re-rolling the paper. As she moved across her yard, she noticed an envelope lying next to a prize rosebush that was addressed to Sherman. The envelope had blown out of the back of the pickup when the boys left the scene. Mrs. Burson made a bee line into her duplex and called Sherman's parents and complained. She would not accept their explanation of who the real culprits were.

Reluctantly, Sherman dialed her number. She had caller identification and answered, "Why hello, Sherman. Are you home early? Did you kill any of those beautiful song birds in South Dakota?"

He ignored that and asked, "Uh, Mrs. Burson, do you know who owns the Corvette that is parked at Rita's?"

Mrs. Burson replied, "Oh no, not at all. But he has been here since just after you left." Sherman's heart sank at the word *he*.

17

Mrs. Burson happily gossiped, "And he sure is cute. But not as good looking as his buddy! And Rita must think so too, for she sure does smile when they hug her!"

Sherman's heart fell into his shoes. Two of them! No! How could she do this to me? After this whole year.

He dropped the phone hearing Mrs. Burson say, "Oh, Sherman, have a nice day!"

Sherman paced the floor trying to think what to do. Then he remembered the license plate. He leaned on his friend Harley Rogers at the tax office. He called Harley and asked if he would run the tag number.

Harley said, "Sure, Sherman. What are you doing home early? Did y'all kill many birds?"

Then he answered, "That number belongs to a Bayen Wilson, address 501 Sugar Lane, Owensboro, Kentucky. And there is no lien on the car."

Sherman thanked Harley and hung up. He felt better because he now had some needed information on this situation. He turned his computer on and went to People Search. The name appeared showing an age of twenty-five. Sherman saw that he was going to have to pay $29.00 to get any detailed information of this person. He was so desperate to get a line on this guy that he would have gladly paid $229.00! He keyed his Visa number in, and the search soon appeared. Mr. Bayen Wilson had graduated from Ole Miss the same day Rita did. He was a member of Kappa Alpha fraternity and Pecan Valley Country Club. He had a condo in Boca Raton, Florida, and was partner with his brother and father in a holding company that owned pizza franchises in ninety-three locations in the Southeastern United States.

Sherman was in agony the remainder of the week. He could hardly sleep, and when he did, it was fitful. Arising early each morning, he would get into his pickup and ride by Rita's place only to see the same thing: the yellow Corvette parked beside Rita's little black Nissan. Since Rita worked most days at the central education office at Poston, she had to leave home earlier than Sherman, who taught at the high school only a few blocks from his house. Sherman would drive by again later to see her car gone and the Corvette unmoved. At lunch Sherman would see the Corvette still there, and it would also be there in the afternoon after Rita came home from work. The situation was driving him crazy. He talked to her each night but never asked about the yellow car. She was the same old Rita, but she wouldn't come over for the next few nights. When she did, he asked who was staying at her place. She explained that it was an old college classmate whose family was interested in buying the local bank, and he had a young bank officer with him. Sherman's jealousy came to the surface. He accused Rita of having an affair with two men at the same time. The argument became huge, and Rita left his house crying. When Sherman dialed her number, Rita would hang up and leave the phone off the hook.

In their last conversation, Rita had screamed at Sherman, "You need to grow up!!"

They hadn't spoken since.

As thoughts about Rita faded, Sherman was thumbing through the Bean catalog looking at their products. When the bottle of wine was emptied, he was on the page that listed the snowshoes. He had always wanted a pair but thought it unwise to spend money on something that might not ever be used. But then again, he might just leave Cade County to forget about Rita. Maine or Montana would be good escapes, and a pair of snowshoes could be used in either place. The snowshoes would be his ticket to freedom from Rita and Cade County. Sherman wrote out the order and mailed it the next day.

CHAPTER 3
AN UNSETTLING DISCOVERY

At daylight on Monday morning, seventy-five year old Wade Sumrall, the chief deputy sheriff of Cade County, sat in his idling car in front of Sherman's house. The thermometer read minus two degrees. The day was gray and the wind was high and still blowing in from the north. Wade had on boots, heavy woolen socks, insulated underwear, canvas pants, a woolen shirt, and a hat. His build was rugged with large hands and a stout torso. His thighs were thick as tree trunks. Even at his age, Wade was hard as nails. A deep scar, a result from fighting Chinese soldiers in hand-to-hand combat in the Korean War, jagged down the left side of his face. Women considered him handsome.

Wade had been a deputy in Cade County for thirty-five years. After being deputy for eight years, he had, against his better judgment, let himself be talked into running for the sheriff's office by some friends who didn't like the front runner in the race. Wade had been soundly beaten at the polls, learning first hand that there was a wide difference in being poplar and being voted for. To the surprise of the voters, the newly elected sheriff kept Wade on his staff. John Dorsey sensed the reason for Wade's entry into the race but realized that Wade was too valuable not to keep.

Wade was a Korean War veteran who had lied about his age to join the Marines. He had enlisted just after high school was out in 1950 and was sent to Paris Island, South Carolina, for boot camp. After basic training, he was assigned to the 1st Marine Division in San Diego. The unit was sent to Korea and was involved in the fighting at the Chosin Reservoir in late 1950.

As the car heater struggled to warm up the air around the front seat, Wade drank hot coffee from his thermos. His thoughts drifted back to 1950 and what had happened at Chosin. He shivered, but not from the cold in Mississippi. After all these years, the memories had not diminished. He remembered how the crowd at Lola's coffee shop in Central City this morning had been complaining of the cold. He voiced these thoughts as he rubbed his hands together, "Hell, they don't know what cold is. How about so cold that when you spit, the saliva froze before it hit the ground? Or the only way to have a fire was to light the gasoline that had been poured on a pyramid of small rocks. Or when your rifle action was so frozen that you had to piss on the metal to thaw it."

A month ago when Sherman's snowshoes had arrived at the post office, Ms. Jonas, the clerk, had noticed that the corner of the wrapper was torn. Curious as she always was, she peeked inside and saw the snowshoes. Ms. Jonas had always suspected Sherman of being a nut, from hearing about his habit of coming to history class dressed like the figure that was the subject of his lecture; the showshoes confirmed her opinion. When Wade came to the window about an hour later to mail a letter, she blabbed her discovery to him.

At this morning's 4:00 a.m. meeting of Sheriff Grady Powers and his staff, Wade had suddenly got the idea of using Sherman and the snowshoes. The sheriff had announced that the county's five supervisors were in the process of having their crews clear the main county roads for traffic. However, they didn't have the manpower or time to clear the secondary roads of the snow and ice. The sheriff wanted his staff to get with the county's first responders and attempt to make contact with residents who lived off the main roads to see if they were all right. All the telephone lines were down, as were most of the power lines, which prevented those who had discharged cell phones from making calls.

Each deputy and responder had been assigned a section to make their contacts. Wade had drawn what had been named Sector Nine, just east of Four Points. In this area were some long, winding back roads that would have deep snow. Since the school was closed, he had come up with the idea of having Sherman ride along. Instead of turning off onto a driveway and risking the vehicle becoming stuck, he would make Sherman walk on his snowshoes to each house while he stayed in the warm squad car and monitored the radio. Wade made the call to Sherman. Sleepily, Sherman agreed to help, thinking how miserable the task would be in the extreme cold but at least he could break in his gear.

Sherman's door opened, and he came out rubbing his eyes. He was warmly dressed, and had his snowshoes in hand. He threw them on the back seat as he got inside.

"How's your love life, young Mr. Tims?" Wade cheerily asked.

Sherman glared at him as he answered, "I was going to sleep late, but not now, thanks to you!"

Wade slyly asked, "Been losing sleep about something?"

"Watch out!" Sherman snarled.

Wade smiled as he backed out of the drive. "Sort of frosty today isn't it?"

"You got that right!"

He handed Sherman a brown bag containing donuts, biscuits, and sausage. "Pour yourself some hot coffee. You're going to need it before the morning is out."

Wade headed down Highway 9 to Four Points, about ten miles away. They passed Mississippi State Highway Department crews spreading asphalt rock on icy bridges. Along the way, they saw several vehicles off the pavement in the ditch. Their windows were covered with ice, indicating they had been there a while. Wade had to drive slowly. What traffic there was had stayed in the center of the road, making furrows for two tires. When cars met each other, both had to give way, taking up one furrow in the middle while making a new one on the outside until the vehicles safely passed.

Sherman drank his coffee, thinking now what a stupid move that had been ordering the snowshoes. He wondered how Wade knew he had them. Sherman had been sober when the shoes arrived. He thought about returning them; Mississippi had not had a snow deep enough to use snowshoes in forty years. It was uncanny how Wade came up with information. Wade seemed to know who was about to commit a crime before he had a chance. He could look at someone and read his mind.

Sherman dreaded the day that lay ahead. He had tromped through the forests in Mt. Ranier National Park on snowshoes several times. Hiking in the snow could be very tiring if you were out of practice. But Wade had explained how necessary it was to find out if stranded people were okay, and Sherman did have students that he was concerned about who lived in Sector Nine.

Wade made the turn off the state highway onto County Road 404 without difficulty. He stopped at the end of the driveway at the first house and waited while Sherman put on the shoes and hiked to the front door. Wade watched him all the way. He was surprised at how effortlessly Sherman walked on top of the snow. Someone in the house opened the door and became engaged in a conversation with Sherman. Sherman was breathing easily when he got back to the car.

The second house was about twice as far from the road as the first one and Sherman's report was the same. Everybody in both houses was in good shape. The occupants had plenty of food and water for the rest of the week. Sherman didn't have to go to the third house. The Jenkins boys lived there. Both Chad and Eric were seniors in high school and were Sherman's students. They were standing at the edge of the road, and when Wade stopped, they pelted the squad car with snowballs. To the boys, it was funny, but when Wade hit the blue lights, they dropped the snowballs in their hands. Sherman rolled the window down and asked if the family needed anything.

Eric replied, "No. We're okay. We hope school will be out for weeks."

"Me too!" Sherman laughed.

As they pulled away, Wade noticed the snow was a little deeper on this segment of the road. When they came to the end of the loop road that went to Mr. Joab's, Wade spied a massive red oak tree that had fallen across the road just up the hill. He could see the telephone wires pinned underneath. He figured the other end of the road would be blocked the same way, so he told Sherman to walk up and check on Mr. Joab. The wind had drifted soft snow across the loop road, and Sherman was sinking somewhat as he headed up the hill. Wade knew it would be a while before Sherman would get back. He called the dispatcher and found that all the first responders were busy, but so far all their reports had been uneventful: just severe cold and deep snow. Wade suspected it would be the weekend before conditions would be even close to normal.

As he sat in the car and watched Sherman disappear over the hill, Wade remembered a trek he had made in the cold and snow, half a world away in the Hudong-ni area of Korea on December 2, 1950. He had been a corporal in the 1st Marine Division. His patrol had been sent from

Hagaru-ri to assist retreating army soldiers who had been routed by Chinese troops that had unexpectedly crossed the Korean border.

Five days earlier, a large force of Chinese had engaged the 7th Infantry Division at Linchiang. The 7th had already moved through the 1st Marine Division units and were ahead on a drive to the Korea/China border. No resistance was expected, but U. S. intelligence had failed to discover the large army of Chinese troops massing for attack. When they struck the U. S. forces, the attack became a disaster.

The 7th's advance was stopped in its tracks. To make matters worse, a piercing wind, which never ceased, set in from the north, and the temperature dropped to twenty-seven degrees below zero. A snowstorm left twelve inches of snow in the flat places. The wind shifted the snow to waist-deep in the ditches and gullies. Wade's patrol had moved along the eastern shore of the Chosin Reservoir. The temperature had frozen the water, so that the ice was thick enough to support soldiers but not heavy vehicles. A motorized task force of Marines was advancing north on an inland road, but foot patrols were needed in areas of the Reservoir that were too rugged for vehicles.

The patrol of one officer and ten marines had left the ice of the Chosin and made its way into the barren hills. The flat places between the low hills resembled the Alaska tundra. Wade shivered as he remembered how cold and desolate those hills had been. About four miles inland at 1400 hours they made contact with twelve U. S. soldiers led by a staff sergeant. Of the twelve soldiers, all but two were wounded. Three, whose wounds were severe, were being assisted by other soldiers. As the two units stopped to rest and assess their situation, Wade was shocked at their exhaustion. The soldiers told how they had fought for forty hours without sleep and food.

The group had hardly begun the walk back to the reservoir when they rounded a hill and were captured by a larger Chinese patrol. The soldiers dropped their weapons for they were overwhelmed. The Chinese marched them five miles to …..

"What the hell?" exclaimed Wade as he stared up the road.

His eyes widened and his jaw dropped. Sherman was racing down the hill as fast as he could in the snowshoes!

When Sherman came to the fallen tree he leaped high to clear it, but the tip of his right shoe caught the trunk; and he fell head first into the snow, disappearing from sight. Wade jumped out of the car and ran toward Sherman, his big legs pushing through the snow. He grabbed Sherman by the shoulders, pulling him into a sitting position.

"What's wrong?" he asked.

Sherman couldn't say anything until he wiped snow from his face. Gasping for breath he exclaimed, "My God, Wade, it's awful! Mr. Joab has frozen to death! You should see him."

Wade jerked him upright and said, "Come on."

Wade didn't wait for Sherman. He broke into a gait that wasn't a walk or a jog, but his lurching movements were effective. Wade reflected that this was not the first time he had shoved snow out of the way with his legs. He outdistanced Sherman as he moved up the road, over the hill, and around the curve to the front porch of Mr. Joab's house. The door was standing wide open. He noticed a patch of discolored snow near the end of the sidewalk where Sherman had thrown up.

"So the kid is not as tough as he had his friends and students believe," Wade laughed.

Wade moved into the house. Mr. Joab was lying in the center of the living room on his right side. His limbs were jutting stiffly away from his body in grotesque angles. His mouth was open wide with his tongue outside. His eyeballs bulged so much it appeared they would burst open. There was a large bruise on his head with blood caked in his hair. Wade stared. He could see how the sight would disturb a young man who had probably never seen a dead person. However, he was not unnerved, except that Mr. Joab was his friend, and this was certainly an undignified death for anyone. Wade had seen many bodies of Chinese and American soldiers in worse conditions than this during his service in Korea.

He heard Sherman walk up on the porch. Wade stepped outside. They tried to call 911 on their cell phones but discovered there was no signal. Wade told Sherman to go back to the car and radio the dispatcher for help. Sherman was also instructed to ask that a piece of heavy equipment be sent to clear the tree from the road so the ambulance could travel up to the house. The wood was frozen, and any attempt to cut the tree with a chain saw would be the same as sawing concrete. Sherman followed directions. Wade knew it would be probably an hour before the ambulance would arrive.

While he waited, Wade took a seat in a wooden chair by the wall and rested from the walk. As his breathing became regular, he avoided looking at Mr. Joab. He gazed around the room. Nothing seemed amiss. Wade had visited here several times before and was somewhat familiar with the room. He could hear a piece of loose tin on the nearby barn making a banging sound as the wind moved it to and fro. A draft of colder air coming from the direction of the kitchen hit the back of his neck. Wade moved to that room and saw the kitchen door cracked open.

He peered outside and saw blood on the back steps. A can was nearby lying on its side in the snow with bird feed frozen inside.

Wade looked around and calculated that Mr. Joab had been coming back into the house from feeding the birds when he had somehow fallen. He must have struck his head causing an injury of some degree. He reflected how terrible it was to die alone this way. He could see that Mr. Joab had managed to crawl inside the house. He went back to the living room and discovered that the phone was off the hook. There was blood on the ear piece. Wade jiggled the button but was not able to hear a dial tone. He followed the blood trail on the floor toward the front door and saw a smear on the door knob. He was not sure why Mr. Joab had been trying to get the door open. He was hurt and couldn't have been able to get to anything outside that would help.

Sherman appeared and reported that the call had been made and that help was on its way.

Wade asked, "Was this door open when you got here?"

"No. It was closed tight. I knocked, but when no one answered, I came in and found Mr. Joab. I guess I left the door open when I ran to tell you about this."

"What's that brown spot out there in the snow?"

Sherman looked off and said, "Oh. It must be where some dog hiked his leg and peed."

Wade turned his head to hide his amusement!

The EMT crew soon arrived followed by a squad car. They stood around with grim faces while Sally Ryder, a deputy sheriff, photographed the scene. When she was finished, they loaded Mr. Joab on the stretcher. Sally knew that there would be a closed-casket funeral.

Joe West, the county supervisor, had also followed the ambulance after the equipment operator had moved the tree out of the road. He stood inside the house watching the activity of the EMT crew. As they finished, Wade and Joe discussed what to do about locking the house. The locks on the front and back doors were old and they were rusted tight. They hadn't been used in years. The two of them went out to the barn and found enough pieces of lumber to nail both doors shut.

Joe told Wade and Sherman to get into his pickup and he would give them a lift back to the squad car. As they rode down the hill to the squad car, Joe remarked, "Man, this is awful! It's unreal that a man could freeze to death in Mississippi. I've never seen anything like this!"

He didn't respond when Wade said, "I have. And worse!"

Joe and everyone else in the county knew about Wade's being in the Marines in the Korean War. There had been rumors that Wade had been awarded the Navy Cross. But no one had ever asked Wade about what he had done over there, and he had never talked in public about Korea.

Then Joe asked, as he shifted a chew of tobacco in his cheek, "Does Mr. Joab have any kinfolks anywhere? Who will get this place? And you know, he is supposed to have a lot of money."

Sherman spoke up, "You wouldn't know it by looking at what's inside his house. And his pickup is twenty-five years old. He had to get an antique tag for it when he paid his taxes this year."

Wade gazed out the pickup window in silence as he listened to them.

CHAPTER 4
MISS EMMA

The Tuesday morning meeting of the Cade County's Sheriff's office started at 9:00 sharp. Sheriff Grady Powers was sitting behind the large walnut desk. He was a short, portly man who always wore a suit or a sport jacket and hat. Around the room was Wade Sumrall, the chief deputy, Deputy Jack Early, Deputy Sammy Baker, Deputy Sally Ryder, and the jailer, Mondel Tutor. Everyone was wearing a uniform except Grady. Absent was the staff's other female officer, Darlene Roberts. Her five-year old daughter, Anna Grace, had awakened with a sore throat, so Darlene had taken her to the local clinic. Grady said they would wait a while in case Darlene was able to get Dr. Taylor to see Anna Grace first, so she could make the meeting. This assembly had been called because of Mr. Joab's death last week. His demise had been a shock; he was well known and very popular. The news of his tragic death quickly spread throughout the county. Lola's coffee shop in Central City had set records of coffee sales. Yesterday had been a double bonus for her business: the death and the extreme cold weather.

The officers had cups of hot coffee in their hands, which they were silently sipping as they were engrossed in thought. Jack was chomping on an unlit cigar stub. He desperately wanted to light up, but he knew that the sheriff would have none of that. The cigar smoke would linger on Sheriff Powers' clothes, and he would not be in the good graces of his wife, Emma. She would ask him which deputy had been smoking in the office. Jack chuckled to himself about what had happened six years ago in this very office.

———————————

Jack was the largest deputy on the force. He was over six feet and weighed two hundred fifty pounds without an ounce of fat on his body.

He owned a cattle farm he tended on time away from work. The chores kept him in shape, and he worked out with weights during slack periods on the farm. His thoughts drifted back to that day when the new sheriff had held the first staff meeting of the term.

———————

Sheriff Powers had been elected to the office for the first time ten years ago. He had won by a landslide and had become the best sheriff that Cade County had ever had to that point. Grady loved the job. He had been successful in holding down crime, and he instituted programs to get young people involved in community affairs. Grady had worked with the local churches to take youths along with their teams that went to Mexico to construct church buildings. He enjoyed being sheriff and would have liked to be sheriff until he retired. However, Mississippi had the archaic law that prohibited elected sheriffs from succeeding themselves in office. Grady would have had no problem being re-elected, if the law had permitted. In the final year of his first term, Grady agonized daily about his predicament.

During the last week before the deadline for candidates to qualify to run for state and county offices, a solution to his problem hit him square between the eyes while on patrol near the back side of the county. Being so astounded by this idea, he nearly hit an oncoming car as he swerved across the center line. Grady pulled off to the side of the road to think this new development through. His thoughts twisted and turned, and finally, he began to smile. He would get his wife, Emma, to run for sheriff!

That night after supper, he broached the idea to Emma. Emma was a small, attractive woman. She had a trim figure, wore glasses, and had a lovely smile. She had taught literature and English to juniors and seniors at Central City High for many years. Emma was immensely poplar in the community and was the most respected teacher that had ever been at Central City High. She did not put up with any nonsense or horseplay at the school. Even the boys that caused the most mischief and those girls who would cut up did not dare confront her with their pranks. Though married, she was known to everyone as "Miss Emma." She was revered as a dedicated teacher who went to great lengths to have her students learn, understand, and appreciate American and English Literature.

In order to pass English Literature, she required all her senior students memorize the first thirty lines of the Prologue to *The Canterbury Tales*. Then, one by one, each student had to appear in her classroom during recess and recite the Prologue in Middle English. This requirement, for some reason, struck terror in the hearts of nearly all the students, especially the jocks. The students had the choice of the time for their recitation, but, inevitably, the ones who dreaded this task the worst put it off until the end of the course. This dread worked in favor of Miss Emma in maintaining discipline in her class. No student, with the duty of the future recital on his/her mind, was interested in any kind of activity that would be disrespectful to Miss Emma.

Emma listened with interest as Grady explained his plan. She knew that Grady was devoted to his job and wanted to continue but couldn't because of the old law on the books. They discussed Emma's campaign for sheriff. If elected, she thought that Mr. Mayo, the principal, might excuse her from being at the school after she had taught her classes, all of which were in the morning. Grady could be on the staff as associate chief deputy. Secretly, Grady was thinking that Emma would be sheriff in name only, and he would continue to run the office.

Early the next morning, Emma went to the courthouse and qualified for the office. Sure enough, with her popularity added to that of her husband's, she won the upcoming election by a landslide.

On the first day of Miss Emma's term, Grady and all the deputies were in the sheriff's office for the weekly meeting. The mood was jovial. They had a job for four more years! Jack remembered that they were all sitting in the same chairs that day, as they were this morning, and were all smoking the cigars that Grady had bought them. Mondel, the jailer, was chewing tobacco and spitting in a green soft drink bottle. The lawmen were telling jokes and laughing. They weren't planning on doing anything the rest of the day unless some problem arose. In the meantime, Miss Emma was in the courtroom, along with all the other county elected officials, being sworn in by Circuit Judge Bill Card.

Suddenly, the office door swung open, and Miss Emma walked in proclaiming, "Good morning, deputies! You all should have attended the swearing-in ceremony. That sweet Bill Card was so nice with his remarks. He especially bragged on me. I always appreciate a compliment from a former student. I'm going to send him plenty of business. It's time that crime comes to a halt in this county. And you all are going to be working harder to accomplish that. Including you, Grady. Now get out of my seat and find one of your own."

Grady and the deputies gaped at her! This was unexpected. They thought she would be going back home after being sworn in and that Grady would be running the office just as he had for the past four years. Meekly, Grady got up and went over to sit in an empty chair in the corner. The room was silent. Miss Emma took her seat in the chair Grady had vacated and rolled up to the desk.

"Now," she said, "let's all get on the same page. Mondel, you get rid of that nasty tobacco and your spit bottle, and the rest of you dump those stinking cigars. Tobacco is not healthy."

The guys chorused, "Yes, Ma'am, Miss Emma!" They quickly snuffed the cigars, and Mondel went out into the hall to trash his spit bottle.

The remainder of the morning was spent with Miss Emma going over what she expected from each of them. Patrol schedules were set. To their dismay, they were ordered to file a written report with her each Friday afternoon of what each had encountered that week. Grady had never required any reports. Emma said she expected the grammar in them to be correct.

"After all," she said, "most of you and your spouses were my students!"

Jack remembered that she had him drive her on patrol on every single road in the county. They stopped at all the general stores, the feed stores, the saw shop in Four Points, the coffee shops, and any place where folks were gathered.

Miss Emma didn't wear a uniform. She just wore the same clothes she wore in the classroom. Jack chuckled at how they would pull up to a country store, and when the male loafers inside saw her get out of the patrol car, the smokers would run out the back door to get rid of their cigarettes. It was well known how dead set she was against smoking. Grown men running from this tiny school teacher! Miss Emma only weighed ninety-five pounds.

The electorate was surprised. For they, also, had expected Grady to continue running the sheriff's office. They thought Miss Emma would be teaching school all day and would show up at the courthouse just to sign off on papers. Not only was she on patrol every afternoon, she had printed rules and regulations about how the Cade County citizens were expected to behave. These rules were posted in a number of public places. Eventually she appeared at all the churches, the schools, and the equipment auctions. Everyone confronted at these meetings was plainly told that crime or unruly and uncivil behavior would not be tolerated. It only took about three months for everyone to realize that Miss Emma was serious.

The last rule on the list was that men couldn't dine in public while wearing head cover. It was not uncommon throughout the county for a man to walk up to the posting, read slowly down it, digesting the content of each rule and start to turn away with only a glance at the last one. Then he would whirl suddenly and stare at it, unbelieving.

Phrases, like "The hell you say!"; "Damn if that's so!"; "You'll play hell enforcing that one!" were overheard.

The men in the county discussed these rules, particularly the last one, among themselves. The consensus was that they would not obey that one, no matter what. However, the rebellion never got off the ground. A week after the rules were made public, Miss Emma walked into Lola's coffee shop to the community table where seven men were downing their breakfast. All wore baseball caps. They became very docile as Ms. Emma stared at them. "Now, boys, I meant what I said about the hats. Momma didn't allow my daddy or any of my brothers to eat at her table wearing a hat. This habit of eating with a cap or hat on in Cade County is not going to continue. The Chamber of Commerce is trying to lure industry here from up North. It's not good for our image. I'm not going to stand for it. I know all of you, and each one of you should be ashamed!" The guys broke out in a chorus of "You're right, Miss Emma." "I'm sorry, Miss Emma." "You can count on me, Miss Emma."

Emma continued, "Okay, boys. Spread the word around. You know, while my husband was sheriff, he let prisoners work off their fines by picking up trash on the sides of highways. I'm going to take that program to the next level. My staff will be instructed to focus on any kind of misbehavior or of anyone wearing a cap while he eats in public. When that man gets arrested, I'm going to put him on the work gang wearing pink pants, like that sheriff out in Arizona does."

Jon David Knox, the town busybody, gasped, "You wouldn't!"

Emma glared at him. "You just try me, Jon David Knox, or anyone else. Now, I'm going to excuse myself. And how will you boys be enjoying your breakfast?"

They all stared at her, their minds blank. Then a light bulb came on in Ben Weaver's head, and he blurted out, "Without our caps on!"

The others chimed in, "That's right, Miss Emma. With our caps off!"

Jack grinned to himself as he reflected how crime had dropped to near zero. The reason was because so many of the people had either been taught by her in school or had heard of her reputation as a dedicated school teacher. Civil behavior had also improved and all because of sheer respect for Miss Emma.

Even big Zeke Tiller, who owned Sleazy's, the joint across the county line at Three-way in Gallatin County, quit selling beer during the four years Miss Emma was sheriff. That irritated a great many people in Cade County, which was dry, for Sleazy's was the nearest establishment where cold beer could be bought.

When asked why he chose to quit selling beer in a wet county, Zeke explained, "Man, it don't matter. I can't sell beer while Miss Emma is sheriff. Not only did she teach me grammar and stories in school, she donated blood to Mamma when she had that emergency operation. Miss Emma and Mamma were the only two people in South Cade County that had O negative blood. And she was always saying in class that folks shouldn't drink. I had to mind her like I minded Mama."

The next four years, Zeke survived by adding a kitchen to serve hot food for lunch and supper. He also put in two gas pumps and added a small line of groceries, and because the distance to the next nearest beer store was fifty miles, beer consumption in Cade County dropped drastically.

During Emma's term of office, the crime rate was so low that it gained statewide recognition. The state legislature honored Miss Emma by declaring August 25th of each year as "Miss Emma Day." The legislature also passed a law allowing sheriffs to succeed themselves. However, Miss Emma decided to retire. She was begged by many to run for election again, but to no avail.

Grady ran for the office and rode back in on Miss Emma's coattail.

Sheriff Powers coughed to get the attention of the deputies. Darlene still had not showed up, but the Sheriff decided to go ahead with the meeting.

He addressed Wade, "You're certain that there was no foul play with Mr. Joab's death?"

"Yes. Best I could tell he slipped, for some reason, in the back yard. He was out feeding the birds. I saw where he hit his head on a rock by a flower bed when he fell. There was hair and blood there. There were no tracks in the snow except his. Looks like he was able to crawl inside the house. He either died from the blow or froze to death. His body was solid as a chunk of ice when we found him."

"Well, an autopsy would determine the cause of death. But what difference would it make either way? As long as no foul play was involved, we'll skip the autopsy. No need of carving up the body. Wade, I talked to the county attorney, and he said I should quickly convene a coroner's jury and get an official cause of death," said Grady.

He continued, "Jack, you call Reese and tell him to be here at two o'clock."

Reese Jones was the county coroner and worked at Gray's Funeral Home in Central City as the undertaker. His employer allowed him time off to conduct autopsies for the county or preside over a jury.

"Also round up six people to sit as the jury."

Wade asked, "Grady, what is going to happen with Mr. Joab's property? He doesn't have any people around here. Since his wife died, he's lived alone out there. Who would know about his relatives?"

The room was silent as Grady pondered. He leaned back in his swivel chair and stared at the ceiling. Grady rocked slowly for a few minutes.

Finally, he stopped, sat straight up and asked, "What about the neighbor, Irv Lackey? He lives a couple of miles away, as a crow flies, on the dirt road that goes off the paved road back towards Four Points. He's such a peculiar old cuss that Mr. Joab has been about the only fellow that would have anything to do with him. Jack, you know him. Why don't you go bring Irv into the office after lunch and let us talk to him? We need to hurry up. And, if he would, he could be the very person to keep an eye on Mr. Joab's house."

Wade spoke up, "Yeah. Last year I had stopped at the store in Four Points, and Mr. Joab was there. He told the regulars hanging out there that, one time, Irv had to go to the VA hospital in Jackson for a check-up. Irv had been in the Battle of the Bulge, and his feet were severely frostbitten. His wife is deceased, and all his children are in California except for his youngest boy that's in the army and stationed in Germany. He lives alone, and he doesn't have a vehicle. Irv always hitches a ride, or walks, to where he's going. Mr. Joab said it was warm weather, and he was sitting on his front porch after dark when Irv walked up. He told Mr. Joab that he had to be away for a few days and wanted him to keep his flashlight and his 1911 Colt pistol. Irv didn't have locks on the doors at his house.

"The next week, Irv came back to get his pistol and told Mr. Joab to keep his flashlight for pay. They argued about that, but Irv insisted Mr. Joab keep the flashlight. Mr. Joab told the store crowd that Irv was the most honest person he had ever known; that you could go away for two years and ask Irv to keep a million dollars of cash for you. When you came back, all the money would be there, and it would be the same identical bills that were left with him!"

Jack Early butted in laughing. "Yeah, but he is indeed a cynical old cuss! I remember one time he was hitch-hiking from Central City to Four Points. Jon David Knox picked him up. You know how tight Jon David is. When he dropped Irv off in Four Points, Irv asked Jon David how much he owed for the ride. Jon David told him a dollar. Irv spit a stream of snuff out the pickup window and told Jon David that fifty cents was all he was going to get because that was all he paid the rest of the sons-of-bitches that lived in Four Points!"

The room rocked with laughter. Grady said, "OK, guys. Ya'll get something to eat. Sammy, you get the jury lined up 'cause Jack needs to run out to get Irv."

CHAPTER 5
IRV

Thirty minutes after the coroner's jury made a unanimous decision that Mr. Joab had died from an accident, Jack Early walked into the sheriff's office with Irv in tow. Irv was a short, unshaven, scrawny man.

He was wearing the coffee-stained, wool overcoat the army had issued him in Europe at the start of the 1944 winter. The hems were frayed from heavy use. Singe marks circled the front and back of the coat where he had stood too close to the hot field stoves in the front lines. It smelled heavily of wood-smoke from home.

Jack was clearly disgusted since about half way to Poston, Irv had rolled down the window of the four-wheel drive pickup to spit out his snuff. He miscalculated the speed of the wind, and the entire wet, nasty stream of snuff blew back inside, splattering against the back window. Irv also smelled like he hadn't bathed since the first frost. Jack was thinking of a good excuse to get out of taking Irv home and to put the return trip on Sammy.

Grady spoke to him, "Irv, thank you for coming in. Did Jack tell you about Mr. Joab?"

Irv twisted his wool cap in his hands. He had backed up to the wall heater to enjoy the kind of heat he didn't have at home but wished he did. The heat elevated his rank body odor causing all the deputies to scoot their chairs back.

"Shore did, Sheriff. I'm sorry to learnt that. Mr. Joab was a fine friend. I been knowing him going on seventy years. He used to give my kids after-school work on his place so they would have spending money, and I know he made up a lot of that work. But them jobs really helped my young'uns. You know my wife was sickly most of her life before I lost her, and I had my hands full raising five kids."

"They did well, didn't they?" asked the Sheriff.

Irv spoke proudly, "Yes, they shore did. Louise and Charles are in Los Angeles. He's a carpenter making big money. Louise has a fabric shop; she always did like to sew. Claudia is in San Diego working in the PX on the Marine base. Cindy Dee is there too, working at the hospital. And Irv, Jr. is a sergeant with them army tanks in Germany. He got a promotion last week!"

The door opened, and Wade walked in. He turned a straight chair around and sat on it backwards, leaning forward with his forearms resting on the top of the chair back.

Grady hadn't expected all these details. He shifted in his chair. "Look, Irv, let's tend to business. We've got a problem here. Mr. Joab's heirs need to be located. We don't know how long that will take. In the meantime, could you look after Mr. Joab's house and place?"

"Why, shore. I'll be glad to. Why didn't Jack say so? I wouldn't have had to leave my fireplace and get out in this cold weather." Irv shivered as he agreed to keep an eye on his neighbor's property.

Grady said, "Well, it's more official if I ask you. Do you know who Mr. Joab's heirs are?"

"What's airs?" Irv asked.

"You know, kinfolks."

Irv's Adam's apple twitched slightly as he said, "Nah, not offhand."

Wade noticed the twitch.

Grady continued, "Do you know who might?"

"No. But I'll think about it."

"You do that."

He looked around to tell Jack to take Irv home. His seat was vacant. Grady's eyes settled on Sammy. "Sambo, take Irv home!" he ordered.

Then he turned to Wade after Sammy and Irv left the room. "Wade, did you see that?"

"Yeah. I didn't know if you noticed."

"When the time is right, check it out. That old cuss knows something."

"Yeah. Irv is a peculiar, suspicious person, and he'll be very protective of Mr. Joab's interests. I'll have to play my cards right, or he will clam up, and we'll never know."

Grady mused, "It's one thing for sure, the lawyers will find out who Mr. Joab's kin is."

CHAPTER 6
THE FUNERAL

Mr. Joab was buried shortly after two o'clock on Thursday in the Mt. Nebo Baptist Church cemetery. The small brick church was located three miles northeast of Four Points on a gravel road in the middle of the woods owned by an out-of-state timber company. Around the turn of the century, the area had been heavily populated, and the church had a vibrant membership. During the depression years, families moved away from the meager existence they were eking out on their farms for a better life elsewhere. Thus, the church membership dwindled as the years went by until services were held only once a month by the associate pastor of the First Baptist Church in Central City.

Despite the cold weather, the sanctuary was full. Folding chairs had been sent out by Reese Jones, the funeral director, and were placed at the ends of the pews and down each wall of the rectangular-shaped building. They were all occupied. Mr. Joab's church in Four Points was well represented. Since school was still out, a lot of young people were there with their parents. Also present was the entire staff of the sheriff's office, all of the county supervisors, Irv, who sat on the end of the back row, and many curious onlookers who had no connection to Mr. Joab, some of whom had not entered church for a number of years. The casket was closed.

The pallbearers sat on the first two rows of the church. They were Laderle Latham, a young man who quail hunted on Mr. Joab's land each season; three of the deacons from Mr. Joab's church; a neighbor; Sherman Tims, who had helped Mr. Joab cruise his timber during the summer breaks while he was in college; Ben Weaver and Ellis Tiller, both longtime friends.

When the pallbearers marched down the center aisle of the sanctuary to their seats, Sherman spied Rita sitting on the dais. He had not expected her to be here, but he quickly figured that she was to sing. Sherman attempted to hang back so he would be on the second row but was out-maneuvered by Laderle, who was bigger. Sherman ended up on the front row.

While Deputy Baker was taking Irv home on Tuesday, Irv told him that he knew Mr. Joab had written down his funeral arrangements. They went to Mr. Joab's house, and the first place they looked was in his family Bible. Sure enough, in between the Old Testament and the New Testament, were the instructions written in pencil on a torn piece of blue lined notebook paper. They were simple. Mr. Joab had listed his pallbearers, where he wanted to be buried, and requested certain songs by a woman who could sing well. These instructions were passed on to the funeral home.

Rita Arnwine was there to sing at the request of the funeral home director, Reese Jones. Martha Spencer, the vocalist at Four Points Baptist Church, had not returned from a winter cruise she had taken with her daughter who lived in New Orleans. The night before, Reese had been at wits end when he had been unable to locate Martha. His daughter, Candy, had stopped by to visit and overheard his telephone calls to various women about singing at the funeral the next day. Candy remembered a friend of hers discussing that she had heard Rita sing at the Methodist Church in Oxford several years ago and that she had a terrific voice. Reese immediately got on the phone and found Rita at home. The school counselor was sitting by her fireplace reading a book. They chatted a while. Reese found that Rita was bored from being snowed in, and she eagerly accepted his request to sing at the funeral. Rita had not been acquainted with Mr. Joab but had heard people talk of him in a gracious manner, including Sherman who had complemented Mr. Joab for giving him summer jobs.

"Mr. Reese, it doesn't matter that I didn't know him. I heard everyone say he was a good man. I'll help you put him away in style!"

A few minutes before the appointed hour, the church became silent and still. Then, exactly at two o'clock, the bell in the tower high above the church somberly rang three times. The sound reverberated sharply through the cold, crisp winter air all the way to the town square of Central City, causing shoppers on the sidewalks to pause. Then Rita, dressed in a simple black suit, arose from her seat and moved to the microphone where she stood proudly and gazed across the congregation.

The service began with her singing "Just a Rose Will Do." The audience was mesmerized by her voice. Most of them didn't know her. Reese was standing at the back of the church where he noticed many ladies leaning toward the person sitting next to them and whispering about the gorgeous young woman who sang so well. As Rita sang, she focused her eyes on Sherman. His face was red, and he kept his head turned down during the entire song. By the end of the song there was not a dry eye in the church.

The funeral service was delivered by the pastor of the Four Points church. The message had been well prepared and was spoken eloquently. This particular pastor, when preaching a funeral, in addition to blessing the deceased, always directed a portion of the service toward those in attendance whom he felt were unsaved. Needless to say, there was a substantial amount of squirming and not from the cold. The pastor sat down after he finished his remarks.

Rita strode back to the mic and addressed the audience, "Will you all please stand and join me in singing 'Rock of Ages'?" She looked directly at Sherman as she said, "And I ask that ALL of you sing."

Rita began to sing, and, as the crowd picked up the verses, her eyes glinted with a show of humor as she watched Sherman mumble along.

The song ended, and she smiled sweetly at Sherman who looked away. The pallbearers lined up at the side door of the church and assisted the funeral home personnel move the casket to the gravesite beside his dear wife in the cemetery. The usual burial ceremony had been waived because the accumulation of snow and ice made the cemetery grounds treacherous.

As the crowd filed out of the church, Sheriff Powers cornered John England, the county attorney. "John, we are going to have to do something about Mr. Joab's affairs. No one seems to know who his heirs are and whether or not he has a will. Somebody needs to take over his business and see about his house and property. If we don't, everything out there will walk off. I don't have enough men to watch that place, way out there, like it needs to be. Irv has agreed to check on the house as much as he can."

"Yeah, I know. This is going to be a mess. I've always heard he had a lot of money even though his lifestyle was frugal. I'll bet somebody will show up to claim the money. Probably more than one," John spoke.

"What do you think needs to be done?"

"Well, I'll call Judge Chandler in the morning. Why don't you go by the bank and see if he had a lockbox. Most people do. If he has a will, it would probably be there."

Sheriff Powers turned away toward the crowd to look for his driver, Deputy Early. He noticed a group of women crowded around Rita. As Grady edged up to listen, he noticed that Norma Sue Riley, who owned a beauty shop on the square in Central City, was speaking to Rita. They were laughing. Grady could see that each was enjoying the other's company. The other women were also smiling. He heard several compliments being paid to Rita of how well she sang and how good she looked.

One lady standing by Grady said, "My goodness, Grady, what a remarkable young woman! We just found out about her living here in Central City. She needs to get out more."

Her companion said, "Yes, indeed. We heard about her breaking up with Sherman. Boy, was he a fool to let that get away!"

He overheard other compliments about her haircut and how well dressed she was. As Grady moved on past the group, he spied Sherman over by his pickup looking wistfully toward Rita. Grady thought that if Sherman ever had any support from the women of Central City toward his breakup, it was lost completely today. Rita had them all in the palm of her hand.

The next morning after he picked up and read his mail, Sheriff Powers and Jack Early rode from the county seat to Central City. They parked at the side of the bank, got out, and went through the front door. There were several customers inside waiting to see a loan officer. The lawmen nodded to them, took off their hats, and approached the desk of Ginger Macon, who was the secretary for Riley Hood, the bank president.

Jack said, "Good morning, Ginger. Is Mr. Hood in?"

"Yes. He's on the phone with the regional office. He'll be through in a sec," Ginger said.

Jack reached into the candy jar sitting on her desk and grabbed a handful of peppermints. He explained, "I'm getting some extra for the poor kids in India."

Ginger smiled.

The door opened, and Riley Hood appeared as he commanded, "Come on in, men. Ginger, please hold my calls." They all went inside. Sheriff Powers and Jack took seats in leather chairs across the desk from Riley. Riley suspected what they were there for but asked anyway, "How can I help Cade County's finest this morning?"

"I know you have heard about Mr. Joab's death. We buried him yesterday. That was a nice stand of flowers the bank sent to the funeral," Sheriff Powers said.

"Yes, Mr. Joab was a fine gentleman, and he was one of our oldest customers. We'll really miss him, especially the ladies here. He was always bringing them fresh vegetables from his truck patch and flowers from his patio on special occasions," Riley replied.

Jack said, "Yeah, that's a true picture of him. Respected by everybody."

"Riley, did Mr. Joab have a lockbox here?" Sheriff Powers asked.

"Sheriff, you know Mr. Joab's business with us is confidential. But between you and me, I know that y'all can get a court order and find out anyway. So, the answer is yes."

"How do we go about getting into the box to see if he has a will in there?"

"That's easy. By law we can open a lockbox only to see if a will of a deceased person is inside. We are allowed to remove any will and hand it to the next of kin or whoever is listed as the executor. Of course, we keep a copy. Then we seal the box. Who is the next of kin?"

"Well, that's the problem. We don't know. In fact, no one that we've talked to knows."

"We can go ahead and open the box. The will may list someone local, like his attorney, as executor. Do y'all have Mr. Joab's key?"

Jack said, "No, but we haven't looked for it either. What happens if we can't find it?"

"Oh, we can drill the box. We'll have to get our locksmith in Memphis to come down and open it. Of course, the estate will be billed for the cost."

Jack thought, "Yeah, you got that right. The bank didn't give anyone a free ride. Not unless they were going to get it back many times over." He was still ill at the bank about the time a couple of years ago when he had written five checks to pay bills. Jack had been in line at the drive-in window to make a deposit for a sum that exceeded the total of the five checks. He had pulled up five minutes before the 2:00 p.m. cutoff for the day's business. But the car in front of him went dead. By the time the driver got the engine cranked and moved away from the window, it was 2:02 p.m. Jack thought that was close enough. But when his bank statement came in a few days later, he became irate when he saw he had been charged with not one, but five overdrafts in the amount of thirty-five dollars each. The balance in his account, before the deposit, was enough to cover the sum of his four smaller checks. But the bank had arbitrarily charged the largest check against his account first, causing all the others to be overdrawn. He had complained to Riley but to no avail. Riley had given him some crap about bank policy and that regional headquarters wouldn't make an exception for customers, no matter who they were.

Sheriff noticed Riley's eyes shift, looking past him through the glass enclosing his office.

Riley exclaimed, "Well, guess what! The locksmith just walked into the lobby. Excuse me a minute."

He left the room. A few minutes later Riley came back announcing, "Well, this is our lucky day. The locksmith was passing through on his way back to Memphis from our branch in Morgan City. He had to drill three boxes there, and he said if you wanted to drill Mr. Joab's box, there wouldn't be a charge."

The sheriff looked at Jack and said, "You know, we might as well. We might look for that key for a week at Mr. Joab's house and never find it."

"Okay. I'll get him started. It'll take about ten minutes," Riley said.

Ten minutes later Ginger stuck her head back in his office saying, "Mr. Hood, he has the box open."

They all left the office and made their way to the vault. Ginger pulled out Mr. Joab's card for Sheriff Powers to sign. As he was signing, he noticed that the last entry made by Mr. Joab was twenty years ago. Riley placed the box on the table outside the vault and lifted the lid. His jaw sagged in amazement! The others crowded around him and saw that the box was empty. Riley turned the box over and found nothing on the bottom.

The guys stood around for a few moments just gaping.

Finally, Sheriff Powers said, "Well, I guess that's that. I don't know what to say."

"Me neither! Most people put their wills in their lockboxes," Riley said. He added, "Maybe it's still at his house."

Sheriff Powers replied, "That is, if he had one to start with."

"That's a good point. I think, before I started going through his house, I'd check with his lawyer to see if one was made for Mr. Joab."

Jack spoke up, "Who do you think is his lawyer?"

"I don't know, but the list for lawyers is short in Central City. We only have three: Ramsey Lockhart, Lamar Mosley, and Archie Baker."

"Okay. We'll go by their offices and see what we can find out," Sheriff Powers said.

They thanked Riley and left the bank. They decided to call on Lamar Mosley first. Jack and Grady had to wait for a few minutes because Mosley had a client. When the client left, the secretary stopped her typing and told them to go on back. They all knew each other. When asked, Lamar told them that he had never done any legal work for Mr. Joab.

Lamar said, "Mr. Joab probably never needed a lawyer. He sort of kept to himself and wasn't involved in anything that would have a need for legal services. I would think if he used a local lawyer, it would be Ramsey. He and Ramsey were bream fishing partners on Gallatin Lake"

Grady said, "Well, we will go see him."

"That may be a problem. I heard that he is under oxygen in the Tupelo hospital. They think he has pneumonia."

Grady said, "I hadn't heard that, and Emma hasn't said anything. She usually knows about sick folks."

"Well, if I can help with anything, let me know. And you should check with Archie. You never know who folks use for a lawyer."

Outside, the sheriff and Jack moved around the corner to get out of the wind. They stood on the sidewalk with their collars turned up and their hands in their pockets and talked.

"I wouldn't think he would use Archie. Talk about a crackpot! How the powers in the state bar association keep letting him practice law is a mystery to me," Jack said.

Sheriff Powers muttered, "I agree. His behavior in the courtroom is obnoxious. He berates witnesses and is rude to the judges and the clerk's staff. He has had numerous bar complaints but somehow weaseled out of them all with only his hands being slapped. But he has few hobbies and does research late on many nights and on weekends. I know for a fact that he anticipates the various motions an opposing lawyer might make at a trial and locates case law to present on the spot that will win his case. I don't think he has ever lost a case. I believe it's because he is probably the most brilliant lawyer in the state. And it doesn't hurt that Supreme Court Justice Maxwell Beasley is his uncle."

"I didn't know that."

They discussed Archie for a few minutes. Archie had grown up on the Gulf Coast and been hired as an adjuster by a national insurance company upon his graduation with a degree in general business from college. He had rented an apartment in Oxford which was in the center of his district. The oldest law school in the state was also located there. In the course of his work, Archie became exposed to the legal aspects of the insurance business and became interested in practicing law. He saw the opportunity. A law school was where he lived, and his company would let him work part-time while he attended school.

Archie was a sandy-haired, slender man, about six feet tall. His interests were few, but complex. He shot snooker, worked the daily crossword puzzle, played in euchre tournaments, and read classic literature. He loved baseball and was a devoted New York Yankee fan. He was a tee-totaler, but did drink Dr. Gilicuddy's Peppermint Schnapps on special occasions. He was married to the former Tena Brock from Clarksdale, a successful artist. She worked in a studio attached to their house which was located in the oldest part of town. On weekends, she traveled to Chicago, Miami, and other large cities to sell her paintings.

Tena was not seen around Central City much because of her devotion to painting and her weekend travel to exhibit her work.

Archie and Tena had been in Central City for eleven years. Archie thought his wife would not have agreed to move to a town of only two thousand people. Before he decided to leave the insurance business and practice law, he discussed the move with Tena. To his surprise, Tena supported him on his decision to leave the insurance business and also to move to Central City.

She said, "Archie, this day and time a small town has just about anything a large city has and much less crime and traffic. I know you don't have the shopping, the plays, and the restaurants that's in a metropolis, but all of that is only an hour or two away. We have friends in Memphis that have commuting time of nearly an hour, but you can be in your office in five minutes."

Between undergraduate and law school, he had been an insurance adjuster for three years in the immediate area. After graduating from law school, he had continued in this job for two more years because he had been reluctant to dive into the sole practice of law. An incident with Harvey Rogers was what caused Archie to reassess his work goals and open a law office.

Years earlier on a day in April, he and Andy Morgan, the insurance company's local agent, had ridden to Harvey's ranch in the north end of the county. Harvey was a cattle rancher. He also was the twin brother of the county tax assessor, Harley Rogers. He and his family lived in a modest house on their land. His pasture ran from the highway south to the Skuna River.

A storm system had moved through the area the previous day, bringing high winds, hail, and heavy rain. Harvey's cows were spooked by the thunder and lightning and had congregated under the single, large, pin oak tree in the middle of the pasture. Harvey's wife had been begging him for several years to cut that tree, but he had never gotten around to doing it. Of course, the tree was a natural lightning rod. And, of course, a strong bolt of lightning popped the tree, splintering it from top to bottom, killing forty-three pureblood Black Angus cows. Only twenty-seven cows survived. The Rogers family saw, heard, and smelled the lightning bolt and feared the worst.

As soon as the storm lifted, Harvey and his oldest boy drove down into the pasture. The sight of the dead cows scattered about sickened both of them. Harvey's thoughts drifted toward the bank note on the cows and how this was really going to set him back. Or, maybe put him under. He had planned to sell enough of these cows to pay the upcoming fall tuition for his daughter Emily, entering her first semester in college. Harvey was crestfallen. If it was not one thing, it was another. Now he couldn't help her at all. He brightened when his boy said, "Pop, call Mr. Andy. Don't we have insurance on the cows?"

Andy found Archie in Baxter, already working another claim. Arrangements were made to meet after lunch on the town square in Baxter and ride out to the Rogers' ranch. When they pulled up in the yard, Harvey and his son were standing outside the house by a tractor shed. Harvey was very anxious, his stomach tied into a knot. He was still thinking about his daughter. She had been very quiet the evening before. She just sat in the corner of the den with a book in her lap. Harvey had noticed she hadn't turned a page in two hours. She knew. The next morning, before he left the house, he overheard Emily asking her mother if now she couldn't go to college. Her mother had replied that if the insurance man didn't help, there wouldn't be enough money to pay for college. On his way out the back door, he had noticed tears streaming down his wife's cheeks. All because of one bolt of lightning, his child's dreams had gone down the tubes.

The insurance men left the car and shook hands with Harvey and his son. Andy had already told Archie the nature and the extent of the rancher's loss. They made small talk, and then Archie said, "Let's get down to business and see about this claim."

From where they were standing, one could see south all the way to the river; all that land was in open pasture. Archie could see the splintered tree and the carcasses of the cows scattered about the tree trunk.

He began to whine, "I don't think my company will pay this claim. It looks like it's your fault that those cows were killed."

Harvey's mouth dropped open in amazement. "What? What do you mean?"

Archie looked down at his shoes and began to talk. At that, Andy Morgan's face reddened. He had been on claim visits with Archie before. Archie had this irritating habit of looking at his shoes and quoting law case cites to the claimant, who usually had only a high school education. Or less. More often than not, this maneuver by Archie intimidated the insured, who usually accepted being low-balled on their claim.

Somehow, Andy didn't think Archie would get away with trying that on this claim. He had known the Rogers twins for a long time, and they had terrible tempers when shoved into a corner.

"Mr. Rogers, that tall tree down there in the pasture, standing by itself, was an attractive nuisance to your cows. Naturally, when the storm came up, in their way of thinking, the cows saw it as their savior. If the oak tree had not been there, they would have milled around in the pasture and the lightning bolt would have sought the nearest highest object. That would have probably been over in your neighbor's woods," Archie said. Archie continued, "Now, I know there is no case on point that has been decided by the State Supreme Court, but there are other cases out there that come close enough."

Archie, still looking at his shoes, began to cite a string of cases and a brief statement of what each was about. Harvey and his son stared at him in disbelief. Harvey began to get a numb feeling in his stomach; he could sense where this was going.

Finally, Archie said, "I can't recommend to my company that this claim be paid. But, I do need to go down there and photograph those dead cows for my file. And the tree."

With that, he got into his car and drove through the cattle gap on down into the pasture. Harvey turned to Andy and screamed, "Do you mean that SOB is not going to pay me? After me paying those high-priced premiums all these years? I could beat the hell out of that guy. And him rattling off all that lawyer talk to me right here in my own yard!"

Andy quickly said, "Now Harvey, cool down! Cool down! Let me talk to his supervisor. This is not the first time I've had to do that."

He was about to continue when the Rogers boy broke in and exclaimed, "Pop! Look down there. Mr. Archie is in trouble!"

Andy and Harvey turned toward the pasture. They could see Archie being chased around his parked car by a huge, white Brahma bull.

48

"Y'all get in my truck," Harvey said.

They crammed into the cab of his pickup, and Harvey sped toward the car.

When Archie parked his car near the tree and dead cows, he got out with his camera and inadvertently hit the door lock. He was busy photographing the dead cows and didn't notice the huge bull, switching its tail, lying in the mud nearby. The bull was still agitated by the havoc the storm had caused; and when he saw Archie standing there, he chose to retaliate. He charged Archie, who quickly recovered from being startled by the charging bull and ran toward his car. Archie knew it was going to be a close call; he had to have time to open the car door. He was looking over his shoulder bug-eyed, realizing he wasn't going to make it, when he tripped on a tree root and fell to the ground. The bull couldn't stop and centered the driver's side door with his massive horns, creating a huge dent and lifting that side of the car up off its wheels. Archie scuttled underneath the car and crawled out on the other side only to see the bull come around the vehicle, his red eyes glaring at Archie.

He fished for the car keys in his pocket. Not finding them, he glanced through the window and saw them in the ignition. Archie went back under the car.

About that time, Harvey pulled up, got out with his shotgun which he leveled at the bull, and fired a load of birdshot into his rump. The bull roared in pain and ran off. Archie, shaking, came out from under the car.

Harvey laughed, forgetting about the denied insurance claim. The front of Archie's pants was wet!

Archie stammered, "My car is locked and the keys are inside! I need to call a locksmith for help. I need to get away from here!"

A tiny smile came across Harvey's lips. "I don't think that's necessary, young man. I can solve this problem right now."

Archie had bent over slightly to look into the car. Harvey poked the end of the shotgun barrel even to Archie's ear and toward the car window. He pulled the trigger and the pellet blast took out the window and the one on the opposite side of the car.

Archie jumped up screaming, "Oh, hell, you busted my eardrums. Why did you do that?"

Harvey sneered. "File a claim and see which one of your high and mighty law cases gets you paid, you sorry piece of crap. And get your ass off my land before I kick it to Timbuktu!"

Archie jumped into the car without noticing he was sitting in a sea of broken glass and fled the Rogers farm.

Tuesday morning, when Mrs. Rogers went to the mailbox by the road, she saw an envelope from the insurance company. Inside was a check for the dead cows, the amount calculated at the highest price per pound for beef that had been given in the previous three months on the Chicago Mercantile Exchange.

Later that week, Andy called Harvey to make sure he was satisfied with the check and to tell him that, on Monday afternoon, Archie had resigned from his job. He opened a law office in Central City on Tuesday and was planning to live there.

Harvey asked, "Why did he do that? He lives in Oxford. I don't think he'll like living in a small town."

"I asked him the same question, and he told me it was because Central City only has two lawyers while Oxford, according to him, has five hundred. And through his insurance work, he already knows most of the lawyers in the area and what kind of law they practice or don't practice."

"Well, Cade County is in for a surprise."

"I agree. I may take my words back later, but it's a big relief for me that he is out of adjusting. You just don't know the business he has caused me to lose over the past few years. I thought I would have it made when he went to law school, but the dang insurance company let him keep working part-time."

"I can see why. If Archie worked all his claims like the way he tried to do mine, he was saving them a lot of money," Harvey said.

"Yeah. But I went over his head and persuaded the claims manager in the Jackson office to pay you what was just," said Andy.

"Thank you. I desperately needed that money!" replied Harvey.

Grady and Jack walked on down the street to Archie's office. It was closed. A note stuck on the door said that Archie was out of town and his secretary was home sick with the flu.

Grady said, "We'll come back later. This probably is a waste of time anyway."

CHAPTER 7
THE SEARCH OF THE HOMESTEAD

A week went by without any progress toward finding a will made by Mr. Joab. Jack Early and Sammy Baker had been sent out to the house by the sheriff with instructions to search all the likely places for where a will would be kept. The deputies took Sally Ryder with them. They really didn't have to have her along, but she was good looking and was a prankster who kept friends in good spirits.

Upon arrival, they noticed that there were no signs in the yard or around the house of anyone having been there since Mr. Joab's body had been removed. The deputies used a crowbar they had brought along to pull the planks off the door that Wade and Joe West had nailed to keep prowlers out.

The house had an entry hall with a bedroom off to the left. The living room was to the right. From there, a door opened into a smaller dining room. Past the dining room was the kitchen which had an outside door, the same doorway which Mr. Joab crawled through after he had fallen in the back yard. All the rooms were well lighted by the many ceiling-to-floor windows. The furniture in the rooms was old and used, but none of the pieces appeared to be antique. The room north of the entry hall appeared to be Mr. Joab's bedroom which contained a homemade bookcase stuffed full of books.

Sally searched the bedroom and went through every book. Before she was through, Jack, who had finished searching the living room, joined her and helped finish the stack of books. A large Bible, in which the funeral instructions had been found, was on the night stand by the bed. Sally thumbed through it's pages and found a couple of letters and some postcards. The pages of the Bible were dog-eared, and many had the corners turned down to mark special passages. She noticed that these verses were underlined in ball-point ink or pencil.

She said, "Jack, would you say that this Bible is worn out? I've never seen one in such condition."

Jack looked over her shoulder at the book. "You're right. I wonder if anyone else in this county has ever worn out a Bible."

"I doubt it, and that's unfortunate. People spend all their time wearing out vehicles and tractors and don't bother to break the covers of a book that has all the answers that they are running up and down the road looking for," preached Sally.

Jack stood silent for a while and then agreed, "Sad, but true."

The deputies spent all morning going through dresser drawers, closets, boxes of papers, and the contents of a two-drawer file cabinet in Mr. Joab's bedroom. Nothing. Only old tax returns, a scattering of letters, various receipts of things purchased, the title to his pickup, some military records, and bank statements.

The house was in decent order but dusty. The officers all sneezed on occasion. Finally, they stopped looking and took a break.

Sally spoke, "I'm convinced there's no will here. If Mr. Joab had one made or wrote one himself, he must have left it with someone for safekeeping."

"Yes. But, you know, most people in this county don't make a will anyway," Sammy said.

Jack was sitting in an old leather chair. "Well, he may have hid his will where no one would look. But what's the point of hiding it, if it wouldn't be found? I mean, the purpose of a will is to set out who you want to have your things. And he should have made one because he has no close kin. For that matter, maybe no way-out kin."

"Well, let's report back to Sheriff Powers. I think his idea is to have the county attorney open an estate so Mr. Joab's business and property can be safeguarded," Sally said.

On the way back to Poston, they discussed the events of the morning.

Jack remarked, "You know, Mr. Joab sure lived a plain life. Besides his furniture, he only had a black-and-white TV set, a case of books, and his Bible. It's like he was living to die. Like he wasn't going to burden anyone with having to get rid of a lot of possessions after his death."

"You're right. There were stacks of the daily *Commercial Appeal*, and I noticed he worked the crossword puzzles. He was good, too. Nearly every puzzle had all the words filled in," Sally said.

"He didn't have many clothes hanging up in the closet either. Nor many boots or shoes. And Wade went back and got his double barrel shotgun and pistol a few days after they found him."

"Well, we've got all the papers with us that look important. I found a small cardboard box of mostly black and white photographs. There weren't very many. I didn't see a camera in the house anywhere so these must have been made by someone else."

The deputies arrived in Poston just before lunch. They told Sheriff Powers what they found and what they didn't find: the will.

"I'll call John England and see if he will open an intestate estate. As county attorney, he has blanket authority to petition the court for legal protection in any matter that I deem urgent. He'll want me to sign an affidavit about the need for urgency to support the petition. We'll go from there and see what happens," Grady said.

That afternoon Grady had a conversation with John England. He reported that the search for Mr. Joab's Will had been fruitless and asked if he would be willing to administer the estate.

"Okay. Well, Grady, y'all did a good job trying. I'll proceed with opening an estate. I don't know who the judge will appoint as administrator, but I hope it will be someone who will devote the right amount of attention to the matter," John said.

The next day, John dictated his Petition to Open and the accompanying documents to his secretary, along with an Order to Open. A blank space was left for the name of whoever would be appointed to manage the estate. John called the court administrator to see which chancellor would be in Poston next. There were three chancery judges in the district in which Cade County was included.

The court administrator said, "John, you're lucky. Judge Chandler will be in Poston on Friday morning to take care of ex parte matters. Why don't you file your petition with the chancery clerk and take the case folder to Judge Chandler. Even if your case gets a computer assignment of one of the other judges, he'll sign the order opening the estate. I've heard the other judges talk. They know about this situation and are curious whether or not a will would be found."

John said, "No, it hasn't. The sheriff went to the bank. There was not one in Mr. Joab's lockbox, and a thorough search of his house didn't locate one."

The administrator said, "This has happened before. A will was produced after an estate was opened in that particular case. But, you all should keep looking."

CHAPTER 8
THE JUDGE'S REMARKS

Friday morning, John England appeared before Judge Chandler with the Joab McMath case file. Court had already begun. There were several lawyers in the courtroom with their clients. Ex parte day was a day when the judge heard uncontested matters like no-fault divorces, name changes, matters agreed to by the parties on both sides, and so forth. Any lawyer wishing to appear on this day would call the chancery clerk's office and request that his case be put on the docket. If he failed to do this, he would have to wait until after all the scheduled matters were heard.

John was late on purpose. He wanted to be last, hoping the courtroom would be clear by that time. Then, his conversation with the judge would not be heard in public. He took a seat behind the rail by the assistant chancery clerk, Crissy Mobley, an attractive young brunette. She shyly smiled at him. John liked her. She was recently divorced, and, being single himself, he was wondering if she would go out with him. But he felt the ink on her divorce decree was still too wet for him to be asking at this point. So John decided to bide his time.

He whispered to Crissy, "What's going on?"

One of the lawyers from Baxter, Wiley Downs, was standing before the judge with an older man and woman who were dressed in scruffy clothes; baggy trousers and faded flannel shirts. John noticed there were a lot of people in the courtroom, more than usual for an ex parte day.

Crissy whispered back, "This is a no-fault divorce. You know Judge Chandler always requests both the man and the woman to be here to testify."

John groaned. This would take a while.

Wiley was hacked off. He was representing the woman even though both she and her husband had come into his office seventy-five days ago seeking a divorce. It was explained that he could only represent one of them or it would be unethical. He was waved off. Both said they didn't care what some jackass ethics committee in the state capital came up with about divorce. None of the members lived up here and didn't know what real life was about. Wiley had been told that both had been married before and both had grown children by their respective former spouses. The couple had met each other in the bait shop during the last crappie spawn while they were buying minnows, had fallen in love, and had married after a brief courtship. They lived in a run-down cabin just inside Cade County, near Three-Way. The cabin was within a mile of the water in Gallatin Lake. The property had been up for sale, and just before the marriage, they bought it because of its convenient location to good fishing. The couple really liked to fish, and they did that every day, no matter what the weather.

The marriage had dissolved, not because of any hard feelings of one toward the other, but because of their children. The children of each spouse had decided that they didn't want their parents to be married. They raised so much commotion and so regularly, that the couple decided to get a divorce in order to appease their children. They would divorce, but they would continue to live with each other. As the wife said, their Social Security checks would be more that way, giving them funds to buy extra bait.

Wiley had called Judge Chandler and explained the background of the parties. He already knew that Judge Chandler was the only one of the three judges in this district that made both parties to a no-fault divorce appear before him to be questioned. Although he was laid-back on most other legal matters, Judge Chandler was a stickler about divorces. He personally thought divorce was too easy to obtain under the no-fault statute. That many married couples, especially the young ones, were too casual about it. That they didn't really think about how serious a marriage was or how much a divorce could affect their future life. So he wanted to question each one at length to make them consider the consequences of what they were about to do.

Wiley was hoping after this unique situation was explained to Judge Chandler, the parties would not be required to be present in court. Just himself to present the divorce order. But Judge Chandler was unrelenting. Wiley had difficulty explaining the need to be present in court to the couple. Each one of them complained. They didn't see the use in having to appear. They wanted to go fishing because the ice, that the severe cold spell had created, was melting, and the crappie were coming to the air-holes. The fish were hungry, and fishermen were catching the limit every day.

Reluctantly, the couple came to the hearing. Before court started, John had heard them out in the hall, grumbling and complaining. They were supported by two other couples who were getting divorces and who also were unhappy about having to be there. The three sets of spouses agreed that was what they paid lawyers for; to take care of their affairs for them.

Standing before the judge, Wiley asked both spouses some basic questions such as their name, address, the county of their residence, and the reason for being in court. Then the judge took over. He only asked each of them if they were sure they wanted a divorce. Their answers were convincing, and the judge signed the divorce order and announced, "Y'all are officially divorced."

The husband stared at Judge Chandler, and the wife announced in a loud and accusing voice, "You mean we lost a whole day of fishing just for this?"

The spectators in the courtroom roared! The lawyers who were present looked away, and the judge's face turned red!

Wiley left the front of the courtroom and took a seat behind the rail on a bench at the rear. Judge Chandler looked over at John and said, "Mr. England, you are next and also last as it appears."

John took his case file and placed it on the bench for the judge to review. He said, "Judge, I'm here to open the estate of the late Mr. Joab McMath. Sheriff Powers and his staff have gone to great lengths to locate a will. So far their efforts have been futile."

"Well, he may not have had one. I'll sign the order opening the estate. And I'll appoint Wiley Downs the Administrator, if you don't mind," the Judge said.

"That's good Judge. I have a lot to do. And me being county attorney could evolve into a conflict down the line. Your Honor, I haven't filed this petition with the clerk yet, so it hasn't been assigned to a judge."

"We'll take care of that in a minute."

The judge called Wiley back to the bench. Wiley had overheard the conversation from his seat. The courtroom had perfect acoustics. Whispers from up front could be heard on the back benches. When the courtroom had been built, the contractor had not planned for acoustics to be that good. He had just gotten lucky.

Standing there, Wiley thought that his day had started badly and was getting worse. He was worn out with having Judge Chandler on any of his chancery matters. Judge Chandler treated him like a child of an unwed mother at a family reunion. This treatment had started in his first year of law practice. He was representing the wife in a divorce case before Judge Chandler. The husband was represented by the judge's son, Hal, who had practiced law briefly in Cade County before going to Washington, D. C., to be on the staff of one of the state's senators. Wiley, as he had been taught in law school, asked the judge to withdraw from the case because his son was representing one of the parties. Judge Chandler was highly offended by Wiley's motion. He dressed Wiley down for accusing him of not being able to be fair and open-minded just because his son was a lawyer on the other side of the case. He denied Wiley's motion. Wiley's request caused the judge to develop a grudge toward him. After that, Judge Chandler refused to acknowledge Wiley's position on the docket on ex parte days, whether it was first or elsewhere, and called his matter last every single time. This had gone on for years. Wiley had to think of a reason to get this case away from Chandler.

"You don't mind doing this do you, Wiley?" Judge Chandler asked.

Wiley replied, "No, Your Honor. It doesn't seem to be much of an estate anyway. Just opening and closing." He added, "Your Honor, it would seem that this case should be handled by Judge Zack Dennis. Mr. Joab was appointed by Judge Dennis to be the administrator in that messy Thomas estate because he had gained the court's highest confidence from assisting on previous occasions in partitioning lands. The judge directed me to represent the administrator. To remind you, Frank Thomas was killed in a train wreck about ten years ago. Frank had children by three former wives and a couple of single women. It was a real mess, for some of the children were minors. Mr. Joab did a good job. He was very patient with all of the family and went out of his way to protect everyone's interest. He made my job and the judge's lots easier.

Judge Dennis became very close to Mr. Joab and commended him highly for the estate work."

Judge Chandler absorbed the comments. He grudgingly said, "I can commend you too, Wiley. I appreciate your referring to the youngsters as children and not 'kids.' You know 'kids' are goats, and I really get irritated hearing a lawyer, or anyone else for that matter, call young human beings *kids!*"

That remark caught the attention of the courtroom audience. They could have heard a pin drop.

"Crissy, come over here if you will," Judge Chandler said.

Crissy stepped up to the bench standing by Wiley and John.

Judge Chandler was the senior chancellor in the district. He asked Crissy, "Who is the next judge to be assigned to a case?"

Being away from her computer which arranged the case assignments and without batting an eye, Crissy answered, "Judge Dennis."

Both John and Wiley looked up at the portraits of the former and present judges mounted high on the front wall.

Judge Chandler replied, "Well, Wiley, you got who you asked for. This case is assigned to Judge Dennis. For the moment, I'll waive bond. John, didn't you say that there is very little personal property?"

"Yes. The sheriff only located a small bank balance, Joab's old pickup, a couple of firearms, and the usual household contents."

"Okay, Wiley. Just have an inventory done. And don't bother to have anything appraised. Doesn't sound like anything found so far has much value. Of course, you understand that Judge Dennis may modify my rulings."

Wiley nodded, "Yes, Your Honor."

Judge Chandler was relieved as he signed the order. In case the estate became a problem, it wouldn't be his.

Wiley went back to his office in Baxter and told his secretary to open a file on the McMath estate and fax the notice to creditors to the local paper, *The Whisperer*. The notice gave instructions to anyone who Mr. Joab owed a debt to file a claim in the estate in order to get paid. The legal ad would be published in the paper once a week for three weeks. The creditors would have ninety days from the first day the ad was published to file their claim, or they would be barred from getting their money.

Wiley told his secretary, "I'll have a small fee coming from this. I shouldn't have to do much work. Just a couple of routine court appearances at Poston."

CHAPTER 9
SLEAZY'S

Wade just happened to be within five miles of the county line when Darlene Roberts, the dispatcher for the day, called at four-thirty on Friday afternoon. "Wade, we just got a 911 call from Darlene Doss who runs the bar at Sleazy's. There's an altercation there, and it's ongoing. Get your ass down there, pronto!"

Wade sighed. Not again! And just when he was going home to grill steaks and watch a baseball game on television. He whined, "Now, Darlene, don't talk to me that way. You know I'm always prompt."

Darlene said sweetly, "I'm not getting on to you, but Darlene said it was urgent. She hung up before I could get any details. And I did hear glass break, a lot of it. It sounded like that bar-length mirror. You know how Zeke will feel about that!"

Sleazy's beer joint, owned by Zeke Tiller, was just across the Cade County line in adjoining Gallatin County, which was wet. One day a stranger, passing through from Illinois to New Orleans, had stopped in for a beer. Zeke just happened to be tending the bar. The stranger asked if his name was Sleazy. Zeke gave the man a cold stare and told him it wasn't. Then the traveler asked why the name of the place was Sleazy's.

Zeke replied, "You should be in here on Saturday night. It's full of riff-raff. This place attracts every low-life from miles around. That name don't tell no lie about my clientele."

In 1948, the U. S. Army Corp of Engineers built a two-mile long earthen levee for flood control purposes near the town of Gallatin, creating Gallatin Lake. The purpose of the lake was to dam up the Gallatin River to control water from flooding the Mississippi Delta cropland. The lake, when full, flooded sixty-five thousand acres, and the shoreline increased from fifty miles to two hundred seventy miles. As a result of the lake contour, a small triangular portion of land on the backside was cut off from the rest of Gallatin County. This area was known as Three-Way. A state highway ran through Three-Way from Oxford to Interstate 55. A dozen households and Sleazy's beer joint were located in Three-Way. The only way the Gallatin County sheriff could patrol the area was to come around the south side of the lake to Central City and then westward to the county line. The trip was fifty miles and took well over an hour. But only twenty minutes was required for the Cade County law or ambulance service to respond to a call from Three-Way. To resolve this difficulty, the boards of supervisors in both Cade and Gallatin Counties entered into an interlocal agreement so this part of Gallatin County would be the responsibility of the Cade County sheriff. Cade County billed Gallatin County monthly for any calls that were made to Three-Way by the sheriff or the ambulance. All of the school children that lived here were bussed to Central City High. The educational cost of these children was also reimbursed by Gallatin County.

After Miss Emma retired as sheriff, Zeke had resumed the sale of cold beer. Since his kitchen had done so well the previous four years, he kept it open. Zeke was the younger brother of Ellis Tiller. Zeke was fifty-seven years old, having been born twenty years after his brother. He was a large man just like all the rest of the Tiller clan but was dwarfed by Ellis who was six foot six, weighed three hundred pounds, and was in tremendous condition.

Even without having been provided any details of the fight by the dispatcher, Wade had a pretty good idea of who was involved. He narrowed the possible list of patrons to his close friends, Ellis Tiller and Coley Wampler. He also suspected Earl Ray Fowler.

Wade made a U-turn in the road and headed west. He called Darlene and instructed her to send him some back-up and added that she might as well send an ambulance. He arrived at the beer joint five minutes later.

As he slid to a stop at the gas pump in front, he saw that the fight was over. He also saw broken windows, smoke coming out of the kitchen, three Harleys on their sides, and three bodies laid out in the gravel parking lot. There also was an Oriental kid on his hands and knees throwing up while a college girl held his head. Several cars with Hinds County tags and Ole Miss stickers were parked there.

The concrete block joint had a door at each end and one in the middle of the front. The tin-covered building was set length ways and forty yards back from the highway. Between the beer joint and the highway was a long gravel parking lot. To the south were several large oak trees. Underneath one of the trees were a couple of wooden picnic tables. It was here that customers would bring their lunch from inside and eat in the shade. A gas grill was by this end of the building, and a large cooler holding bagged ice was against the wall. Wade jumped out of the squad car and ran to the door at the south end of the beer joint.

On the way to the door, Wade also noticed Ben Weaver and the Musician leaning on the fender of Ben's pickup that was parked in the shade. When he spotted the Musician, Wade did a double take; he had not seen him in a while. What was he doing here? He could tell the two men had not been in the fight. Their clothes were too clean, and there was no blood on them. Both silently watched Wade arrive.

Wade drew his 1911 .45 Colt automatic and slid inside the door, putting his back against the wall as his eyes became accustomed to the darkness of the barroom.

As his eyes adjusted, he glanced around and was not surprised at what he saw. Brawls had happened here regularly over the years, but he believed the damage was the worst this time. Darlene had been right. A long wooden bar ran down the entire back wall. The mirror behind the bar was now on the floor in a million pieces. Several of the bar stools were demolished, and the tables on the main floor were in a disarray. Many were upside down, and broken chairs were scattered around. The only people in the room were Darlene, Ellis, and Coley. Coley, an undersized man, was slumped against the inside of the front door holding his bloody head in both hands and moaning. His crushed eyeglasses lay at his feet. Wade went over to Coley and pulled his hand back. There was a gash on his forehead, and his nose was smashed. Wade could see that the cut would require a lot of stitches.

He asked Coley, "Got any broke bones, Coley?"

Coley moaned, "Nah, Wade, I'm okay. I just tripped coming in the door and bumped my head on the floor. Go see about Ellis."

Wade just shook his head. Coley was tough as seasoned leather.

Wade strode across the room to the table where Ellis was sitting. Darlene, a forty-year old blonde, was sitting by Ellis with her arm around his shoulder. Ellis had his head in his arms that were down on the table, and was sobbing like a baby. Sheepishly, Darlene looked at Ellis with big eyes.

"Are you hurt, Ellis?" asked Wade.

Ellis stopped sobbing and replied, "Yeah, Wade, I'm hurt real bad. I should be. Me and Coley had our hands full with those Outlaw bikers and that smart-ass Korean college kid."

Wade noticed that Ellis' hands were swollen and the skin on all his knuckles was gone. There was a cut on his head, and his hair was matted with blood. His shirt was torn to remnants, and he smelled strongly of whiskey.

Ellis apologized to Wade, "I'm sorry, Wade. I just came apart, and I had been doing so good lately. But when the fight started, I came unglued. It just all came back, and I couldn't stop!"

He began to weep again.

Seeing that Ellis' wounds weren't severe, Wade went into the kitchen. A large aluminum pot of gumbo on the stove was boiling over, sending smoke up the vent. Wade moved the pot to the counter and turned the stove off. He went back to the barroom and started righting the tables and bar stools.

He heard the ambulance arrive with its siren wailing. The paramedics began to tend to the bikers lying in the parking lot. Wade could see the emergency medical technicians would need help, so he told Darlene to call Darlene to have another ambulance sent.

About that time, he heard one of the parked cars crank up and leave the parking lot, slinging gravel against the tin front of the building. Through the open front door he saw two red-headed girls jump into the remaining car and head south. Wade glanced at them. He recognized the Swaney sisters. The redheads were from Jackson and were in school at Ole Miss. They went home one weekend a month to visit their mother. As the girls passed by Sleazey's on Friday afternoon on their way home, they would always stop to drink some cold beer. Every time they stopped, they caused some kind of commotion with the crowd of boys in the bar. It didn't help that in warm weather they wore cut-offs, tight t-shirts, and baseball caps with their pretty red-haired pony tails hanging through the loop in the back. They liked to flirt with Earl Ray Fowler who had been a Friday regular at Sleazy's. For some reason, the sisters were fascinated with him. The trouble they caused had become so frequent that Wade warned them to quit stopping at Sleazy's. The girls had obeyed him for only one weekend. Then they fell back into their routine. Every time Wade started in on them, Hannah, the younger sister would twitch her behind and smile sweetly at him, and his heart would go soft. She reminded him of Evelyn Nobles, his high school sweetheart.

He would end up begging, "Now, girls, I've got to keep law and order here, and ya'll are not helping me."

Robin, the older sister, would lean against him and say, "Aw, Mr. Wade, we'll do better next time."

But next time was always the same.

The trouble toned down when Wade told Earl Ray to stay away from Sleazy's on the Fridays when the Swaney sisters came through. Earl Ray obeyed. But he made Wade think he was doing him a favor even though he didn't care one way or the other about the Swaney sisters. And, he had all the other days in the month to drink beer at Sleazy's.

Wade asked Darlene, "Was Earl Ray here when this fight broke out?"

"No. He wasn't. He has been keeping away just like you asked when those Swaney sisters come through."

The second ambulance soon arrived followed by Sammy Baker, the deputy. They were able to load all the injured except for Coley, who said he would call his sister to come and get him. Wade consented; he knew Amy Wampler would get him to the hospital. She was an RN and was off duty today.

Ben and the Musician eased inside and began helping Wade and Darlene clean and straighten up the mess. Both were small men. The Musician was pale-skinned with blondish brown hair whereas Ben was a wiry, swarthy man from many years of working outside. He had a perpetual squint from looking into the face of the glaring sun and blowing wind. He was sometimes mistaken for an Indian. Ben worked for a construction company during summers and trained dogs for quail hunting in the fall and winter. The Musician was tidily groomed, wearing his customary silk shirt, size small. His pale hands were smooth, indicating he was accustomed to making a living from dealing cards or shuffling papers of dubious origin. The Musician's real name was Henry Childs, but few knew him by that. The true nature of Henry's occupation was vague and sometimes suspect in the eyes of the community.

Wade asked, "Darlene, where is Zeke?" He wondered, for Zeke hardly ever left the place on Friday, the day he paid his suppliers.

"He went to Memphis to get some new bar stools and some more tables from that furniture place on South Front Street."

Ben said, "That will work out really good. Most of these here are destroyed."

Darlene said, "Yeah. And Zeke is going to be real mad when he finds out his mirror is gone. He really liked it. I don't know where he'll get another one that long. This one was an antique that came from an old bar in Virginia City, Montana. Zeke picked it up on an elk hunt out there."

They finished getting the room back in order. They swept the broken glass into a dust pan and carried it, the broken chairs and tables to a garbage bin behind the building. Darlene went behind the bar and opened cold beers for Ben and herself. She poured iced tea into a glass for Wade, who didn't drink alcohol.

The Musician objected to her opening one for him. "Nah, Darlene, you know I haven't had a beer in two years. And, anyway, I've got a record, and I still have papers outstanding. The Feds might catch me. It's pushing the point just my being here in a beer joint."

Wade mused about that and asked, "Why are you back here in Cade County? I haven't seen you in months."

The Musician replied matter-of-factly, "I just got tired of Memphis. You know all that rush hour traffic and the crime. I want to take it easy for a while."

Wade chuckled inside. There was more to it than that. Ever since the Musician graduated from high school, he had lived in only two places, Memphis and Central City. Nope, make it three places; he had spent several hitches in federal prisons. The Musician preferred to operate out of Memphis, and when he surfaced in Cade County, Wade knew the heat was on in Memphis about something. In time he would find out what it was on this occasion.

Wade, Ben, the Musician, and Darlene took seats around one of the few tables not damaged. "Ok. Tell me how all this got started," Wade instructed Darlene.

Darlene had been divorced for five years. She was a decent looking woman for her age. Darlene wore her hair short, and on her left bicep was a tattoo that read "Love is Hell." She lived in a trailer that was placed behind the beer joint. Her hours at the bar were from ten in the morning, when the bar opened, to midnight. Zeke helped her most nights, but during the days, he was usually away, feeding the herd of cows at his home place or baling hay. During the winter, he put in a lot of time deer hunting. Darlene had worked for him at the bar going on twelve years now. When Zeke was away, he never thought about the bar. He trusted Darlene wholeheartedly.

Darlene said, "Well, it had been a slow day for a Friday; had a few customers in for lunch. We had red beans and rice. Several stopped in for beer in the afternoon. Ellis and Coley came by about 2:00. A few minutes later those three Outlaw bikers wheeled in. I could tell they were looking for trouble, as usual. Ellis started out drinking beer, but I could see he was about to tie one on when he switched to Jagermeister. Zeke will wish he had never stashed that bottle in the kitchen. The bikers were drinking beer and shooting pool at the table over there in the corner. Around 3:30 those college kids came in: the Swaney sisters, the Oriental kid and his girlfriend, and two boys I've never seen in here before. They all sat at the same table except for the Swaney girls who sat over by the juke box playing Patsy Cline records. Ellis and Coley went back to the kitchen for a refill on the Jagermeister. They cleaned up the sinks and counter and took out some steaks to marinate for tomorrow's grilling. I guess they had decided to leave because they came out going toward the side door. When they passed the table where the kids were eating beans and rice, one of the boys made a face at Coley, who was carrying a hammer to break up all the ice that had lumped together in the cooler outside.

"Then the Oriental boy smarted off to Coley. 'Hey, redneck, you don't have but three fingers on your hands. Are your parents cousins?' The kids snickered which angered Ellis.

"Ellis looked down at the kid and sneered, 'Hey, gook, eat your flied lice and then hit the road!'

"The boy sneered, 'I'm not a gook, Gramps, I'm a Chink. Why don't you drink some Karo and run out and play in the traffic?'

"Ellis turned on his heel, went back into the kitchen, picked up that pot of rice, came back, and jammed it upside down over the kid's head. That's when all hell broke loose!

"Coley swung the hammer and whammed the top of the pot. Man, did it make a noise! That kid won't hear anything for a month. His girl friend let out a shriek and kicked Coley square between the legs. About that time two of the bikers came at Ellis. The other one let Coley have it across the head with a cue stick and put him out of the fight. Ellis had his hands full. I've never seen him in such a rage. He had his two whipped, but the third one was 'bout to wipe him out with the cue stick when that Swaney girl threw the nine-ball and hit the biker dead between the eyes. Her sister would have hit him with the ball she threw but the biker fell and the second ball sailed past him and hit the mirror, causing it to shatter from end to end."

"What were the other two college kids doing?" Wade asked.

"Nothing. They were standing against the wall, bug-eyed."

Wade laughed. "You mean they let the Swaney sisters show them up? Well, well! I'll have to go easy on them from now on. I didn't know they had that much backbone."

"Hah! I hope their mother doesn't hear about this. You should have heard the language they used when they threw those pool balls."

"Which girl hit the biker?"

Darlene replied, "The one that you are sweet on."

Wade's face turned red as he stammered, "How do you know I'm sweet on one of them?"

"Why, Wade, a woman just knows. And maybe you have a sign hanging on you. Why do you like her?"

Wade was slow to reply, "She just reminds me of someone I knew a long time ago when I was about her age."

Darlene gazed intently at Wade, "That figures. You have a lot of ghosts, don't you, Wade?"

Wade's eyes took on a faraway stare, and for a moment, he seemed lost in thought. "Yeah. I guess so. I have had more than my share. But they are not as fierce to me as the ones Ellis has," he said.

Ben and the Musician looked at him, thinking he was going to talk about his past, but Wade changed the subject and said, "I'll have to give a report to the Gallatin County sheriff in case any of these characters decide to file charges."

Wade asked Ben if he would haul the bikes to the jail. He said, "When they bring those guys there from the hospital, I'm going to have them hit the road. Zeke will just have to eat the damages. I don't want those bikers back here. They don't have any money anyway."

Wade, Ben, and the Musician went outside and removed the dog boxes from Ben's pickup. After they loaded the bikes and strapped them down, Ben and the Musician got into the cab and headed to Poston.

Wade stuck his head into the door of the bar and asked, "Darlene, there's no need to tell Zeke who broke his mirror, is there?"

Darlene smiled and winked. "No, Wade. I've got you covered. Not to worry. As I recall, one of the bikers broke it."

"You're a good woman, Darlene," Wade replied warmly.

CHAPTER 10
THE SMUDGE POTS

A few days later, Wade remembered the remark that Darlene said the Oriental kid had made about Coley's fingers. The image of Earl Ray's hands flashed before his eyes. He had a missing finger also. Wade also remembered a bizarre incident concerning Earl Ray earlier in the year. On one of Wade's trips to Three-Way, Zeke Tiller had mentioned that a lady, Lou Bertha Eason, who collected his empty beer cans to sell for scrap metal, told him about finding Earl Ray drunk in the middle of the isolated road near her house late one night. She said that Earl Ray looked like he had been beat up.

Wade turned off the highway into the dirt drive that led up to a small, white wood-framed house that belonged to Lou Bertha Eason. He stopped at the end of the drive, stepped out of the patrol car, and walked around the side of the house to the back yard. Lou Bertha was sitting in a straight chair under the shade of a large oak tree. She was shelling field peas into a pan placed on her lap. Wade had expected to find her here doing some task. Lou Bertha was an ample black woman about seventy-five years of age. She was wearing a tattered dress, a white cloth wrapped around her head, and worn sandals on her feet. She was a jovial, likeable person who was a friend to everyone she met.

She welcomed the deputy. "Hello, Mr. Wade. Grab a seat. How you dewin this morning?"

Wade smiled, "All right, Lou Bertha. How's the pea shelling going?"

"Pretty good. I'm on my last bucket. I got up early this morning and picked a couple of bushels before it got too hot!"

Wade grabbed an extra pan, filled it with peas, and began to shell as they talked. "That's smart thinking. They say it's going to get up to ninety-five today. This will be the first real hot day we've had."

"Sho-nuff."

Wade grinned. "I heard you laid it to those white boys from Jackson down on Gallatin Lake in that fishing contest!"

Lou Bertha bellowed. "You got that right! They'll know better than to mess with Lou Bertha next time, won't they?"

Wade chuckled. Back in April the U.S. Crappie Association had held its annual crappie fishing contest on Gallatin Lake. There had been one hundred seventy-one entries. This year, instead of having the usual two-day event, the board of directors had decided to experiment with having just a Saturday contest. Fishermen came from all across the South for the grand prize of twenty-five thousand dollars for the largest fish. The sight of all those expensive rigs that showed up early that Saturday morning was awesome. The motels in Gallatin were full. Some of the entrants had to sleep on the seats of their pickups because rooms were not available for everyone. The start was from the marina area of the lake near the levee. All of the fishermen had the latest model bass boats with trolling motors, live wells, 200 HP motors, lights, horns, extra gas tanks and, generally, all the accessories that the manufacturers offered. The pride of the lot was the expensive fish locators. The boats were towed by costly club-cab pickups.

And there was more. Premium fishing gear was in abundance. Some of the entrants even had custom-made poles. The tackle boxes contained the full selection of the popular lures on the market. To say the least, money was not an obstacle when it came to being outfitted for tournament fishing.

As expected, it took an hour to get all the boats into the water. Each boat roared away from the launching ramp at top speed. For a while, the noise was deafening as the boats buzzed out in all directions to spots where each fisherman was convinced the big crappie would be lurking.

Lou Bertha's son, James Henry Eason, had to go to Gallatin that afternoon to have a set of tires put on his car. He already knew about the crappie contest. He wanted to be a participant but didn't have a boat. At least, not that kind of boat. All he had was a used fourteen foot, flat-bottom aluminum skiff with a thirty-year-old 10 HP Mercury motor. James Henry would have been embarrassed to have shown up with his rig in front of all those pros. They would have sneered. Since his mother loved to fish, he would take her to the launching point where she could fish off the bank. There, she could watch all of this contest activity while he was at the tire store. Lou Bertha agreed. James Henry also wanted to be present at check-in time to see who won.

When they got to the boat ramp, James Henry helped Lou Bertha get her fishing gear to a good spot on the bank where she might catch some fish. On their way down to the water, they passed the registration booth. James Henry started talking to the contest officials and found that the entry fee for bank fishermen was only ten dollars. The form was colorful, and the contestant's name was typed on its face in an unusual, bold font. James Henry thought that one with Lou Bertha's name on it would look good on her fireplace mantle, so he entered her in the contest.

That afternoon, the boats began to return for check-in. The deadline was four o'clock. One by one, each fisherman had his largest fish weighed. The guys gathered around the scales to watch. They were popping tops on their beer cans, passing out high fives, and, in general, just being jovial good ole boys. No one noticed Lou Bertha trudging up the hill with her registration papers in one hand and her cooler in the other.

James Henry was late getting back. A wreck on the highway held up traffic. The fishermen were already loading their boats on the trailers. He saw Lou Bertha standing to one side clutching a paper in her hands while talking to the outdoor editor for the Jackson *Clarion Ledger*. He walked up to a small crowd peeking at the bulletin board on the side of the registration shack.

He looked over their shoulders and saw the contest posting of the winners.

$5,000 Third Prize -- Benson Carr, IV,
                    Brandon, Ms
                          Quantum graphite rod, Davis reel,
                          monofilament line

$10,000 Second Prize -- Dana Ford-
                    Ridgeland, Ms
                          Shakespeare graphite composite rod,
                          Abu Garcia reel, Berkley transoptic line

$25,000 First Prize--   Lou Bertha Eason,
                                  Cade County, Ms
                                  Cane pole and minnow

"What have you done with your money, Lou Bertha?"

She smiled. "That's mo money than I can spend in one week. But I'm not going to quit my day job. First thing I did on Monday morning after I caught that fish was to carry my check to Mr. Riley's bank and got him to keep it for me. Except for a thousand dollars, which I gave to James Henry. If it hadn't been for him signing me up, I wouldn't have had nothing but some fish bones after I ate that crappie."

Wade chuckled. "You just added it to the million you already got there?"

"I ain't saying no mo," laughed Lou Bertha.

Then she asked, "You didn't come by here to shell peas did you, Mr. Wade?"

Wade replied, "Nah, I didn't. I wanted you to tell me about finding Earl Ray Fowler by that construction site down the road, back during that cold spell in January."

"I sho did. If I hadn't gone out there and drug him into my house, he'd be stone dead."

"What happened?"

Lou Bertha said, "Well, the wind was blowing real hard that night. A few hours after midnight my little feist dog, Lucy, wanted to go outside. I let her out and was standing by the door waiting for her to finish her business so I could let her back inside. She started barking and growling and looking down the road. I saw taillights on a pickup stopped down where them construction folks had a bulldozer across the road, blocking where that bridge was out. I thought maybe somebody had hit the dozer. I called Lucy back in and kept on looking. Then I saw something move on the ground in the truck's head lights. That was odd. I put my boots and overcoat on, got into my car, and drove down there. Lord, what I saw! There on the ground in the mud lay Earl Ray. Was he drunk!! He had took his shirt off and was trying to blow out a smudge pot, of all things!

"When he saw me, he laughed and said, 'Come on, Lou Bertha, get down here and help me blow out these pots. Then we can go tell all them sissies at Sleazy's who the real tough guys are around here.'"

Wade said, "Boy, he had to be bad drunk. You can't blow out a smudge pot with the exhaust of a jet engine."

"You got that right. That's why they use them for warning lights 'cause it don't make no difference to them little things what the weather is. They works 24/7." She continued, "So I grabbed him and drug him, mud and all, into the back seat of my car and drove back to the house. That was ruff on me 'cause he built like a linebacker! He told me he had left Sleazy's when Darlene closed the place but he wasn't ready to go home."

"What did you do next?"

"I got him into the house. It liked to have wore me out. I got his clothes off and got a cloth and a pan of warm water and cleaned him up. I ain't never seen a naked white boy before."

Wade broke in, "Did anything you saw surprise you?"

She replied, "Nah. All you mens is all alike. All shriveled up in cold weather."

Lou Bertha continued, "Then I put some of James Henry's clothes on him and made him sleep on the sofa under a pile of quilts. He was going in and out and talking crazy."

Wade asked, "You mean like drunk talk?"

"Nah, not that kind of talk. I've heard plenty of that before. It was some kind of foreign talk. I couldn't understand it."

Wade was puzzled at this revelation. He asked, "Wasn't Earl Ray in the Guard with your son?"

Lou Bertha beamed. "He sho was. They went off to their training together to that fort in Missouri. I remember that well cause I didn't know what might happen to James Henry. It was New Year's Day, 1968. We were in the middle of that Vietnam War. One of Earl Ray's buddies carried both of them to the bus station at Houston. The bus left about nine o'clock that night. James Henry wrote me that it took them twenty-four hours to get to the army base from Houston. It snowed north of here, and the bus slid off the road at Trenton, Tennessee."

Wade asked, "When did they get back here?"

"Well, that's the thing. James Henry got back here at the end of April. But Earl Ray didn't come back."

Wade perked up. "What do you mean?"

"James Henry and Earl Ray were in the same company. He said not long after they started going out to the rifle range, Earl Ray bowled out or something."

"Oh, Lou Bertha, he boloed."

"Yeah, that's what James Henry said. He got sick or something, and they were going to make him start all over again. You can talk to James Henry. He can tell you mo."

Lou Bertha said, "You know, I never thought about it before now. My son served his six years in the Guard, and I don't remember Earl Ray being in the Guard no mo."

She added, "And that sure was a bad scar on Earl Ray's back. It was some sign and it looked like it was burned into the flesh. Boy, somebody did him bad. Somebody done flung some powerful evil on Earl Ray. That had to hurt!"

Wade stared at her, lost in thought.

"Did you ask him about that crazy talk the next morning?" he asked.

"Nah. That's not none of my business. Anyway, I was glad he was okay. Boy, did he put away the eggs, sausage, and biscuits I cooked for him. Course, it was near dinner time before he felt like crawling out from under them blankets. He thanked me plenty for getting him out of the cold and left me a fifty dollar bill. I didn't want to take it, but he wouldn't have it any other way. Earl Ray asked me if I was superstitious about a fifty. I told him them kind of thoughts wasn't between my ears about money that could slide into my hands."

Wade laughed and said, "I'll talk to James Henry. I've got to go. Take it easy, Lou Bertha."

He was nearly to the corner of the house when he heard Lou Bertha laugh and call after him, "Wade, you know about that fish I caught? I done fried a lot more over the years that was bigger than him!"

The next day at 5:00 p.m., Wade was outside the plant where James Henry worked. He was parked at the back of James Henry's car waiting for the plant to close for the day. James Henry was a supervisor, so Wade knew he would be one of the last to leave the building. The workers came out, got into their cars, and left the parking lot. Soon, Wade saw James Henry headed toward his car carrying a black lunch box.

Upon seeing the deputy, James Henry spoke, "Hello, Mr. Wade. How are you?"

Wade replied, "All right, James Henry," and got out of the squad car. The two men spent a few moments talking about the weather and how the Cubs were in a losing streak and twenty games out of first place. James Henry wanted to use some of the money Lou Bertha gave him to take his small son to Chicago for a weekend to see them play. But now, he was not so sure it would be worth the trip.

Wade said, "I saw your mother yesterday."

"Yeah. She told me about it last night. Said you were asking questions about Earl Ray."

"That's right. Nothing that important. Lou Bertha said he didn't come back from Fort Leonard Wood with you. How come?"

James Henry said, "Well, he boloed. We went up there together and were in the same training company. He was shooting better than any other soldier at the rifle range. One day while we were standing behind the firing line and the shooting was going on, a jeep pulled up with a bird colonel and a Green Beret major in it. They got out and went to where our company commander, Captain Dooley, was. They talked a while. Then Captain Dooley called the senior drill instructor over and said a few words. The SDI and the three officers came to where we were standing.

"The SDI told all of us except for Earl Ray to move away. We could see them talking to Earl Ray, and they looked at his score card. After a while, Earl Ray came back to where we were, and the officers left.

"As the officers walked by us, I remember the colonel saying, 'Look what dropped into our lap,' and the Green Beret major replied, 'Didn't we get lucky? This may be our ticket to the Pentagon.'

"I asked Earl Ray what was going on. He seemed embarrassed and said the officers were bragging on his shooting. They had his zero target card showing how the bull's eye had been shot out with his nine practice rounds. The paper was gone leaving a hole the size of a nickel. They had asked him how he had learned to shoot so well."

Wade asked, "What did he tell them?"

"That he had bird hunted since he was twelve and had a .222 that he shot a lot."

"Yeah, I know about that. His football coach, Slick, and his friend, Phil, both had .243s. All three of them would all ride around in the lake area shooting crows at long distances when it was legal. Man, were they good! That was before Earl Ray went off to the army."

James Henry continued, "The next day, he didn't come out to the range with us. Or the next few days. We both were in Easy Company, which was the last one in the battalion, but not in the same platoon. When we were assigned barracks, E Company was split up to fill in the parts of the barracks that Alpha, Bravo, Charlie & Delta Companies didn't. So, Earl Ray and I were in different buildings. It was the end of the week before I had a chance to ask some soldiers in his platoon where Earl Ray was. They said he got a severe case of upper respiratory infection and was sent to the hospital. They heard he was going to be recycled. That happened to a lot of guys because the weather was really cold up there. It snowed a lot, and we had just spent a night bivouacked in the snow while the temperature was 13° below zero. I never saw him again at Fort Leonard Wood."

Wade asked, "When was that?"

"About the end of January, 1968."

"Did he have all his fingers?" Wade asked.

James Henry turned his head toward Wade and said, "Of course."

"Did he have a large tattoo or scar on his back?"

James Henry said nervously, "Now Wade, I don't make a habit of looking at men's backs."

Wade laughed. "Hell, I know that, but didn't y'all take showers together?"

"Yes, we did. If something like that had of been there, I would have noticed. And some wiseass in the company would have run off at the mouth about it. So I would say he didn't."

Puzzled, James Henry asked, "Why are you asking all of this, Wade?"

Wade looked off in the distance and answered, "Aw, I don't know. I guess I don't have enough to do. I was just thinking that it was a coincidence that Earl Ray and Coley Wampler don't have a left little finger and they are big drinking buddies."

James Henry said, "Well, Coley doesn't have a right little finger either."

"Yeah, but Coley got his right little finger cut off in a table saw about thirty years ago. Somehow, he lost his other finger in the Korean war."

Wade mused. He knew why Coley didn't have a left little finger. Wade was there when he lost it. Wade wondered where Earl Ray was when he lost his.

James Henry added, "You know, Earl Ray never came back to the Guard. In fact, I didn't see him for over a year after I got back. Then I saw him in town one Saturday. We talked about Fort Leonard Wood, and I asked what happened. He muttered something about getting a medical discharge."

Wade thanked James Henry and was getting back into the squad car when James Henry remarked, "Wade, one thing I've always wondered about. Growing up, I was around Earl Ray a lot. Before we went to the army he never drank more than a few beers, and that was on weekends. Now he drinks like a sailor."

Wade drove away leaving James Henry standing there scratching his head wondering about the mysterious questions he had been asked.

CHAPTER 11
EPISODE AT THE FUNERAL HOME

On the last Thursday of July at 5:30 in the evening, Trip Bowen and his cousin Miles Lennox were standing outside Gray's Funeral Home, located a few blocks north of the town square in Central City. Trip and Miles were seventeen years old and would be seniors at the Central City High School. Both were starters on the football team, the Hornets. They had begun to run twice a day to get into shape before fall practice started in two weeks. They dreaded the upcoming sessions because it was hot and steamy in August in Mississippi. Standing to one side was their friend, Toby Teller, running his mouth about silly nonsense, as usual. They could barely stand him, but they also couldn't do without him. His father owned nine hundred acres of the best hunting land in the county. Mr. Teller had the land posted and was very vigilant in watching for poachers during deer season. However, he would let any of Toby's friends hunt on the land. As Trip and Miles saw it, as long as they could put up with Toby, it was the same as owning the land themselves. Toby was fifteen and would be a sophomore this school year. He also was on the football team but wasn't good enough to start.

Trip and Miles prided themselves as being "cool" and being in demand by the best looking girls at Central City High School. In their minds they were already men of the world.

Inside the funeral home lay Oscar Sappington, age sixty-five. He had died at home Tuesday from a massive heart attack after drinking bourbon into the wee hours of the morning. Oscar had been a regular drinker since coming home from Vietnam where he had been a member of the 101st Airborne. He had been in-country for two hitches and was present at the battle for Hue. His platoon had been trapped behind a stone wall near a palace occupied by the North Vietnamese Army, and had taken heavy fire on and off that day. By the time a rescue force arrived just before nightfall, all of the soldiers in the platoon had been wounded. Oscar had taken rounds in his shoulder and thigh. He was transported by helicopter to the hospital at Da Nang where he recovered. He was then sent to Fort Campbell, Kentucky, and was honorably discharged two months later. Three of his buddies did not survive their wounds. The news of their deaths came to him while at Fort Campbell, and Oscar began a lifetime of heavy drinking.

When Oscar came home, he didn't do anything for a while since he drew a disability check from the army. His wife, Arlene, whom he had married a year before joining the army, was a nurse at the local hospital. She was paid very well, which guaranteed a comfortable lifestyle.

Being bored from doing nothing, he had opened a small, used-car lot on the edge of Central City. Business was good. Oscar would buy his cars at a dealer auction in Memphis. His technique on a car sale was to get, as a down payment, the amount of money that had been paid for the car, plus fifty dollars. The balance of the sale would be financed, and, if the car had to be repossessed, no money would be lost. Oscar was poplar with his customers; if he had been ambitious, he could have sold ten times more cars than he actually sold. But he was content to sell only a certain number each year. To be busier would have interfered with his whiskey drinking and his other favorite pastime, chasing women. His interest in women had no bounds. Oscar always ate supper late and went to bed late or, as the case might be if he drank more than usual, early the next morning. Most morning awakenings were accompanied with hangover headaches. Therefore, he was not an early riser. However, that didn't repress his business, since hardly anyone in Cade County shopped for a used car before noon.

He didn't have any office help. An arrangement was made with the secretary, Alicia, in a local lawyer's office to do the necessary paper work when a car was sold. Mose Wooten, an elderly black man, worked in the afternoons for Oscar, cleaning and servicing the units on the lot. Mose was loyal and trustworthy and, most of all, kept his mouth shut about Oscar's affairs. That, in itself, guaranteed Mose's job security. On occasion, Mose took liberties with this knowledge and would not come to work for days at a time when the fish were biting in nearby Gallatin Lake. Sometimes that caused inconveniences for Oscar, but he never complained.

Oscar had not been selective about his female companions. It didn't matter if they were young, old, thin, heavy, pretty, or ugly. Over the years he had discovered a few things about females. To him, the one thing they had in common was that they all needed loving, and Oscar was dead set on accommodating as many of them as possible. Common knowledge in Central City was that Oscar always had a side woman. The interest was in who he was seeing next.

Strangely enough, the community unwittingly aided Oscar in keeping his affairs secret from Arlene. No one wanted to be identified as the blabber-mouth who spilled the beans to Arlene. Arlene had no direct knowledge of Oscar's pursuit of women although she was continuously suspicious of him. From time to time, she did try to track his movements. One such effort blew up in her face and made her a joke in the eyes of the coffee crowd at Lola's.

Ten years ago, Arlene went with a car load of her friends to a Central City High School girl's basketball tournament in a town seventy miles away. The games started at noon and continued into the night. Central City High's game was scheduled at 6:00 p.m. She and all her friends had played high school basketball, and they enjoyed the games played by teams other than Central City High. As soon as the women arrived at the tournament site for the first game, she hired a taxi to sneak her back to Central City with the intention to catch Oscar with a woman. Arlene had not asked the taxi driver how much the fare would be and was surprised, upon arriving back at her home, that it was ninety dollars. A fifty was all she had in her purse, and the bank was closed on this particular afternoon.

The only way Arlene could cover the fare was to have the cabbie take her to the car lot and get the money from Oscar. Oscar was caught by surprise when he saw Arlene get out of the cab. It just so happened that this was one of the few days he wasn't with a woman.

When Oscar asked why she was coming back to town in a taxi, Arlene, already deeply embarrassed, screamed, "You SOB. I was coming back to catch you with a girl friend!"

Oscar began laughing and couldn't quit. Arlene started beating him over the head with her purse. Mose had to step out from under the shade tree and pull her off Oscar. Mose drove Arlene home where she sat on the couch and fumed the rest of the day. A local customer, who had been on hand during the confrontation, made a beeline to Lola's coffee shop with the news. This event was easily the talk of the town, and Arlene was the butt of jokes for several days.

Deputy Wade Sumrall exited the funeral home after paying his respects to Arlene, passing by Trip, Miles, and Toby. They all spoke, "Hello, Mr. Wade. How are you doing?" Although they were friendly to Wade, they were also afraid of him.

Just as Wade went out of sight in his squad car, a long, black Hummer limo with Shelby County, Tennessee, plates eased around the corner. The boys focused on the vehicle. Limos were not uncommon in Cade County ever since the casinos had opened at Tunica, but they had never seen a Hummer. The vehicle stopped directly in front of the funeral home entrance. The smartly dressed driver got out, left his door ajar, went down the side, and opened one of the double doors. Trip and Miles were staring at the instrument panel and didn't really see what happened next, even though later they claimed they did. A tall blonde with substantial breasts swung her long legs out of the limo, open for a brief moment then closed as she stood up on her spike heels. She was wearing a low cut, very short, expensive black dress. The top was unbuttoned nearly to her navel, revealing much flesh. The boys stared!! As she walked past them, she squeezed Toby's cheek, smiled "Hi, Cutie," and strutted into the funeral home.

In the parlor, Arlene was sitting on a sofa near the casket, sobbing and clutching a tissue in her hand. Three of Arlene's closest friends were sitting beside her trying to give comfort. Several visitors were awkwardly standing nearby. Before anyone fully understood what was happening, the blonde had breezed by them leaving the scent of exotic perfume in her wake. No one recognized her.

As the ladies stared, she approached the casket, bent over and kissed Oscar on the cheek and said in a husky voice, "Oh, Sweetie, I'm going to miss you so much!! Especially those Tuesday nights when you would take me to the Rum Boogie on Beale Street after the car auction! You were such a man! Bye, Baby."

The ladies and the visitors looked on in shock. Before anyone could react, the blonde disappeared from the room.

Arlene's friend Mary, her eyes wide, exclaimed, "Who in the hell was that?"

Lola, the coffee shop owner, blurted out, "I've never seen her before. And I don't think she was wearing any underwear!"

Arlene had stopped sobbing and was looking on with her jaw dropped wide open. Suddenly, she jumped up and charged the casket shrieking, "Why, you son-of-a-bitch!! So that's what's been going on behind my back all these years."

She started pummeling the corpse, jerking at Oscar's tie causing the casket to shift on its platform.

She screamed, "I knew it! I knew you were two-timing me while I was working my tail off at the hospital and cooking for you and washing your clothes. All this time you were making me the laughing stock of this two-bit town. I should have kicked your ass out long ago!"

Arlene had become red-faced and was frothing at the mouth. One of the three ministers she had hired for the funeral services to pray Oscar's soul to Heaven appeared, his mouth agape. He had never heard Arlene, or any other woman for that matter, speak this way. He was fresh from the seminary and had been sent by his church, six months ago, to the denomination's branch in Central City.

Since it was the peak time of visitation, some of the visitors had intended to socialize in the lobby of the funeral home as a means of putting off having to go on into the parlor to view the corpse and talk to Arlene. But when they heard the commotion, all of them quickly moved in, jamming one of the doors in the process. Jo Ann Mathis, who worked in the funeral home and was also Oscar's sister, grabbed at Arlene trying to pull her away from Oscar. Arlene jerked back. Jo Ann tugged harder at Arlene. Arlene was in a rage. She was already chapped with Jo Ann, for word had drifted back to her that Jo Ann was telling around town that Arlene was the reason Oscar drank so much. She slapped Jo Ann. Jo Ann grabbed Arlene's hair, and, to her amazement, it came off in her hands. Everyone stared; no one in town knew Arlene wore a wig. The sight was comical: the woman standing there bald-headed, shrieking obscenities, and grabbing at Jo Ann. Amos McPhail, the young preacher, thought that someone needed to get these two women separated. He was a small guy, and both Arlene and Jo Ann were larger than he. He grabbed Jo Ann to pull her away from Arlene just as the crowd came into full view of the fuss. Jo Ann and Arlene's struggle was slinging poor Amos around. It appeared to the crowd that Amos was attacking Jo Ann, and Arlene was trying to pull him off her.

A matronly lady who was a member of Amos' church, exclaimed, "Goodness sakes! What kind of heathen preacher did they send to us?"

In the meantime, the blonde exited the funeral home, blew a kiss at the three immobile boys, and got into the limo. The chauffeur closed the door and got behind the wheel. The limo disappeared in the direction it came.

Sam Gray, the owner of Gray's Funeral Home, was called at home by his undertaker, Reese Jones, who was on funeral duty. When the telephone rang at Sam's house, he became irritated upon seeing his business number on the caller ID screen. Reese had been instructed that he was not to be bothered because his favorite movie "*The Good, the Bad and the Ugly*" was on TMC tonight. Sam had already seen it seventeen times but was looking forward to enjoying it again.

When Sam answered, Reese urgently said, "Boss, you need to get down here and do something. Some young floozy just walked in here and kissed Oscar lying dead on his back. Arlene has lost it again, and she and Jo Ann are fighting in front of the whole Methodist Church!"

As Sam muted the sound on the movie, he thought how those Methodists had always caused him grief. It was always something.

Sam asked Reese, "Has Wade Sumrall been by yet?"

"He just left."

"Call 911 and have them get him back. He is the very one who can get those women settled down."

Sam hung up. He didn't give a damn if they destroyed the whole damn funeral home. He was not leaving his movie! With that, he scooted forward, turned up the sound on the TV, and promptly forgot the whole matter.

Wade was on the outskirts of town, headed toward the county line, when the 911 operator contacted him with instructions to return to the funeral home. By the time he got parked and entered the parlor, the commotion had ended. Arlene had replaced the wig but not before several church members had snapped photos of her with their cell phones. She was back in her former spot on the sofa being again comforted by her friends but now for a different reason. Jo Ann had disappeared to the ladies room, and several of the men present were getting Oscar's body back in a proper position in the casket. Others were picking up the floral arrangements that had been knocked over.

Wade just stood there with his hands on his hips shaking his head in disbelief. He turned and walked up to the office where Reese was getting off the phone. Wade asked him what had happened back there. Reese explained. Wade was standing in the door and Trip, Miles, and Toby had inched up listening intently to the conversation.

Wade asked, "Well, who was that blonde woman? Apparently, she is the cause of this ruckus."

Reese replied, "Wade, I've never seen her before. And I saw her twice tonight. Once when she breezed by my doorway, and once when she flew by again and out the front door, all for a total of five seconds. But man, was she good looking!"

Trip blurted, "You got that right, Reese. She is better looking than Norma Sue Riley!"

Wade whirled facing the boys. "That's not possible. Nobody looks better than Norma Sue."

Toby snickered, "If you had seen what I saw, you wouldn't be saying that."

Wade asked, "What did you see?"

All eyes latched onto Toby. Toby's face turned red from the sudden attention. He muttered, "Nothing," and retreated to the nearby water fountain for a drink.

Wade was curious. "Where were you boys when all this happened?"

Miles spoke up, "We were outside when this black Hummer limo showed up. The blonde got out of the back and smiled at me and then went inside."

Trip said, "Naw, that's not what happened. She smiled at me."

"That's a lie if I ever heard one!" Miles replied.

Wade spoke, "Okay, boys, knock it off. Now tell me, was that limo from Tunica?"

Toby had regained his courage and had ventured back. He said, "I don't know about that, but it had a Shelby County, Tennessee, tag. My aunt lives in Memphis, and when I go to visit her, I see those tags on all the cars up there."

Trip sneered and said sarcastically, "That's a sharp observation, Toby. Do you think they would have Michigan tags on their cars in Memphis?"

Toby ignored him. He had thought of something which would elevate his status in the eyes of Wade. He eagerly said, "Mr. Wade, I know what her name is."

"What is it?" Wade demanded.

"It's Coco Chanel."

"How do you know that?"

Toby said, "I saw it stamped on her black leather purse that she left on the limo seat when she went inside."

Wade wondered what might pop up if he ran that name on the internet tomorrow.

Reese sniped, "That's real cool, Toby. Only about ten thousand women in America have that name. You dunce, that's the name of the purse maker!"

Wade scowled. "I've about had enough of you boys. All of y'all come to the sheriff's office in the morning. I want to get a report on what y'all saw."

Wade was late getting to the office on Friday morning. The boys were already there talking to the 911 dispatcher. Wade invited them into the front office where Sally Ryder was busy retrieving e-mails from the computer. Wade told Toby and Trip to wait there and had Miles follow him into Sheriff Powers' office. He sat in Grady's leather chair facing Miles. Deputy Jack Early came in, closed the door, and sat in a chair by the window.

Wade quizzed Miles about what happened the night before and what he had observed. Miles repeated what he had told Wade and Reese. He added nothing new. Wade dismissed Miles and had him tell Trip to come in.

Trip entered, took a seat in the chair Miles had vacated, put his feet up on the sheriff's desk, and smartly asked, "Am I a suspect? Do I need to have my lawyer present?"

Wade glared at him. Trip lost the war of the stares, put his feet on the floor, and straightened up. Wade went through the same questions he had asked Miles, and from Trip's answers, was convinced he had been told everything they had seen.

Trip left the office, and Toby, the youngest of the three young men, entered.

"Okay, Toby, tell us what you saw last night," Wade said.

Toby replied, "Well, when that woman got out of the limo, I saw up under her dress. She wasn't wearing any panties. I think she wanted me to notice."

"Is that a fact?"

"Yeah."

"Well, tell me Toby, was her body hair blonde?" Wade asked.

Toby exclaimed, "Are you trying to trick me, Mr. Wade? She didn't have hair! She was naked like all women are."

At that, Wade had to look down real hard at the desk blotter. Jack turned in his chair, looked out the window, and became strangled, trying not to laugh aloud. Aha! Toby had never seen a naked woman!

Toby looked over at Jack and then asked Wade, "What's wrong with Mr. Jack?"

"Oh, he is having trouble with his allergies."

Wade leaned back in his chair, rocked slowly and stared up at the ceiling. He said, "You're very observant, Toby. Maybe we could use someone to be our eyes around town. You know, we don't have enough officers to be everywhere."

Toby brightened up. "Why, thanks, Mr. Wade. I'd like to do that. When can I start?"

"Oh, we'll let you know. You go on. I'll talk to the sheriff about it."

As Toby started toward the door, Jack asked, "Say, Toby, did you like what you saw?"

By now, Toby was feeling included and he cockily replied, "Nah, Mr. Jack, not really. When you see lots of naked women, it sort of gets old."

After the door closed, both Jack and Wade laughed so hard their sides hurt.

Wade said, "The only thing we learned this morning that we didn't find out last night is that the blonde is shaved."

CHAPTER 12
THE SPEEDING TICKET

Wade Sumrall had pulled over to the side of a gravel road that intersected the highway at the north end of Cade County. A large tree with low hanging branches was there, and he was parked in its shade with the car windows rolled down, catching the breeze. He was about twenty yards from the highway and in a good position to see the traffic. It was Friday, the first day of August. Wade had been sitting there for an hour, just resting and watching the cars go by. He had a lot to think about. So much had happened since the first of the year.

Carl Spencer and his wife, Eunice, sped by heading north. Most of the drivers that passed by had not noticed the sheriff's vehicle, but Carl did. Since the car didn't have an air conditioner, the windows were down in his Chrysler. Carl's huge, gnarled left hand went out the window and upward in a wave to him. Wade grinned and flipped the overhead red lights acknowledging the wave. They were his neighbors, and he knew they weren't going to Oxford for beer. He figured that Eunice giggled at the lights coming on.

A few minutes later Earl Ray breezed by, also heading north. Alertly, Earl Ray spied him and flipped Wade the bird with his left hand, a finger missing. Wade hit the siren. He knew Earl Ray was going after beer, or bourbon, depending on his mood and how far he intended to carry his feelings.

Seeing the hand started him thinking again about Earl Ray and Coley. He was lost in thought when a southbound BMW blew by going at least one hundred miles per hour. Wade was startled at the rate of speed. He cranked up, hitting the highway with his lights on and siren blaring. Both cars covered several miles before Wade was able to overtake the BMW and get it pulled over. Wade noticed a Shelby County, Tennessee, license plate which was personalized with the letters *ISUEU*. Although the rate of speed of the car didn't really concern him, this bit of egotism did.

Wade approached the driver's side of the BMW. The driver had already rolled the window down.

Stanley Robbs, a thirty-year old lawyer with a large downtown Memphis law firm, was speeding south toward Poston, the county seat of Cade County, Mississippi. Today was the deadline to get papers filed in a case in Cade County. Stanley was also in a dark mood. The day had started wrong and had gone downhill ever since. A service truck had flipped over at the Mallory Street exit causing a huge back-up of traffic headed to the business area of downtown Memphis. The wreck caused him to be late for work.

Entering the front office of the high-rise building four blocks east of the cobblestones on the Mississippi River, he saw several people sitting in the waiting room. Actually, Stanley smelled the people before he saw them. The scent of stale sweat filled the entire room. He nearly gagged. The three arm chairs and the sofa were occupied. That was a surprise. The prestigious law firm of Janes, Knobly, and Stilt, rarely had visitors. The firm had forty-three lawyers on its staff and represented clients in a variety of legal issues. Most of the clients were corporations or individuals who were established with the firm. These clients made contact with the law firm by telephone, email, or fax and had no need to be in the waiting room. A visit there was a waste of time for the clients. Actually, the lawyers didn't want a physical visit anyway since it also took up their time that could be devoted to work.

In fact, in his three years with the firm, Stanley had never seen anyone in the waiting room and was shocked at the sight of the people present. To him, it looked like a whole family of white trash. The only grown man in the bunch was dressed in overalls and a faded, red Carhartt t-shirt with the sleeves cut off. He had on worn black dress shoes without socks. One of those silly Arkansas Razorback caps with a hog snout on the bill was atop his head.

Next to him on the sofa was a heavy-set woman wearing a sack dress that appeared to be home-made. She was wearing flip flops on her dirty feet. A boy, about sixteen, wearing canvas pants that hadn't been washed in weeks and a New Orleans Saints jersey with the number torn off sat in one chair. The other two seats were occupied by junior high school girls.

Both wore glasses and were reading magazines from the end table. Two younger girls were busy playing hopscotch in the middle of the room. They had marked off the game lines on the expensive hardwood floor of the waiting room with a piece of blue chalk from their mother's purse. They had already knocked a pretty Chinese vase off its stand and had caved in the shade of the lamp standing in the corner. As they jumped through the hopscotch squares from one end to the other, the girls squealed loudly and ground the plaster of the broken vase into the floor wax with Mary Jane shoes. No one in the room was paying any attention to their antics except Leah Fornet, the receptionist/typist. She was glaring at them through the glass in front of her desk.

Stanley had stopped just inside the door staring in disbelief! As he moved past the visitors to get into Leah's office, the woman on the sofa gave him a huge smile. She had no teeth! Stanley shuddered!

Stanley entered Leah's office and demanded, "Who are those people?"

Stanley had been raised in Baltimore in an exclusive neighborhood and had attended an up-East law school, finishing fifth in his class. His father was a successful stockbroker, and his mother taught math at a nearby college. Stanley's undergraduate education had been in a private school located near his neighborhood. He had never seen people like these, not even in the shopping malls in Baltimore.

Leah smiled sweetly. "Oh, Hon, these are your clients! And you need to get them off my hands."

Stanley stared at her in disbelief. "Why are these my clients?"

"Because Mr. Nutt said so." Josh Nutt was one of the five senior partners in the firm and was the one who assigned the member lawyers to new clients.

She was beginning to enjoy Stanley's discomfort; she really couldn't stand him. During his first week at the firm, Stanley had demanded that Leah give him the parking space in the garage where she had been parking for years. It was near the elevator. She had refused. Ever since, Stanley had gone out of his way to be rude to her by making snide remarks about her social life or falsely accusing her in front of the senior partners of making errors in her work. Leah and all the secretaries and paralegals at Janes, Knobly, and Stilt agreed that he was arrogant, egotistical, and spoiled. In short, he had an attitude. Stanley was single, and the ladies could understand. He had no friends among this crew, a fact which would haunt him in the days to come.

"I thought Dudley Cook was next on the list," Stanley replied.

Leah smiled. "He was. But he got to work before you. On time, I might add, and he saw this bunch of freaks out there. Dudley grabbed several files and went to the courthouse to run those land titles you haven't got around to doing. Mr. Nutt said he didn't want those people to be out there any longer than necessary. When he looked at Dudley's empty desk, he moved you up the list. You get them back to your office fast! I have had all of this that I can stand."

"Why didn't Mr. Nutt run them out of here?"

"That's the best part, Hon. You should read the intake sheet. Here, look at it."

Stanley took the sheet from her and noted the client's name was Jeb Shaw. Then he skipped down to the explanation box for the reason for needing counsel. By the time he reached the end, his eyes bugged. Essentially, the man claimed to be the next of kin to Mr. Joab McMath, a resident of Cade County, Mississippi, who had died in January. Jeb said that his cousin's estate was worth seven million dollars, and he wanted to file a claim for all of it. Wow! As much as he was repulsed by the Shaws, Stanley thought that he had better check this out. If he refused to investigate this claim and it turned out to be true, he would find himself a defendant to an interoffice malpractice situation before being fired!

Stanley went to the door, held it open, mustered his best ambulance-chasing smile, and said, "Sir, why don't you and your son come back to my office."

The man and boy stood up. The man directed an exaggerated wink toward Stanley and said, "Well, that's my wife's son. But I'm not sure if I'm the father!"

The woman gave out a very masculine sounding guffaw, slapped her leg and said, "Now, Jeb, you know better than that. Don't you remember that day in the barn loft?"

The boy smiled and hit Jeb on his shoulder with his fist. "Aw, Pa!"

They had started past Stanley when Jeb turned toward his wife, took a pair of false teeth out of his mouth and handed them to his wife, a string of salvia drooling down from them to the floor. She took the teeth and placed them in her mouth.

Stanley stared. As she smiled at him again, he was amazed at how well they fit! Jeb spoke, now in a different dialect and one more appropriate for his appearance, "Mabel might need them if you keep me back there very long. She gets hungry a lot, and them Nabs in that machine downstairs might be hard to chew on with her gums."

Stanley thought that this would be one of his shortest interviews ever. He led them back to his office; and when they were seated, he proceeded with some of the usual small talk.

"I see y'all are Razorback fans."

The boy spoke up, "How did you guess?"

Stanley's face turned red and he replied, "Oh, I got lucky I suppose."

Stanley continued, "I apologize about only having two of your family back here. But we are having renovations."

The father spoke up, "Well, you don't mind us. Just go ahead. We had some fried sauerkraut, biscuits, and buttermilk before we left the house this morning."

Stanley stared uncomprehendingly. Then he realized the man thought that renovations were some kind of city food. He just waved his hand. "Oh, never mind. I'm not hungry right now. I'll just save them for later."

Jeb and the boy were sitting in the chairs across from his huge desk. Stanley had sat down in his leather chair and rolled back as far as he could on the chair mat. He fully understood the in-office theory of having large desks in order to put distance between the lawyer and his client so that the client could be further intimidated. But today, Stanley was thankful for another reason! Now the body odor of these clients would be more distant from his nose, making it bearable to stay in his office.

Stanley studied the intake sheet. He noticed that the whole family, except the two small girls, had cell phones. The boy's name was Jeb Shaw, Jr. He laughed to himself thinking how cruel it would be to Jeb if he did someday find out that he was not the boy's father! Stanley didn't recognize the Arkansas town on the address line. He would look it up later, if the town could be found on any map.

The information was written down in Leah's handwriting. Stanley wondered if Jeb could read or write but didn't want to get into any subject with Jeb that would keep him in the room any longer than necessary. So he didn't ask. It didn't matter anyway. Jeb stated that he was a distant cousin of Joab McMath, a late resident of Four Points, Mississippi. Jeb also claimed that he was the sole heir of Joab and entitled to all his assets. Stanley looked up and saw that both males were watching him.

"Mr. Jeb, I see that you are a cousin to Joab McMath. Could you explain how you are kin?"

"Why, shore, Mr. Stanley. You see, Joab was my mother's mother's baby brother's grandson."

At that, Stanley shook his head from side to side trying to digest this revelation. He took out a sheet of paper and diagramed the family tree. The Shaw men grinned, and Jeb asked, "You need any help in figuring that out?"

"No, I don't. I'm not stupid," Stanley snapped.

Jeb, Jr. grinned. "Well, we wuz wondering!"

Ignoring the remark, Stanley said, "It looks like you are his third cousin."

Jeb smiled. "That's right. And the only one! And there ain't no second cousins or first cousins or yard chilluns. I'm Joab's only heir! Any way you figure it."

Stanley looked across the desk. "Do you think your cousin left a will?"

"I doubt it. I don't think anybody in our family ever had a will. Never was nobody who ever had any money to leave. Just usually some land. And the children always split that up."

"I see you put on this sheet of paper that your cousin had seven million dollars. Why do you think that?" Stanley asked.

Jeb explained, "Well, Joab wuz always going to Texas. I mean by that about once a year. Before my grandma died, he always stopped by to see her either on the way out or on the way back. But she died fifteen years ago, and we haven't seen him since. Joab did send my Momma a Christmas card every year, though. I wuz there the last time he saw Grandma. We were out under the shade tree in her front yard talking. Us and that nosy Tommy Baldwin and his son from down the road. Tommy asked him what he was going to Texas for. Joab winked at me and said, 'To check on my oil wells. I settle up with the oil company once a year.'

Tommy asked, 'How much money are you getting out of them?'

Joab told him, 'Oh, I think I've got a couple of million by now.'

Tommy blurted, 'Wow! If I had some wells that gave up that much, I'd move out there and buy a house next door to them so I could listen to them pump at night while I slept.'"

Jeb continued, "But you know that two million ought to be worth about seven by now. Maybe more."

Stanley groaned to himself. He reflected that this was pure speculation and he should consult with Mr. Nutt because it is beginning to look like a worthless case.

To the pair seated in front of him, Stanley said, "Excuse me. I need to discuss this information with my boss. I'll be right back."

Stanley walked down the hall to Mr. Nutt's office which, of course, was a corner office. From there you could see the north bridge over the Mississippi River in one direction and across the river toward West Memphis in the other. The door was open. Stanley knocked on the frame and proceeded into the room where Mr. Nutt was hanging up the telephone.

"Mr. Nutt, ah, I don't know what we have here with this new case," Stanley began sheepishly.

"Tell me about it," the older man said.

After Stanley explained what Jeb Shaw had told him, and they had discussed the situation in detail, Mr. Nutt said, "Step outside and close the door. I need to call a colleague."

Fifteen minutes later, Stanley was back in his seat in front of Mr. Nutt's desk.

Mr. Nutt said, "I called my good friend, Frank Poley, in Tupelo with Waltz, Poley, and Prod. They're the largest firm in town, and we have worked together on many cases over the years. Frank has contacts all over northeast Mississippi. He called the clerk in Cade County and found that the Joab McMath estate has been opened. After the man's death, no one stepped forward with a will to probate, so a lawyer named Wiley Downs in Baxter was appointed by the chancellor to be the administrator. The clerk said nothing has been filed in the case since it was opened except a few small claims. And she said that other than a small balance in the bank, a section of land with the residence, and some worn-out personal property, nothing else has been located. But down there within the community, it's believed that this man had wealth, even though he never wore it."

Mr. Nutt added, "And there's a problem. Today is the deadline to file any claim at all in that case. By their law, if no claim has been filed and someone came forward later with a will, it could be admitted for probate, and it couldn't be contested no matter what it said. That means Shaw's claim has to be filed today. If he is proven to be related and no one comes forward with a will, he will inherit. If a will is found, then we will be in a position to contest it and hopefully prevail. I'll get the staff busy with the filing, and you will have to drive it down to the courthouse. I can't use a runner because if there is any problem with getting this claim filed, I want a lawyer there - someone who would know how to handle any filing issue."

Mr. Nutt called the office manager and instructed her what needed to be done. She said that it would be about one o'clock before the typing and proofing would be complete. Stanley looked up the route to Poston, Mississippi, by way of Holly Springs and Oxford, and calculated that he could make the drive in two and one-half hours.

Stanley sat fuming in his BMW as he looked in the rearview mirror and watched the deputy sheriff approach. He noticed the deputy limp slightly as he walked forward. The guy looked old. They must be desperate for help down here if this man is all that could be hired for law enforcement, he reflected.

Stanley wouldn't have been this late if he had not taken the wrong turn south of Holly Springs. His mind was on the McMath case as he sped southward. By mistake he had taken a right on Highway #4 and had driven twenty miles toward Senatobia before he realized this was the wrong road. Stanley had stopped at a service station in the middle of nowhere to ask for the quickest way to Oxford, which was on the way to Poston. An unshaven guy in greasy coveralls was changing the oil in a car up on the rack in a bay. He walked over and asked the attendant for the directions. The guy grinned at Stanley's agitation of being lost and having to admit it. He patiently listened without interrupting to Stanley's explanation of why he took the wrong road and then said, "You know, I don't live here. Go over there by the welder and ask my boss, Billy Bob Bishop. He can tell you."

At that, Stanley's anger increased. His pet peeve since moving to the South was that nearly everyone, man and woman, had double first names. Billy Bob! Then, as he moved by the rack, the trouser leg of his tailored suit rubbed against the air compressor, leaving a streak of dust and grease on the material. He had just gotten the suit out of the cleaners yesterday. He nearly came unglued when Billy Bob told him that the shortest way to Oxford was to backtrack on Highway #4 to Holly Springs. Stanley tried to argue with Billy Bob because, as a lawyer, he knew there had to be a shorter way.

But Billy Bob, detecting his slight up-East accent, sternly looked at him and asked, "Fool, who's lost, me or you?"

Anyway, valuable time was being lost so Stanley dropped the subject and headed back the way he came.

———————

Stanley had his license ready by the time Wade reached the door. He spoke in a subdued tone, "Good afternoon, Sheriff."

Then he took a good look at Wade. Stanley noticed the western style white hat on top of his head with a badge pinned to the front, the scar on his face, and the sunglasses with reflective lenses, known in the profession as "Cool-Hands." Stanley could see his reflection in both lenses which caused him to think that this was the Hollywood stereotype of a Southern lawman!

Wade hitched his pants and replied, "Son, it's deputy sheriff, but thanks for the promotion."

"Could you go ahead and write the ticket? I'm in a hurry."

"Well, the hurry is obvious. So what is the hurry?"

"I'm with the law firm of Janes, Nobly, and Stilt in downtown Memphis, and my boss has sent me to file some papers at the courthouse in Poston."

"Is that a fact? Why didn't you mail them? Everybody else does."

Stanley explained, "Because today is the deadline, and I have to get there by five o'clock. If you don't hurry up, I won't make it."

Wade looked at his watch. It would take twenty minutes to get to Poston, and it was now 4:35. He smiled to himself. He could tell the young man was under a lot of stress.

"You know, I wasn't going to give you a ticket, only a warning. But since you told me to go ahead and write one, I'll accommodate you. But I'll tell you what. I know Mrs. Few, the clerk, very well. I'll call and have her wait for you."

Wade wrote out a ticket, handed it to Stanley, and said, "Now be careful and watch your speed going through Baxter. Their cops are out early on Fridays. They have a retired book salesman for a mayor down there and he is a loose cannon. He's made his cops get out of their squad cars and patrol the town on foot, among other things. And they are not in a good mood."

Stanley proceeded down the highway, driving exactly at 55 miles per hour. Wade got back into the car and called Mrs. Few on his cell phone. He explained why she was about to have a visitor and asked her to stay there until the lawyer arrived. Then he called Sheriff Powers and told him that he had seen the lawyer's papers sticking out of a file folder. At the top of the paper were the words "In Re: Estate of Joab McMath."

The sheriff said, "I figured someone would come out of the woodwork. And I'll bet you five dollars it's coming from Arkansas."

Linda Nell Few, the Cade County Chancery Clerk, was standing at the front counter when Stanley stormed through the door. It was 5:10 p.m. He had caught up with a slow-moving vehicle and the chain of other vehicles that the car was delaying just south of Baxter. Stanley was fifth in line. Even though this stretch of highway was flat and straight, there had been no opportunity to pass because of the oncoming traffic. It was as if someone up ahead was opening a gate and letting cars out at appropriate intervals to prevent passing. He was forced to move at a speed of twenty-five mph the entire distance from Baxter to Poston, all the while fearing that the clerk wouldn't wait for him that long.

Stanley had run from his car in the parking lot to the clerk's office and was out of breath. Ms. Few was alone. Her staff had already gone home for the day.

She smiled sweetly. "Shug, are you the one that Wade called me about?"

Her remark irritated him. This was his second pet peeve about being in the South. Most of the females, young and old, greeted acquaintances and strangers alike, with personal names like *Hon, Shug, Sweetie, Darlin.*

He gasped. "Yes, ma'am!"

"How can I help you?"

"I need to file this claim in the Joab McMath estate," he parroted, exactly as he had been told and handed her the documents.

Ms. Few took them and stamped the filing date and time on the face page.

Stanley protested. "Wait a minute. You put 5:10 p.m. on them. Can't you put 5:00, the hour the courthouse closes?"

"It doesn't matter. The law says a document is deemed filed on time if the courthouse is open."

Stanley blurted, "That's not what we were taught in law school."

Ms. Few peered over the top of her glasses at him. "And where did you go to law school?"

He told her the name of the school which had a prestigious reputation, thinking she would be impressed.

"I've never heard of it. But that doesn't matter. This is my office, and what I say goes. If I said this claim is filed on time, then it is filed on time." She pointed her index finger at him and demanded, "Is that clear?"

Stanley stammered, "But, what if someone contests this claim as being filed after the deadline?"

Linda Nell reached over and gently patted his hand that was resting on the counter. "Why, young man, you just call me as a witness, and I'll clear that up. I drink wine with the judge and his wife over at their house every Saturday afternoon. You don't have anything to worry about! That is, as long as you stay on the good side of me."

Stanley breathed a sign of relief. This was the first break he'd had all day. He even felt better now about being called *Shug*.

CHAPTER 13
THE PLAN

On Monday morning, Stanley was in the office on time. He didn't want to have another Friday. He was ambivalent about the McMath case. Stanley felt like this was a wild goose chase because he sensed those Shaws were not credible. He didn't believe any money or anything of value would ever turn up, and the firm would be out expenses for proceeding in the matter. On the other hand, if money could be found, he, as lead lawyer on the case, would get a double share of the firm's fees. He gloated! That would serve Dudley Cook right. His long, tall colleague was sort of aloof toward him because Dudley had finished first in his law school class. Dudley's constant efforts to ingratiate himself with Mr. McNutt was particularly galling. Just see how much money Dudley would get out of the title files he had grabbed to get out of having to deal with that white trash family!

The firm had a meeting at eight-thirty every Monday morning. All of the attorneys who didn't have court appearances were required to be in attendance. The chair of the meeting rotated among the three most senior lawyers. Today, Mr. Nutt was chairman.

As Stanley went past Leah, he handed her the speeding ticket to take care of on his behalf.

She smiled sweetly. "Oh, Stanley, what is this? Your grocery shopping list?"

Stanley reddened. He had dreaded having to confront Leah and to admit what had happened. Stanley had thought about paying the fine out of his own pocket, but his frugality overcame that urge. He would take any insult over the ticket in exchange for the fine being paid from the firm's travel account.

Stanley went to his office to go over some files before the meeting started. When he entered the conference room, all the seats except his were filled. He noticed a couple of the lawyers grin and turn their heads. Stanley became suspicious.

Mr. Nutt called the meeting to order. He went around the table from his right asking each lawyer to give a status report on their respective cases. Stanley was next to last with his. When he got to the McMath case, all the lawyers listened intently.

After Stanley was through, Mr. Nutt asked, "How did your trip go? Did you have any trouble on the way?"

Stanley squirmed. "Not really. Except I got a speeding ticket from a deputy just across the county line, about twenty miles from the courthouse."

At that, the room roared with laughter. Dudley was beating the table with his fists.

Stanley demanded, "Okay. So what? Everyone gets speeding tickets. And this is my first one since I started working here." He now knew that the busybody, Leah, had spread the word about the ticket.

Dudley Cook chortled, "Hey, a sheriff or his deputies can't give a speeding ticket on a state highway in Mississippi! You got snookered. I'll bet those lawmen down there are spreading the word about the Memphis rube that turned up. Now, won't our law firm look good the next time we go there for court?"

Stanley spoke sharply, "Just go to hell, Dudley!"

That outburst brought another round of laughter.

Mr. Nutt smiled. "Okay, ladies and gentlemen, knock it off. I want this case thoroughly investigated before we continue with it. Get our skip tracer busy with a property search. Start locally and expand it nationwide if you need to. Stanley, I'm going to assign Lillie Bess Dorgan to assist you. She is good at will contests and estate matters. I would advise you to listen to her. Okay?"

Stanley mumbled his consent. He didn't really get along with Lillie Bess, but she was admired by the senior partners. He knew not to rock that boat.

The meeting ended, and Lillie Bess trailed Stanley to his office. She spoke to him, "Stanley, we need to move this claim of the Shaw's forward as quickly as we can. If someone finds a will, we have serious problems."

"What good is that going to do if that man didn't have money? Or has money, and it can't be found?"

"That's true. But Mississippi has a two year statute of limitations that begins to run from the date an estate is closed. If a will is found after that, it won't do any good."

"The claim I filed Friday also asks for attorney Wiley Downs to continue in his position as administrator. Mr. Nutt said to leave it that way. Mr. Downs has to account to the court on the money he takes in and spends. That Tupelo lawyer knows him and said Downs is credible."

"Yeah. Just hope something doesn't happen that causes him to resign."

Stanley repeated, "Yeah."

"But we're going to have to do what's called a determination of heirship proceeding at some point."

"What's that?" Stanley asked.

Lillie Bess said, "It's a court hearing to prove that Jeb Shaw is the next of kin. You have to bring witnesses in to prove Joab McMath's family tree. You know, that he didn't have children, who his parents were, who their brothers and sisters were, and who died when. It can get sort of hairy."

"This sounds complicated."

"It is. You have to run a legal notice in the local paper directing anyone who claims to be an heir to show up in court. If money is found, you know someone other than Jeb will show up."

Stanley replied, "I just hope that character, Jeb Shaw, knows what he is talking about. How are we going to find out who knows who Joab McMath's heirs are?"

"Oh, we'll have to associate a local lawyer to assist us. We'll be groping in the dark if we don't."

"Does that mean we'll have to cut him in on our fee?"

Lillie Bess smiled. "Why, yes, sweetie. And that means your cut, whatever it is, just got smaller."

Stanley ignored her jibe and said, "Oh, well, zero times zero equals nothing."

Lillie Bess admitted, "That's a universal math equation."

"Yeah. I think we'd better get Mr. Nutt to locate a local lawyer. It would be best for us if he made the call, just in case the guy turns out to be a dud. You never know about those small town lawyers."

Later that day, Josh Nutt called Frank Poley again. "Hey, Frank. We've taken on a client who is a relative of a Joab McMath. That's the case I called you about last week. We filed a claim Friday on his behalf to the entire estate. Our client says he is a third cousin. You know we're going to have to confirm McMath's heirship in court. We need to associate a local lawyer, preferable one who practices in Cade County to assist us. Do you know one who would be suitable?"

Frank said, "Yes, I would recommend Lamar Mosley. He has been practicing law in Central City for over thirty years. He also knows most of the people in the south end of the county which is good for the heirship petition. There are a couple of good lawyers in Baxter if he can't do it for you. I wouldn't use Archie Baker though."

"Why not?" Josh asked.

"That guy is a nut. He knows the law, but his behavior is very erratic. He is always doing the unexpected. I guess the best description for him is that he is a loose cannon. He seems to deliberately antagonize the judges in his every courtroom appearance to the chagrin of his clients."

Josh said, "I'll take your word for it. We'll see if Mr. Mosley will help us on this matter."

"Well, we're always here. Call us if you need help."

Josh thanked him and hung up. He had his secretary locate Lamar Mosley's number and call him. Josh Nutt found that Lamar was willing to help. They talked a while and came to terms on the fee arrangement and who would do the paperwork for the proceeding.

CHAPTER 14
AUGUST WEEKENDS

Wade and Sheriff Powers were sitting in the sheriff's office just after lunch. They were sitting there not saying anything at all, just letting their lunches settle. The ceiling fan was turning steadily, stirring a stream of air down on the two men. Wade's eyelids began to droop.

He was just about asleep when Grady spoke, "Wade, I think that thing with the young blonde at Oscar's funeral was some kind of set-up."

"Why do you say that?"

Grady rocked back and forth in the chair, his hands clasped together over his stomach as he answered, "Well, she was a stranger to everybody at the funeral home and arrived in a limo from Memphis. Plus, she caused a tense commotion in the funeral home. It's as if she knew exactly which sore spots on Arlene to rub, like she intended to get Arlene to react just as she did."

Wade said, "I've been thinking the same thing. That whole episode was suspicious."

Grady said, "I wonder who could have been behind that and why."

"Well, no law was broken."

"That's right. Just a lot of hard feelings on Arlene's part came to the surface."

"Yeah, right in front of the entire Methodist Church and most of the town."

"I sort of feel sorry for Arlene having to put up with Oscar's drinking and women chasing all of those years," said Grady.

"I feel the same. Any other woman would have left Oscar years ago," said Wade.

"You got that right. I guess she must have really loved him or just didn't have anywhere else to go."

"I agree. Nowadays, too many women get stuck in a rut and find out too late that they've paired off with the wrong man."

Grady said, "I can't argue with that. That's what a good minister or marriage counselor would say."

"Speaking of counseling, what do you think of the school counselor, Rita Arnwine?"

Grady said, "She's not from here, so we didn't have the advantage of watching her grow up. But Emma really likes her. Since she and Stanley broke up, Emma has sort of taken Rita under her wing. The girl hasn't been in the county long enough to have made a lot of friends."

"Do you think she and Stanley will make up? They sure would make a good pair."

"The problem is Stanley. He can be hard-headed. I found out what they broke up about. And it was his fault. He jumped to conclusions about some of her school friends and let jealousy move in front of common sense."

"You can't be jealous unless you care for someone," noted Wade.

"Well, he must have really cared about Rita because his reaction to those Kentucky friends staying with her was over the top."

"Maybe he'll cool off. From some remarks she has made to Emma, I feel sure she'll take him back if he'll approach her the right way."

Grady said, "Well, Stanley will have to do it the right way. If he makes matters worse, she will be through with him. That girl has too much on the ball. She can have about any man she wants. Emma said that she has made remarks about going to medical school."

"Yeah. I've noticed some of our single guys going out of their way to drive by where she lives," Wade laughed. "Especially on those days when she is out washing her car wearing those short cut-offs. Those Swaney sisters would be pushed down a notch if she hung out at Sleazy's."

"I hope she doesn't get to be a regular at the beer joint. We have enough problems down there as it is."

"Yeah. But that would help us in a way because all the single guys would be at Sleazy's, and any trouble that they would be causing would be at one spot. We wouldn't have to be flitting all over the county to put out the fires."

Later that afternoon Wade drove down to Four Points to make a presence in the south end of the county. Sheriff Powers had discovered long ago that the voters were pleased if they saw a squad car in their community on a regular basis. They felt secure and safe with the thought that the sheriff did really care enough for their welfare to have his deputies drive by. Wade pulled in at the Stopwatch, a general store carried over from years past. The Stopwatch, the only store in the village, was a long rectangular building with lapped-wood siding. The peaked roof was covered with tin, now rusty. A porch was across the front of the building, the floor of which was two feet off the ground. Windows were to the left and right of the double front doors and were behind steel burglar bars.

On the inside, the wooden floor was soaked with coal oil from many years ago and generated a unique scent. The walls on both sides were shelved from waist high to near the ceiling and held the store's wares. Counters, spaced a few feet away from the walls, ran the length of the building. Four ceiling fans were mounted, in line, on down rods fastened to the ceiling. They whirred slowly the year round. Even though there was a pot-bellied stove near the back of the store that burned wood or coal, the owner had installed modern space heaters to keep the whole building warm. The owner had also installed a bank of coolers and freezers.

At the end of one counter near the stove, a salt meat box covered with a lid doubled as a seat for loafers. Around the stove, a few wooden straight chairs and some empty wooden drink cases also served as seats. Old fashioned candy and cookie jars rested on the counter top. A customer could still buy one huge cookie at a time to go with a slice of bologna. Besides the Stopwatch, the only other businesses in town were a chain saw repair shop, a feed mill, and a pulpwood yard.

Just as Wade pulled into the parking lot of the Stopwatch, the Jenkins brothers walked out with soft drinks and bags of potato chips in their hands. They were headed toward their father's pickup when Wade rolled down his window and hailed, "Hey, guys, come over here for a minute!"

They both ambled over and Chad asked, "What's up, Mr. Sumrall?"

"Not much. What are you boys doing this summer?"

Chad replied, "We've been helping Uncle Joe with his crops. He gave Eric and me a job this summer so we would have money to go to college this fall."

"That was good of him. And he did need help. By the way, how old are y'all?"

Eric chimed in, "I'm eighteen and Chad is nineteen. When Chad was in the 8th grade, he came down with rheumatic fever and had to lay out a year. That's why we graduated together this year."

"By any chance, was either of you at visitation at Oscar's funeral?"

Chad replied, "Nah. But we heard about the commotion there. I wish now we had of gone. We would have liked to have seen that fight!"

Eric said, "But we weren't left out completely. We saw the woman that caused the scene."

Wade became all ears. "You did? Where?"

"Oh, we were at the BP station on the south end of town filling the pickup with gas. A black limo pulled in past the gas pumps and stopped near the pay phone. This good looking blonde got out and made a call. She stood there probably five minutes talking. The woman laughed a lot, sometimes so much she would bend over," Eric said and raised and lowered his eyebrows.

"Yeah. We got our eyes full. No woman in this county wears skirts that short! Wow!" Chad said.

Eric laughed. "I won't forget that. We were both staring, and Chad let the tank run over. I'll bet two gallons of gas spilled out on the concrete before he let go of the hose handle."

Chad joined, "Yeah. But the wasted gas was worth it. And that limo driver died laughing when he saw what I had done."

Wade soaked in their conversation. He asked, "Look, if either of you saw the woman again, would you recognize her?"

Both nodded vigorously, and Eric said, "Heck, yeah, Mr. Sumrall. I'd recognize either her face or that good looking butt anywhere!"

"What do you boys do on Friday and Saturday nights?" Wade asked.

Chad said, "We've been hanging out at Sleazy's a lot. Sometimes we go to Gallatin. More girls are over there. And they are not as skanky."

"Would you boys be interested in having some fun and getting paid for it?"

They both chorused, "Yes!!"

Wade talked to them a few minutes. They listened intently. Wade pulled a roll of cash from his pocket, peeled a few bills off, and handed them to Chad. Then he cranked up and headed north to Central City. The boys did high fives and left for home in the pickup.

At 10:00 a.m. Monday morning Wade showed up at the sheriff's office. Sally was sitting at the front desk working on some files. Darlene was on vacation this week, and Sally always filled in for her. Sally and Wade exchanged good mornings, and she said, "Chad Jenkins called for you earlier. He needs to talk to you and said to call him during the lunch hour at his uncle's house. He and Eric are hauling hay today for their uncle and can't be reached till noon. They are off in Sabougla bottom and out of cell phone range." .

At 12:30, Wade called Uncle Joe's house. His wife, Kate, answered and Wade asked for Chad. Kate laughed. "Wade, I'll try. He has his feet stuck under my dinner table. Today, we're having crusty fried chicken, mashed potatoes, string beans, field peas, okra, fried green tomatoes, and corn bread. My dessert is hot blackberry cobbler with vanilla ice cream on top."

Wade groaned, "My stars, Kate, why didn't you invite me?"

"Wade, you would gain too much weight. You are big enough as it is."

She lowered her voice and asked, "Chad is not in trouble is he?"

"Oh, no. I just want to know if he and Eric will wash our squad cars next Saturday."

Kate put the receiver down. Wade heard her footsteps go to the dining room and tell Chad that the phone call was for him.

Chad came to the phone. In a low voice, he said, "Mr. Wade, I can't say much. Aunt Kate could hear me."

"Ok, I'll make it brief. Did you and Eric find out anything?"

"No, we didn't. We went to the place you told us to go on both Friday and Saturday nights."

"Well, it might have been an off night. Go back again this weekend."

Chad asked, "Saturday night, too, if we don't see anything on Friday night?"

"Sure. Do y'all need more money?"

"Yes, we do. We made some friends and had to spend money on them. But we only have one more weekend after this one because college starts after that."

"Yeah. This is a long shot anyway. If y'all don't see anything by then, I'll go to plan B. I can't finance your weekend fun forever. This is costing me more than I thought it would. I didn't think about y'all making friends, but I should have known that would happen."

"Well, we are sure having fun. We never imagined this kind of thing goes on."

Wade laughed.

Chad begged, "You won't tell anyone about this, will you?"

"Nope. No one will ever know."

"It would be embarrassing if our folks or Uncle Joe and Aunt Kate found out where we've been."

"I'll keep you covered," Wade assured.

Chad said urgently, "Hey, Mr. Wade, I've got to go. Eric and Uncle Joe are getting ahead of me at the table. If I don't hurry up and get back, there won't be any chicken left. When Uncle Joe said the blessing, I had my head down but kept my left eye open and saw that Eric already had his hand on the pully-bone. He beat me to the best part of the chicken."

Wade chuckled and hung up.

.

CHAPTER 15
MARLA

Saturday night, just as the weather report was beginning on Channel 33, the telephone rang at Wade's house. That irritated him to no end. A storm had developed earlier in the day in the southwest part of the state and was moving toward Cade County. Wade was a weather bug and enjoyed stormy weather. His favorite television shows were simply the news, weather, and "Wheel of Fortune" if he was in the house when the program came on. He had quit watching other television programs, except for ball games, a long time ago when "Gunsmoke" and "Rawhide" had been dropped. Wade didn't want to miss any storm warnings.

He got out of his comfortable recliner and picked up the phone, and he grumpily answered, "Hello!"

There was a moment of silence. Then Eric Jenkins replied, "Uh, Mr. Wade. Did I call you at a bad time?"

Wade could hear a lot of loud music and noise in the background. He said, "That's all right, Eric. The weather was coming on, and I wanted to see when the storm would get here. We may have some damage tonight. Go ahead."

Eric said with eagerness in his voice, "Hey, we've hit pay dirt! She's here. She just got here. And we're seeing a lot more than that day in Central City. Man, you won't believe it!"

"Are you sure it's her?"

"There's no doubt about it!"

"Have y'all seen anyone else in there you recognize, like anyone from Central City?"

Eric admitted, "No. But we really haven't looked around, not since she came in, and it's sort of dark in here anyway."

"Look, you boys stay till pretty late and watch who comes and goes. I want to know if anyone from Central City comes in there. If they do, sneak out without being seen. Ok?"

"You got it."

"And find out, if you can, what's going on there next weekend. And her name. I want to know that."

Eric said, "I don't think that will be a problem. I have to go. Chad is waving for me."

Wade put down the receiver and walked back to the leather recliner. By now the weather was over, but it didn't matter because his mind was focused on Eric's report.

He uncapped another cold diet Dr. Pepper and took a long swig, gurgling it down. He began to formulate a plan for the next weekend. The answer to that whole mysterious funeral home episode might be just around the corner.

Wade was occupied all day Monday. The weekend had been a busy one for Cade County law enforcement, the emergency medical technicians, and the fire departments. There had been a drunken brawl among a bunch of migrant workers in Vena, the third largest town in Cade County. It had rained all day Saturday keeping them out of the fields. Their usual weekend beer drinking had started early. They were all single or married with their spouses still back in Mexico. The sheriff's office had to send assistance to Vena's police department to get the brawlers under control.

The fight had started in the middle of the afternoon at a local sweet potato warehouse. The workers had gathered underneath an open shed with coolers of beer. A game of marbles had been started in the dry dirt. Only two could play at the same time. So, the player next in line would play the winner and the loser would go to the bottom of the list. To see who got the first shot in the game, the players "legged" at a straight line drawn in the dust some distance from the circle of marbles. The marble that landed with the least distance to the line entitled its player to the first shot. It was really a boy's game, but the workers were a long way from home and were bored. This kind of game fit nicely into their down time.

An argument arose over whether Manuel's or Artiz's marble was the closest to the line. Manuel's marble had carried past the line and Artiz's marble had stopped short by about the same distance. It really looked like a tie, which would call for a retry, but neither would agree. And it didn't help either that two days ago, when the workers were culling rotten potatoes out of the crates that were to be shipped to market, Manuel hit Artiz in the head with one. The mushy potato had splattered all over his hair leaving an awful stench on his face and shirt for the rest of the day. Artiz accused him of doing it on purpose. Threats were exchanged, and their argument became so heated that the supervisor had to call them down. Manuel had been placed on a crew at another farm by the supervisor to keep the two separated.

They were bent over facing each other across the line when Artiz grabbed a handful of dust and threw it into Manuel's eyes. While he was rubbing the dust out, Artiz reached down and rolled his own marble over one revolution toward the line using his sombrero to shield the move. However, Manuel's friend, Teco, saw this and jabbered in Spanish to Manuel what he had seen. Manuel slapped Artiz, and the watching crowd joined in, escalating an argument between two marble players into a free-for-all. Knives came out and were used as well as an occasional two-by-four turned into a weapon. A dozen workers had to be transported to the emergency room. Three were severely cut and had to be sent to the Med in Memphis.

The jail was full. The county jail was the only one in the county, and it took care of the prisoners of the police forces from all the towns. In addition to the migrant prisoners, there was one person jailed awaiting a lunacy hearing, nine prisoners arrested for DUI, and a scattering of others in for domestic assault, suspended drivers license, and shoplifting. It took the sheriff's office and both justice court judges two days to sort out the weekend's problems.

Wednesday, Wade started looking for Chad and Eric but found they were gone. They were taking their clothes to the dorm at the college they were to attend. He finally found them at the Stopwatch on Thursday stocking up with snacks for the first week at school.

Wade said, "Look, boys, I'm going to Memphis Saturday night, and I need y'all to come with me to identify that woman. I need to ask her some questions. The night will be on me."

The boys agreed to meet him on the north side of the town square in Central City at 6:00 p.m.

Wade dressed up in street clothes and went to the square to wait for the Jenkins brothers. He chose to wear a baseball cap instead of his usual white western hat, just in case someone might be in attendance who could recognize him. A car that had been seized in a drug stop had been checked out of the in-pound lot. An out-of-county tag from the sheriff's evidence room was mounted on the rear.

The Jenkins boys arrived on time, and the three headed out of town. The boys were in a good mood, excited about leaving home to be on their own at college and about the upcoming night.

Wade was driving. When they got into the outskirts of Memphis, he asked the boys to guide him to their destination, for it had been a while since he had been in this area of town. They pulled into the parking lot of the Clothes-Hangers Gentleman's Club about 8:30. Darkness was falling. The parking lot was nearly full. As they got out of the car, they were enveloped by big city odors: diesel fumes, hot asphalt, frying hamburgers from a nearby restaurant, and cigar smoke. Also, big city sounds - a train whistle, screeching tires, car horns, and sirens - filled the air.

They approached the door which was guarded by a huge black bouncer. He was dressed in black jeans and a black t-shirt. His biceps were so big that the sleeves had been cut up the sides so he could slip the shirt onto his torso. The bouncer watched Wade pay the usual cover charge for the three to the cashier without comment. Wade and the boys moved on inside. A well lit stage in the shape of a semi-circle was at the back of a huge room. Three stripper poles were in place. At the moment, a top-heavy blonde with slender legs was performing on one of the poles to the side. Her movements were in sync to the music that blared from Peavy speakers hung from the ceiling. All of the seats around the stage were filled, and Wade could hear the guys seated there encouraging the stripper to keep dancing.

Chad led the other two over to an unoccupied table to the right. About half of the many tables on the floor were filled by customers. The three were barely seated when a skimpily attired waitress approached them for their order. They all asked for beer.

The boys didn't consume alcohol but had been informed on their first visit that they would be kicked out if they didn't order drinks. So they ordered beer which they found to be exorbitantly priced. Then they learned that additional rounds were expected to be ordered at regular intervals. They remedied this dilemma by pouring the beer on the floor under their table when the waitress wasn't looking in their direction. Then the bottles would be empty by the next time she came by.

The waitress brought their drinks right away. The boys had their eyes glued to the action on the stage, but Wade began to survey the audience. When satisfied there was no one in the room he recognized, he shifted his chair around so that his back was to most of the crowd.

Eric asked, "I wonder why this place is called 'Clothes-Hangers'? That's a catchy name."

Wade replied, "It's obvious if you compare the name to what you see in here. You boys haven't been out of Cade County enough to know what all goes on in the real world."

The girl on the stage finished her routine by stripping down to a tiny red g-string. The guys at the stage's edge hooted and clapped and threw currency onto the stage. The dancer moved closer allowing some of the patrons to stuff bills into her garter. She left the stage, and a tall brunette with an even larger chest took over.

All three were engrossed in the second dancer's movements and were surprised when a very attractive young blonde slid into the vacant chair between Chad and Wade. Wade's eyes traveled over her. She was gorgeous.

Eric caught his attention and mouthed, "That's her."

Wade was about to decide, as Toby had said, that she was prettier than Norma Sue. In the partial dark, anyway. He would need to see her in broad daylight to know for sure.

"Hello, boys. Good to see y'all again."

Eric stammered, "Yeah!"

"Y'all have become regulars. And I like both of you. Especially, since you left me good tips the past two weekends."

Chad's face turned red as he looked down toward the floor.

All of a sudden Eric stood up and said, "Excuse me, ma'am. I have to go to the restroom."

Wade grabbed his arm and said, "Just hold on a minute, Eric. That can wait. I need to find out a few things."

He asked the woman, "You said two weekends?"

She smiled. "Yes. Paul and Barry, here, came down from the Bootheel in Missouri and sat at the stage while I danced. That was the first time I had danced in a month, and I do remember. Both Paul and Barry stuck a $100 bill into my pink garter."

Wade stared at the boys. They wouldn't look directly at him. Wade thought how he had been set up by "Paul" and "Barry." Those rascals! So, they had found her on the first visit and had been stringing him along so they could have him pay for their entertainment on the other nights. On the way home he would figure out how to get some of his money back. Along with chewing them out.

She asked, "Big Man, what's your name?"

"Uh, George." Immediately, Wade wondered why he had said that for he was single and his name didn't matter.

"Oh. That's a nice name. Just about every other man that comes in here is named George. Especially the married ones."

Wade asked, "What's your name?"

She smiled sweetly. "Marla."

"Real or stage?"

"Both." Marla added, "I've never seen you in here before."

"Where have you seen me?"

She shrugged. "Oh, nowhere. But I regret that. You are so handsome and so strong," she said as she ran her fingers over his shoulders. "Have you seen me anywhere before?"

Wade blushed. He replied, "No. Unfortunately."

"Well, you've missed a lot. I dance here and I'm good. So good that I get to set my own appearances. If I were dancing tonight, this place would be packed. But I'm off."

Wade thought there was no doubt that this was an exceptional woman. And she came across as educated for she spoke perfect English, unusual for a stripper. He wondered why she was wasting her talents in a place like this.

Marla seemed to read his mind. She looked directly into his eyes and said, "This is not the only thing I do. I have a degree in chemistry. My day job is to do medical research for a hospital here in town. I'm good at that too."

This revelation shocked him. "Then, why this?" Wade asked.

She shrugged again as she answered, "It's an outlet for the stress I'm under. We've been working really hard for several years to find a cure for a children's disease. A lot of lives could be saved if we can find the answer. My team and I are really focused in our research. A lot of dedication is there. And I'm a woman. I like the attention."

Wade asked, "Do the people you work with know you strip?"

She replied hesitantly, "Not really…... sort of …….. maybe."

"That is a definite answer. Do your co-workers come here and watch you?"

"No."

"Why not?"

She frowned. "I think somehow that coming here would compromise their respect for me."

The boys were hanging onto every word exchanged between Wade and Marla. But they didn't interrupt. This was obviously an adult conversation, and they also felt that Wade and Marla were bonding, even though there was a wide gap in their ages.

Wade became aware that more patrons were entering the building and filling the empty tables. He caught her looking past him to the far corner of the room.

She took her hand off his shoulder and said, "Boys, have fun and excuse me. A friend just came in, and I need to talk to him." She leaned over and kissed Wade lightly on his scarred cheek.

Then she stood up, swinging her hips as she walked over to a table in the corner that was occupied by one person. All three at the table stared at her perfect body as she moved away.

The man seated at the table turned his head upward to her as she came to his side. A wave of light from the stage swept across his face, and Wade gasped. He recognized him! It was the Musician!

He quickly asked, "Boys, do you know that man Marla is talking to?"

They shook their heads.

"Well, I do. And he knows me. Both of y'all stand up and shield me so I can get out of here without being seen by him."

They did. Wade got out of his chair, pulled his cap low over his eyes, crouched over, and quickly moved to the door. The boys followed looking over their shoulder. Outside, Wade asked if the Musician had looked their way. Chad said, "Naw. He was having too much fun talking to Marla. You could tell they knew each other."

———————

As Wade drove down I-55 toward home, he began to think through the night's events. He lit a cigar and cracked his window to let the smoke drift out. He became lost in his thoughts. Both boys had leaned against the car doors and were dozing. Wade realized they would get home sooner than planned because the entrance of the Musician at the club had caused them to leave early. But that was okay; Wade had found out the girl's name, what she did for a living, and that she knew someone from Cade County. He should have already listed the Musician as a suspect because of his long history of living in Memphis at different intervals. The more he thought of the Musician, the more Wade became convinced that he was behind the commotion at the funeral home. But, why?

Wade looked at his watch and calculated that they would be home before midnight. He knew that Reese Jones, the undertaker, would still be awake because he stayed up late watching "Saturday Night Live." Reese would answer the telephone if he called him.

Wade dropped the boys off at their car. They quickly thanked him for the trip and scrambled into their car, squealing their tires as they left the square. Wade was so preoccupied with having seen Marla with Henry Childs, the Musician, that he forgot to scold the brothers for fleecing him on the strip club trips or to ask them to repay some money.

He went on home and called Reese.

Reese answered, "Hello, Wade." He had caller ID. "Why are you up so late? Trouble?"

Wade replied, "Nah. Just wanted to ask you some questions."

"Okay"

"Sheriff Powers and I have been trying to figure out who was behind the ruckus at Oscar's funeral."

"Me too."

"Was Henry Childs at the visitation?"

Reese exclaimed, "Why, yes the Musician was! And I have a reason for remembering."

"What's that?"

"Well, he got a call about ten minutes before that blonde came inside. It was on the office phone. You know, cell phones don't work inside the funeral home because of the metal roof we put on last year."

"Go on."

117

"A man was on the other end. He said he knew Henry was there and asked if I would give him a message. I said I would. He wanted me to bring back Henry's reply."

"What, then?"

"I laid down the phone and found Henry at the door that opens from the viewing room to the room between it and the chapel. I told him his friend Leland was on the line and would be delivering his heifer to the show barn. Henry grinned and told me to tell Leland that if he could deliver the heifer in five minutes, the show could start."

Wade asked, "What did that mean?"

Reese said, "I have no idea. But that's not all."

"Go on, Reese."

"After the commotion was over and we got the women and the church people back there settled down, I came up to my office. I needed a strong drink. Imagine Mr. Gray leaving me all alone to handle that mess."

Wade accused, "You're getting windy, Reese."

"Yeah, yeah. But when has anything like this ever happened in Cade County? And right in my yard, so to speak. Anyway, I had just poured myself a straight shot of Jack when the phone rang again. It was a young woman, and she asked to speak to Henry. I thought that he sure was popular tonight. So I went after Henry. I didn't know if he was still there."

Wade asked, "Was he?"

"Yeah. He was still at the same spot as before when I told him he had the first call. Henry went up the hall to my office, and I got busy sweeping soil that had spilled from some potted plants that were kicked over in the melee."

"And?"

"I stopped sweeping and went back toward the office. The door was open and I could hear Henry. He was mostly laughing at what the woman was telling him. He was laughing a lot. I went back to where the plants were and got caught up in a long conversation with that pest Jon David Knox. By the time he shut up and I got back to my office, Henry was gone. And he wasn't the only thing that was gone," added Reese.

"What else?"

Reese snarled. "My shot of Jack and the bottle it came from that was hid in my desk drawer. I have to make a special trip to Oxford for my Jack Daniels."

Wade laughed.

Reese snarled again. "Go to hell, Wade!"

Wade snickered. "I never would have imagined that Henry would do a thing like that!"

Sunday afternoon, Wade was in his back yard cleaning out his fishing boat and tackle box when Sheriff Grady drove up. Grady asked, "Any news, Wade? Anything going on?"

Wade said, "Yeah. A lot."

He proceeded to tell Grady what he had found out in Memphis and all about the events that had led up to last night.

Grady listened in awe and asked, "Tell me, what led you in that direction for the answer?"

Wade uncapped a couple of diet Dr. Peppers and handed one to Grady along with a bag of shelled peanuts. They both took long swigs of their drinks to lower the level of the liquid in the bottle. Then, they each made a funnel with one hand and poured their bag of peanuts into the bottle, which created a fizz. Grady tipped up on his bottle, gathering some peanuts into his mouth which he began to chew.

"This is the only way a soda should be drunk, with a kicker of good peanuts."

Wade said, "You got that right. Only in the South."

He continued, "To answer your question, I thought a lot about that melee. First, the limo came from Memphis, not to say the girl could have been picked up anywhere. Second, she was good looking, according to Toby and the cousins, and was not the type of woman you would find living here. Then, as we were told, she was clean shaven, which is probably not what women around here do and would point for a special need to be that way."

Grady said, "Well, I wouldn't know about that. At my age, I've sort of moved past what all this younger set does."

Wade said, "Yeah, I agree. Anyway, all of those clues pointed to Winchester Street in Memphis."

"Strip clubs?"

"Yeah."

"But you sent the Jenkins boys to only one. And there are a bunch of them on Winchester. And a few elsewhere up there."

Wade said, "I have my contacts. From what I've been told, Clothes-Hangers is the classiest one in town, if you can say that. I just had a feeling that if the girl in question was a stripper, she would be high class."

Grady said, "I have to say you figured out what she was and where she was, and rather quickly, too."

"Yeah. But I got real lucky when Henry walked into the club, and I saw that Marla knew him. That nailed it."

Grady responded, "That knocks out the question of who was involved in the ruckus, but it leaves the question of why."

Wade said, "Yes. If you think about it, Henry was out some money to have her come here. And in a limo."

"Yes. She was out, say, five or six hours. And she doesn't work cheap if she is the top stripper in that club."

"Why would he go to the effort and expense to cause all that trouble at Oscar's funeral? No doubt that Arlene was humiliated in front of the whole county."

Grady said, "Look, what happened then has spread all over North Mississippi. Every time I have a conversation with a sheriff in another county, I'm asked for all the details. It was real funny to people who didn't even know Oscar and Arlene."

"Well, I got the answer to part one. I think you should get the answer to why."

Grady was thoughtful for a while. He chugged down the last swallow of his Dr. Pepper and all the remaining peanuts in the bottle came with it, leaving the bottle clean empty.

Wade noticed. "You're good, Grady. You got the last peanuts with the last swallow. That way you don't have to slap the bottom of the bottle to get out any that's stuck."

Grady smiled and claimed credit. "Sixty years of practice."

Then Grady said, "Let me ask around. I would say Henry was trying to get even with Arlene about something."

"I'm thinking you might check with Zeke Tiller. Or Earl Ray, if you can get him in a mood to talk. He is so secretive."

"Yeah. About the only time you can get anything out of him is when he is drinking. And then he doesn't say much."

Wade replied, "An idea about that. Maybe we could get someone who is close to Earl Ray to press for Henry's reason."

Grady said, "Uh, I'm not sure who that might be. Maybe Darlene Doss? Customers usually tend to confide in bartenders, especially the ones they are comfortable being around. Or Norma Sue? She cuts his hair. Maybe we could recruit her to help."

Wade volunteered, "I'll talk to her. She also cuts my hair, and I'm always looking for an excuse to talk to her. Man, she is so pretty."

"I'll agree with that. Chief Wayne Bowen told me that last week an out-of-town trucker was navigating around the square as she was closing the beauty shop and walking across the street to her parked car. The trucker was staring at her, forgot what he was doing, and jackknifed his eighteen-wheeler across the curb. The chief had to call a wrecker to get the truck unstuck."

Wade laughed. "That's what she can do to a man."

CHAPTER 16
SPILLED MONEY

August was nearing its end, and the heat was unrelenting. The heat would carry well into September making it rough for fall football practice. Each day the temperature toyed with the 100° mark. However, the heat didn't curb the amount of coffee consumed at Lola's.

Lola's coffee shop served breakfast, lunches, menu items after the noon hour, and lots of coffee. Her shop faced the west side of the highway where it left the north edge of Central City. A sprawling, gravel parking lot wrapped around the front and the north side of the shop. Teenagers and college students filled the lot on weekends and kept the carhops busy. On the busiest nights, a parking space at Lola's could be more valuable than a free meal. The youths passed their time cruising the town square, making multiple trips to check out the activity at Lola's and returning the mile to the square. Inside the shop were five plywood booths to the right of the door. A long community table filled the center of the room with a counter to the left. Nine stools accompanied the linoleum covered counter. In the back were a dozen tables that seated four diners each. This spot generated a sense of privacy while the community area was generally boisterous.

This morning, Ben Weaver, Jon David Knox, Reese Jones, Andy Morgan, and Todd West, the mayor of Central City, sat at the large community table. These guys were regulars. They liked to come in early for coffee and a breakfast sandwich. None of them punched a clock, and they got a small sense of pleasure watching other people scurrying in for food to take to work. To add insult to injury, they would tarry.

Drinking coffee called for a round of conversation each day. The topics of conversation usually fell into two categories: that which had just happened, which could be local, statewide, or nationwide; and gossip. The gossip could also be about what had just happened. This morning, the group discussed some of the national news stories that had been broadcast over the old, clunky television set that sat high on a shelf behind the counter.

Ben Weaver was the last one to arrive. Because of the cooler weather up north, he had been in Canada and the Dakotas for six weeks to train his bird dogs. All of his fellow coffee drinkers were glad to see him, for he was usually the life of their conversations and was a man of dry wit. Ben was behind on the local news.

After being caught up on a number of topics, he asked, "Did they ever find Mr. Joab's money?"

He was answered by a chorus of "No's!"

Andy brought him up to date on the efforts that had been made to locate any money that Mr. Joab might have. The administrator, Wiley Downs, had made an inventory and appraisal of the personal items of value that had been found at the house. These reports had been deposited with the chancery clerk and, needless to say since the file was public record, a copy had been obtained by one local snoop. From this copy, many others had been made and circulated.

In fact, Jon David pulled a folded copy out of his hip pocket and handed it to Ben. Ben had been a friend of Mr. Joab for many years. He bird hunted on the farm and also helped Mr. Joab with cutting firewood and other chores. In the wintertime, Ben would visit, and they would sit by the fireplace swapping news. Ben had found Mr. Joab to be an interesting fellow. Mr. Joab was also a good-natured man, which was probably why he had been successful in buying timber from landowners over the years.

Ben unfolded the paper and slowly read. The others became silent as they watched him. The inventory set forth items in numbered order with the values listed in a column to the right. Ben was familiar with most of the assets on the list because Mr. Joab had showed them to him. Wiley Downs had hired a local, experienced appraiser to perform the task on behalf of the estate even though the judge had excused an appraisal. The appraiser inventoried the house, room by room. Instead of listing every single item in the house separately, he had lumped things like pots, pans, knives, forks, towels, sheets, and bedclothes into categories styled "kitchen contents" and "linens." Most of Mr. Joab's furniture was so worn and worthless that it did not qualify for a category. In fact, there were few items that gained a separate line. These were the Seth Thomas mantle clock, a Boston rocker, a glassed-in oak curio cabinet, a marble-top wash stand with a green tiled back, a big cookie jar shaped like a red apple, a bookcase that Mr. Joab had made when he was in high school, and a wooden sea chest. Also listed were sets of dog irons, pokers, and tongs for the two fireplaces in the house that had been made by Mr. Joab's grandfather, a blacksmith in his day. Next were the personal items: The Purple Heart for his wounds on Okinawa, his wallet and contents that included $973 in currency, assorted coins that totaled $97.10, a worn, gold Omega wristwatch, a sapphire ring that was appraised at $2,500.00, assorted books, and his Bible.

The outside items included an 8N Ford tractor, a rotary cutter, trailer, wagon, a stack of heart pine lumber, a hand-turned corn sheller mounted on a wooden catch box, lawn mower, two chain saws, and several tool boxes containing wrenches. An old pickup and the guns the sheriff's office was holding were listed separately.

Ben reread the list and frowned. Something was missing. Reese Jones noticed the hesitation and asked, "Ben. Is something wrong?"

"Nope. Just noticed that his twenty-foot log chain wasn't on the list," Ben quickly countered.

Jon David spoke up, "Well, that's not a surprise. A log chain is something that is always borrowed out at Four Points. Usually, it's not returned. You have to go get the chain if you want it back."

Todd scoffed, "Do you think the chain will be brought back?"

"That will depend on who has it. This won't be the first time that a death has caused title to property to change without a bill of sale," Andy said with a nod.

Ben let out a sign of relief at the remarks. Now he was clear of further questions.

Andy remarked, "After you read that list, if we didn't know any better, you would say that Mr. Joab was a poor man."

"Well, how is it that we know better? I mean, how did everyone in the county come to think that Mr. Joab was wealthy?" Todd responded.

Reese said, "I can explain that. It was part of how he lived and part something else."

Jon David asked impatiently, "What else?"

Reese snapped, "I'll get to that, Jon David!"

Reese didn't particularly care for Jon David. Neither did anyone else. Sixty year old, chubby John David Knox sold accident insurance for a national company to poor people in the county. He had a slew of time to hang around the barber shop or Lola's to run his mouth. He contributed nonsense to every subject broached. He was largely supported by his wife, Edna, who worked on the line at a textile plant in Central City that was four blocks from their house. She trudged to and from work daily because Jon David was always too "busy" to transport her. Except on Friday afternoons, the payday, when he parked directly in front of the plant entrance in his shiny red pickup to haul Edna to the bank with her check. He was loathed by every woman in town.

He continued, "All of their lives, he and his wife lived frugally. They never really bought anything they didn't need. And then, it was secondhand. Mr. Joab never owned a new vehicle. And they didn't have any children."

Todd broke in, "That, right there, is enough to make anyone rich these days."

Everyone around the table chuckled to themselves. For they all knew about Todd's presently having a son and a daughter in college. He had bought each of them new automobiles when they started school and the girl, apparently, was trying to be a one-woman fashion show on campus. From what they had heard, she was trying to out-dress the sorority girls from Dallas, which was a losing cause. They knew the kids were costing Todd an arm and a leg.

"Anyway," Reese said, "Mr. Joab never made a whole lot of money at buying timber. He was too soft-hearted and would give the landowners more than any other company, so there wasn't a lot of profit. But he still saved money."

"Yeah. We know that Wiley found an account with a stockbroker firm in Memphis that had a $100,000 balance," Jon David said.

Andy said, "That's not a lot of money this day and age. You would think that from the way Mr. Joab scrimped and saved for all these years, he would have had more than that."

"That's what I'm getting to," said Reese. "One day in January about thirty years ago, Mr. Joab was coming to town from Four Points. His pickup broke down just about a mile away at the river bridge. It was a raw, cold, cloudy day. A northerly gale was blowing leaves and debris across the square and clean through town. He had to walk to town into the wind; there was no traffic from which to hitch a ride. He had on a baseball cap and a jeans jumper over a short-sleeve shirt. No gloves or ear muffs. When he got to Joe Bob's Diner, his face and his calloused hands were beet red. I was in there drinking coffee with some others. He was carrying a large paper grocery sack. Mr. Joab sat down in the chair next to mine and put the bag on the floor between us. Lola, who was working here before she bought Joe Bob out and changed the name to Lola's, came to the table and fussed over him like an old hen. She poured him hot coffee and laced it with chocolate syrup. Then she went and heated some towels and put them around his hands and neck. Mr. Joab was shivering when he first came in, but the hot towels and the coffee brought him back to normal.

"After he got warm and rested, he asked me to watch his bag and went over to the pay phone on the wall. He made a call and talked a few minutes. While he was at the phone, someone at the table got up and, in the process, a table leg was moved against the bag causing it to tip over.

"Bundles of $100 bills spilled out on the floor, and everyone at the table saw them. I quickly gathered the bundles up and put them back into the bag before Mr. Joab turned around. When he finished his call, he came back and sat down. Not a word was said to him about what had happened."

Todd said, "And I know that everyone in Joe Bob's kept quiet later on."

Ben's chortle expressed his doubt.

Reese said, "Oscar Sappington pulled up outside a few minutes later in one of the cars off his lot. Mr. Joab paid his bill, thanked Lola, picked up his bag, got into Oscar's car, and they headed north."

Jon David asked impatiently, "What does that have to do with anything?"

Reese snapped at him again. "Let me finish. That weekend, the Sunday *Commercial Appeal* had an article about how two out-of-town men showed up at Merci Hospital and made an anonymous cash donation for a certain patient."

Jon David blurted, "Who?"

Ben warned, "Shut up, Jon David. Don't mess with Reese's story!"

Reese said, "That's what was so unexpected. The reporter slipped up. She made mention of a tattoo on the donor's arm and the description fit the one on Mr. Joab's arm to a T. Putting together that description and the timing of us seeing him with all that cash on the same day, left no doubt of who the giver was. That Mr. Joab gave money to help someone, even though he didn't spend money on himself, was no surprise to anyone. He was that kind of man. But the newspaper article went on about how the money was intended for the medical expenses of a baby girl. Of course, the hospital wouldn't release her name. The reason why the gift had any publicity at all was that Merci was so grateful. And they wanted the public to know there was someone out there who really cared. The gift did cover the medical expenses of the little girl with a substantial amount left over to help others."

Ben asked, "Did anyone ever find out who the baby girl was?"

Reese thought before he replied. He knew that his boss had found out. When this news broke, Mr. Gray called a college classmate who was a doctor in Memphis and a consultant with the hospital. Mr. Gray's friend, under a sworn oath of secrecy, had told him. But the doctor said the donor didn't explain his connection to the baby. Reese, being a young man at the time, had asked Mr. Gray for the name. He well remembered Mr. Gray's response. "Reese, some things are better left unsaid."

So he explained, "Ben, the papers never told."

Andy wondered how Mr. Joab would have known the little girl was in the hospital and who she was, if he didn't know her or her family. Or, did he know her?

All of the guys sat there reflecting on the round table conversation. Lola came by and refilled their cups. "What are you guys discussing?"

"Why Mr. Joab had the reputation of being wealthy. Reese was just telling about the time he came in here with that sack of money. Did you see it?" Andy asked.

"Yeah. I won't forget that. I was over by the counter, and I had a clear view. I had never seen that many $100 bills before. All the next week there was a lot of speculation of how much money was in the sack."

"How much?" Jon David asked.

Lola laughed. "It was funny. Heated arguments arose over how much money was in the sack. Everybody had his own opinion of the amount. I thought two of the guys were going to fight over who was right. Several men went to the extent of finding bags the same size as the one Mr. Joab had and measuring them to see how much money they would hold. A bill is six inches long and two and one-half inches wide. And someone called down to the bank and found out that a ten thousand dollar stack of new $100 dollar bills would be an inch high. Everybody wanted to agree that about seventy bundles would fit into the sack, which would amount to $700,000. That is, if all the bills were new."

Reese added, "But I don't think they were. When that sack tipped over I could smell the odor of moth balls."

"Sounds like the money had been stored in a trunk," Andy said.

Lola continued, "Then an argument arose whether or not all the bundles were $100 bills. It could have been an Oscar deal. Everyone knew about Oscar's habit of covering a fat roll of ones with a hundred and flashing it at every opportunity, trying to come across as having a lot of cash."

Todd explained. "His prank got discovered one Saturday night back in 1980 at the county fair. Oscar was juiced up and was trying to impress some high school kids about how much money he had. When he pulled the roll from his pocket, the rubber band around it broke and dollar bills flew all over the place! The kids laughed and spread the news. Oscar really lost face."

Reese interjected. "Yes, I remember all that happening. But no one believed that Mr. Joab would feign his cash. There was no reason to because he just wasn't a flashy man. The coffee crowd came to a general agreement that Mr. Joab probably had $350,000 in his sack."

Andy whistled, "Man, that was a lot of money back then!"

They all nodded.

Reese took a long sip of coffee. He knew more than he could tell. One night at the funeral home, he and Mr. Gray had opened a new bottle of Jack. They had buried a twenty-year old boy that day that had been killed in a car wreck. The funeral had been difficult as always when the deceased was a young person. The crowd had been large, which was usual, for the youngster had not had the chance to outlive his friends. The funeral service had been long. The air was hot inside the chapel. Emotions had been high. A great deal of distress, anxiety, tears, and some low-grade anger. Reese and Mr. Gray were drained.

Mr. Gray was usually a tight-lipped man. But that night the Jack in him, from the bottom of the bottle, started talking. He told Reese that his doctor friend in Memphis said that every year the tattooed man would show up at the hospital with a cash gift. It was not always the same amount but each gift was substantial.

Lola said, "Our coffee sales tripled that week. I was caught by surprise and nearly ran out. I was even selling the New Orleans chicory flavored coffee which only three customers in the entire town drank."

Andy said, "Maybe he gave all his money away before he died."

CHAPTER 17
MR. JOAB'S WILL

The news spread! Mr. Joab's will had been found! Just after noon, Archie Baker had walked into the chancery clerk's office with a Petition to Probate a Copy of a Lost Will of Joab McMath and Other Relief. The clerk, Linda Nell Few, had taken the afternoon off to go shopping in Tupelo with some friends. She had left Crissy Mobley in charge of the office. Crissy had been working there only two years but knew the duties of the office very well.

She had walked up to the counter when Archie came in and asked, "Can I help you, Mr. Archie?"

He replied, "Don't call me 'Mr.' That makes me feel old."

"Well, I have to call you something. You're not exactly a spring chicken!"

They had been going through this same ritual ever since Crissy had started working in the clerk's office. Archie was aware that she spoke to him this way on purpose. He didn't really know why she insisted but suspected it was because of his representation of her sister's ex-husband in their divorce. The sister had cleaned her husband out, but still Crissy wanted to pile it on.

He changed the subject and said, "I need to file this petition," and handed the documents to her.

Crissy looked them over. She had never seen this sort of filing before. She said, "This says you want to file a copy of a signed will. That the original can't be found?"

"That's right."

Crissy asked, "Where did you get this copy?"

Archie sneered, "That's confidential! Underlings don't need to know."

Taken aback, Crissy replied in a cold, clipped tone, "Well, you can't file a copy."

"Why not?"

"The statutes on wills says you have to file the original will."

"Well, young lady, there is more law out there than statutes. There are Supreme Court cases on this subject that says you can, and I have cites of those cases."

Crissy smiled. "You may be right. But I hope they are better than the ones you used on Mr. Harvey Roger's dead cow claims."

Archie's face turned red.

"I'm not going to file this petition," Crissy said.

Archie demanded, "Yes, you are."

"No, I'm not."

"Where is Linda Nell? I need to talk to her. And I'm going to complain about you. You're a smart...."

Crissy's brown eyes flashed. Her back stiffened. "Watch out! Don't you say that word. Not to me. You may talk uppity to other women. But not to me. Not today. Not ever!"

Archie backed off. "Ok. Ok. Don't get hot under the collar. Just call her. Where is she?"

"She is in Tupelo. And she doesn't want me to bother her. But I think I should let her know about this matter. Hold on."

She stepped into Linda Nell's office so Archie couldn't hear her.

Linda Nell was sitting in the bar of The Catch, a seafood restaurant in Tupelo, with friends and was halfway through a second glass of wine when her cell phone rang. Linda Nell frowned when she checked the caller ID, perturbed that her office was calling on her afternoon off. But she answered, thinking Crissy wouldn't interrupt unless something important had occurred.

"Hello."

Crissy replied, "Miss Linda Nell, I hate to bother you. But there's some big news! Archie has shown up with Mr. Joab's will."

"What? You don't mean it?"

"Yes! I haven't read it yet. But there's a problem. He's trying to probate a copy of a signed will. He says the original one is lost."

"Where did he get that? And why Archie?"

Crissy said, "I don't know. He refused to tell me! But I told him he couldn't do this and he got really mad. We had words."

Crissy started crying. "He said he was going to complain to you about me."

"Oh, hush, Crissy. Archie needs his ass kicked. Don't worry about him. I'm always having to call him down."

Crissy sniffed.

Linda Nell said, "Look, this has never happened since I've been in office. Go ahead and file his petition. Judge Dennis can decide whether it is proper or not. Boy, if he can, this filing will really stir up those Memphis lawyers."

"Yeah. And the whole county."

"File those papers, and when he leaves, scan the will and e-mail it to my cell phone. I want to see what is in it! And look at his affidavit of service and tell me to whom he has mailed notice of this filing," Linda Nell instructed.

There was a pause as Crissy looked for that page. Linda Nell took another sip of wine. Her mind was racing about this new development.

"He served Wiley Downs, John England, Judge Chandler, and Judge Dennis," Crissy said. "But he asked me to issue a summons for a process server to serve the petition on the law firm that is representing the Shaw cousin. While I was getting the form for him to fill out, he was looking out the window and sniggering, like it was some kind of private joke!"

Linda Nell frowned. Then she asked, "Why did he serve all those people? He only needed to serve the Memphis law firm and Wiley Downs. I guess he's up to some of his usual shenanigans that are always getting him into trouble with the Court."

Crissy added, "Archie always goes overboard with his pleadings. That's so he can bill his client more."

Linda Nell agreed, "Yeah. I've caught on to that. Just tell him we will file his petition. And don't let him get under your skin. Life is too short for that."

Crissy went back to the counter and said, "Ms. Linda Nell agrees with me, but she said to file it and let Judge Dennis worry about the legality."

Archie gave her an "I told you so" look.

Crissy smiled. "And she said you were a nice man."

Archie sneered. "Like I believe that. She stays on my case every chance she gets."

Archie left. Crissy looked at the will attached as an exhibit to the Petition. Her eyes widened as she read through it. She said aloud, "My gosh!"

Linda Nell ordered another glass of wine for herself and her two friends. She proceeded to tell the friends, who also were from Cade County, about what Crissy had reported. They all got very excited and started talking about the estate. About twenty minutes later Linda Nell heard her tone for an e-mail message and opened it. Her friends eagerly waited as they watched her read the screen.

Linda Nell exclaimed, "What a will!"

When Archie returned to his office, he instructed his secretary to mail a copy of the will to Earl Ray Fowler and to the Merci Hospital in Memphis. He remarked, "I'm sure we will hear from the hospital's lawyers, whoever they are, and soon. But I'm not sure about Earl Ray. Depends upon what else he has going on."

CHAPTER 18
SKIP TRACER

The same day the will was filed for probate and before the Memphis firm representing Jeb Shaw was served, Stanley Robbs was in his office meeting with Roxy Malone. She was the senior skip tracer with Dodge and Trace, Inc., a local bonding company. They specialized in finding and returning criminals who had skipped out on their bond. The company also had a staff to locate debtors who had left town without paying their bills and to find unclaimed property throughout the nation. They were successful in these endeavors and especially in finding lost property. Dodge and Trace, Inc. took on clients for a percentage of what they found, usually one-fourth or one-third, sometimes one-half. If nothing was found, the company received no fee for its efforts.

Roxy had tried to sign Janes, Knobly, and Stilt on for a one-third recovery fee. Mr. Nutt would have gone for it and was backed by the other senior partners, for they knew that this search would be difficult. It had become obvious that there was little McMath property in Cade County, and the search would have to be expanded away from there. However, before the law firm could commit to the bonding company, the deal had to have Jeb Shaw's approval. When the offer was explained to him, Jeb would have none of it. Stanley had called him hoping to get his agreement over the telephone, but Jeb insisted on coming to the office to discuss the matter.

He said, "I don't mind. I'm not doing nothing." Which was no surprise to the law firm.

Then their luck turned. He continued, "But is it all right if I come by myself? My wife is up under the trailer wrapping the water pipes. Winter will be here before you know it and its cool up under there right now. And my boy has carried the other children to the dollar store to buy school supplies."

He was assured that he was more than welcome to come in without the rest of the family. Jeb showed up in the front office about two hours later. Leah sent him back to Mr. Nutt's office because Stanley was in court in the justice complex. Mr. Nutt had Dudley sit in as the firm's best negotiator. They couldn't make Jeb understand that it would take a professional to find any money or other property owned by Mr. Joab and the property locaters would incur a lot of expenses in their search. If they didn't find anything, it wouldn't cost Jeb a dime. But Jeb dug in. He told them the search should be simple. The money was coming from oil wells in Texas just like his cousin had said. They could find that themselves. And the oil wells were probably named after Mr. Joab.

Dudley pleaded with him. "Mr. Shaw, there are tens of thousands of oil wells in Texas. We don't have the expertise here to make that kind of search. We just can't pick up the phone and call around and expect to get an answer. We have to have something to go on."

Jeb admitted, "Well, I did see a show on TV one time about that drilling out there. There were a lot of wells. But a third is too much. I used to work cotton and corn on Mr. Handley's land over on the White River. That was when I was a young man and didn't know any better."

Dudley asked, "What kind of rent arrangement did you and he have in you contract?"

Jeb asked blankly, "Contract? What's that?"

Mr. Nutt rolled his eyes. "You know, what kind of deal did y'all have in your papers?"

"Oh. Why didn't you say so? I paid him a fourth of what I sold my crops for. And he paid me a fourth of what my fertilizer and diesel fuel cost. But we didn't sign no papers. A man's word is good enough. At least it was back in them days. I can go for a fourth on this deal."

Mr. Nutt interjected, "Would you settle for somewhere between a fourth and a third?"

"I dunno. As it is, if I give up a third to that treasure hunter and then give up a third to you lawyers, I'm not going to be able to buy Mabel that fur coat I promised her."

Dudley pointed out, "Mr. Shaw. These are just figures. They don't mean anything if no money is found. So just go ahead and agree to a third!"

Jeb shook his head. "Nope. No way. But since you didn't take my offer for a fourth, I have a different number I'll give you."

"What?" Dudley eagerly asked, as he leaned forward.

Jeb leaned back in his chair, hooked his hands under the galluses of his overalls and said, "A fifth. That's more than a fourth."

Mr. Nutt and Dudley were crestfallen. They tried to explain fractions to him. But they just couldn't make him understand. Finally, Mr. Nutt gently suggested, "Jeb, if you cooked two apple pies and cut one into four pieces and one into five pieces, which pie would have the smaller pieces?"

Jeb smiled. "I like that kind of talk. Just so happens that Mabel makes the best apple pies in the world."

He thought for a while and then said, "Oh, the pie with the five slices has the smaller ones. Since it was your idea and you explained it so well, I'll give you the smaller slice. A fifth. That's it. Take it or leave it. Or you can find the money yourselves."

By this time the lawyers were worn out. They didn't believe the property locators would accept a contract with the percentage this low. Mr. Nutt left the room and consulted his partners. They finally gave their consent to twenty percent. Mr. Nutt returned and told Jeb they had a deal.

Jeb stood up and said, "You boys are smarter than I thought you was. Listen, I'll have Mabel bake a couple of apple pies, and I'll bring them over next time I'm in Memphis."

Dudley hastily replied, "Oh, don't go to that much trouble. Most of our staff are on diets and those pies would be fattening." Not to say, probably deadly. He shuddered at the thought of what the condition of Mabel's kitchen might be.

The bonding company hit the overhead when Mr. Nutt called in the percent that Jeb had requested. The vice-president in the property section screamed, "Nutt, you are always tightening the screws on us. And we are always finding lost assets for you! "

Nutt reminded him what could be at stake, "A little bit of something is better than nothing."

The vice-president cooled down. "Okay. We'll agree if your firm pays our expenses."

They argued about that, and finally it was agreed that the bonding company and the law firm would split the costs of the search.

Roxy was sitting directly across the desk from Stanley. She was thirty-five and divorced, with two small children in her custody. She was tall, with a trim figure. Her clothes were immaculate, her haircut fresh, and her nails done. She wore a gold bracelet on her right wrist, a Rolex on her other, a small gold chain around her neck and a sapphire ring on her right ring finger. And red, high-heeled shoes. Roxy was wearing a short skirt exposing a lot of her nice legs. Stanley had never dealt with her before. As he sat there looking at Roxy, he thought, "High Maintenance", which could be a good reason why she didn't have a husband.

She noticed Stanley inspecting her, and to throw him off balance and have the upper hand in the meeting, she asked, "May I smoke?"

Stanley was startled. He snapped, "No! Uh, I mean, it's not allowed in here."

Roxy thought, 'Touché!' She smiled. "Okay, Sugar. I can wait."

Stanley asked, "Let's go over your progress, if you don't mind."

"Sure, honey."

He cringed. She was the worst yet with those cozy name references. But he was beginning to feel attracted to her. Leah had warned him about Roxy. Leah said she was active on the Memphis bar scene. Roxy went out nearly every night. Her children were still pre-school and her kid sister, who lived with them, baby-sat. The guys in the office called her "Foxy Roxy" behind her back. Stanley could agree with that name. It definitely fit.

Roxy said, "I've been working on this case off and on for the last few months. I've also had my assistant, Joe Oakley, helping me. He's going to law school but has time to help. Joe lived in Texas when he was in junior high. His father is professional military. He also has lived in San Diego, Minot, and Ft. Walton, Florida. So far we've found nothing."

"We knew going in that this would be a tough cookie."

"Yes. It would help if we had more leads than that angle about oil wells in Texas. Like, if we had the man's social security number or his tax returns. This case is really cold."

"We're working on that. Right now we don't have the privilege of obtaining much information. As soon as we prove that Jeb Shaw is the sole heir, we will have the court's authority to proceed with discovery on everyone and everybody."

Roxy said, "Mostly, we have been only searching in Texas. Maybe we can narrow the areas where Mr. McMath might have property. If you could get that heirship nailed down, we would have the right to inquire of all the oil companies that have production in Texas whether or not Mr. McMath was drawing royalties from them."

"Yes. We have already associated an attorney in Central City to find some credible witnesses to testify as to Mr. Joab's heirs."

"Is there a hurry?"

"No. Not right now. We are in the catbird's seat. The time has passed for any other would-be heir to come forward. The only thing the administrator can do is turn the assets over to the state if we don't prove Jeb Shaw the only heir, or to devisees in any will which might be produced, which has not happened."

Roxy said, "Keep me posted, Hon."

She stood up and walked to the door. Opening it suddenly, Roxy whirled, catching Stanley staring directly at her body. He blushed.

She smiled coyly. "Shug, you should see me when I'm wearing Daisy Duke denim shorts. You would write home to your mother about that!"

She winked and walked through the door leaving him speechless. When the door opened, Leah had turned in her chair and caught it all.

Leah laughed. "Ha! Ha! That's the first time I've seen a lawyer in this firm at a loss of words."

A week later on Friday night, Josh Nutt and his wife were attending the 50th wedding anniversary of Randy and Martha Belue, two of their closest friends. Randy was the retired manager of the local office of a national stock brokerage firm. He had been very successful. Randy was active in church and community affairs. His wife had spent a lot of her time being involved with fund raisers around town.

The event was held at the most prestigious country club in Memphis. The socialites were dressed to the nines. The best caterers had been engaged. A full sized, carved ice statue had been flown in from the west coast as well as a renowned violinist from the Big Apple. This was the social event of the year, and to have received an invitation meant that one was included in the town's highest level of society.

By seven o'clock, the party was in full swing. The weather was pleasant. The music was mellow. The liquor was flowing. Couples were swirling around the dance floor. Guests were still arriving, many by limo. By eight o'clock the big room was packed, and the crowd had begun to spill out onto the patio. Josh Nutt, who had been selected to honor the Belues with opening remarks, stepped up on the bandstand. From the cornet player came a blast of catchy music to get the attention of the crowd. The room fell silent. Josh pulled a note card from his pocket, straightened his tie, and cleared his throat. All eyes were upon him. He reveled in this moment. More than anything, Josh loved attention, whether it is in the midst of a sensational trial, making opening and closing arguments, pleading a motion with deep passion, or at an exclusive social event, such as this. He planned to be witty and wise to the extent that he would be the talk of the party. Josh was eyeing some senior members of other downtown law firms standing at the back of the room. He knew they were envious, wishing they could be in his position. Lots of wealthy, potential clients could be seen in the gathering. Some were with original wives on their arms and others were accompanied by trophy wives, usually former secretaries. And some with dates. This was a prime opportunity to connect.

Josh took his time. When he felt the moment was right, he began to speak.

"Ladies and gentlemen, and those who wish to be." At that the crowd roared. "Tonight is a wonderful night. It feels so great. I am honored to be in the presence of so many elite, beautiful people."

"Yes, indeed, one more time!" squealed a drunken, elderly Mrs. Turner, the richest woman in town. Peals of laughter followed her outburst. They all knew her.

Josh felt warm inside. This was going to go well for him.

He continued, "We are gathered here to ….. "

About that time, a comical figure stepped out from behind the wall where the drums were stationed. The person was dressed in a colorful Mardi Gras court jester's costume. At first, he stood facing the crowd giving them time to notice him. Josh had halted his speech. He noticed the eyes of every person present shifting from him to slightly to his right.

As he began to turn in that direction, the jester moved swiftly by and, without stopping, stuck a white envelope under his tux jacket, and finished Josh's speech very loudly... "Get served, you pathetic bumbling barrister!"

The jester spun on his pointed slippers, jingled the red balls in his "Fool's hat," and exited through the back door to a waiting pickup. The vehicle disappeared into the darkness before anyone could react to observe the license plate.

Mouths dropped open. Josh stood there shocked. Then shouts of laughter broke from his competitors. The laughter caught and spread around the room. Josh even noticed some of the younger lawyers in his firm joining in, particularly Stanley Robbs. Josh's face turned red. He was irate. Immediately, he suspected someone in the law firm of Ricks, Tyson, Tinsley, and Arnoff to be responsible for this prank to embarrass him.

Josh struggled to regain his composure. A large portion of the crowd left the room for the patio bar. Josh realized that he had lost his momentum. Mr. Belue was frowning and staring at his shoes. Mrs. Belue had a worried look on her face.

Josh continued with his congratulatory words, but the din spilling in from the patio drowned most of what he said. He found himself in the similar position of being in court trying to absorb the testimony of an adverse witness and attempting to make notes for later cross-examination, while his client was pulling at his sleeve and telling him to make an objection.

He noticed that no lawyer remained in the room. They were outside, apparently laughing their rears off about him getting served in such an embarrassing manner.

What was in the envelope? He was dying to know. As soon as he finished his remarks, Mr. and Mrs. Belue stood for accolades from the audience. Many couples moved forward to embrace them giving Josh the opportunity to escape to the restroom.

Dudley Cook told his wife, "Honey, go get me a strong drink. I'm going to talk to Josh."

Dudley entered the restroom just as Josh tore open the envelope and stared at the contents. It was a copy of the petition to probate Mr. Joab's will that Archie Baker had filed earlier that week.

He said to Dudley, "Look at this. This is bad news for us. I was dreading that this might happen."

Dudley read the papers rapidly, "Oh my! This is not good."

"I'm going home. I can't face those hyenas out there. If I appear where our fellow lawyers are, I'm afraid I'll punch the first one who makes a wisecrack," Josh snapped.

"You can bet your boots they're waiting for you."

"I won't give them the pleasure. You go home and call every lawyer in the firm. Have them be in the office tomorrow morning at 10 o'clock."

Dudley protested. "But, Mr. Josh, can't it wait 'till Monday? Everyone has already made plans for the weekend."

Josh snarled, "If they want to have a desk Monday morning, they had damn well better be in tomorrow!"

Dudley's shoulders sagged. He was supposed to play in a golf tournament with his usual partner, and they were predicted to win. But he conceded, "You got it."

———————————

Saturday morning found all the lawyers in the conference room of Janes, Knobly, and Stilt seated around the huge, oblong table. This was a first. The entire firm had never met on Saturday. The junior attorneys had been puzzled as to what attire was expected of them. Through a series of early morning calls, they all agreed that wearing khaki pants and preppy shirts with another man's name on the breast should suffice. Leah Fornet and two other secretaries were also there. No one was talking. Stanley was sitting in his usual chair with a long face. He had called Roxy on Wednesday. She had agreed to go with him to St. Louis for the weekend Cardinal games. When he let Roxy know the trip to St. Louis was off, she had told him not to ever call her again, for she had not believed that he was serious to begin with. She had slammed the phone down saying, "You tightwad!"

Dudley was leaning back in his chair staring at the ceiling. He was already tired of the mandatory Monday morning meetings. He was beginning to wish for his own practice. Dudley began a mental tally of what the overhead might be if he were on his own and which clients might be lured from this firm. He was also thinking what all the other lawyers were thinking about this: Josh was adding insult to injury by demanding this meeting. It could have waited until Monday.

Leah passed out copies of the court documents to everyone. Josh sat there waiting for all to digest the content of the petition. His face became redder and redder.

Then he stood up. "I want to get to the bottom of this. I have never been as embarrassed as I was last night and in front of all my dear friends and our best clients. This damn redneck lawyer could have mailed the petition to the firm. That, without exception, is what all lawyers do in an adversary proceeding. It's obvious that he went out of his way to have personal service and in doing so, to humiliate this firm. And myself."

He began to talk louder. "There is no way that small-town lawyer in that po-dunk county that far from here could have known where I would have been last night. He obviously had inside information. And it had to come from up here. I want input. Do any of you have thoughts about this?"

There was a lot of squirming around the table. Finally, Lillie Bess spoke. "Uh, Mr. Nutt. I was standing over by the bar in the corner. Some of the lawyers from the Ricks firm were there too. They seemed to enjoy the situation more than anyone else."

"Why do you say that?" Stanley blurted

She continued, "Well, just as you stood up to speak, I heard Ken Arnoff tell Ernest Tinsley to go get everybody back in from the patio, that the fireworks were about to begin. When that jester stuck the papers in your tux, I heard Ken say that he had it coming."

Mr. Nutt screamed, "That proves it! They are behind this. We will retaliate and retaliate. We will leave no stone unturned until we get even. More than even!"

Some of the lawyers looked upon him in alarm. They thought he might be about to have a stroke.

Leah rushed a glass of water to him. He turned it up, spilling some which dripped down his chin onto his expensive sport shirt.

He gasped for breath and said, "We're opposite them in the Embry medical malpractice case. I want every motion in the book filed against them. Maximize our discovery. If the rules limit the number of questions, I want each question to have as many subparts as possible and as many ridiculous subparagraphs as the IRS does in their regulations, enough that they have to hire a math major to keep track of where they are when the answers are being prepared. Give them no quarter!"

Mr. Janes joined in, "I fully agree with Josh. I'm going to pull a few of you off your current cases to devote time to research as to what all is out there that we can use to harass them. Especially that obnoxious Ken Arnoff. Damn him!"

Josh asked Leah, "Can you get up with Frank Poley in Tupelo? I'd like to get his view about all this."

Leah left the room. A few minutes later she stuck her head in the door and said, "He's on the line."

Josh picked up the receiver and spoke, "Hey, Frank. I hate to bother you on a Saturday morning, but the entire firm is in a meeting here. I'm going to put you on the speaker phone so everyone can listen."

"Boy, this sounds serious for the entire staff to be there on Saturday."

Josh reiterated the previous night's events to Frank.

Frank agreed. "That wasn't necessary to have personal service on those papers. It is normally done by mail. I mean there is no hurry to have that kind of pleading served."

Josh said, "I think I'll file a motion against that lawyer for harassment. I'd really like to sue him."

"Listen, Josh. I can tell that your feelings are badly hurt. But I warn you about Archie Baker. He does things like this for a reason. He wants to get under his opposition's skin to throw their focus off the case. You should see him conduct a trial or a motion hearing. A lawyer in our firm was down in Poston last year to argue a motion in circuit court. He said Archie was scheduled to have a client plead guilty to a crime of burglary. Archie walked into the courtroom dressed in a New York Yankee uniform!"

Sounds of disbelief were uttered around the table.

Josh asked, "What happened?"

"According to our lawyer, the judge went berserk. He chewed Archie out in front of the whole courtroom. Astonishingly, the judge was not that concerned about his wearing the uniform. He got on to him mostly about wearing cleats because they were marring the wooden floor. Archie wasn't fazed at all by the butt chewing. It rolled off him like water off a duck's back. The court reporter stepped up to the bench to have the judge sign a document. While his attention was diverted, Archie turned sidewise and discovered a captive audience across the room. The jury box was filled with bored prisoners dressed in orange 'pumpkin' suits awaiting their turn to be sentenced. Archie went through a set of coach's signals, tugging his ear, pulling his nose, bumping his knee with his elbow, and pawing on the floor. The inmates came alive and sniggered, most of them returning signals, causing Archie to respond with frantic body movements. The judge turned his head toward the racket to discover that the prisoners had immediately become somber. The district attorney was so amused and preoccupied with the episode that he didn't object when Archie asked the judge to cut the prison term for the defendant in the plea deal by half."

Stanley exclaimed, "Unbelievable!"

Frank said, "Yes. I'm telling you he had a reason to have the papers served by a jester. You'll probably hear more about this. Archie can be really bizarre."

"Do we need to do anything about that will being filed?"

"Yes. To protect your client, you need to file a caveat to contest the will."

"Thanks, Frank"

"Sure. If you need more help let me know."

Leah disconnected the call and asked, "What now, Mr. Nutt?"

Mr. Janes spoke, "Look, Josh. Let's all go home and try to salvage our weekend. We can go over our strategy on Monday."

All the lawyers left the building without a single one wondering what connection Ken Arnoff and his firm might have to Joab McMath's estate.

CHAPTER 19
MR. JOAB'S BEQUESTS

On Monday, the lawyers were back in the conference room. Mr. Nutt had decided that the entire firm should be involved due to the contents of the will. He had never seen a will containing the terms this one did.

When they all were seated he asked, "Have all of you read this will?" All heads nodded.

He looked at his copy and read it again to himself.

STATE OF MISSISSIPPI
COUNTY OF CADE

LAST WILL AND TESTAMENT
OF
JOAB MCMATH

I, Joab McMath of the County of Cade, State of Mississippi, a single person, being over the age of twenty-one years and being of sound and disposing mind, knowing of the certainty of death and of the uncertainty of life, in the name of God, Amen, do make, publish and declare this my true Will and Testament, hereby expressly revoking any and all Wills, Testaments and Codicils hereto made by me.

IMPRIMIS

FIRST
I commit my soul to God who gave it and my body to Mother Earth from which it came.

SECOND
I desire that my body be decently buried, and that, at the head of my grave, a suitable and proper monument be erected in keeping with my station in life.

THIRD

I hereby appoint the Executor of this my Last Will and Testament, attorney Archie Baker. I hereby waive the necessity of his making bond but require that he make inventory and appraisal of my assets and an accounting to the Court.

FOURTH

I hereby give unto my friends, Laderell Latham and Irv Lackey, the title to my land located near Four Points and all improvements situated thereon. This land was made by God and of which in my lifetime, I was a mere and lowly caretaker. May they be such also and permit others to enjoy the beauty it portrays.

FIFTH

I hereby give unto Ben Weaver all of my firearms and ammunition.

SIXTH

I give unto Lola Hobbs, my friend who always laced my coffee with chocolate syrup, the contents of my house and the sum of $500.00 to furnish free coffee to her regulars at the coffee shop until it is expended. I also give her the sum of $25,000.00.

SEVENTH

I give unto my friend, Zeke Tiller, all my vehicles, wrenches and farm equipment.

EIGHTH

I give unto my friends, Ellis Tiller and Coley Wampler, the gallon jug of wild muscadine wine that is underneath my staircase (should be anyway) and when they partake thereof may it aid in momentarily expelling the demons that dwell in their minds. I direct that Coley shall have first swallow.

NINTH

I give unto those listed below all of my out-of-state property, which is substantial:

75% to Merci Hospital, Memphis, Tennessee.

25% to Earl Ray Fowler, for what he did. I inadvertently discovered his feat and commend him for sacrificing a prime year of his youth for his country.

TENTH
In the event, and in that event, that any of my above devisees predecease me or decline to accept my respective designated gifts to them, I will and devise those gifts unto a charity or charities to be selected by Reese Jones, Emma Powers, and Phil Mayo. Their selection will be final and binding upon the representative of my estate.

ELEVENTH
All the rest, residue and remainder of my property, real and personal and wherever situated, I give, bequeath and devise unto the Four Points Baptist Church.

TWELFTH
I specifically disavow and disinherit all of my blood kin.

Further, I state, in public and before mankind, that I never robbed God.

Finally, that I have confessed my sins and shortcomings and have received mercy and forgiveness.

In witness hereof, I have this day signed, published and declared this instrument as my Last Will and Testament, in said County and State. This the 13th day of March, 2000, Anno Domini.

_____

Joab McMath

Witness: Norma Sue Riley
Witness: Kayla Weeks

After reading the will, the lawyers all waited for Mr. Nutt to speak. He looked around the table and said, "Well, the will speaks for itself. He provided for his friends and so forth."

Mr. Janes spoke up. "Yes, he also added personal beliefs."

Dudley said, "I think what has and should get everyone's attention is paragraph nine, specifically the words *Out-of-State* and *Substantial.*"

Mr. Nutt said, "I agree. And that puts us back to square one. No wealth has been found in Cade County. We were correct in employing the property locator."

Lillie Bess had input: "But notice that will was made about ten years ago. He could have disposed of everything he had by this time."

Josh said, "Excuse me a minute. I'm going to my office and call Lamar Mosley and see if he has any news."

In his office, Josh dialed Lamar and found him free.

Josh asked, "Lamar, we have just obtained a copy of the McMath will. Have you seen it?

Lamar chuckled. "Yes, along with just about everyone else down here!"

Josh asked, "What are they saying?"

Lamar replied, "Everyone's excited. Especially, the crowd at Lola's. Each day her coffee sales are more than the day before. I hear it's the same way over at Baxter and Vena. The public focus is mainly on the fact that his wealth is located somewhere away from here and on who gets it."

"What do you mean?"

"Well, Merci Hospital gets most of his property. A lot of people here donate to that hospital because so many local children have received care there, which, most of the time, is free. But the most comments are about Earl Ray being in the will at all and of why he gets so much."

"Nothing significant has been located so far. And there may not be anything, as one of my lawyers has pointed out."

"I agree. But you can't convince anyone here about that. You should hear some of the rumors going around. Like he owned oil wells, was moving drugs in from South America, was growing Mary Jane on his place, that Archie's wife was stealing art and he was fencing it for her, and that he was laundering cash for the Mafia. Ridiculous! Mr. Joab was one of the most honest men I've ever met."

Josh laughed. "The will does leave room for active imaginations."

"Yeah. And for small minds to wander."

Josh said, "Tell me about this Earl Ray Fowler."

"Well, there's not much to tell. He's around sixty years old. He has a college degree but never used it for work. He's a highly skilled carpenter and works Monday through Thursday for an out-of-town contractor. On weekends, he stays busy searching for arrowheads or old bottles. He has quite a collection. He's not seen much around town, sort of a loner. His parents have been deceased since he was in college. Earl Ray's only known vice is his occasional drinking sprees. He hangs out at one of our county-line beer joints and gets into fights often. He's always taking up for those who are bullied there. I've never heard of him getting whipped, and it's common knowledge that no one has tried him twice. "

Josh said, "Sounds like quite a character. Why did Joab provide for him in the will?"

"That's the puzzle. No one can explain why. The main question going around is 'What did Earl Ray do?'"

"Why doesn't someone ask him?"

"Hah! That'll never happen. At least not by anyone who knows him. Earl Ray is the most closed-mouth person you'll ever meet. He minds his own business. You could ask him but he wouldn't tell."

"I can see why everyone is agitated. The fact that there is a secret out there, and the person who knows it won't tell."

"You bet."

"I've talked to Frank Poley again, and he says we need to file a caveat opposing the will."

Lamar replied, "That's right. Because it's not the original will. But first, we should prevail on our Motion for the Heirship Determination to get Jeb Shaw qualified to contest the will."

Josh said, "If you don't mind, my firm will prepare the caveat which we will send to you for your approval."

"That's good. I'm sort of spread out right now. And I'll let you argue the motions. Of course, I'll be sitting in the courtroom to help. I have to anyway because you are an out-of-state lawyer."

"I know you are running the legal ad for anyone who claims kin to Mr. Joab to appear. When is the date of that hearing?"

"Friday. Next week."

"I was going to let you handle that. But after this development, I think someone in my firm should assist. Don't you?"

"Yes. I may need help with that crazy Archie being involved now."

"Have you found anybody to come and testify at the heirship hearing?"

"Yes, I have. Mrs. Ruby Shows, a ninety-two year old lady that lives over in Gallatin County, will be our witness. She grew up at Four Points. Her family is one of the oldest down here. She taught school all her adult life at Gallatin High School. After retiring, she became involved in tree-climbing."

"What?"

Lamar laughed. "That's what we call people who are involved in genealogy. She, with others, has put together several family trees in Cade County. And it just so happens that she did one on Joab's family."

"How does it look?"

"Good. All we have to do is get proof that certain family members are deceased. And have Mrs. Shows testify to the tree, how she did her research, and how she verified the information she used to compile the tree."

"Can we help?"

"Yes. I'll fax you the name of cousins who supposedly died in Arkansas. Could you expedite getting death certificates from the Bureau of Vital Records in Little Rock?"

"We'll do that. I'll send a staff member over there tomorrow for the certificates. We don't have time to wait on a mail request."

Lamar replied, "I don't expect anyone to show up except Jeb."

"Well, you can think again about that."

Worriedly, Lamar asked, "What do you mean?"

Josh laughed. "Not another heir. I mean Jeb will probably bring his whole family."

CHAPTER 20
THE HEIRSHIP HEARING

On the day of the hearing, Josh Nutt, Stanley Robbs, Dudley Cook, Lillie Bess, and Leah left Memphis early. They were in Josh's BMW, but Dudley was driving. Josh told Dudley he was selected because he didn't get speeding tickets, looking sideways at Stanley as he spoke. Leah turned away and smiled. Stanley remained silent thinking that he would never live that trip down.

The staff pulled into the parking lot of the courthouse at Poston thirty minutes early. As they got out of the car, they noticed two Mercedes automobiles with Shelby County, Tennessee, plates parked in front. The vehicles, a tan one and a blue one, were the current year's models.

Dudley remarked, "I wonder what happened in Memphis last night? Looks like a mass exodus."

Stanley laughed. "Yeah. That blue Mercedes looks exactly like the one Ken Arnoff drives."

"Ken wouldn't be caught dead in this place," Josh sneered. "He's back in Memphis padding his client's bills."

They were still smiling when they walked through the front door of the courthouse and down the corridor past several doors to the one that appeared to be the lawyer's entrance to the courtroom. Josh was leading the way. As he entered the courtroom, he stopped in his tracks and stared. At one of the tables in front of the bench sat Ken Arnoff, five of the lawyers in his firm, and two paralegals! They were all looking straight at him with wide grins.

Josh regained his composure and strode to the table. "Well, hello, Ken and all. Have y'all snared a big insurance case down here?" he inquired.

Ken kept smiling. "Oh, no, Josh. We're here on the McMath estate."

"What?" blurted Josh.

"Yes. We're here to enter an appearance in the estate. We've been employed by Merci Hospital to represent them and to protect their interests against unscrupulous people."

"And lawyers," piped one of his associates.

Josh asked shortly, "Are you saying that I'm not of principle?"

Ken said. "Ah, come on, Josh. You know I wouldn't insinuate that about you. Of all people!"

"I would," said a voice from the jury room.

All heads turned. Out of the nearby room walked Archie Baker with Wiley Downs. Josh's crew took stock of Archie. He had on un-ironed khaki pants, red high-top tennis shoes, a navy blazer that looked to be fifteen years old, a faded, French-blue shirt and a clip-on, green bow tie.

He asked, "Who might you all be? I'm Archie Baker, and I represent a dead man!"

Taken aback, Josh said, "Well, I've never heard it expressed that way. But that can't be argued with, can it? I'm Josh Nutt. I represent Jeb Shaw."

Then he introduced the rest of his people. As Lillie Bess shook Archie's hand, she noticed a brief twinkle in his blue eyes as they met hers. She thought that this guy was dangerous. Josh may have met his match.

Judge Zack Dennis was sitting in his chambers along with his court reporter Ashley Anderson. He had entered the building through the back door and was unaware of who was present in the courtroom. The judge was due on the bench at 9:30. Judge Dennis was a short, heavy man. He had a solo practice his entire career until being elected chancellor twelve years ago. He was in good health and had few hobbies; his major vice was eating too much. In the early days of his law practice, he had been a hard drinker.

Zack abruptly quit drinking because of what occurred late one night on his walk home from a bar just off the square in downtown Oxford. He took a wrong turn down a side street and ended up in a seedy part of town. Three young toughs, who were sitting on the tailgate of an old pickup drinking whiskey, accosted him. Unwisely, he became belligerent. They didn't like his smart talk. One of them picked up a stick of firewood lying in the bed of the pickup and hit Zack upside his head, knocking him to the ground. When they started toward him, Zack pulled a pistol out of his pocket and fired. The shot missed, but the three toughs hit the trail. He became sober, instantly. Zack wildly looked around to see if this brawl had been observed. He didn't see anyone on the street or anyone looking out of a window. Zack ran all of the way home thinking of how his law practice would have been devastated if he had shot one of the toughs while under the influence, self defense or not. He didn't sleep the rest of the night. The next morning, Zack poured all the alcohol in his house down the sink and vowed never to drink again.

––––––––––––

A couple of lawyers breezed through his chambers having him sign routine orders. Then Linda Nell Few walked in.

She greeted the judge and Ashley and then said, "Judge, this estate is about to get heated."

Judge Dennis perked up. "What do you mean?"

"It looks like Brooks Brothers has set up shop in the courtroom. There is a ton of Memphis lawyers out there all dressed in tailored clothes. And it seems like one set of them brought most of their library. I do know one, the young lawyer who filed the claim for the heir some time ago."

"I thought I was here to hold a hearing for an heirship determination. That should be short and simple."

"That's what's on the docket. So I don't know why it's necessary for so many people to be here. And I think Archie has some motion to argue." The judge's face became red. "Uh, oh," thought Ashley, "he's losing his temper!"

Judge Dennis expected to be back in Oxford to eat fish at the Mudcat for lunch. Fried catfish was their special on Fridays, and he hardly ever missed that meal. It was an all-you-can-eat event, and many of his friends gathered there. The meal was a great way to end the work week. He instructed Linda Nell to get the case file for his review. She did and sat there in silence with Ashley while the judge read.

The judge opened the file jacket and flipped past the petition to open, the few small claims, the inventory returned by the administrator, the claim made by the purported heir Jeb Shaw, Archie's petition to probate a Lost Will and the caveat filed by the firm of Janes, Knobly, and Stilt. All appeared to be in order and contained no surprises. Then he carefully examined the Petition to Determine Heirs, the subject of today's hearing.

He looked over his reading glasses and asked Linda Nell, "How many sets of Memphis lawyers are out there?"

"I'm not sure, but it looked like two."

Judge Dennis said, "Well, let's get moving. I need to get this sorted out. Anytime Archie is involved, simple matters usually turn into a mess. But I know one thing, I'm not going to put up with any of his shenanigans."

As he entered the courtroom wearing his black robe, the bailiff called the courtroom to attention, "All rise. The Chancery Court of Cade County, Mississippi, is now in session. The Honorable Zack Dennis presiding."

All the lawyers, court personnel, and spectators rose.

Judge Dennis sat down and declared, "Be seated."

He looked around and asked, "Are all of you lawyers present for the Estate of Joab McMath?"

They all nodded.

"I'll have one of you from each law firm to stand and announce who you represent," said the judge.

He looked at Wiley first who stood and said, "Your Honor, I'm the duly appointed administrator of the estate, and I replace the Honorable John England who initially opened the estate." He sat down.

Then Archie stood and announced, "I am the Executor of the Last Will and Testament of Joab McMath. If a situation arises during probate, I might need to be represented by counsel; but since I'm an attorney, I will proceed without one."

He looked around the courtroom and added cockily, "I'm the best lawyer in the state anyway. So it's redundant that I would need advice."

The Janes lawyers stared at him. Ken Arnoff smiled.

Judge Dennis saw the opportunity to say, "Mr. Baker, there's many a slip between the fork and the mouth." Then he looked over the bench down at Archie's shoes and smirked, "You're not in the court you're dressed for, Mr. Baker. In this one, foul-outs can come rather quickly for misbehavior!"

Snickers were heard coming from the Janes lawyers.

Judge Dennis said, "Next."

Josh Nutt stood up. "Your Honor, I'm Josh Nutt, a senior partner with the Memphis firm of Janes, Knobly, and Stilt and these are my associates." He introduced each of them.

When he finished the Judge asked, "Do any of you have a Mississippi license?"

Josh replied, "No, Your Honor, but we have associated Mr. Lamar Mosley of Central City."

Lamar stood and confirmed, "That's correct, Your Honor."

The judge said, "Okay. Would each of you leave your business card with the court reporter before you leave?"

When he looked toward the larger group of lawyers, Ken Arnoff stood and stated, "Your Honor, I'm Ken Arnoff with the Memphis firm of Ricks, Tyson, Tinsley, and Arnoff." He then introduced his associates. Ken continued, "My firm has been employed by Merci Hospital to represent their interest as a devisee under Mr. McMath's will. We are here to enter an appearance as such."

Judge Dennis was astonished! He couldn't believe that all those lawyers showed up in court just to enter an appearance. He thought there must be a power play of some sort going on between these two Memphis firms.

"Do you have any further business today in this case?"

"No, Your Honor. We will remain and observe the hearing."

The judge looked around and said though a smile, "I can't believe that we don't have a Tupelo lawyer here or one from Batesville." The judge asked, "I will also ask you. Do any of you have a Mississippi license?"

Ken replied, "No, Your Honor. But we also have associated a local lawyer, Archie Baker."

Josh stood up and protested. "But, Your Honor, we object. That's a conflict. Mr. Baker is the executor of a will that has been proffered but has not been admitted by the court."

Ken smiled smugly. "No, it's not a conflict. His position is to probate the will."

Josh countered, "But we have contested the will. He has to defend the contest. He can't do that and assist Arnoff."

The judge hit the bench with his gavel as he spoke, "Now, fellows. I don't allow running arguments in my court. When you make an objection, I expect to rule on it before anyone else speaks. Is that understood?"

They meekly nodded.

The judge said, "Here's the deal. The personal representative is expected to defend the caveat. After that, if the will is admitted, he just hands out assets to whoever is entitled to them. And the Ricks firm has an interest in the will being admitted. That's the only way the Merci Hospital will get anything. You know, in this state, the rule is 'will or no will'. A will can't be admitted in part, only in its entirety. Anyway, the court has not yet issued letters testamentary to Mr. Baker because of the will contest. Mr. Downs will continue to administer this estate. I hereby appoint Mr. Baker to represent him until further orders of the Court and he is allowed to assist Mr. Arnof. Mr. Nutt, your objection is overruled."

Judge Dennis continued, "This hearing for the heirship determination is premature since this issue of the will has arisen. First, the will contest should be resolved which I am setting three weeks from next Monday. If it's not admitted, then the heirs-at-law inherit."

Lillie Bess rose. "Your Honor, we are prepared to go forward with the heirship matter today. We have all our witnesses here and our documentary evidence. We could at least resolve this issue now. And we need to establish Mr. Shaw as an heir so his caveat will be valid."

Judge Dennis smiled at her as he added, "You've made a good point, young lady. Of course, there may be others here today to assert a claim. I see a lot of people in the courtroom, and this is the only matter I have scheduled."

Those lawyers seated at the tables turned and looked toward the spectator area of the room. It was about three-fourths full. The people there were absorbing the conversation of the judge and the lawyers. Obviously, there was a lot of local interest in this case.

The judge said, "If you are ready, call your first witness."

Lillie Bess said, "Your Honor, we call Mrs. Ruby Shows." Then she walked through the opening in the center of the rail to where a frail, elderly lady was standing up with the aid of a cane and the help of a younger woman. As Lillie Bess and the other woman guided Mrs. Shows past the lawyers' tables to the witness box, the judge addressed the audience, "Is there anyone here that has business in the Joab McMath estate?" No one answered. The judge repeated his request two more times as the law required, pausing briefly between. Still, no one answered.

By this time Mrs. Shows was seated in the witness box. She turned toward the judge and said, "How are you, young man?"

The judge smiled and said, "I'm fine and thanks for the compliment."

Those in the gallery tittered.

Mrs. Shows smiled back and said, "I may be sort of nervous. I've never testified before in court. In fact, I've never been in court for anything."

Judge Dennis became friendly. It was election year, and he couldn't lose ground by catering to the elderly. "I'll bet you have always been a good girl, then."

Mrs. Shows answered, her voice slightly shaky because of her age, "Well, if you don't count that time my friend, Julia, and I put the live bream we had caught in the creek into her mother's tank of rainwater she used to wash her hair."

The gallery laughed. The judge and all the lawyers chuckled.

The judge asked with a grin, "What did Julia's mother have to say about that?"

"Well, about two days after we did it, Julia and I were playing in the yard. Miss Oma came out of the house with a towel wrapped around her head and a bucket in her hand. When she peered into the tank and saw the fish, she started saying bad words. After I got older, I realized that she was doing some heavy-duty cussing."

Another round of laughter arose from the courtroom.

Then the judge told Lilly Bess to proceed.

Lillie Bess asked, "Would you state your name and where you live?"

"Ruby Shows. 1073 Palm Street, Gallatin, Mississippi."

"Briefly give the court your background, like where you grew up, your education, your work career and your family status."

"Sure. I was born at Four Points many years ago. Ninety-two years ago, in fact. My parents, Ed and Joy Lucas, lived in the community all their lives. I graduated from the local high school. It's not there anymore because it consolidated with Central City High after I left. I went to college at an all girl's teacher's school in Georgia. I graduated there and was hired as an English teacher in Gallatin. A few years later, I married

Kenny Shows, who worked for the railroad. We raised our family in Gallatin, and now we have great-grandchildren."

Lillie Bess interrupted, "That's commendable."

The gallery noticed the judge nodding in approval.

Lillie Bess said, "Please continue."

"After I retired I started working in genealogy. I wanted to establish my own family tree. That took a lot of research and correspondence with many, many family members. And it took a lot of time. In fact, my husband said he wasn't getting the attention he wanted from me and would divorce me, except all of our life savings was in my personal bank account."

Everyone in the courtroom laughed. The spectators had come to the hearing to be entertained, and Mrs. Shows was accommodating them.

"Along the way, friends joined me in this work. Our group sort of became a club. It made the chore easier for me."

Lillie Bess asked, "Did you ever complete any other family trees?"

"Yes, we did."

"Would you name them?"

"Trees for the Caraway family, the Pittman family, the Vance family, the James family, the Cooper family, the McMath family, and the Doler family. And we have many more that are in the process of being finished."

"Did you do much work on the McMath tree?"

"Yes. I did nearly all the work on that one. It turned out there weren't that many branches. I had a lot of reliable feedback from some good sources."

Lillie Bess walked over to her table, picked up a bound manuscript and handed it to the court reporter, "Would you please mark this as Plaintiff's Exhibit One?"

The court reporter placed a sticker on the cover and marked a "P-1" on it.

Then Lillie Bess handed the book to Mrs. Shows and asked, "Would you please identify the manuscript you are holding?"

"It's the family tree of Josiah McMath, who was born in 1791."

"Would you read to the court the name of the author?"

"Yes. The author is me, Ruby Shows."

"What is your title as listed on this manuscript?"

Ruby proclaimed seriously, "Top Branch."

All in the courtroom smiled.

"I ask you, is Jeb Shaw one of the members?"

"Yes, he is."

"What chronological information does this tree show?"

"It shows the dates of birth, the dates of marriages, and the dates of death of all those listed. If a date was unknown or uncertified, then a question mark or a note is set forth by the name."

"What else is shown?"

"Where the deceased are buried and the names of their descendants."

"Is Joab McMath included in this tree?"

"Yes. He is a direct descendant of Josiah."

Lillie Bess asked, "Was Joab survived by direct descendants?"

"No," replied Ruby.

"Was Joab survived by any nieces or nephews or any descendant of them?"

"No," replied Ruby.

"Please look at this tree and tell the Court how Joab McMath and Jeb Shaw are related."

Mrs. Shows peered over the top of her glasses as she slowly thumbed through the volume. Finally she located the page she wanted. "They are third cousins," she reported.

"Did Joab McMath have any first, second, or other third cousins?"

"Yes, but all of those in those degrees of kin are deceased except for Jeb."

"Did those that are deceased die before Mr. Joab?"

"Yes. The latest one died about four years ago."

"Do you know Jeb Shaw?"

"No."

"Did he furnish any information about this tree to you?"

"No. We sent him an information sheet to his Arkansas address, but he didn't reply. Someone thought that he might not be able to read or he was suspicious and might think that there was an ulterior reason for needing the family information."

"According to the McMath family tree as shown here, who is the closest living relative of Joab McMath?"

"Jeb Shaw," answered Mrs. Shows.

"Did you know Joab McMath?"

"Yes. I knew him well. He was the same age of one of my younger brothers. They used to quail hunt together after school and on Saturdays. Quail hunting was better known around here as bird hunting."

Lillie Bess said, "Your Honor, I tender the witness."

Mrs. Shows started to get up from the witness chair with effort.

The judge extended his open palm toward her. "No, Mrs. Shows. Remain seated, please. The other lawyers may want to ask you questions."

Mrs. Shows sank back down.

The judge addressed the Arnoff group, "I really don't see why any of you have standing to ask any questions. You are trying to get a copy of a lost will admitted, and it shouldn't make any difference who an heir might be."

His red shoes made a squeak as Archie stood to say, "Well, Your Honor, I disagree with that. Since no one else besides this Jeb Shaw is making a claim as an heir here today, if he was proven not to be one, then our will couldn't be contested."

Judge Dennis thought for a minute and replied, "Yeah, I guess you're right. I see your point. Proceed."

Archie strode up to the witness chair. He needed to cast doubt on Mrs. Show's testimony, but he had to handle her with kid gloves. Otherwise, he would lose the judge's favor if he was seen being rough with a ninety-two year old lady.

He had the full attention of the gallery. They were waiting to hear what Archie would ask and if he was going to be as rude with Mrs. Shows as he usually was with witnesses on cross-examination.

Judge Dennis squirmed in his chair. If Archie got out of line the least bit with Mrs. Shows, he was going to slam him. He watched Archie intently.

With his hands locked together in the small of his back, Archie paced back and forth, back and forth. Mrs. Shows began to get nervous as she watched him. She wondered why the judge allowed him to appear in the courtroom dressed so freakishly.

Then Archie turned and said, "Mrs. Shows, I commend you and your fellow limbs and branches....."

Judge Dennis immediately interrupted, "Mr. Baker, are you trying to be smart with the witness?"

With his head down, Archie replied, "Oh no, Your Honor, I just was trying to put the correct nomenclature on these tree climbers."

The judge spoke sternly. "You look at me when you are talking. For your information, the correct reference in my court is 'Mrs. Shows' and her fellow 'researchers.' Is that clear?"

The gallery smiled gleefully!

"But, Your Honor, it says right under the title, *Ruby Shows, Top Branch.*"

His face red, the judge half rose from his chair, leaned over the top of the bench and shouted, "I said, 'Is that clear?'"

Archie replied, "Yes, Your Honor."

"Then proceed. And be civil."

"But, Your Honor, you're the one that's upset."

"Archie!"

"Okay. I'll move on."

Archie said, "Let me rephrase my question, Mrs. Shows. Has your research of the Josiah McMath family been concluded on all members of the tree to the extent that there remains no doubt at all that anyone has been left out?"

Mrs. Shows quickly replied, "Young man, there could always be a left-handed child out there. But no, this family tree is iron-clad."

"Thank you." Archie turned to the judge and said, "Your Honor, I have no more questions."

The judge was startled! He couldn't believe that Archie was ending his cross-examination with only one question. He turned and smiled at Mrs. Shows. "You are dismissed and thank you for coming."

As Mrs. Shows stood and looked over the courtroom, she said, "Judge, I enjoyed my first experience testifying. I already feel like an expert witness."

All of the lawyers smiled.

Lillie Bess rose and said, "Your Honor, I request that the document marked as 'Plaintiff's Exhibit 1' be admitted into evidence."

Judge Dennis said, "So ordered. And where is the heir, Jeb Shaw?"

Josh replied, "Oh, Your Honor, we didn't think it necessary to haul him such a long way. We'll rest on his sworn affidavit that he is the sole heir of Joab McMath. We also move that the court rule him established as the sole heir."

The Judge said, "So ordered."

Then he addressed the lawyers, "Is there any more business before the court in this matter?"

There was a chorus of "No, Your Honor" from all the lawyers.

Archie had intended to bring a motion before the court but decided after the turn of today's events that it could wait until another day.

The judge stood up to exit the bench when, from the middle of the courtroom, came a firm, clear voice, "I do."

The judge froze. He looked out to the gallery. There stood a man dressed in clean work clothes with his head up and looking toward him.

Judge Dennis asked, "And who might you be?"

"Earl Ray Fowler."

"What is your business in this estate?"

"I've been named in Mr. Joab's will."

"Well, sir, that will has not been admitted for probate as of yet. It's being contested by the heir, Jeb Shaw."

"Judge, I'm aware of that. I want to protect my rights."

"Do you have a lawyer?"

Earl Ray stood there with his cap in his hand. "No, Sir, I don't."

The lawyers in Josh's firm were all turned in their seats watching him and absorbing his every word.

Judge Dennis paused, surveyed the array of legal minds seated before him, and said, "I think you might ought to get one."

"I have to disagree with you, Sir. God is on my side."

At that, Stanley strangled a laugh in his throat. Lillie Bess, a devout Baptist, glared at him.

The judge looked down and smiled. He looked up and said, "Well, if you see it that way. It's your call."

Then Earl Ray made a request that silenced the entire courtroom: "I want my cause heard by a jury."

The judge sat back down. Linda Nell Few nearly stroked out. She had never been involved in seating a jury. Never. In fact, in the chancery court there were only two kinds of cases where a party was entitled to a jury. One was a divorce, and then the jury's decision was only advisory. The judge in the case could ignore the jury's finding and rule contrary.

The other situation upon which a jury could hear the facts and could give a binding decision was a will contest.

Judge Dennis sat there reflecting. During his career on the bench he also had never had a jury on a will contest in any of the counties in his district.

Finally, he declared to Earl Ray, "I'll grant your request. You have that right under the law."

All the lawyers were silent. Even Archie was speechless after this unexpected development. He thought he had this whole scenario figured out. Now he would have to regroup in a hurry because the trial started in three weeks.

Judge Dennis addressed the courtroom, "You know, this seems to be much ado about nothing. I've already examined the administrator's inventory, and if you sold everything that's listed from the courthouse steps, it wouldn't pay for all your lawyers' suits."

No one replied, but everyone in the courtroom had the same thought. There had to be something valuable somewhere, or the testator would not have made mention of it in his will. Why had he been so vague about the details?

CHAPTER 21
TOBY'S PUSH

On Monday morning, Wade was sitting in the office of Phil Mayo, the Central City High School principal. The football team had won their first game of the season the previous Friday. They had defeated the visiting Kelso Owls by a score of 35-14. All the students and fans were happy, except for two: the parents of Toby Teller. That was the reason Phil Mayo had asked Wade to come by his office. The Tellers' unhappiness had been caused by the football team of which their son was a member or by some unidentified member or members of the team. The problem had arisen not before the game or after the game. It had happened at halftime and not on the field. At halftime Central City had found itself behind 14-0. The team had been the preseason favorite to win the conference, primarily, because of having fourteen experienced seniors returning from last season. Kelso wasn't even in the same conference. Kelso was a smaller school, some eighty miles to the south, which was playing at Central City because Mr. Mayo had paid them a $2,500 fee to come there. Their principal had wanted Central City to come to Kelso and split the gate. Mr. Mayo wisely countered their offer with the $2,500. He was well familiar with the local support of the Hornets. Central City High School could bank more money this way. Kelso had a young team, and Mayo knew they wouldn't draw many fans to their own home field.

Apparently, the Central City players had been reading the sports coverage and had let the pre-season accolades go to their heads. They entered the game with a too casual attitude. A 125-pound sophomore for Kelso took the opening kickoff and returned it all the way for a touchdown. On the ensuing kickoff, Miles Lennox fumbled the ball on the ten yard line, and, after kicking it up field while trying to cover it, a Kelso player picked the ball up and ran back to the ten before being tackled. Two plays later, Kelso put the football into the end zone, and the Central City fans, players, band, and cheerleaders sat in stunned silence.

The rest of the half saw the Hornets fumble, blunder, and stumble. Their coach was content to get his team into the field house dressing room being behind only 14-0.

The team had sat in silence as their two coaches threatened, screamed, cussed, and begged throughout the halftime. The three managers kept their heads down to escape the coach's wrath as they taped the player's feet and ankles. They had been lax in their duties themselves during the fall practice and had been called down more than once. They had to be constantly reminded to sweep the field house floor. The wrench used to replace broken cleats had become misplaced by the managers one day, and most of the team had to scrimmage without shoes. All three had been accused by the band director of removing the turf markers used by the band to key their formations for the half-time performance.

Then the players were startled as Larry Poe walked in and pushed the coaches aside. He stood up on a bench in the front of the room and began speaking words of encouragement. He had played in the backfield for Central City nine years ago. Larry now owned a feed store in town and had done well with the business. The players were unaware that he also bet on football games, including this one. Larry began to rant and rave so much that he began to foam at the mouth. He pumped his fists in the air. His words began to take effect on the team. Slowly, they began to lift their heads. Larry's antics were lifting their spirits. The team began to get worked up.

The straw that broke their negative mood was when Larry finished his speech with the promise, "If y'all beat Kelso, I'll buy the team a hamburger steak supper after the game with all the French fries you can eat!"

Larry had a huge bet on this game and the cost of the supper was peanuts to what was on the line. The team began to howl, "Go! Go! Go!"

Then Larry added, "And your girl friends."

The team captain screamed, "That's it! Let's go guys. Let's send Kelso home with their tails tucked!"

The players poured out of the room holding their helmets high in the air. Their coaches stood to one side, speechless. The captain led the team down the hall of the field house amidst a mighty roar. The players charged out to run across the wooden bridge over Indian Creek, a deep channel that ran between the field house and the north end of the football field. The lead players, four wide, had to slow down to keep their cleats from hanging in the spaces between the planks that floored the bridge which caused the players who followed to stop. But they were worked up, and they pumped their legs up and down, standing in place, screaming all the while. The second-team players were the ones at the back of the squad, and Toby Teller found himself on the outside near the edge of the narrow bridge which had no banisters.

Toby had been a pain to the entire football team all during fall practice. He ran his mouth incessantly. He was always getting out of the hard parts of practice with imaginary injuries or by mentioning that his father was on the school board. By the first game, even the coaches, both who had been starters in the Southeastern Conference, had a bellyful of Toby. But they had to put up with him because of Mr. Teller's position on the school board and the fact that he let the coaches hunt on his land.

The line of players resembled a string of cars leaving a red light. As the lead players got off the end of the bridge and ran toward the field and the stands where the fans were coming to life after hearing the team's enthusiastic cheering, the back of the line began to move across the bridge. At that moment, Toby got carried away and churned his legs even more viciously while still standing in place. As the players moved by him, an unknown hip bumped Toby, aided by an unknown push, which knocked him off the bridge into a deep hole of water ten feet below. Toby let out a ghastly scream as he fell, which caused the stands to go wild, for they mistook the shriek for a secret rally cry.

The over-the-top enthusiasm of the team caused another event that, at first, appeared to be a disaster. Central City had won the opening toss but had deferred. Their coach elected to kickoff at the second half. The team ran out on the field all pumped up. When the kicker settled down to tee the ball, he realized he had not brought the tee with him. From the middle of the field, the huge right tackle, "Bogey" Bailey shouted toward the bench, "Throw me the tee."

The senior manager, Porter Webb, opened the lid of the huge first-aid box where the tee was always stored. To his dismay, it wasn't there. He had been caught up in the team's fervor and had left it in the field house. His heart sank; he feared this would end his career as a manager. That meant he wouldn't get a leather football jacket at the year-end banquet. In a panic, he tore off running to the field house to retrieve the tee, as if the game would be held up that long. The referee was becoming impatient and shouted, "Let's go, Coach! Get moving!"

The coach yelled to the kicker, "Kick it flat!"

The players on the field gawked at him. "Bogey," possessed with a strong back and a weak mind, wasn't sure he heard the instruction correctly. "Huh?"

"I said kick it flat!"

"Bogey" took the football from the referee and laid it on its side on the spot where the tee should have been. The crowd buzzed with excitement. They had never seen this tactic before. The fans collectively thought, how innovative!

As "Bogey" backed up for the kick, the coach put his arms around the shoulders of each of the other two managers and said sternly, "Boys, you have fallen from my grace. If one more stupid little thing happens the remainder of the football season because of you two, y'all are gone!"

The young managers moved to stand behind the bench, their chins on their shoes.

The kicker's foot struck the ball, lifting it head high and it sailed swiftly away resembling a brown, oblong knuckle ball as it traveled downfield. It hit a front-line Kelso player in the chest. The ball bounced back into the arms of a charging Central City player who carried it to the one-yard line. On the next play, Central City scored. The momentum built, so the game became a rout.

No one noticed Toby as he came dragging up to the bench, soaking wet. He began to demand who pushed him off the bridge. No one would admit to the act. The whole team soon learned what had happened, and they all felt that Toby deserved the dunking. The incident could have developed into a major problem except for the fact that before the game was over, everyone on the squad, including Toby, was put into the game.

However, the next day Mr. Teller walked into the barber shop and overheard a group of men laughing about Toby "falling" into the creek. He also heard comments to the effect that Toby had deserved his tumble. Mr. Teller called Principal Phil Mayo Saturday afternoon and demanded that he find out who did the pushing and that he be punished.

Phil told Wade, "Thank you for coming by. I need a second opinion, and I value yours."

Wade had already heard about what happened at halftime at the ballgame. Phil and he talked about how to handle Mr. Teller. They both knew that whoever pushed Toby wouldn't admit to doing it and that anyone who had seen the shove wouldn't either. They finally agreed that if the coach would punish the entire team, Mr. Teller would settle down.

Phil picked up the telephone, called the head coach, and discussed their suggestion. The coach agreed. He also saw this as a way out of the mess. The coach said, "I was going to run the stew out of them at practice today, anyway, because of how sorry they played in the first half. I'll have a team meeting and ask who pushed Toby off the bridge. Of course, no one will admit it, just like you say. Then I'll explain that since no one will tell, they will all have to suffer. That should build some comradery."

Mr. Phil hung up and breathed a sigh of relief. "Well, that's that. I wish my other problem could be solved that easy," he grumbled.

Wade raised an eyebrow. "What other problem?"

"Oh, last week I received a notice from the State Board of Education that all high schools in the state are going to have to offer a foreign language to the seniors next semester. That means I will have to hire a new teacher. Add that to our budget woes!"

Wade asked, "Don't you have a teacher who took a foreign language in college?"

Phil pointed to a stack of files. "That's the college transcripts of all the teachers in the county. Would you believe not one of them had a foreign language?"

"That is a surprise."

Phil added, "There is one person in the school system that had one, though. But it's not a widely spoken or written language around the world. Teaching it would be sort of a waste."

"Who is the person?"

"Rita Arnwine, our school counselor."

"Oh. What language does she know?"

Phil told him.

Wade mulled over that a while. He admitted, "That language is hardly spoken outside of its native country. I guess you will have to hire a Spanish or French teacher. Good luck."

On his way to his car, the chief deputy bumped into Trip Bowen, the team quarterback. Wade congratulated him on the win and how well he had managed the offense.

Trip said, "We were lucky to win. If Larry hadn't came by the dressing room and got us pumped up, we would have lost. Everybody was really down. But he started acting wacky just before we scored that last touchdown."

"What do you mean?"

"We were getting close to the goal line. A huge crowd had been standing there all night, just past the north end zone by that oak tree. Larry was in the middle. All night he had been waving us in to score. But on this drive he had his palms open and was making pushing motions toward us. I guess he wanted us to be good sports and not run up the score.

"After the game, the team went to the Blue Apron on the square to eat the hamburger steaks he promised us. Larry was sitting at the table by the front door. We all thanked him when we left. Since I'm the team captain, I thanked him more than the others and said if it hadn't been for his locker-room speech we would have lost the game. He didn't seem interested in our win. He shrugged, 'You win some and you lose some.' He wasn't nearly as excited as he was at halftime. I don't understand."

Grady said, "Oh, well. Shake it off." He thought, that rascal Larry! Not only does he bet on the games, he bets on the point spread. Sounds like he won the game bet and lost the spread. I need to put a stop to this.

That night after supper, Wade called Rita. She had learned to like Wade. She and her associate had been assigned by the superintendent to stay at her office in Poston on Friday nights during football season to receive the gate proceeds from all the countywide games. Wade would stay with them, providing security until Rita locked the money in the safe, and then he would follow her home on the dark highway. They had spent a lot of time together talking, and Wade had given her bits of fatherly advice on a couple of issues that she had divulged.

He asked if she would help him solve a mystery. She eagerly agreed, "Sure."

He said, "I can't tell much. For one thing there is a lot of speculation on my part. And there may not be anything to it. But it's about Earl Ray Fowler and what he did that got him included in Mr. Joab's Will."

Rita said, "Everyone is trying to figure that out. That's all my co-workers have been talking about lately."

"I have some hunches. Something I was working on even before the will was found."

"What do you want me to do?"

Wade said, "I need for you to go on a date with me to Sleazy's bar."

Rita laughed. "Ha ha! Why, you dirty old man! That's the most unusual pickup line I've ever heard, but ok... I'll take you up."

"And it has to be on short notice. Like maybe nine or ten o'clock at night."

She laughed again. "Ha! You do put a girl on the spot. That is short notice. Which night?"

"I don't know yet. That's why it'll be on short notice."

Then he explained what he wanted her to do and how to dress.

She agreed, "I like the part about how I'm supposed to dress. That way, no one will talk about me the next day."

Wade slyly asked, "Does that include Sherman?"

He caught her voice being tight as she said, "Oh. That's over."

"Okay, if you say so."

A couple of days later, Wade ran his patrol to Three-way in the middle of the afternoon and caught both Zeke and Darlene at Sleazy's. To his relief no one else was in the bar, so he asked if they would call him when Earl Ray showed up to drink beer. He only wanted them to call when it was obvious that Earl Ray was going on one of his benders. They agreed but said the hour might be late before they could identify that it was going to be one of those nights. Both were itching to know what this peculiar request was about, but they knew not to question Wade about why he needed the tip.

About a week later at 10:30 on Thursday night, Wade got a call from Darlene, "He's here. And he's on one. Earl Ray was loaded before he got here."

"Who's with him?"

"He's alone."

"Who else is in the bar?"

"Oh, it's full. A lot of guys who have been getting dove fields ready for the hunt this weekend are in here."

Wade said, "That's good. Really good. Look, can you see that there'll be two seats open by him an hour from now?"

"You got it."

About an hour later, Wade walked into the bar dressed in khaki pants and a sport shirt with a young woman on his arm. He looked around the barroom and recognized only a few who were from Cade County. They nodded, looking his date over. She was good looking. They had never seen her before. Jon David Knox was there, and he came over offering to buy them a drink.

Wade knew Jon David was really being nosy if he was going to buy drinks in exchange for the opportunity to find out the name of his date. Jon David held his hand out to her and said, "I'm Jon David Knox."

"Pleased to meet you. I'm Wade's date," the woman replied as she shook his hand.

Jon David was taken aback and hummed, "And does Wade's date have a name?"

"No!" she sweetly replied.

That clinched it for Jon David. She had to be a hooker, or she would say her name. Or somebody's wife. Wait till I get back to Lola's!

He was exalted! "Well, you're the prettiest brunette that's been in here in a while."

"Thank you."

Jon David walked away. Wade caught Darlene's eye. She nodded her head down the bar to where Earl Ray sat. He and his date moved that way. The young woman took the vacant stool on one side of Earl Ray and Wade took the one on the other side.

Wade observed that Earl Ray was so drunk that he was having trouble sitting on the bar stool.

Darlene sat a bottle of Coors Light down for the young woman. As Wade's date lifted the bottle for a swig, she deliberately spilled some beer onto Earl Ray's arm and said, "*Shilye hamnida!*"

Earl Ray waved his hand nonchalantly and replied, "*Alge sumnida.*"

Wade's date smiled and clicked her bottle to Earl Ray's. "*Gombae!*"

Earl Ray vigorously repeated, "*Gombae!*"

The woman asked in English, "Do you own this place?"

Earl Ray laughed. "*Aniyo.*"

The thought of owning Sleazy's caused him to shake with laughter. So much, he had to grab the bar to keep from falling off the stool. He raised his head and wiped the tears from his eyes. He turned to say something to the girl.

She wasn't there. Neither was Wade.

The next day Earl Ray awoke at noon. The sun was streaming through the bedroom window. His head was splitting with pain. Earl Ray swore if he could ever get over the effects of last night's drinking, he would never take a drink again. As he lay there on his back looking up at the ceiling fan turning lazily, he admitted to himself that he probably would drink again. That promise had been made many times, and they all had been broken.

Then a chill ran down his spine. Earl Ray had a thought that made him feel violated. He tried to remember the conversation with an unfamiliar woman at Sleazy's the night before. And Wade was there too, but maybe not with the woman, since they had sat on each side of him. But what was bothering him was whether or not he talked to them in English. That was a fear he had carried for many years. He had taken an oath that he would never discuss with anyone the burden he had volunteered to take upon his shoulders. Earl Ray knew he shouldn't drink to excess as he did; a time when his guard could be let down. But the lingering stress would build, and build, and the only escape he had ever found was his irregular drunken benders.

CHAPTER 22
THE HORSESHOE

Ben Weaver went to see Sheriff Powers to let him know he would be running bird dogs on the Teague property the next few weeks. Ben would be firing blanks from his shotgun to train the young dogs from being gun-shy. He figured that a stranger might be passing by and assumed someone was hunting out of season, which would prompt a call to the law. To save the sheriff an unnecessary trip to investigate, Ben wanted to give him a "heads up." Ben wasn't concerned with the locals; they were accustomed to his pre-season activity.

No one was in the outer office, so he walked through the open door into the sheriff's office. Grady was there talking to Jack Early about switching patrols from Four Points on the weekends to the north end of the county. Ben took a seat by the door.

When Grady was through talking, he asked, "What's going on, Ben?"

Ben told him his reason for dropping by. Then all three began to discuss a variety of subjects. Glancing around, Ben noticed an object placed on the floor in the corner of the room.

"So that's where Mr. Joab's letter holder got off to," he said.

Grady turned his head toward the corner. "What do you mean?"

"When I got back from South Dakota a while back, I was in Lola's. The guys there had a copy of Mr. Joab's inventory that had been made by Wiley Downs."

"And?"

"I noticed that the letter holder was not listed and wondered why."

Grady spoke, "It wasn't on the list because we had removed it from the house before the inventory was made. The stand it was on had been knocked over. The holder was lying next to Mr. Joab's right hand. Blood was on the base. At first, the cause of his death was not certain. Since Mr. Joab had a bloody wound on his head, we had to rule out that someone had used the letter holder as a weapon to strike him. The object was sent to the lab. We just got it back last week. We also thought, since it was by his hand, that he may have intended to use it as a defensive weapon against an intruder."

Then Grady asked, "Why is it you remembered the letter holder?"

"Oh, Mr. Joab showed it to me one time when I was at his house. He said his brother out in Texas made it. His brother gave the holder to Mr. Joab many years ago just before he was killed in that car wreck. The workmanship was good, and Mr. Joab was really proud of it."

Jack walked over, picked up the holder, and examined it. The base was a horseshoe. A metal rod was welded in the curve of the shoe. At the top of the rod was a spring clip. It was designed so that the holder could sit on a desk and papers could be placed in the clip, calling attention to them. The entire holder, except for the clip, was covered with gold paint.

All three studied the object, thinking of Mr. Joab. Jack turned it around in his hands.

Jack mused, "I wonder if Mr. Joab considered this horseshoe lucky?"

"That's not a horseshoe," Ben announced.

Jack looked up, puzzled. "It's not? Then, what is it?"

Grady looked at Ben.

"It's a muleshoe," Ben replied.

"I didn't know there was a difference," Jack said.

Grady said, "Oh, sure it is. A muleshoe is smaller. Any blacksmith can tell you that. I hadn't even noticed that it was a muleshoe."

Jack looked at the holder some more and then put it back in the corner.

Ben said, "To change the subject, I have something to tell you."

"What?"

"Wade and I were talking the other day about Henry, the Musician. Wade was telling me about how he pretty well had figured out that Henry was responsible for getting that floozy to stir up the trouble at Oscar's funeral. I thought about that off and on all weekend."

"So?"

"I have an idea of why he did it."

Jack and Grady perked up.

"Why?" Jack asked.

"You remember how apprehensive Henry was about getting old? He had been heard, on several occasions, talking about how he dreaded reaching forty. Well, the last time Henry was in the federal pen, a full page ad appeared in *The Whisperer*. It was an earlier picture of Henry standing in front of his pink Cadillac convertible. He was smiling really big. The caption under the picture was in large letters which said, 'Happy Fortieth Birthday, Henry! Wish you were here and not there!' The ad was signed, 'Paid for by Oscar Sappington and Olney Shelton.' The ad was the biggest news in the paper that week. The day the paper came out, a large crowd gathered at Lola's discussing it. People started telling old stories about Henry and all the escapades he had been in over the years. After a while I said that I didn't realize that Henry was forty years old. Several more at the table said that was exactly what they were thinking. No one knew for sure, but after much speculation, a consensus was reached that Henry couldn't be more than thirty-seven."

"That's a big difference at that age," Jack said.

"Yeah. I remembered that a few weeks after the ad appeared, someone got a letter from Henry. He was having the paper sent to the pen and had seen the ad. In his letter, Henry said he was indeed thirty-seven, which Oscar and Olney knew. Henry was really mad about the ad being in the paper, but he was in a place where he couldn't do anything about it. That made the prank safe for Oscar and Olney. At least until Henry got out."

Jack asked, "Henry never did anything about it when he got out?"

"I never heard of him retaliating. I guess he had cooled down by then. But what Mose said has a meaning now."

"What do you mean?" Grady asked.

"I went by Oscar's car lot a month after the ad came out to borrow a fishing rod from Mose. We were laughing about the ad and how much fun the joke had created. Then Mose told me that Mr. Oscar and Mr. Olney didn't do that. I quizzed him and he said that Miss Arlene put the ad in the paper. When I pressed him how he knew and why she did it, he told me about overhearing Arlene and Oscar in a heated argument in the office. Arlene was shouting to Oscar that she knew he was running around on her and that Henry was lining up women for him. She screamed at Oscar that she was going to catch him sooner or later and that she put that ad in the paper to make Henry miserable for his part. Then Mose heard Oscar say that the ad would cause Henry to blame him since his name was under it. Mose said Arlene stormed out of the car lot office screaming that she hoped they killed each other."

"Wow! That makes sense," Jack said.

"Yes. Sounds like that the Musician just patiently bided his time to get even," Grady added.

"I wonder how Henry found out that Arlene was responsible." Jack asked.

Ben said, "I imagine that Mose told him. He always did like Henry because Henry would bring Mose the whiskey he couldn't get in a dry county."

Later that afternoon while Jack was filling out reports, Wade showed up. Jack told him the news that Ben had brought about Henry.

Wade confirmed, "That's a logical explanation. I remember Reese Jones telling all about how Henry enjoyed that ruckus more than anyone else in the funeral home."

Jack laughed. "I learned something today."

"What's that?"

"That some horseshoes are actually muleshoes."

"Oh?"

"Yeah. That letter holder of Mr. Joab's over there is a muleshoe. Ben said Mr. Joab's brother out in Texas gave it to him."

Wade turned in his desk chair and studied the object for a while. He pulled the file on Mr. Joab from a desk drawer. He flipped through to the photographs that Sally had made when Mr. Joab's body had been discovered. He slowly examined at each one. They had all been taken from different angles. The clip holder was in three of them. He absorbed the images they projected. He saw nothing that had any meaning.

Jack interrupted his thoughts. "Wade, I have to run a patrol. Earl Ray called for you about an hour ago. He said he needed to see you."

Wade said, "I want to go talk to Irv. I'll run by Earl Ray's house on my way back."

Wade changed his mind and decided to stop off at Earl Ray's before going to see Irv. Earl Ray's house was a little out of the way of the route to Irv's place. He lived about two miles off the main highway on a gravel road which made its way through timber company lands to a paved county road. Since Earl Ray was the only one who lived on the road, there was not much traffic, just some occasional log trucks, deer hunters in the winter, and the usual late-night beer drinkers. Earl Ray enjoyed the isolation. He minded his own business and never bothered anyone. For company he had an Australian Shepherd dog, a six-year old male named Jake. Jake went everywhere Earl Ray did. He let the dog ride on the seat of his pickup. Jake, like most dogs that rode in a vehicle, loved to stick his head out the passenger window to catch the wind in his face. There were days that Earl Ray really wanted to have the window up and the air conditioner on. He knew how well Jake enjoyed the wind, so he suffered the heat to let the dog have his way.

Earl Ray's neat, white wooden house was small. It was probably sixty years old but was kept up really well. The yard, an outlying shed, and barn were also in good upkeep. As Wade drove into the yard, Earl Ray was sitting on the front porch reading a newspaper and drinking a soda. Jake was lying at his feet.

When Wade got out of the car, Earl Ray said, "Come on up, Wade. I'll get you a Coke."

As Earl Ray went inside the house, Wade pulled a chair away from the wall and sat down. Jake got up, stretched and came over for some petting. Wade was scratching Jake's ears when Earl Ray came back, handed him the cold drink, and said, "Jake sure loves to have his ears scratched."

Both guys sat there slowly rocking, sipping their soda, and enjoying the cool breeze that was coming across the porch.

Finally Earl Ray spoke, a little awkwardly, "Say, Wade, I need to know something."

"What?"

"The other night at Sleazy's, I was out of it. I vaguely remember you being in there. A really pretty woman was there too."

"My date."

Earl Ray's heart sank. "Y'all were together?"

"Yeah."

"Wasn't she sort of young for you?"

"Love is not bounded by age."

"Oh, are you two in love?"

"Why don't you ask her?"

"But I don't know her."

"Maybe you do, and maybe she is usually not a brunette."

That remark caused Earl Ray to pause to think. Then he continued, "What I want to know is what I said while you two were there at the bar with me?"

Wade began to pet Jake. "You didn't have time to say much because we weren't there very long."

"You're dodging me. I mean, did I talk funny? Did I slur my speech?"

Wade's gaze directly met Earl Ray's. Wade thoughts were confirmed. There is something here, just like he suspected. Earl Ray is on edge because he's supposed to be keeping something secret. Now he's afraid he has compromised the secret while he was drunk. Wade decided to show a card. "No, you spoke really clear. You talked to us in Korean."

Earl Ray's face turned white. "How did you recognize that language?"

"I fought in Korea in 1950 and 1951," Wade said.

"Oh, I forgot about you being there. Ellis and Coley were there too, weren't they?"

"Yeah, but not long enough to learn to speak Korean. They got wounded severely enough to be sent home early. I was wounded too, but not as bad as them."

"I knew about Coley being shot up, but I never heard that Ellis was hit."

"He wasn't. His wounds are between his ears."

Earl Ray said thoughtfully, "Yeah. That can happen."

Wade realized that he now had the upper hand with Earl Ray. "Where did you learn to speak Korean?" asked the deputy.

Earl Ray laughed bitterly. "When I was in college, two of my buddies and I had a course in business statistics taught by Dr. Kak, a Korean. He was twelve years old when the Korean War broke out. He lived in the North, and his parents escaped to Seoul with him and his sisters. They finally moved to the States where Dr. Kak went to college. That course was really difficult, but Dr. Kak was a super instructor. He went the extra mile to have his students learn the subject. He even invited any of us to come to his house for extra tutoring. My two buddies and I were struggling at first, so we took Dr. Kak up on his offer. None of the other students did. We discovered that Dr. Kak and his wife were the only Koreans on campus. They were just lonely. They were delighted to have us over. The sessions developed into a social event. We would be studying in their den, and Mrs. Kak would bring in hot tea and cookies on a silver tray. I became interested in their native language, and when Mrs. Kak found that out, she offered to teach me Korean. By the time I graduated, I was fairly fluent in the language and also knew many Korean customs."

"What kind of grade did you get in the course?"

"I got a B+. A high school classmate of mine that took the same course under Dr. Kak the year before only got a C+. In high school, he always had to help me with math problems."

Wade laughed. "That figures. I'll bet he didn't have tea and cookies with the Kaks either, did he?"

Earl Ray smiled broadly. "Nope!"

"What happened after you graduated?"

"I got a job. But I would visit the Kaks on some weekends until I got into the army. The next year, Dr. Kak took a position with a college on the West Coast. We stayed in touch until they both died a few years ago."

"I've found out you didn't come back from basic training with James Henry Eason like you were supposed to. How come?"

Earl Ray squirmed. "I got sick with some unknown fever. I never could get over it. I was in and out of the hospital so much they finally gave me a medical discharge."

Wade looked out across the pasture in front of the house. He studied the heat monkeys that were dancing in a long line in the late summer heat. Then he turned to Earl Ray and said, "I've been reading some newspapers at night. Nothing good is on the television this summer. Does the date January 23rd, 1968, mean anything to you?"

Wade noticed Earl Ray's throat move. Earl Ray replied, "You sure are reading old newspapers, Wade."

"My job gets me behind on my reading."

Earl Ray paused, "It's just another day on the calendar."

Wade realized that this subject was closed, at least for today. He asked, "What did you want to see me about?"

Earl Ray relaxed, "I need your help on something."

"What?"

"You know that Mr. Joab left me a fourth of certain assets. Neither Wiley nor anyone else has located where that might be. It could be anywhere. I know you have a way of finding out things. And you have access to the computer and to informants. If you could find Mr. Joab's property, I'll give you a fourth of what I get."

Wade started rocking and thinking. Then he agreed, "Okay. I'll do that for you. I'll need to tell Grady and make sure it's okay with him. But I might have to call on you to be my leg man."

Earl Ray agreed.

Wade added, "If that property is under lock and key, like in the possession of someone else, we may have to use a lawyer to get our hands on it."

"I've thought about that."

"Well, you need to be thinking of who you want to use. And that means we'll have to give him a cut."

"That's true. But let's see if we can find it first."

Wade said, "We need to hurry. You know those Memphis lawyers will be looking, too. And if the property is something that can walk off, there's a good chance that what shows up in court may have already been raked off the top."

"Yeah, like meeting with the lawyer to divide and him saying, 'One for you and one for me,' after he has already stuck four in his pocket."

Wade laughed. "That's it! We don't want to get into a game of Chuckle-Up with all those lawyers."

"Chuckle-Up?"

"Yeah, that's gambling talk. Like, how the dealer in a back-room poker game calls 'Let's play a game of Chuckle-Up, the more you put down the less you pick up'."

"Ha! Ha!"

Wade left. Earl Ray sat there watching the dust from Wade's wheels settle back down in the road. He wondered why Wade was interested in his whereabouts in 1968. He realized that Wade had set him up in the bar. He was drunk and that girl was so pretty. When she spoke to him in Korean, his guard was down, and he reacted and responded just like they had expected. But 1968 was all over, or at least was supposed to be. "I'll make a call to see if something new has developed," he muttered aloud to his dog Jake.

Wade caught Irv down by the mailbox at the end of his driveway. Irv's shirt was soaked with sweat. He had been hoeing weeds in his watermelon patch. Wade positioned himself so that Irv was downwind to the breeze that was blowing. Irv was known not to take a shower any more than he had to, and his body odor could be rank, especially in hot weather.

"Say, Irv. I didn't realize that Mr. Joab had a brother that lived in Texas."

"He shore did. Jerry McMath. He was a good bit older than Joab. Jerry was bornt about 1907. He moved to Texas right after that stock market went broke and all them people jumped off tall buildings in them big cities."

"What did he do out there?"

"Jerry was a mechanic. He learnt to run a lathe and welders. He was sort of a jack-of-all-trades. Jerry got to where he could repair most anything, according to Joab."

"Did you know him?"

"Oh, shore. I knowed him before he left here. Jerry would visit back home some."

"I guess he was too old to have been in the War."

Irv spit some snuff onto the ground. "Well, he would have been 'cept he was sangle. The draft applied to sangle men up to age thirty-eight. Jerry was drafted in 1944 just before he turnt thirty-eight. Jerry was in Europe just like me, but in a different part. One time, while he was on leave, he looked my unit up to see whur it wuz. My unit had been pulled off the front lines to Montherme, France, whur he came to see me. There was another friend of his close by who he visited too. I shore was glad to see someone from back home. It was like Jerry to visit his friends instead of going to Paris and partying. That's the kind of man he wuz."

"What did he do after the war? Did he do well? Like get rich?"

Irv kicked some dirt around with the toe of his work boot. "Nah. I rode with Joab out there one year to see him. He just lived in an ordinary house. If Jerry had anything, you couldn't tell it. Drove an old pickup. He was still sangle."

"What happened to him?"

"Jerry was kilt in a car wreck in 1951. A drunk came across the center line and hit him head-on. Joab was real tore up about that for a while. Joab and his wife went out to the funeral. I don't think anyone else from here went. It was too fur."

"Do you remember the name of the town where Jerry lived?"

Irv chuckled and spit out snuff again. "I shore do. It was a funny name, but a good one, I thought."

"What was the name?"

"Muleshoe."

Wade drove back to Poston. He needed to get back into the Joab McMath file. He called Sally to his office. They sat there looking at the dozen or so photographs she had made.

He asked Sally, "Is the body and everything else in the exact position as when you arrived?"

"Well, yeah. It seems to be."

Wade said, "I didn't disturb anything. After I looked around, I sat in a chair and waited for the ambulance."

Then a thought struck him. Of course, Sherman had been the one to find Mr. Joab's body. He might have noticed something. Wade called Sherman on his cell phone. Sherman just happened to be in the courthouse buying a car tag. A few minutes later he walked into the sheriff's office.

Wade said, "Look at these pictures and see if everything is in the same place as when you found Mr. Joab."

Sherman pored over the pictures. "Yes. As far as I remember. Oh, wait a minute. The letter holder is not. I moved it."

"Why?"

"It was an accident. When I walked up close to the body, the tail of my snowshoe knocked it over."

"Knocked it over? The stand it was on was over on its side. The letter holder should have been on its side too."

Sherman said, "It wasn't. You see this nail head sticking up just a little bit out of the wooden floor? The holder was clipped upside down to the nail."

"You mean like fastened to it?"

"Yes."

Sally said, "That's a curious place for the holder to be."

Wade said, "Yes. That indicates that Mr. Joab fastened it to the nail before he died."

They all three agreed that was very odd. Why would he do that?

CHAPTER 23
PAY DIRT

After Sally and Sherman left his office, Wade called Earl Ray. "What are you doing in the morning?"

"Nothing I can't get out of."

"Meet me at Mr. Joab's house about nine o'clock. Bring a tape measure and a shovel."

Earl Ray was sitting on the steps of Mr. Joab's porch when Wade drove into the yard. Wade had the photographs with him. He told Earl Ray what Sherman had revealed the day before. Then Wade fished a key out of his pocket and opened the lock that had been installed on the door, and they both went inside to the living room. Wade held the end of the tape measure by the protruding nail in the floor and had Earl Ray measure from the nail to the wall, and then to the opposite wall. The nail was exactly the same distance from each wall. When the cross direction was measured, the same result was had. The nail was the same distance from all four walls. They examined the plank in which the nail was driven. Everything about the nail and the plank was normal. They looked like all the other nails and planks in the floor.

After a while Wade said, "Earl Ray, this old house has a crawl space. Why don't you take my flashlight and crawl underneath and see if you notice anything. I think Mr. Joab was trying to pass on a particular message when he fastened the letter holder to the nail. There would be no other reason for him doing that. I mean, he was laying there dying, and he knew he was."

"I'm going to get dirty. But we need to follow what few clues we have."

"Crawl up to the center of this room. When you get close, I'll thump the floor to guide you."

Shortly, Wade heard Earl Ray say in a muffled tone, "Okay, Wade, hit the floor."

Wade started banging the floor with the end of one leg of a straight chair.

Earl Ray said, "Okay. I've located the center."

"See anything?"

"I'm looking."

Wade sat in the chair and waited. Then he heard sounds of Earl Ray dragging himself out from under the house. Wade went out on the porch as Earl Ray came around the corner, grinning. He walked up to Wade and opened his hand. In it was a flat brass key.

Wade asked, "Where did you find that?"

"That nail was driven through the floor next to a joist. Someone had taken a power saw and cut a deep, narrow slit in the joist just beneath the end of the nail. The key was in the slit. And someone had carved a piece of wood to fill the slit to hide the key. They did good work for it was difficult to see. No one would have found that hiding place unless they had a hint of sort of where to look."

Wade grinned. "Am I doing a good job earning my share?"

"Yes, you are. Now we have to figure out what lock this key goes in and where it is."

They examined the key. The number thirteen was stamped on one side and underneath the number was the letter *L*. To the top right of the letter was a small symbol of a single star.

It appeared to be a key to a bank lockbox.

"I've seen a number of lockbox keys over the years. If that's what this is, it's an old one. They are not made like this anymore," Wade said.

"That's a lot of help. Just think of how many banks there are in America. Are we going to have to call every one? That'll take forever."

"I think I know how we can narrow our search," Wade mused.

"How?"

Wade said, "Sit down on the steps and let me explain."

Wade spoke, "There are a lot of coincidences stacking up. It's like a voice is screaming out as to the location of Mr. Joab's property. One of the last things Mr. Joab did before he died was to fasten that letter holder to the nail. As it turns out, the key was hidden directly under that nail. I mean, he could have laid some other object on top of the nail. There were several things handy, so why did he choose the letter holder? Well, we found out yesterday that it was made by his brother who lived in Texas.

No one had noticed, until Ben Weaver came by, that the horseshoe was actually a muleshoe. That was unusual because most folks think in terms of horseshoes. Then when I talked to Irv yesterday, I found that Jerry McMath lived in, of all places, Muleshoe, Texas."

Earl Ray brightened and questioned, "So you think the key fits a lockbox in Muleshoe, Texas?"

"You got it. I also think that letter L with the star by it means 'Lonestar,' the nickname for Texas. Now we need to find out what bank is there. If Muleshoe is a small town, it probably won't have one."

Wade added, "I still think you are going to have to get a lawyer involved."

"Why?"

"If that's a key to a lockbox, the bank won't let you use it unless you have a legal right. Like have your name on the signature card."

"My name is not on any card in a Texas bank," said Earl Ray.

"Let's just say that the key fits a box in Muleshoe, Texas. First, we have to find out if Mr. Joab had a right to enter the box. Then you'll have to show them how you have the same right to get into his box."

"At this moment, I don't because the will has not been allowed to be probated," Earl Ray said.

"That's coming up in a few weeks. We need to know more about this key before then," Wade said.

They locked the house, and Earl Ray followed Wade to the Stopwatch at Four Points for a snack. After getting drinks and chips inside, they went around the corner of the store to a shade tree to talk awhile.

Wade said, "Look, Earl Ray, we need to have a plan. Someone needs to go to Texas, like tomorrow. That's about a two-day drive out there. I can't go. I need to stay around and be on standby in case help is needed here. Can you go?"

"Sure. I can leave this afternoon if you think I need to."

"We need to figure how we can approach the bank and find out if this key belongs to it."

"Well, actually this key belongs to Wiley Downs, the administrator."

Wade said, "I know that. But you are a devisee, and you have as much a right to pursue this search as him. Besides, we know a lot more than he does at this point."

"Yeah. If we gave it to him, he may have to disclose that fact in discovery to the Shaw lawyers. Then it would be a free-for-all race for the loot. I don't trust those lawyers. We need to be the ones to locate this property."

Wade said, "We have the edge. That key is old, which means that the box was rented before banks required a Social Security number. I've noticed that lawyers' thinking is predictable. When Mr. Joab's number is made available by Judge Dennis, they are all going to use it to find out if there is an active account with any bank outside Cade County."

Earl Ray chuckled. "Hah! That move will never get any of them away from square one."

"Yeah! While they all are thinking, we will be looking."

Wade added, "The bank is not going to tell you if the box that key fits belongs to Mr. Joab. We will have to trick them."

Earl Ray replied, "That's right. They may admit the key fits their boxes, but they won't say who owns box number thirteen."

"We will need help from someone who is good at obtaining that kind of information, and I know the person that would be perfect for this job."

"The Musician?"

"Yeah. He's the perfect choice with his prison background and his exposure to all kinds of con men."

"He'll want a cut."

"I'll give him ten percent of my share. All we need to know is if the box that this key fits belongs to Mr. Joab. We can take care of getting into the box later."

"I agree, and I'll give Henry the same part of my share. My share is dwindling, but it's a gift I never expected."

Earl Ray continued, "I'll let you explain this deal to Henry. I'm going home to pack."

"I'll take care of Jake for you while you are gone. While you are out there, see if there are any oil wells in the area. If there are, I have an idea how that information might be useful."

CHAPTER 24
CASING THE BANK

Earl Ray and Henry were checked into a new motel on the outskirts of Muleshoe, Texas. They discovered the town had a population of three thousand people. It had the usual number of fast food restaurants for a town of that size, so the matter of getting something decent to eat was resolved. Muleshoe had only one bank which was located near the center of town. The town was thriving and had a great deal of traffic on its streets. That was good; the chances of being noticed would be less while they were out and about.

At lunchtime, Earl Ray had walked into the lobby of Ranchers Bank with the pretense of busting a couple of one-hundred dollar bills. There were only two tellers working and one person occupying a manager's office. As expected, the bank was short-handed at lunch. The two tellers were busy with customers. While Earl Ray stood in line, he inconspicuously cased the lobby. The vault was located at the back of the lobby. The door was open and he could see that an entire wall and the back of the vault was filled with lockboxes of various sizes.

A customer was near the vault signing the ledger to gain access to his box. The customer, an elderly gentleman, was talking to a middle-age bank employee. It was obvious that they knew each other. Earl Ray noted that their conversation couldn't be heard in the teller area where he stood. And none of the tellers were giving any notice to the vault.

When he returned to motel, Earl Ray gave Henry a thorough description of the bank lobby. Henry asked some questions and was finally satisfied about the layout.

The next day at noon, Henry walked into the bank lobby. The activity there was similar to what Earl Ray had seen the day before. He made his way to the vault. Sitting behind the desk was the same lady that had apparently been there yesterday. She was an attractive woman with short black hair. He spoke to her in a friendly manner. The lady looked him over and was pleased with what she saw. Henry was a handsome guy with a smile that inspired trust. He was short and slender and had a gold tooth that complimented his appearance. A tattoo was on his left forearm but he had wisely worn a long sleeve, silk shirt to cover the ink. This seemed to be a conservative town, and Henry didn't want to give cause to suspect his political views weren't the same.

He glanced down at the name plate on the woman's desk. The plate read, "Otye Henley."

"Well, that's a pretty name. I've never seen that one before," Henry said.

Otye smiled proudly. "I'm glad you like it. That's a family name. You see, I'm part Indian."

Henry smiled. "Are there any little Otyes?" He had a way with women.

Otye giggled. "Why, yes there are. I have twin daughters."

"Would you tell me their names?"

"I'll have to, for you would never guess."

"Come on now. What are they?"

She smiled broadly. "Otye Dell and Otye Nell."

Henry laughed as Otye joined him. Then she asked, "How could I help you?"

Henry wiped tears from his eyes and said, "I'm from Mississippi. I'm on my way to Durango, Colorado, to watch the aspens turn their color. It's so pretty out there when they do that."

Otye agreed, "Yes, indeed. My husband and I go out there most years. But we usually get to the Antonita and Monte Vista area."

Henry thought, "Here goes. This will make me or break me. I have to say the correct words at the right times and I have to control my voice tone to make it accommodate my remarks."

He said aloud, "Anyway, my uncle, Joab McMath, has a lockbox here. He's thinking about closing it, and, since I was coming through, he wanted me to stop in and find out what kind of paperwork the bank needs to do that."

"He didn't have to have you come by. He could have called."

"He doesn't have a telephone anymore. My uncle is so tight with his money," Henry laughed.

Otye hesitated, "I understand. But I can't even discuss whether or not he has a lockbox here. It's against the rules."

"Oh, I know that. Here, I have his key. He said that was good enough."

He handed her the key. She took it, noticed the number thirteen and looked in the ledger. Then Otye pulled the signature card from the metal bins that held all the cards and laid it flat on her desk. About that time her telephone rang. A lengthy conversation developed with the calling party. When she turned her head down to make some notes, Henry stared at the card. During his three stints in the federal pen, Henry had learned many skills, none of which were exactly legal. On the outside, he had to shelve most of them or he would be back in trouble and in the pen again. He had a variety of cellmates while serving his sentences: a paper hanger, a second-story man, two embezzlers, a hit man, and a couple of common thugs who excelled in being street wise. He had picked up an assortment of tricks from all of them. With plenty of time on his hands, Henry had taught himself how to read upside down and also reverse, while holding a mirror or some other reflective object.

Typed at the top of the card were the names, Jerry McMath or Joab McMath. The card had been set up by the bank on September 10, 1945. Henry quickly glanced down the spaces for the signatures. The first five lines contained what appeared to be the signatures of Jerry McMath in September, 1945. He couldn't tell the dates. Thereafter, all the signatures were those of Joab McMath. There was one in 1951. The rest started in 1979 and there was one for every year thereafter. The signatures were always in December, although he couldn't make out those days either. Henry was able to absorb this information in a flash for he couldn't be caught staring. He filed these details in small compartments in his memory for later retrievals.

When the call ended and Otye looked up, Henry was facing the tellers. He turned when Otye said, "I'm sorry I was interrupted. We are short-handed at lunch."

Henry calmly replied, "Oh, I understand. And I 'm sorry to be a bother."

"Oh, shush, you're not. Just tell your uncle that all he has to do is give us a letter about closing the box and whoever comes to claim the contents needs to have a power of attorney."

Bingo! Henry had what he had come to Texas for. He was ecstatic! He thanked Otye for her help. They talked a little more, a technique

Henry often used. Just be patient, don't leave too quickly, don't arouse suspicion.

He turned and was leaving when the message she called out stopped him cold in his tracks. "If you will be the one to carry out the contents, you might should bring some help. Those three boxes are the largest ones we have. You look to be a little light in the britches to be able to tote very much."

Henry assured her, "Oh, don't worry. I'll have plenty of help."

His heart was racing as he left the bank. Three boxes? They hadn't expected that! His imagination became vivid as to what was in the boxes. He may have hit the home run of a lifetime.

Henry went straight to the motel and blurted his success to Earl Ray, who became very excited. "This may be big league for sure! I wonder where the keys to the other two boxes are."

"It don't matter. If my 'uncle' owns them, they can be drilled. We don't need keys."

Earl Ray said, "Let's check out and go home. That bank lady may realize that she talked too much, and we don't want the local law to run us down for questioning. Do we?"

"Nope. I'm allergic to lawmen. I'm ready to go. We need to get with Wade. And whatever is in those boxes isn't going anywhere."

They met with Wade the day they arrived back in Cade County and gave him their report. He was elated! They discussed what to do next. Wade and Henry thought Earl Ray should get a lawyer to represent him, especially since they were now in the hunt. Wade noted that if Mr. Joab's will stood up, they would have to get a court order to open the boxes. And Earl Ray couldn't obtain the order since he wasn't a lawyer.

Earl Ray asked, "Who will we use?"

"I hate to admit it, but I think that Archie is the man," Wade replied.

"That's what I was thinking. He sure is abrasive, but he is good as they get."

Henry said, "Okay. It's a deal. I wonder what he will charge us. He'll probably want a cut."

Wade said, "You never can tell. He may just want fees."

"Most likely a cut and fees. Reckon what is in those lockboxes? I'm going to be there when they're opened," Earl Ray said.

Henry chuckled. "I hope it's not going to be like Geraldo opening Al Capone's hidden room in his basement. Nothing but stale air!"

CHAPTER 25
SEATING THE JURY

Linda Nell Few, the chancery clerk, was on the telephone with Judge Dennis. She was in a better mood than the one she had developed the day Earl Ray requested a trial by jury. She had inquired around the courthouse. Someone remembered that forty years ago there had been a will contest that was heard by a jury. Mrs. Alicia Davis had been working in the clerk's office at that time. She was now retired and lived in Vena. Linda Nell had called her to discuss having a jury trial. Linda Nell knew her as a friendly, intelligent woman. Mrs. Davis remembered in detail the process of jury selection and was delighted to explain how the jury was selected in the old case. She volunteered to help Linda Nell if needed.

Linda Nell repeated to the judge how the jury had been seated.

Judge Dennis said, "Look, that will contest is set soon. I want you to call those lawyers and tell them to be here on Monday, a week before the trial, to select the jury."

Linda Nell interjected, "Judge, isn't that short notice?"

"Yes. But I want the jury selected before the first day of trial. Selecting twelve bodies to sit on the jury shouldn't be such a big deal, although it will take some time. Anyway, there are so many lawyers in those firms they should be able to have someone who is free on that Monday."

He continued, "Get the sheriff's office busy. I would draw about thirty names out of the jury wheel. Give the names to the sheriff. When they serve the summons on the jurors, he should emphasize that they are to be here that day. If they don't show up, I'll have them put in jail."

Linda Nell hung up and told Crissy to go to the circuit clerk's office and borrow their jury wheel. Then she called Grady and gave him the judge's instructions. The sheriff assured her that all his deputies would be put on the task that afternoon. He had become more interested in this case since Wade had asked for permission to help Earl Ray.

The jury wheel already contained the names of the qualified jurors in the county. Crissy spun the wheel and within a few minutes she had retrieved, at random, the thirty names. Deputy Jack Early was standing there watching the wheel turn and the names drop out.

Crissy and Linda Nell quickly filled out the jury summons and handed them to Jack, who drove them over to the sheriff's office. Grady and the deputies looked them over and recognized most of the names. Jon David Knox was one.

Within two days, all of the jurors had been found and served. Most of them complained. They were told that if the summons was a problem to call the clerk, or, if they had the backbone, the judge. That quieted most. The judge didn't get a single call of protest, but Linda Nell did get five; all at home. Three of the selected had basically the same whine: they would miss work or they had to go to the doctor that day.

One caller, Ceclia Beckett, had three or four excuses. Her first one was that she had to carry her child to school and pick her up afterwards. Linda Nell pointed out that a school bus came by her house. Then Ceclia complained about her dog that had been diagnosed as neurotic by the vet. The dog had to be given his medicine every two hours, and she had no one to help her with that. Linda Nell thought, "I'll bet the circuit clerk has never heard that one before." Linda Nell told her to bring the dog with her, and the bailiff could administer the medicine. Ceclia's final complaint was that her flowers would die if she wasn't at home to water them.

Linda Nell told her that she knew for certain that it would be raining on Monday. Ceclia gave up in a huff and threatened, "Next election, I'm going to haul voters to the polls to defeat you!"

"Don't bother. I'm retiring after this term," Linda Nell announced.

Then Jon David called. He stayed on the phone for a solid hour and caused Linda Nell to miss the local news, which really nettled her. He wasn't trying to get out of sitting on the jury; he just pumped her for information. Jon David wanted to know what was in the case file, the names of the lawyers and who each represented, an update on what she knew about any property being found, and how much he would get paid. Then he asked, "What will we have for lunch?"

"I don't know. It will probably be catered by Lola," Linda Nell snapped.

Jon David replied, "Well, if that's all we're going to get, I'll bring my own."

"And what would that be?" Linda Nell asked.

"Probably Vienna sausage and crackers and maybe a slice of hoop cheese."

Linda Nell warned, "I don't care what you bring. But you better not make a mess."

Jon David changed the subject, "Who else got summoned besides me?"

"I can't tell you that."

"Why not?"

"Because that part of my office is, by law, confidential. I can't tell you or anyone else."

"Well, who knows besides you?"

"Crissy and the deputy sheriffs."

Linda Nell became curious, "Why do you want to know?"

"I want to go around and talk to them about Mr. Joab. We might be able to get this thing settled before the trial. It would save the judge a lot of time and trouble and save the county money."

Linda Nell nearly fell off her bar stool upon hearing his statement. "Oh, hey, Jon David! You do that, and the judge will put you under the jailhouse."

"Well, I don't see that as a problem."

"Jon David, your problem is that you think you know more than anyone else."

"You know, that makes me feel good about myself. Over the years, I've had a number of people tell me the same thing. Thank you, Linda Nell," and he hung up.

Linda Nell went to the kitchen and poured a glass of wine after taking the phone off the hook.

On the day of the jury selection, Linda Nell and Crissy took all of the necessary court documents from the clerk's office over to the courtroom. They were forty-five minutes early. The courtroom was already full. Linda Nell thought, "Wow, this case is really attracting attention."

Linda Nell had made the jury list in the order they had dropped out of the wheel. She walked up to the rail that separated the audience from the jury box and the area where the tables for the lawyers were placed. She announced that the jurors should come forward and be seated in the benches to her left when their name was called. To her surprise, she noted that everyone who had been summoned had appeared. Later, the circuit clerk said that had never happened in her court.

Linda Nell stepped into the hall. Several people were hanging around, including Red, a tall lanky guy who was a regular at Lola's. Red had built a successful furniture manufacturing concern in Baxter. At age fifty-five, he had received an offer from a Florida company to buy his business. He took them up on their offer and retired. Now, he really had nothing to do but watch his investments, play poker with his friends, work crossword puzzles, and hang out at Lola's. Because of his regular visits to Lola's, he pretty well knew about all the gossip. Linda Nell called him over, "Hey, Red, I'm surprised at all the people in the courtroom. Do you have any idea why so many people are here?"

Red laughed. "Yeah. The word is out that Earl Ray has found Mr. Joab's fortune."

"How did they reach that conclusion?"

Red laughed again through his beard. "Well, lately Wade has been seen riding around the county with Jake, Earl Ray's dog, sitting on the passenger seat. The windows were down and Jake had his head out enjoying the wind. Several people thought the county had bought its first drug dog. Then someone realized that it was Earl Ray's dog. Earl Ray has never been seen without Jake except on the nights he goes to Sleazy's. Obviously, Earl Ray has been gone somewhere."

"And?"

"Well, the busybodies became busy. Next, it was noticed that Henry's Cadillac was gone at the same time Wade had the dog. Then some early risers saw that it was back at daylight one morning. The Cadillac was parked in the carport with the front facing the street. You know, Henry's house is close to the street, so it was easy to see that the entire grille and the windshield was covered by mating lovebugs. Henry has the reputation of keeping his car spotless. When it's raining, he'll walk around town doing his errands rather than getting the clean car out on the streets. So it was concluded that Henry had ended a trip after dark. And those lovebugs have an oily content. You need to get them off pretty quick or they will mar the paint. Lovebugs are also a giveaway. The only place you find them mating this time of the year is in the Gulf Coast area."

"So that means that Henry has made a trip to the coast?" asked Linda Nell.

"Yep. But that could be anywhere from Florida to Texas, except for the bumper sticker that has just appeared on his car."

"What?"

"A Dallas Cowboy Cheerleader sticker. Henry does have a weakness for younger women."

Linda Nell smiled. "So, both Earl Ray and Henry have been out of the county at the same time, and the conjecture is that they took a trip together to Texas?"

"You got it. There was already talk that Mr. Joab owned some oil wells in Texas. Word got around rather quickly about the trip. Everybody assumes that Earl Ray has found the oil wells. Also, Wade, Henry, and Earl Ray were seen going into Archie's office the day they got back. That's the reason the crowd is here."

Linda Nell left Red and walked into chambers to tell Judge Dennis she had the jurors ready for the *voir dire* process. She also told him that the courtroom was full and the reason why.

Judge Dennis shook his head. "I'll never understand why people are more fascinated with fabrication rather than the truth." Then he asked, "What lawyers are out there?'"

Linda Nell said, "Not as many as last time. Stanley Robbs, from the Janes firm, Ken Arnoff from his firm, and of course, Archie, Wiley, and Lamar Mosley."

"Yeah. Those local lawyers are necessary since we have the Tennessee lawyers here."

Linda Nell said, "I need to tell you something. That nosy Jon David Knox is on the jury list. And he called me the other night asking about who else was on it."

"Why?"

"He said he wanted to discuss the case with the others to see if they could go ahead and decide whether or not this will is the real one."

The judge's jaw dropped. "You mean before they have heard any evidence?"

"That's what he said."

"Go tell the lawyers to come in here. And get the court reporter in case we need to record any motions. They need to be aware of this."

The lawyers filed into the chambers followed by the reporter, Ashley Anderson. Stanley quickly grabbed the chair in front of Judge Dennis' desk. The others leaned against the wall.

Judge Dennis cleared his throat. "I need to disclose something to all of you. One potential juror, Jon David Knox, told the clerk a few days ago that he wanted to approach some of the other jurors for the purpose of making a decision on the outcome of this trial in order to save time. I can't strike him from the jury unless he either admits to me, or one of you, that he indeed has approached another juror."

Archie spoke up, "Well, Your Honor, I think he should be removed. I don't want him on the jury anyway."

Stanley's ears perked up.

"Why not?" the Judge asked.

"It's a long story. I sued the hunting club that he's in a few years ago for running their dogs on my client's property during deer season. Most of the dogs were his. Jon David hasn't liked me since."

"I can see why. But you will have the opportunity later to move to strike. You have to have better grounds than just not being liked. From the reputation you have developed, I might never find twelve people that like you."

Archie admitted, "I've thought about that. That's why I wanted to have a bench trial."

Stanley gloated and thought that his firm now might have an edge.

Judge Dennis said, "Here's the way I'm going to do the jury selection. First, I'll *voir dire* the panel. If I detect from a juror's answers to my questions that he or she is not qualified, is biased, or has an interest in the case, I will excuse that person. Then Archie will go next with his questions. And finally, Mr. Robbs. Both of you save any objections you might have until we come back into chambers. Then you can make your motions. After we address the objections, Linda Nell will make a list of all that remain. Since the jury pool is small, each side will be allowed to automatically strike only two from the list that is presented to him. Is that understood and agreeable?" They all nodded. The judge said, "All right, guys. Let's get started."

The lawyers went to their respective tables, and the judge followed in his black robe to the bench. He waited until Ashley Anderson made her tape recorder ready.

She signaled and the judge addressed the jury panel: "Ladies and Gentlemen of the jury panel, you have been summoned to appear here today for the purpose of a jury selection to decide whether or not the will of Joab McMath that has been filed in this case is his true will. Twelve of you and two alternates will be selected from the group. First, I will ask you some questions, and then a lawyer from each side will follow with his own questions. These questions are not intended to be personal or embarrassing. They are merely to find out if you can hear the testimony of witnesses and view any evidence that is presented and be impartial in your deliberations on this issue."

Then the judge began his questions while the lawyers observed the panel.

"First, are any of you related to Joab McMath?"

No response.

"Have any of you ever been a party to a will contest?"

No response.

"Have any of you ever received any property through a will?"

A few hands went up. The judge quizzed each one and was satisfied that no prejudice existed.

"Have any of you ever sat on a jury in Cade County Circuit Court that involved a non-criminal matter?"

A few hands went up. The lawyers made notes of the names of those who responded. Then the judge introduced the lawyers to the panel and explained who each represented.

He asked, "Do any of you here have a grudge or dislike against any of these lawyers, to the extent that your grievance would prevent you from making a fair and impartial decision in this case?"

There was no response, but the judge noticed several reacted by squirming and looking away. He repeated the question and got the same reaction.

Wiley also noticed. There's something here that could be a problem.

The judge moved on. "Have any of you discussed this matter with any other potential juror?'

No response. Jon David wondered why that question was asked. It shouldn't make any difference. And he had not. When Jon David had found out that the trial was going to be a week later, he had decided to wait and see if he got on the jury and who else would be selected. That way he would have a week to talk to thirteen people rather than to some out of the twenty-nine who wouldn't even be there. Therefore, he wouldn't waste any money on gas that would be used in riding to twenty-nine people's houses.

The judge waited to see if anyone would change his or her mind. Then he asked the panel if anyone had excuses for why they would have trouble sitting on the jury for a period of time of up to a week. Several responded. One young guy told the judge he was in college and was starting school the week of the trial. He and his roommate were moving a trailer to a mobile home park in Starkville that week.

The judge grinned. "That would be a good excuse except you are going to the wrong school." A strong response came from the courtroom for everyone knew to which college the judge owed his loyalties.

Then Ceclia brought up the matter about her neurotic dog. The judge and the audience gaped at her. They couldn't believe she was serious. A couple of others had decent excuses and the judge told them all he would rule later.

He addressed the lawyers, "Gentlemen, that's all the questions I have. Mr. Baker, you may address the jury panel."

Archie stood up and walked to the lectern. He looked the courtroom over and then asked, "Would those of you who held up your hands when the judge asked if you had previously sat on a circuit court jury, please hold them up again?"

They did, but Archie noticed there was one hand less in the air. The one belonging to Jon David Knox. Unbeknownst to the jury panel, Archie and two of the paralegals from the Arnoff firm had done a thorough background check on all thirty potential jurors. They knew everything that could be found on the background of each one. Archie would have been content to try the case in front of any twelve on the strength of his prowess. But Ken Arnoff would have none of that. Archie was amused at Arnoff's willingness to spend whatever money it took to accomplish his intended results. The law firm was approaching the will matter like a law school casebook problem. He wondered if they had inside information about Mr. Joab's wealth or was it just because Mr. Joab had been such a generous giver to the hospital and they were locked in on believing that his resources were endless. If they only knew that he was now aware of the probable location of Mr. Joab's wealth. Archie had figured out a way to capitalize on this knowledge. This case would bring him more than just his usual hourly rates.

Archie asked routine questions of the ones who had held their hands up. Then he zeroed in on Jon David Knox. "Mr. Knox, didn't you sit on the jury three years ago in the Wall case?"

"Well, yeah, I did."

Archie demanded, "Why didn't you hold up your hand when I asked my question?"

"Oh, I just forgot."

"Wasn't that the case when Mr. and Mrs. Wall were hit by the beer truck running through a stop sign because the truck's brakes were faulty and had been for a week with the company's knowledge?"

"Yes, it was."

The entire courtroom was paying attention to this, beer drinkers and non-beer drinkers alike.

"Wasn't Mr. Wall hurt badly? To the extent that he lost his left leg? And Mrs. Wall was laid up in the hospital for six months recovering from her injuries?"

"Well, yes."

"As I recall, the jury awarded them two million dollars from the beer company."

"That's right."

Stanley rose and argued. "Your Honor, I object to this line of questioning. All of what happened in a civil case in another court has nothing to do with this contest."

The judge replied, "Well, this is thin. But we are only selecting jurors, so you're overruled."

Stanley said, "But, Judge, in......"

"No 'But Judge'! You're overruled. Sit down."

He obeyed.

Archie continued, "Mr. Knox, how did the jury vote?"

Stanley jumped up. "Your Honor, I object."

"Sit down, Mr. Robbs. I, myself, want to know the answer."

Jon David replied, "Eleven to one."

"Who was the one who voted against recovery?"

Jon David spoke directly to the judge, "Do I have to answer?"

"Yes."

He said, "It was me."

"Why?"

Stanley jumped up again. "Your Honor, I object. This has nothing to do with this case."

"Yes it does, young man. This goes to the heart of impartiality. Mr. Baker is attempting to identify any prejudice Mr. Knox may have toward reaching a particular verdict. You're overruled."

"Mr. Knox, answer the question," the judge instructed.

Jon David's face turned red. All eyes in the courtroom were upon him.

He muttered in a low voice, "I just didn't think the Walls should have that much money."

"Why?"

He looked away. "I just don't think anyone should have any more money than I have," he blurted.

A murmur ran through the courtroom. The ones who had followed the Wall trial always wondered why Jon David voted against the Walls. It was obvious to those on the street that the beer company had been completely at fault.

Archie said, "I'm through, Your Honor."

He sat down. Ken winked at him. They had made a bucketful of points with that *voir dire*.

Stanley went through his *voir dire*. He had never done this before and came across as clumsy. But he managed to struggle through his questions. He purposefully didn't pose any questions to Jon David Knox. Nothing of consequence came to light.

"We'll take a brief recess and then you lawyers come into chambers," the Judge said.

Fifteen minutes later they were all present. Ashley had moved her equipment into chambers.

"I didn't hear any comments that would cause me to strike anyone for cause," the judge said.

Archie said, "Your Honor, I move to strike Mr. Knox from the panel because of his disclosure of why he voted the way he did in the Wall case. That clearly shows that he is against awarding large amounts of money, even when it's obvious the plaintiffs are entitled to it."

Stanley replied, "Your Honor, I oppose the motion. All the jury is going to do is decide whether the will is valid or not. The will itself decides who gets what and how much. The jury has no control of distribution of property."

Archie countered, "Even though the will does direct the distribution, if everyone on the jury has the same attitude of Mr. Knox or is influenced by him if he is selected to the jury, then they can control the distribution by refusing to accept the will as being valid."

The judge rubbed his chin for a while and then said, "Those are both good arguments. However, the case file does not reflect Mr. Joab McMath having substantial wealth so, Mr. Baker, your argument is close to being moot. Therefore, I overrule your motion."

Stanley smacked his fist into his open palm. "Yeah!"

The judge looked at him sternly. "Don't be so hasty with your celebration, Mr. Robbs. I wasn't finished. I'm making that ruling with the reservation that if substantial wealth is located before the trial, I will revisit the motion."

Archie was standing to one side of the judge and stuck his tongue out at Stanley. Stanley thought, "How juvenile!"

Of the thirty people summoned, no one was struck for cause.

The judge said, "I'm going to let the college boy and those other three who had good excuses off. And that idiot woman with the insane dog!"

He told Linda Nell to prepare the list with the remaining twenty-five people in the same order.

A few minutes later, Linda Nell re-appeared with the new jury list.

The judge said, "Okay, guys. I've talked to Bill Card, the circuit judge. He said I should do a coin flip to decide whether to begin the jury selection from the top or the bottom of the list."

He pulled a fifty cent piece from his pocket and said, "Heads, I'll start at the top. Tails, I'll start at the bottom. Okay?"

He flipped the coin high in the air and it landed on the floor heads up. The lawyers began to mull over the names at the top. As the judge had already noted, Archie was to select first since he had the burden of proof to prove the will. Archie began to sweat. The one person he didn't want on the jury was Jon David Knox, and his name was number fifteen. It would be a close call to keep him off this jury.

Everyone else also noted that Jon David's name was number fifteen. With only twelve jurors to be chosen, Archie's two strikes had to come from the top fourteen names. After he did that, the other side would have the opportunity to strike two names from the original sixteen names, less Archie's two strikes. That would leave Jon David being juror number eleven with the two names past him being the alternates. Archie was on the spot. The only way he could keep Jon David off was to waive his allowed two strikes.

Ken motioned Archie to follow him into a vacant witness room to discuss the jury list. Ken had seen the dilemma and urgently asked, "What about these people? Is there anyone in this group who would be worse for our client than Jon David? Our opponents want him to be seated on the jury. I noticed Stanley and Lillie Bess whispering and making notes when you were questioning Knox. Is there any way we could refuse our strikes and be comfortable?"

Archie said, "I don't know."

Archie's focus was directed to juror number one. Uh, oh, he thought. That one will hang us. Felix Moore was first on the list. Felix had filed multiple, bogus claims with Archie's former insurance company when a major hurricane had hit the coast. When the storm left the coast, its center had traveled through Cade County. Weakened as it was, the storm still blew over many trees, knocking power lines down as they fell. Felix lived just outside Vena with his elderly mother, who had a homeowner's policy that covered storm damage.

Mrs. Moore had surveyed her yard the morning after the storm and saw no damage, she thought. After lunch she took a long nap. She looked out in her yard again about three hours before dark. To her amazement, two large pines were on top of her detached garage. She didn't remember any pines standing in her yard. She thought all her trees were oaks. Mrs. Moore then noticed a puddle of water in her front room which had a hole in the ceiling. Strange, she thought. Maybe a second storm came through while she slept.

When Felix came in for supper she quizzed him about the damage she had discovered. He assured her that she had been mistaken. That the storm indeed had caused the damage.

Felix, a burly unshaven man wearing blue coveralls and knee high black rubber boots, showed up the next day in the Central City high school gymnasium which all the insurance companies had rented to locate their respective claims centers. Each company had set up folding tables and chairs at different areas on the gym floor. Felix was directed to his mother's company. He had brought photographs of the damage with him. Felix had found out from an earlier claimant that the company didn't have time to visit all damage caused by the storm. They would approve small claims from viewing photographs.

Archie had been assigned this particular claim, and a company secretary pointed Felix to his table. When Felix approached, Archie had his head down looking at another claim. Felix stopped and coughed. Archie looked up, startled. His eyes widened upon observing this huge man standing before him. Felix was glaring at him while he shifted a cud of Canonball chewing tobacco from one cheek to the other. A brown trail of dried juice ran out of each corner of his mouth to the bottom of his jaws. Archie sighed in disgust. Still, Felix would have had his claim approved except for the fact that he had a revolver strapped to his waist, which Archie thought a little weird. Felix also came across as belligerent and demanding. Archie chose to scrutinize the photographs carefully. He noticed that the end of one large pine had been severed by a chain saw. When Archie asked Felix about that, he replied that he had cut the tree from the stump to relieve pressure that the trunk was putting on the roof.

Archie said, "Mr. Moore, I think I'll visit your mother's property to view this damage."

"My mother is to be in the hospital in Birmingham this week for surgery. Just go ahead and approve the claim. She needs the money for her bill."

Archie balked. "Nope. I'm coming out."

Two days later, Archie was able to make the visit. What he saw didn't surprise him. There were no stumps to match the severed ends of the trees. It was obvious that Felix had dragged the trees from elsewhere.

Archie denied the claim. Later, Felix came into the gym still wearing the pistol. He threatened Archie and gave him a thorough cussing. Security had to remove him. After Archie started his law practice, he would be met with icy stares every time he met Felix in public.

Ken agreed that Felix should be struck. They would take their chances with Jon David. Only nine votes were needed to prevail. Surely, Jon David couldn't influence more than two other people. They went back to chambers and dictated their strike into the record. Gleefully, Stanley made his two strikes, and Jon David moved up to number twelve.

All this while, the judge had been reflecting over his decision to select the jury a week in advance of the trial. The prior revelation by Jon David to the clerk now meant that he would have lots of time to ride the roads to visit the other jurors.

The judge cleared his throat again. "Fellows, I'm making an order from the bench. The jury selection will remain sealed until the morning of the trial. I will instruct all twenty-five people that they will all have to be present on the morning of the trial. Then I will announce the names of the jurors."

Archie said, "Thank you, Your Honor. I have a motion."

"What's that?"

"I move that the trial date be continued for two more weeks."

"Why?"

"We have property locators that are busy searching for the McMath property. And at this time we think we are close to the location."

Stanley was all ears.

The judge said, "I'll grant the motion. In fact, I'll give you three weeks. A case that was set for trial that week has been settled."

Stanley traveled back to his office and went over the jury list with Josh and Mr. Janes. When he announced the new trial date, Josh beamed, "Oh, thank you Judge Dennis for this gift?"

"What?" asked Stanley blankly.

"Now we have three more weeks to really investigate the background of these jurors and see what makes them tick," beamed Josh.

Mr. Janes smiled. "We'll get Dodge and Trace to send a couple of their sleuths down there and take care of business."

Stanley asked, "Won't that cost us a lot?"

"Yes. But hopefully we'll come out ahead. We always have in the past when we relied on Dodge and Trace," replied Mr. Janes.

Josh chortled. "They know how to take care of business. Our business!"

Stanley sat there perplexed after Josh and Mr. Janes left the room. They seemed eager to use Dodge and Trace on what should be a mundane matter.

CHAPTER 26
MILITARY RECORDS

Wade was curious about what was in Earl Ray's military records. So after lunch one day, he slid by the National Guard Armory in Central City. Only one person was in the office, CWO4 Leroy Goza. Wade walked into the office and took a seat by the desk. Leroy spoke and then asked what Wade needed.

Wade said, "I'm involved in an investigation that may involve one of your former soldiers."

"Oh. Who?"

"I can't say at the moment. But I need to look into this person's file."

Leroy complained, "Now, Wade, You know I can't let you see any of these files without a court order."

Wade sighed. "Leroy, a court order is a pain in the rear. It's aggravating and usually unnecessary to have to get one. I really need to get into that file cabinet over there without bothering the judge."

Leroy protested, "Now, Wade, if the commander at Fort Lee found out I let you see a soldier's file, I could be sent to Leavenworth."

Wade ignored the remark and asked, "Have you forgotten Saturday night two weeks ago?"

Leroy's face turned red. That night he had gone to Three-Way to get a case of beer. When Zeke pulled the hot case out of the storeroom and brought it to the cash register, he, as he always did with his customers, pulled one six-pack out and replaced it with an ice-cold one from the cooler behind the counter. Leroy had bought long-neck bottles for a reason. On the way home he had opened a cold bottle to drink. He saved the cap in case he was stopped by the law.

The route he took was the most direct from the dry county to the beer joint. From time to time, law enforcement agencies would set up a check-point on this road to nab those in possession of alcohol. And business was usually good. Sure enough, he came to a roadblock manned by the State Highway Patrol and assisted by the Cade County Sheriff's Office.

Since the roadblock was on a county road, the Highway Patrol didn't have authority to make arrests unless a sheriff's deputy was on the scene. Sheriff Powers always cooperated with the Patrol's request and rotated his deputies on these assignments. That night was Wade's turn.

Several cars were coming through the roadblock at the same time as Leroy. There were three patrolmen there with Wade. Two of them happened to be writing tickets to motorists. Wade recognized Leroy and stepped in front of the other patrolman to Leroy's vehicle. Upon seeing the road block, Leroy had capped the half-empty bottle and stuck it under the carpet on the floorboard. He had to stop behind a vehicle that was being checked. When Leroy's turn came to move up, his foot slipped on the brake pedal which caused the car to jolt. The cap came off the bottle, spilling beer on the floorboard.

Wade could smell the alcohol. So could the patrolman who had stepped up behind him. About that time a carload of teenagers stopped behind Leroy, their music blaring and their seatbelts unbuckled. The patrolman's attention was distracted. Wade urgently motioned Leroy to move on through the road block. When the patrolman turned his head, all he could see of Leroy was his tail lights disappearing into the night.

Leroy coughed. "Wade, I'm going to go to the post office and get the mail. I'll take the phone off the hook. If anyone comes by, tell them I'll be back shortly. If you would do me a favor, stay here for a while so I can go by Lola's and drink coffee with my buddies."

"Sure, Leroy, take your time."

After Leroy left, Wade moseyed over to a file cabinet that had a tag, "Prior to 1980." He opened a drawer and thumbed through the files to one styled "Earl Ray Fowler, PFC."

Wade pulled the file and sat at Leroy's desk. He opened it and searched for a particular page. He noticed that there was a medical discharge dated January 31, 1968. But that was not the sheet he was looking for. He shuffled down through the folder to the page he was seeking. It was an army form that listed the history of Earl Ray. He read down through the background: name, address, birth date, name of parents, marital status, work history, education records, and test scores. Wade noticed that Earl Ray did have a college degree. Next on the page was a list of achievements. Earl Ray had listed that he had ridden bulls on his college rodeo team, had a carpenter's license, and, under the section for foreign languages, had listed that he could speak and write Korean.

As Wade read, he learned that when Earl Ray was in basic training the Army would have been aware that Earl Ray could speak Korean. And it just so happened that while Earl Ray was in basic, the North Koreans had attacked and captured the *U.S.S. Pueblo* on January 23, 1968. That could explain what James Henry Eason had told him how all of a sudden the demeanor of their training had drastically changed. Instead of the troops going back to the warm barracks at the end of each day after firing on the ranges, the cooks brought the evening meals out to them. After chow, the soldiers went on forced marches through the night to biovac areas where they slept in extreme cold, sometimes in snow. They underwent cold weather tactics: training all day without hot meals, night firing, and setting up biovac areas with extra guards.

Wade wondered why these files showed Earl Ray with an early medical discharge when no one in Central City remembered him showing up for nearly a year later. And what about those body scars that Lou Bertha had seen that night when she had pulled him away from the smudge pots on the construction site? And the perplexing devise in Mr. Joab's will to Earl Ray because of his sacrificing part of his life for a just cause.

Leroy returned with an armload of mail. Wade was back sitting in his chair, reading a magazine.

Leroy asked, "Anyone come by while I was gone?"

Wade looked up. "Nope. Have a good day."

CHAPTER 27
THE DOUBLE FIX

The morning after the jury selection, Archie had a meeting with Wade, Earl Ray, Henry, and Wiley Downs in the law library of his office. Archie opened the meeting as he noted, "Fellows, we need to make a move on getting into those lockboxes in Muleshoe. Wiley and I made some phone calls yesterday evening to find out what needs to be done to have the bank out there open them. It seems that we will have to open an ancillary estate in that county."

"What does that mean?" Earl Ray asked.

Wiley spoke, "We have to employ a local attorney to file papers in the Texas court to open an estate, sort of like we did here. A legal ad will have to be published in the papers giving creditors notice to file claims. While the ad is running in the paper, we can get an order to open the boxes. The bankers will inventory the contents and hold them until the time period for the claim filing has expired. Then the assets will be released to me or to Archie, if the will has been allowed here."

Archie replied, "And here is a hitch. I'm trying to probate a copy of a signed will. That's not a slam dunk, but I think Wiley, Merci's lawyers, and I can get that done. But I don't want to give Nutt an additional defense. Wiley and I think it best if we notify the Nutt firm of our intention to enter those boxes."

"Why is that necessary?" Henry asked.

Archie continued, "Because there could be a later will in those boxes. Or a codicil, which would make changes to the will. Lockboxes are where most people keep their wills. So, if Nutt is present when they are opened, he will have a firsthand view. Then he can't say that we found a will and destroyed it because it provided for a different disposition of the property."

"That makes sense," Earl Ray said.

They all nodded.

Henry asked, "Why don't we hedge our bets? If that Shaw cousin wins in court, they will have a free ride to the assets on our time and trouble."

"What do you propose?" Wade asked.

"Let's somehow approach the Nutt firm and ask for a cut in exchange for telling them the location of the property," Archie said.

Wiley said, "That's a good idea. But, Nutt is hardheaded. We do need to get a commitment from them before we go to Texas, that's for sure."

Henry said, "I have a friend in Memphis who is active on the singles scene. He was at a downtown bar a few weeks ago. Late that night, he gave a girl named Roxy a ride home. Her car wouldn't start when the bar closed. They had known each other for several years although they had never dated. This Roxy had too much to drink, and it was really good that my friend gave her a ride. Anyway, she started griping about her job and her co-workers. Roxy complained that she was getting pressure from her boss to find some property in Texas that an old man in Mississippi had when he died. My friend got interested when she said it was believed the man owned oil wells there, or parts of them. And her chief gripe was that her company had to take on the case at a twenty percent recovery fee. They usually got a third to a half for this kind of case. Roxy told my friend that the old man had better owned a lot of wells for her to get decent money for the work she had done."

Archie laughed. "This information is good to have. Let's ask for half."

"Go for it," Henry said.

Archie left the room to call Josh Nutt.

He came back a few minutes later and said, "He'll see me next Monday at 1:30. Who wants to go with me?"

Wade said he couldn't because he had duty.

Earl Ray shuddered. "I don't like big cities at all, especially when I don't know anybody there."

Wade said, "Take Henry. Memphis is his second home. He could be useful."

One-thirty on Monday found Archie and Henry seated in the waiting room of the Janes, Knobly, and Stilt law firm. Across from them sat a man dressed in blue coveralls, straw hat, sweatshirt, and work shoes. He was already there when Archie and Henry walked in. Leah had told them Mr. Nutt was on the phone. She rolled her eyes toward the man and mouthed silently, "Jeb Shaw." They nodded.

Henry got into a conversation with the man. "You look familiar. Were you in the pen in 1995?"

The man in overalls grinned, showing toothless gums. "Nah. But I wish I had of been. I was working a corn crop over on the edge of the White River that year. And it was hot! I heard all you had to do in jail was eat, sleep, and watch TV."

"Well, there's more to it than that."

The man said, "Yeah, but you don't have to put up with a wife and younguns like I got."

"I guess you're right." Henry had been married eight times. He guiltily remembered the feeling of relief when the federal judge sentenced him to his second prison stint and how it would take him from his fifth wife who continually nagged for money to buy furs and jewelry. But he had to admit she wasn't as undesirable as his next wife whose appetite for money was insatiable.

Archie got up to speak to Leah. While Archie had his back turned, Henry made an obscene gesture toward him and also made a face. Jeb burst out laughing. When Archie turned to see what had happened, Henry had resumed his former position of looking directly toward the man. Archie turned back to Leah, and Jeb gave an exaggerated wink toward Henry. Henry sensed that Jeb was now bonding with him.

Henry said, "Man, I sure am sleepy. I was up late last night with my fox hounds. They had one running down in the river bottom."

The man exclaimed, "I have fox hounds, too! I love to run my dogs."

Henry grinned. "There's nothing I like better. Especially running them on posted land."

The man squealed and moved his arm chair next to the end of the couch where Henry was seated. "We need to get together some night with our dogs and run a fox. You need to come to my place. I know where a red one stays," he related.

"Oh, pshaw!"

"Hey, that's my name. Shaw. Jeb Shaw. Glad to meet you," and held out his hand.

Henry shook it thinking that he would need to remember not to touch himself anywhere until he would get to the washroom.

Henry replied, "Really, you need to come to where I live. I have the best fox hunting territory around."

The man asked, "Is that right?"

"Yes, my uncle owns ten thousand acres of the best fox hunting ground in the country."

At that Archie looked sternly at Henry.

"Wow. You don't mean it? When will he let us hunt on it?"

"Oh, anytime we want to. And you can bring your buddies with you."

"You don't say?"

"Yes, we can camp out down by the river."

"My wife and kids like to fish. Can they come with me?"

Henry replied, "Sure. They can set out bank hooks for catfish. There are some big ones in the deep holes."

"Man, I'm glad I met you! How long can we stay?"

"You're welcome to stay there as long as you want. I have this older house trailer on a lot next to my uncle's land."

As Jeb listened, he had his hand deep inside his coveralls, scratching. In dismay Henry wondered if he had been doing that before they shook hands. He put his right hand under his thigh to keep from touching his face.

Jeb exclaimed, "That's where we live! In a house trailer. We would be right at home."

"Mr. Nutt is off the phone. Follow me," Leah announced.

Jeb jumped to his feet and said, "Oh, no, young lady. You keep on typing. I know the way. I'll show my friend and his boss where to go."

He eagerly led them down the hall to Stanley's office. Stanley looked up startled. He wasn't aware of the meeting. "What's going on?" he barked.

Jeb took control. "Junior, we're having a meeting with Mr. Nutt. Why don't you join us?"

Stanley followed them to the small conference room. He deliberately took the seat farthest from Jeb's. But Henry chose to sit by Jeb.

Josh entered the room and greeted them, "So y'all have news about finding some property?"

"Yes. We have definite results."

Jeb beamed. "You have? How many oil wells did you find?"

"We'll get to that in a minute. Let me explain. I had a team conduct an out-of-state search for Mr. Joab's assets. A lot of effort and expense was put into it. Some dim clues were discovered from which we were able to capitalize."

Dudley Cook had just entered the room and overheard Archie's remarks. He took a seat across from Henry.

Josh asked, "So tell us what and where?"

Archie countered, "Not so fast. That information is available to you, but it's not for free."

"I was expecting to hear that. What's the deal?" Dudley asked.

Archie looked at Henry and said, "We'll tell you where the property is for one half of its value."

Josh left his seat. "No way! That's highway robbery!"

"Do you expect to win the will contest?" Archie asked.

Josh screamed, "Yes! Without a doubt. We just have to show up at Poston and go through the motions. You don't have a leg to stand on."

Archie laughed at him. "If you say so. But if you do win, all you're going to have is an empty bucket. You'll never be able to find the assets. Your girl Roxy hasn't, has she now?"

Stanley looked at him suspiciously. "How did you know Roxy had a contract with us?"

Archie nodded toward Henry. "The Musician found out. He knows more of what goes on in Memphis than the police. In fact, the police here have used him as an informant."

Stanley looked Henry over. Curiously he asked, "Why do you call him the Musician?"

"Because he can work the slide better than any man alive. Or dead."

"Oh, so he plays the trombone? I didn't know anyone in that rural, redneck county knew anything about music except how to turn the knob on a radio."

Archie coldly replied, "Not the slide on a trombone, you fool. The one on a twelve gauge Remington pump shotgun."

The room became very quiet.

Henry looked away embarrassed.

"What?" asked Stanley.

"Yeah. He was point man for a line company in Nam when they went on patrol in the boonies. Or pulling drag from time to time. He was the best in the army."

Several expressions formed on the faces of the men in the room. In the silence, Archie added, "Yeah. That's how he medaled up. And more than once, I might say."

Stanley sunk down in his chair.

A few moments went by. Mr. Nutt coughed and reminded the men, "Well, let's get back to the matter at hand."

Archie said, "We've located a lockbox in a Texas bank that belongs to Mr. Joab."

The Janes lawyers began to take notes. Henry became aware that the tempo of Josh's breathing increased.

Archie confirmed, "Wiley Downs, in his capacity as administrator, has already employed a Texas lawyer to open an ancillary estate of Joab McMath. We did that so Wiley will be able to have the box opened."

Stanly protested. "When did he do that?"

"Two days ago."

"Why weren't we notified?"

"Because you don't have to be."

"Yes, we do. All parties to this case have to be," Stanley said.

"Nope. Wiley only opened the estate there. No notice to anyone is required. Only when a motion is filed is notice to your firm necessary."

"Does Ken Arnoff know about this?" Josh asked.

Archie said, "No. We have a meeting with his firm tomorrow to discuss the association of the Texas attorneys."

"About that lockbox. Can you show us proof it exists?" Dudley asked. "Sure."

Archie fished in his jacket pocket, pulled out a key, and placed it on the table. All the lawyers half rose from their chairs and inspected it with wide eyes. It was a worn brass key bearing the number thirteen.

Stanley demanded, "How do you know what bank the key belongs to?"

Archie was enjoying having these lawyers rocked back on their heels. "You'll just have to take the word of a fellow lawyer, whether you like it or not," he smugly replied.

Josh muttered, "You're right. If we discredit you, we'll be talking about ourselves. Won't we?"

"Yep. You're catching on." Archie added, "Anyway, we're going to have that box opened this Friday, and we want at least one of you to be there."

They all looked at him and wondered why he was being so generous.

Dudley asked coolly, "Why do you want us to be there?"

Archie replied, "So you can't say there was another will in the box and we destroyed it."

Josh assured him, "We will be there."

Archie reached into his briefcase and pulled out a document. "This is a contract between your client and me, as attorney for my clients, for half of the property that we have located inside the Texas bank. For half," persisted the lawyer

"No way," said Dudley.

Jeb spoke, "Now wait a minute, boy. I have a say in this."

Josh squirmed, wondering what was coming next.

Jeb turned and asked Henry, "Are you getting any of this?"

"Yes, Jeb, I am. I'm getting ten percent of what you sign off on."

Jeb turned his head toward the ceiling and mumbled to himself. Finally he turned his head to Josh. "Mr. Josh, I am willing to give forty percent. I want my good fox-hunting friend here to have a fourth. Ten percent times forty percent equals a fourth. Like I told you before, I used to give a fourth to the landlord when I farmed."

Dudley protested. "But, Mr. Jeb...."

"It's Jeb."

"Okay. Jeb, your math is incorrect."

"Incorrect?"

"I mean it's wrong."

"Nah, it's not. I learned percents in the second primer and fractions in the third reader. That is when I wasn't chasing Miss Jones, that good looking teacher just out of college. I started young," said Jeb with a sly grin.

Stanley reflected, yeah, and look what you ended up with.

Jeb confirmed, "It's forty percent. Anyway your treasure hunter didn't find anything, did she? And I was giving her a fifth. I can give away forty percent of something and still have more than four/fifths of nothing."

He put his arm around Henry's shoulders, hugged him and asked, "Is that good enough, ole buddy?"

Henry wanted to escape his grip. It was all he could do not to gag. Thank goodness Jeb doesn't dip snuff. He was aware that Archie had placed a cold, warning stare on him. Archie's eyebrows went up and down several times indicating that Henry should accept the offer.

Henry replied, "Yeah, ole buddy. That's it, and I'm grateful for the handout."

Dudley threw up his hands in disgust. "Okay, sign the contract."

Archie filled in the blanks on the contract for forty percent, and then he and Jeb signed multiple originals of the contract. One was handed to Dudley. Archie picked up his briefcase and went out of the building to his car. Several minutes later Henry got into the car. He smelled of restroom soap and hot water.

"Phew! I had to spend more time talking about fox hunting. Man! The body odor coming from that guy would gag a maggot!"

Archie said, "That's true." Then he scolded, "I can overlook you lying about fox hunting but what about your uncle owning ten thousand acres of land?"

Henry puffed out his chest as he explained, "You didn't catch on. I was talking about Gallatin Lake, the Corp of Engineers lake. Uncle Sam owns that! I'd make a good lawyer, wouldn't I?" Henry was proud of his deception.

As they left downtown Memphis on Riverside Drive, Henry mulled aloud, almost as an afterthought, "You know, that Jeb Shaw looked vaguely familiar. It's like I've seen him somewhere before." Henry watched a tugboat carefully push a string of barges downstream under the Harahan Bridge while a northbound tow treaded water against the Arkansas bank, leaving the channel clear for safe passage. He noticed the distant deckhands move about the tugs and wondered if that was the kind of career he should have chosen when he was younger.

Henry added, "I noticed you didn't tell them specifically that there were three lockboxes rented by Mr. Joab in the bank."

Archie smiled slyly. "That was for a reason. But my contract commits them to all property in the bank. So I didn't have to get into any detail about numbers of boxes."

After Archie, Henry, and Jeb Shaw left, the Janes lawyers sat there amidst their own thoughts.

Stanley was the first to speak, "Our chances of winning this case are less than theirs."

Nutt replied, "I agree. We need to hedge our bets if we can. Like they just did. We need to figure out a way to take a cut from the hospital's share. They get the most."

Dudley said, "Yes. It would be a waste of time to approach Earl Ray. From what we've been told, he seems to listen to a different drummer than the rest of us."

Stanley agreed, "He and that Musician seem to be peas from the same pod."

Dudley looked at Stanley. "Well, well. Listen at that. City Boy, where did you learn that old country saying?"

Stanley's face turned red. "I've been drinking coffee with our female staff. Several have grandmothers that live on farms outside of the city. I'm learning a lot."

Dudley said, "The hospital won't play ball with us on any kind of straight forward offer. We will have to approach them through the back door."

Nutt said, "Excellent idea. And while they are not looking or thinking in that direction."

Stanley offered, "I have a plan that will work."

Nutt told the paralegal to close the door to the room. Everyone huddled around Stanley as he went into the details of his plan. When he was through, they all relaxed. Josh told the paralegal to draw up a contract between the hospital and the law firm.

Josh said, "We might as well take the document with us. If they agree, we must attain their signatures before they have a chance to back out."

Dudley pressed, "We need to meet with them this afternoon before Archie sees them tomorrow, or it will be too late."

———

Stanley had Leah call Merci Hospital for a meeting. One was arranged for four o'clock at the hospital's offices. Stanley bragged to Leah how he had come up with a plan to beat the hospital out of a large portion of the property devised them under Mr. Joab's will and embarrass Ken Arnoff's firm at the same time. To Leah, he was obviously gloating. It was of concern to her that Stanley would stoop low enough to take, legal or not, from one of the best charities in the nation. Doesn't anyone have a moral backbone anymore? Is it always about money and the desire to win at all costs? Leah was becoming disgusted with what she was seeing happen around the office. No wonder the public held lawyers more devious than the lying, used car salesmen. By Leah's estimation, a lot of lawyers should be ranked below whores.

Stanley and Josh arrived at the meeting at Merci Hospital. Others present were Monsieur Paul; the CEO of the hospital; a staff member; Ken Arnoff, Earnest Tinsley, and a paralegal from their firm. Everyone took a seat around a carved walnut conference table.

Ken began, "So y'all have a proposal?"

"Yes. We know the location of Mr. Joab's property or at least a substantial portion of it. For us to reveal the location, we are asking for a share as a reward," Stanley said.

The hospital people looked at each other. This plan was unexpected. They thought Josh Nutt wanted the meeting to concede to have the will contest settled and for all parties to share in the estate.

Ken cleared his throat and sternly responded, "Well, the hospital's position is that it has been devised seventy-five percent. We expect to receive that amount."

Stanley said, "Our property locaters have been looking for Mr. Joab's assets. We have always believed that the man had substantial property, just as he stated in his will. There was reason to believe that he owned interests in oil wells in Texas. Reliable information has been furnished us to that effect." Then he lied, "And we have found his property." He had the full attention of the hospital people.

Ken said, "Cut to the chase. What do you want?"

Stanley said, "We won't be greedy. We will settle for a fourth of your share."

"That's too much," replied Ken.

"Take it or leave it."

Monsieur Paul spoke up, "Would you all leave the room and let us discuss this?"

"Sure." The Shaw representatives left with their files under their arms.

Monsieur Paul addressed his counsel, "Look. I'll agree to that. Don't clients normally give their lawyers a third or more contingency on a lawsuit?"

"Yes. That's a normal agreement," Earnest Tinsley said.

"Then we'll agree."

Josh and Stanley came back into the room and took their seats on the opposite side of the table. They were told they had a deal, but Ken wanted to know the location of the property. Stanley said that was a part of the contract. Then he pulled out the contract for their signatures. Ken read through it. It committed the hospital to split with the Nutt Firm twenty-five percent of their share of the property identified in Exhibit A attached to and made a part of the contract.

Ken asked, "Where is Exhibit A?"

Stanley smiled. "I have it here in my hand. But I'm not giving it to you until Monsieur Paul signs the contract."

Ken was suspicious. His chair moved forward with a loud squeak as he asked, "Why not?"

"Because I don't want you to see the location of the property and then not sign the contract."

Ken didn't like being maneuvered this way, especially by a young lawyer from his rival firm. But they didn't have a choice. There were thousands of oil wells in Texas. They needed to know which ones.

Monsieur Paul looked anxiously at him. Hesitantly, Ken said, "Go ahead and sign."

He did. Then Josh Nutt signed and handed the contract to Stanley. He stapled the exhibit to the contract and beamed as he handed it to Ken.

Eagerly, Ken took the contract and turned to the exhibit with Monsieur Paul and Earnest looking over his shoulder. Instantly they became crestfallen. The exhibit identified the property as "Contents of lockbox number thirteen in Ranchers Bank, Muleshoe, Texas."

Ken became irate and spoke very loudly, "Damn it. We already knew about that! You said this was involving oil wells! You lied. We know about property in a bank lockbox!"

On one of his trips to Merci, Mr. Joab had confided to Monsieur Paul that the money he gave them came from property he had stored in a lockbox in a Texas bank. His bank at home wasn't used because he wanted to maintain privacy, but he had never told the hospital which bank held the box.

Standing and pointing a finger at Ken, Josh snapped, "It doesn't matter what you know. We didn't know what you knew. We just said we had reason to believe Joab owned oil wells, and we still do. We just haven't found them. But we have found the lockbox, and your agreement is legal and will stand up in any court in the land!"

Both Ken and Ernest looked as if they both had been told that their mothers-in-law were moving in with them. Stanley and Josh didn't even try to hide their glee.

Josh gloated. "Hah! Y'all got who-doed. Ha! Ha! It serves you right for embarrassing me at Randy Belue's party by having me served with process in front of all my friends! Let's go, Stanley."

They left. The atmosphere in the room was comparable to a funeral. Ken put his head down in his hands. In his entire legal career, he had never been outsmarted like this. He was always the one who did this to other lawyers. He moaned.

Monsieur Paul came over to comfort him, "My son, do not despair. What goes around comes around. Anyway, it's only money. Surely God will not desert us on this matter."

Ken moaned, "Yes, but I have let you and God down!"

"But you must remember I was the one to agree to this contract. No repercussions will come your way from us." Monsieur Paul added, "I will ask God for his grace. He has always stood by us here at Merci. Our entire operation is based on faith."

The next day, Archie called Ken to tell him about their discovery in Texas. Ken listened as Archie gave the details of how the key had been found, how it was determined it fit a box in a bank in Muleshoe, and how that had been confirmed.

Ken exclaimed when he was through, "Clever! Very clever!"

Then Archie added the kicker, "There are three boxes, not just one."

Ken sighed with relief, "Oh, boy! They may get me off the hook!"

"What do you mean?"

Ken explained how they had been tricked by Josh Nutt into giving his firm a portion of the hospital's share. But the contract only involved the contents of box thirteen.

Archie chuckled. "There's hope for you. Henry noticed that box thirteen had been entered regularly over the years. There may not be much left in that one. We have no information about the other two."

Then Archie told Ken how they had got a commitment from Jeb Shaw in the event he won the case. He added, "My contract applies to all property owned by Mr. Joab in the bank. So we're safe."

Then their upcoming trip was discussed. Archie had found that there was an airport at Muleshoe with a landing strip long enough to handle a small business jet. Ken said his firm would lease a jet to fly them to Muleshoe. Archie said he and Wiley would fly with them, but Wade and Grady were going to drive. Neither liked to fly, and they also wanted to view the countryside. It wouldn't be too far out of the way to visit the steakhouse in Amarillo that offered a free seventy-two ounce steak to any diner who could eat it all. Neither were big eaters, but they could watch others try it.

CHAPTER 28
SURPRISE!

On Friday morning, Wiley Downs and Archie were sitting in the law office of Mike Holland, located on the main street of Muleshoe. The office was within walking distance of both Ranchers Bank and the courthouse. Small trees had been planted the length of both sides of the street between the curbs and the sidewalk.

Mike was the lawyer that Wiley had hired. He was a seasoned member of the local bar and had been able to quickly obtain the necessary orders from an accommodating judge to move the Texas estate of Mr. Joab forward. He was eager to be involved. He explained that Mr. Joab had employed him to make his will on one of his trips to Muleshoe. He told them that Mr. Joab was afraid that the identity of his devisees might slip out if he used a lawyer in Cade County.

Wiley asked, "Do you have the original will?"

Mike answered, "No. I mailed it to him. I explained that he could get his signature witnessed by two people in Cade County. When I further explained that the witnesses didn't have to know the content of the will, he was satisfied. But it could be in one of the boxes that are about to be opened."

Archie asked anxiously, "Did he say why he wanted me to be the executor?"

Mike smiled. "Yes. Mr. Joab said you were the only lawyer in Cade County that had a business background and you should know how to take care of his business better than the others. He felt that in the event there was an uproar over the probate of his estate, you were insolent enough to deal with any oncomers!"

Archie's face reddened. After a few moments of silence he blurted,

"Mike, do you know what's in those bank boxes?"

Mike replied, "No. But it has to be a lot of something for him to keep three big boxes rented all these years."

Mike continued, "I got the judge to sign an order yesterday that will allow the bank employees to open any lockboxes there owned by the deceased. I've already talked to the banker, Silas McCarver, about this matter. He confirmed that there are indeed three boxes to enter. When I explained that you all don't have the keys to two of them, he said there would be a locksmith present to drill them."

Wiley thanked him.

Mike asked, "Who all will be present?"

Archie replied, "There will be several. The heir, who is claiming the estate, will be represented by Josh Nutt and Stanley Robbs from Memphis. Besides us, the Merci Hospital will be represented by Ken Arnoff. Also our Sheriff, Grady Powers, and Chief Deputy Wade Sumrall are here. They want to be introduced to the banker."

"That's good."

"Everybody flew in yesterday except Grady and Wade, who drove. They got here a couple of hours ago," reported Archie.

"I'll call Silas and tell him how many folks will be over. Sounds like we'll have to open the boxes in their meeting room. Let me treat you to lunch. We have some good ole Texas barbeque out here. It will be different from what they cook in Memphis."

"Sounds great," agreed Wiley with a wide smile.

Archie said, "Oh, by the way. There is one other person, a fellow back home that we call the Musician will be here."

Mike raised an eyebrow. "The Musician? That's a weird nickname."

Wiley laughed. "Yeah, it is. There are several long stories of how he got that name. He's quite an interesting fellow."

At the last minute, Archie had asked Henry to tag along. Archie had been reflecting upon what could be in the bank. According to Merci, Mr. Joab had contributed quite a bit of cash to them over the years. Henry, when he cased the bank, noticed that Mr. Joab had signed off on his entry card a number of times. There was no way one box could hold the amount of cash that Mr. Joab had given away. There had to be something else in there that was very valuable. Archie believed that Henry might somehow be useful again on this trip. Henry had balked at first. He said that if Otye was at work, she would recognize him and would soon realize that he had flimflammed her in a way. Henry prided himself as coming across as straight and honest, a cover for his many years of deception. Archie pointed out that he could dress in a different way, perhaps, or maybe the bank lady wouldn't be at work on Friday.

Wiley told Mike, "We know that we have three boxes to open. You will be running the show today. Could you see that the last box to be opened is number thirteen?"

"Sure. I'll get Silas aside and arrange that."

"Thank you. I have a reason for asking that favor. I'll explain to you later. I think you will really appreciate my reason."

When Mike, Archie, and Wiley walked into the bank at 1:30, the lobby was crowded. Most were there for the box opening. Grady and Wade were having a conversation with Ken Arnoff. Josh and Stanley were off to one side talking on their cell phones. There were also several local customers in the lobby doing business. Otye's desk was vacant. The employees were curious about what was going on with so many strangers present. Mike could see that the locksmith was busy in the vault. Silas, the banker, came out of his office and led them all to the meeting room. There, he was introduced to the visitors.

"Why don't you all have coffee?" he asked.

Josh chortled, "I really would like some good Texas whiskey!"

"Me too!" Stanley said.

They were both as high as a kite. They could smell money. Big money.

Silas smiled. "When we get through here, I'll treat everyone to a drink at the Settler's Bar across the street. It's Friday, and I'm ready to end my week." Then he added, "The locksmith is about through with his drilling."

Stanley became wary, "Drilling? Why is that needed? Did Archie forget the key?"

"I'll explain that in a minute," said Silas.

Stanley looked at Josh with a puzzled expression. Silas winked at Archie. Then he left the room for the vault.

A few minutes later, he came back into the room carrying the tray from a lockbox. Following him was two of the bank clerks. They also were carrying trays from boxes. Their two were bigger than the one Silas had.

Mike motioned through the doorway, and a female court reporter came in with her recording equipment. Mike announced that she was present to make a record of the inventory of the content of the boxes. The other lawyers thought that an excellent idea.

Stanley looked intently at the three boxes. Tied to the handle of each was a cardboard tag with a number written upon it. The boxes were numbered *nine, eleven, and thirteen.*

"What's this?" he demanded.

"The three boxes that were rented by Jerry McMath on September 10, 1945," Silas answered.

Josh was incredulous, "Archie, you told me that there was only one box! Number thirteen."

Archie sniped, "No, I didn't. I showed you the brass key that was numbered thirteen. You jumped to conclusions. But my client's contract with you is for all property owned by Mr. Joab that's in this bank."

Ken caught on, jumped up, shook his fist, and exclaimed, "Hallelujah! You did it to yourself, Josh. Merci Hospital's contract with you applies only to that one box."

The banker joined in, "I don't know what's in the boxes, but thirteen is the only one that's ever been entered, according to the signature cards."

"What?" Stanley asked.

"That's right. You can look at the cards. Whatever was put into nine and eleven on September 10, 1945, is still there." He laid the three yellowed-with-age signature cards on the table for all to see.

Ken began to glow inside. Boxes nine and eleven and their contents were outside the hospital's contract with the Janes firm.

Silas looked around the table, made washing motions with his hands, and announced with anticipation, "If y'all are ready, I'll open number nine first."

Everyone around the table rose eagerly, leaning forward so they could get a good look. The lid went halfway down the top of the tray whereupon it was hinged. Silas flipped the lid up and off the tray of box nine. A collective gasp came from the onlookers as they all stared in shock and disbelief! Josh Nutt farted. The tray was full of loose diamonds! The room was quiet. Everyone stood there grinning. Then a wave of laughter began to spread around the room. It grew into a din. The men began to swap high fives and to slap each other on the back. Tiny rays of light glittered from the box, sending beautiful sparkles around the room.

Archie's legs began to wobble. He slumped into a chair in disbelief. As everyone looked on with expectation, Silas lifted the lid to number eleven. The men's brains had difficulty absorbing what their eyes saw next. This box was also full of loose diamonds. The diamonds jubilantly winked as a chorus at the men, as if they were giving thanks for finally being freed from the dark recesses of the bank vault.

Ken Arnoff was on cloud nine. He didn't care what was in the last tray. The value of the beautiful stones had to be in the millions, and every single one of them was free of the dumb contract he had recommended that Monsieur Paul sign.

All eyes were upon Silas as he lifted the lid to the last tray, number thirteen. At first, he couldn't see anything. He frowned and tilted the tray. Something from the back slid forward and clunked against the front of the tray. It was two Country Gentlemen tobacco sacks. The old cloth still reeked of tobacco. Silas opened the drawstring of one, turned it upside down, and diamonds spilled out. The result was the same with the second one. Ken beamed across the table at Stanley and Josh. They glared back.

Ken said, "Looks like you guys won't get much out of this deal. If you get anything substantial, you'll have to win the trial next week. And that is not going to happen."

The only other item in the box was an envelope. Scrawled across the front in shaky handwriting were the words, "To be opened after my death." The top edge had already been slit.

Silas poured the contents of the first tray onto the table. Everyone was stunned. No one present had ever seen that many diamonds. There were thousands. And they were beautiful! Henry was fascinated by the sight. He loved diamonds. A sideline of his in Memphis was to buy and sell diamond jewelry. Sometimes his ice was hot, but never enough to melt. He quickly determined that every stone appeared to be from one to four carats in size. As Silas spread out the mound, Henry also noticed that only a few were the size of five to seven carats. Henry was puzzled that there were no large or small diamonds in the cache.

"I've never encountered this kind of situation before. All I can do today is make a count of the diamonds. I'll make photographs of them, also," Silas said.

Mike agreed, "That's all you can do. When you are finished, give all of us a copy of the count. I'll need to go back to the judge and get permission to employ an expert from Dallas to come here to size, grade, and appraise each one of the diamonds."

"I'll have to get approval from Judge Dennis to pay the cost of that," said Wiley.

"These boxes will be sealed and the contents held until they are appraised. The diamonds will be released when you lawyers get the proper court order to me," the banker said.

Henry slipped from the room, went out the front door, found a quiet spot on the sidewalk, and made a call on his cell phone.

"The locksmith is installing new locks. I plan to give Mr. Holland the other keys to the boxes," Silas said.

"That will work. Then they can't be opened without proper monitoring from the court," Mike said.

"Are we through except for counting all these diamonds?" Silas asked.

Archie replied, "Yes. But I need to open this envelope. I want everyone present to see what's inside just in case it's another will. Okay?"

He carefully spread open the top edge of the aged envelope. Inside was a sheaf of faded papers. Attached to the front page with a rusty paper clip was a typed sheet signed by Joab McMath. They all watched as Archie somberly read one page, then the others in turn.

Finally, he looked up. "This is obviously not a will. These yellow papers are from Joab's brother, Jerry. The note on top explains a lot."

Archie asked Silas if he would make a copy of the documents for everyone else. Silas called Otye, who had returned from a late lunch, and had her make copies. Archie waited until everyone had read his copy before he asked, "Is everyone satisfied this is not a will? It's pretty clear it's not."

No one objected.

"This letter will be of most interest to Monsieur Paul," Ken said.

Mike, the local lawyer, invited them to a steak dinner that night. They all accepted except Stanley and Josh who immediately left for the airport.

There was nothing in Muleshoe for them to celebrate.

———————————

After the dinner was finished, Ken, Archie, Henry and Wiley boarded their jet that was parked on the tarmac at the Muleshoe air strip, and headed for Memphis. The night flight would take a couple of hours so they relaxed in their seats. Their mood was really upbeat. The shock of seeing two entire trays of sparkling diamonds had not worn off.

"I don't think I'll be able to sleep at all tonight," Wiley said.

"It's just another day's work," Archie laughed.

"Yeah. That's why I keep on practicing law in a small town. You never, ever know what will walk through your front door."

"I agree. Every day is different. But I would have to say this day has topped them all. Who would have ever imagined that a thrifty old man in our backwater county would have access to a fortune of this size and sat on it for all these years?"

Henry said, "I feel like a rich man."

"I guess this is how Mel Fisher's divers felt when that first gold chain was pulled from the ocean sands off the Florida Keys in their search for the wreck of the *Nuestra Senora de Atocha*," Archie replied.

"That was some kind of rush. Seeing so many beautiful diamonds. I just wanted to dip my hand in those trays and let the stones spill out of my palms," Henry said while wiggling his fingers on his upturned hands.

Archie laughed. "Did you see the expression on the women's faces at the bank when they saw the display on the table?"

"That good looking, young blonde with the short skirt squealed that she wanted to marry whoever got those diamonds so she could wear a different diamond on her finger every day of the year," laughed Henry.

Wiley said, "Boy, won't this deal be the talk of Muleshoe?"

"That's what worries me. I'm afraid this news will reach Cade County. And this does up the ante in the will contest," Archie replied.

"I've already called Monsieur Paul. He's very excited. Especially when I told him how empty box thirteen was compared to the other two," Ken said.

Henry said, "While y'all were still inside the bank, I called a friend of mine in Memphis who is a free-lance diamond broker. Without letting him onto what we found today, I asked him what diamonds are going for per carat. I had to run several sizes of stones by him. I think it is safe to say that our stones will sell for fifteen hundred dollars per carat. What was the final count?"

Wiley took out the inventory. He said, "There were 12,063 diamonds in box nine, 12,197 diamonds in box eleven, and 201 diamonds in box thirteen."

"Yeah! Tell me one more time how many were in box thirteen?" Ken exclaimed.

Archie smiled. "Two hundred one."

"I can't hear that enough. Oh, does that give me a lift!"

They all laughed.

Archie handed his copy of the documents from the lockbox to Henry, who had left the room when the letter had been opened. "Read this!" he ordered.

Henry settled in his seat as the plane sped toward Memphis and began to read silently.

Dear Joab,

If I die before you do, the contents of my lockboxes are yours because your name is on the bank cards as my survivor. I need to explain how I came to possess these diamonds. In the spring of 1945, my unit, the 27th Armored Infantry Battalion, had crossed the Rhine River after the bridge at Remagen had been taken. We had been fighting for weeks. Not long after we had crossed the river, we were relieved by another unit. We were trucked back during the night to a small town in Belgium near the border. I never knew the town's name. We took shelter in small groups in abandoned buildings. The entire town was unoccupied by civilians. Before daylight, we were counter-attacked by a German armored column which had been bypassed earlier and was fighting their way back to the homeland. They were in an ill mood.

Four of my buddies and I took refuge in a building in the center of town. Eventually, the fighting moved away from us. When morning broke, all gunfire had ceased. My buddies were PFC Michael Joe Busby, Sergeant Paul Clark, Technician Garcia, and Lieutenant Maxie Orwell, who we called M.O. I was the First Sergeant and called 'Pops' because of my age. All of us had been together since the first of the year.

When daylight appeared, we began to observe our surroundings. We were in a bank that faced a town square filled with early spring flowers. M.O. told Busby and Clark to search the town. While they were gone, we looked around. There was a tiny vault in a room off the main lobby. An artillery shell had blown the roof above this room off, and the floor was filled with debris. Shortly, Clark and Busby came back and said we were alone. The Germans were gone as was our unit. Apparently, they had pulled out without us. We had no radio, so we were stranded. We started gathering up wood to build a fire. The weather in the early morning was still cool, and a drizzling rain had begun to fall.

Clark was moving timbers out of the vault when he discovered a small metal door in the floor with a combination lock on it. We were curious about what was under the door. We had explosives with us, so M.O. gave the order to blow the safe open. That was easily done. Inside were several containers. M.O. pulled one out and took the top off. We were stunned! It was filled with loose diamonds. M.O. kept pulling more containers out. Every one of them was filled to the top with stones. Boy, was that a beautiful sight! We had no idea how many there were or how much they were worth.

We planned to sit around all day resting. We figured there was no hurry to get back to our unit, and we thought it might be dangerous to move until the Germans cleared the area. Busby played with the diamonds for hours. We watched him as he would lift double handfuls up and let them spill back down. The stones would catch light rays from the fire, which would make the room glitter like Christmas. As we sat around the fire, we discussed what we had found and what we were going to do. A lot of ideas came forth. Naturally, we decided that the loot would be split five ways. The hard part was trying to figure out how to get the stuff home. We felt the war was about over and we knew that our unit was overdue to be sent to the rear for a much needed rest. Our discovery had to be kept secret. If we disclosed the find to the officers, we would never see a single stone again. Like Clark said, we needed to take care of ourselves. We would be set up for life when we got home. At that time, the only thing that could be done was to bag the stones and try to reach our lines. Busby found an abandoned duffel bag to put the stones in, and we stuffed some extra clothes on top.

In the middle of the afternoon, a mounted patrol came by and found us. The commander explained where our unit had gone. He radioed back and a truck was sent to pick us up. Sure enough, the next morning we were told the unit was being sent to a camp near Paris for rest and equipment repair.

We had only been there two days when I was called to the company commander's tent. He informed me that I was being sent home. The captain said that a plane load of decorated soldiers were being sent to Washington to be involved in a War Bond Drive and then to be discharged. I was to be included because of my age. M.O. was elated when he heard the news. He gathered Busby, Clark, and Garcia and explained that the diamonds should be carried to the States by me. M.O. was sure that no one on that plane would have their gear checked because of its special mission. I was trusted by all of them. We agreed that I would take the stones on home with me. When each soldier got back to the States, he could come to Muleshoe and get his share. I gave them my address and told them I would be easy to find.

It went as planned. A brigadier general and three colonels were flying on my plane. When I saw them load cases of wine, dozens of pieces of artwork, and a captured German machine gun, I knew this plane wouldn't be searched. It reaffirmed our decision not to report our find to the officer corp. If those officers had only known what I was piggy-backing on their loot! I made it to Washington without my belongings being checked. For a few weeks we went around to several nearby cities promoting the Bonds. Before I went on the tour, I placed the duffel bag in a locker at the NCO Club on the Pentagon's grounds. Then I was discharged, and I retrieved the bag and headed home on the train. At the stop in St. Louis, I was sitting at a lunch counter in the depot drinking coffee when the cute little waitress, Renee, heard over the radio in the kitchen that the war had ended. A wild celebration broke out in the café and out on the street!

After I arrived home, I hid the duffel bag in the attic of my house. I got back into my daily routine of working and waiting. Finally, a letter arrived from M.O. He said he and the other three had been kept in Europe for post-war military work, and it would be some time before they would get home.

On Sunday morning, September 9, 1945, just as I was

finishing breakfast, I heard a knock on my front door. It was M.O.! He had ridden the train from the Bronx in New York City, where he lived, to St. Louis. From there he had taken the bus to Muleshoe. He was worn out from the trip. I was really glad to see him! I made a fresh pot of coffee and scrambled some eggs for M.O. As we sat at my kitchen table, he told me that Busby, Garcia, and Clark had been killed. The plane that was taking them to England had crashed in the Channel. He asked about the diamonds. I got the bag from the attic and poured them onto the table. Neither of us had much of an idea of where our three buddies were from. We knew Garcia and Busby were drifters before the war started, and Clark was an orphan. M.O. said it would be bad luck to take any part of their share. He said he would be satisfied with what his share would bring. I felt the same way. He told me to give their shares to charity. He trusted me.

We visited the rest of the day. We talked about our three buddies and their attempt at humor while under stressful circumstances; Clark, who would mock Hitler and make speeches whenever he was drinking; Garcia, who would cry out when an enemy round came very close, "He couldn't hit a bull in the ass with a bass fiddle!"; and Busby, who was continually squealing like a sow hog after everyone else had finished laughing at a joke.

Then we talked how we excited we had become when our patrol came to the edge of the Rhine River Valley and far below we could see the Ludendorff Bridge. To our amazement, we could see that it was not damaged. We laughed about when Commanding General Hodges called headquarters to report the find and how a ranking officer told him not to send troops across because it would conflict with Montgomery's plans for a crossing elsewhere. That's when Ike got the news. He ignored what Montgomery might think and ordered General Hodges to send everything he had across the bridge, including the kitchen sink, and to hold the bridgehead against all odds.

M.O. went to bed early. After breakfast the next morning, I took him with his share of the diamonds to the bus station. The last I saw of him was when he waved to me from the bus window.

Later that day, I went to the bank and rented lockboxes to store the diamonds. Three were needed to hold them. It took me several trips to the bank to get them all stored.

Joab, as I write this letter, I have not decided on which charity to give the three shares. M.O. and I had talked about why so many diamonds were in a bank in such a small Belgian town. M. O. came from a place where organized crime was a way of life. He speculated that this bank had to be a front for a Belgian or International crime syndicate or a major financial backer because the little bank couldn't have had the assets necessary to purchase this amount of diamonds. We figured, because of the German occupation, the diamonds couldn't be moved by whoever owned them. And this little bank would not be of interest by the troops.

We had another idea. That bank where we took shelter wasn't far from the German border. We figured that when politics began to change in Germany and when the Nazis began to get control, German citizens would flee across the border. They would bring diamonds with them to exchange for Belgian francs at the bank. They were afraid to bring out marks, which might be devalued or be declared worthless by European countries.

After I got home, the news came out about the concentration camps in Poland. M.O. said before he left Europe he had talked to soldiers that had liberated a few. According to them, it was awful. So, M.O. had a more disturbing idea. He believed that the stones were taken from the victims at the death camps. The Jews would have had their valuables with them. They were removed from their homes under the pretense that they were being temporarily relocated. Only the officers at the camps would have control of the records and the diamonds. He said it would have been easy for rogue Nazi officers to sneak the stash across the border and hide it in the bank to be retrieved when convenient.

I thought about that a lot and decided that I couldn't live with myself if I profited from the misfortune of others. I was healthy, could work, and could get by without this extra wealth.

I would hope that you would consider my concerns and devote the value of these stones to a positive progression of mankind.

Your brother,
(S) Jerry McMath

P.S. There is a nice lady and friend of mine here in Muleshoe named Ethel Cooper. If I haven't already, would you pick out the largest, prettiest stone and give it to here in memory of me? She kept up my house for the year I was in the Army and cared for my dog, Shep. And she wrote to me regularly. Getting a letter in Europe about news at home was a big deal and kept me going. There is nothing more depressing than being the only soldier at mail call that doesn't get a letter.

Henry put the papers down. He said, "I think Jerry was right. Since WWII we've seen how the Nazi high command looted the European art collections and seized tons of gold. Lower level officers would jump at any opportunity to pirate any treasure that fell into their hands."

"I agree. The Jews would have hoarded smaller diamonds. If they had to exchange them for food or security, their wealth would go farther," Ken added.

"I say that Mr. Joab would make his trip to the bank to remove diamonds. Then he would sell them to a broker somewhere for cash, which he would then give to the hospital."

Wiley said, "It makes sense that the broker would be in Dallas which is on his way home."

Henry then read Mr. Joab's note that was clipped to his brother's letter. It was short.

To the representative of my estate, whoever it might be:
I have taken the position of my brother. I have been notified that there is a child in need of expensive medical treatment at the Merci Hospital in Memphis, Tennessee. It will be the recipient of the first donation. If they prove to be a worthwhile charity, they will receive future donations from this charge, and to include my brother's share.
12/07/79
(s)_____
Joab McMath

CHAPTER 29
MISS ETHEL

Before they left the bank in Muleshoe the afternoon before, Wiley asked about Ethel Cooper. A couple of the ladies there had known her. They said she had died about 1985. One remembered that she had a single child, a daughter who lived in another state. The bank lady referred them to a Mrs. Ruth Whitney, the town librarian. Mike called her. She was willing to meet them on Saturday morning at her house. Wiley asked Grady and Wade to go with Mike and see if Ruth might know about Ethel.

They were led into a cozy den by Ruth where she served coffee and homemade teacakes with blackberry jam to her company. Ruth was a charming lady. She was told about Mr. Joab's death and why they were in Muleshoe. Grady informed her of Jerry's written directions about giving Ethel a diamond.

Ruth exclaimed, "I'm sorry to hear about Mr. Joab. I knew Mr. Jerry when I was growing up. My family and he lived on the same street. My sister and I would sneak off to watch him weld on broken metal at his shop. That whole procedure fascinated us, the sparks and the flame and the hissing and the odor of the burning welding rods."

She talked more about Jerry and how she remembered his coming home from Europe when she was very small. There was a welcoming committee that met him at the bus station. Her father held her up on his arm so she could see over the crowd. Jerry was wearing his army uniform that had ribbons and medals pinned to his jacket, which impressed her.

She said, "Oh, I knew Miss Ethel, too. She was a widow woman who worked at the dry cleaners doing sewing and alterations. She really had a tough life. Her husband had been killed in an accident on a well-drilling platform. In those days there was no insurance to help the family. She had one daughter, Catherine Elizabeth, who was my age. We went all through school together."

"Do you know where she is now?" Mike asked.

"Yes. She and her husband live in Tiptonville, Tennessee. She became a school teacher after college and taught in Dallas, where she met her husband. They lived in Dallas for a few years until his company transferred him to Tennessee. Both are retired now."

Grady asked, "You say you knew Jerry's brother, Joab?"

"Oh, sure. Mr. Joab was such a nice man. He visited here from time to time. For many years after Jerry's death, his shop was rented to another welder and he would come out to check on it." Grady told her about Jerry's note in the lockbox asking his brother to give a big diamond to Miss Ethel. Ruth exclaimed, "Oh, she got the diamond! On his trips here, Joab would visit Ethel. She told me that Joab got it out of the lockbox just before Christmas one year and brought it by her house." She never wore the diamond because she thought it was too gaudy for Muleshoe. Miss Ethel never even had it mounted in a ring or necklace."

Grady asked, "What happened to the stone?"

"Catherine Elizabeth has it."

"That's nice!"

"Yes, it is. I guess the keepsake will be passed on to her daughter. She had such a time with that baby."

"What do you mean?"

"Oh, Catherine Elizabeth and her husband, Dale, never had a child until she was forty-one. They had tried so hard. Then the baby was born premature and had to stay in the hospital three months. But she grew up to be a normal, healthy young woman."

"That's good," Grady said nodding his head up and down.

"Yes, and what's so ironic is that the child became a medical researcher and now works at the same hospital that cared for her."

"Well, we certainly thank you for the information. We just wanted to find out whether or not Mr. Joab gave her the diamond. I'm glad he did," Grady said.

Wade said, "Got a long trip ahead of us but we enjoyed the visit. We have to go."

"Come back to see me if you're ever in Muleshoe," Mrs. Ruth invited, in keeping with the usual Southern custom.

"Thank you. We may have to come back later to pick up some property that belonged to Mr. Joab," Wade said. "Maybe we can stop and see you again."

CHAPTER 30
THE LONG RIDE HOME

Wade and Grady were back at the motel at 10:00. They loaded their clothes into the car and pulled under the awning at the front of the motel. Wade went inside to check out. While he was in the lobby, Grady's cell phone rang. Emma's number came up on the screen.

Emma said, "Grady, I have some bad news. Ellis Tiller died in his sleep last night. James Henry Eason went over to his house early this morning to borrow a tractor. He couldn't get Ellis to come to the door, which was peculiar, for Ellis is a light sleeper. He went around the house and peeped into the bedroom window. James Henry saw him on the bed, not breathing, and called 911. Jack followed the ambulance there. The EMTs thought it was a heart attack."

"This is bad news. And unexpected. Somehow you get used to thinking that all the people around you are going to live forever. I'll tell Wade. This will hit him hard because they were close."

Emma said, "It looks like it's going to be a long ride home for y'all."

"It will be."

"Be careful. I love you!"

"I love you too. We'll be home as soon as we can. When you learn the arrangements, will you call me?"

"Yes." There was silence. Then Grady heard her crying.

"Emma, are you okay?"

"No. I'm not. Grady, I love you."

"I love you too, Emma."

"Please be careful."

"I will."

"I was close to Ellis, too. He was just such a big baby."

"I know."

"One day he brought me tomatoes that he had raised. We were sitting in the carport talking, and he broke down. It was pitiful. Ellis got into one of his crying spells, and I didn't think the tears would stop. I went over and put my arms around him. I asked him to just talk to me. He said he wanted to but just couldn't. I asked him if it was about Korea. He nodded and sobbed that it was. Ellis said since Korea, he had been living in misery every single day of his life. He kept saying over and over, 'I'm guilty! It should have been me and not them! Why did I leave them?' Finally, he stopped crying. I asked if he felt better. Ellis said he did and then started apologizing. He was so embarrassed. I assured him that a woman can understand why a man cries. He thanked me and left."

Grady sighed. "I know. Ellis had a big monkey on his back. Now, he is finally free from his living hell."

"That's for sure."

"Maybe Wade will tell me what happened over there. He has always known why Ellis cried. Here he comes now. I have to go."

Wade got into the car. He sat without moving while Grady told the news.

When Grady finished he said, "I dreaded this day, but I knew it was coming. I wished Ellis could have worked all that out of his system so he could have enjoyed life."

Grady came to the highway that led home. "If it's okay with you, I'll drive straight through."

Wade agreed. They were silent for an hour. The miles passed. Then Wade said, "I have to tell you about what caused Ellis to live in mental agony. Out of respect for Ellis, I never discussed with anyone what I'm about to tell you. Now, I'm released from that obligation." He told the story as Grady headed down the highway, eastward toward home.

"I was on patrol with ten other marines on the east side of the Chosin Reservoir on December 2, 1950. Our orders were for us to make our way into the low hills on the east side of the lake and locate retreating U. S. soldiers. The Chinese had entered the conflict in the middle of the night on November 27th by sending thousands of troops across the border from Manchuria. The army had already advanced to the north through our Marine lines and took the brunt of the attack. They fought quite hard for a while but were overwhelmed and had to withdraw to the south. The lines became fluid. Sometimes army units found that the Chinese had already gotten behind them. They would find the enemy attacking both ends of a column. And the severe weather made matters much worse.

Casualties were mounting, both from the enemy and the weather. Re-supply didn't exist. There were some air drops but most of those fell into enemy hands. The temperatures at night would drop to more than twenty below zero. The days were only a few degrees warmer, and the snow was really deep.

"My patrol made contact with twelve army stragglers. They were exhausted. They had fought for forty hours without sleep. Their motorized column had been shot to pieces. Many of the soldiers in the column had been captured, and the rest fled in small groups in different directions. All of the twelve were wounded, and three were being carried. We had just begun our way back to the reservoir when a larger force of Chinese captured us. We were marched five miles to a small village where a command post had been set up, staffed by both Chinese and North Koreans. It was a holding area for prisoners. We were put in a shed that had one stove in the center. Wounded soldiers were lying on the floor by it. The stove wasn't doing much good, and the wounded were miserable that night.

"About 2:00 p.m. some more prisoners were brought to our shed. They were members of the point unit that was to advance to the northern border of Korea. These troops were unshaven, dirty, and covered with blood.

"I heard my name called, 'Wade!' I looked in that direction and recognized Ellis. I already knew that Ellis and Coley were in the same company somewhere in Korea. My mother had written me about it. She was excited that three boys from the same county were stationed near each other. Ellis had just placed Coley on the floor. He was wounded and unable to walk. Man, were they glad to see me! I hugged both of them. We cleaned a place by one wall for Coley and made him as comfortable as possible. They were starved. I had some rations in my field jacket that I gave them, meager as they were. We spent some time discussing what was happening. Ellis said they had been in a truck and armored vehicle convoy moving south to the marine lines. They had been involved in some bitter fighting, but they were finally overwhelmed. Some of the soldiers managed to escape, but most were captured. Ellis, Coley, and the group they were with got caught later.

"While we were talking, some North Korean officers came in with a table and some chairs. They seemed to be in command of the prisoners instead of the Chinese. We were ordered to line up and come to the table where a young captain was seated. A clerk was recording the names of each soldier along with some basic information. Suddenly, the door burst open, and three of our soldiers were shoved inside. They had been caught trying to escape. The captain could speak broken English, and he strode over to the three soldiers. He became irate. He said, 'You not escape. It is bad to try, see.'

"He pulled out his pistol and shot one of the three in the kneecap. The guy fell to the floor screaming in pain. The captain was obviously very upset. When he got back to the table, Coley was there being held up by Ellis. He shouted 'Example!' and had another officer hold Coley's fingers over the edge of the table. The captain pulled a hatchet from his belt and whacked off Coley's left little finger. Coley fainted. He was hurt too badly to overcome the new pain. That's when I charged the captain. I hit him in the face with my fist and broke his jaw. I kicked and stomped him until one of the Chinese hit me in the head with a rifle butt, knocking me out. When I came to, I was in a hut tied to a post. The Chinese soldiers beat me severely with fists, belts, and rifle butts. When they were satisfied, they drug me back to the shed."

"Man! That was tough!" Grady said.

"Yeah. I slept between Coley and Ellis that night. By the end of the next day, I was able to hobble. Luckily, I had no broken bones," Wade said.

Grady said, "That treatment to you and Coley was bad enough, but surely that didn't cause Ellis to behave as he has all these years. Did it?"

"Nah!" Wade said.

"What was it then?"

"He was haunted by what happened at the truck convoy before they were captured. Ellis said the officers in charge finally realized the advance toward the Korean-Chinese border had stalled, and it was time to move back to the marine lines. They had no communication with the rear command. The officers had no idea where the enemy was or their strength. The marine observer assigned to their ranks was able to communicate with the Corsairs, whose mission was to provide air cover to the convoy. Many of their vehicles were disabled. They had taken a tremendous amount of enemy fire. One night, the officers decided to start moving back the next day. There was no hope of reinforcements. The convoy needed to begin moving out early in the morning because there were only eight hours of daylight at that time of the year. The trucks were full of wounded. The dead were used as a source for weapons and ammunition. The troops were already worn out from the days of fighting. The weather was growing worse.

"An attempt was made to bury the dead, but the ground was frozen. The bodies were stacked in rows under an overhang of a cliff and left.

"Then a desperate situation evolved into a fiasco. The column didn't begin to move until noon. As it started out, the entire column came under an assault by hundreds of Chinese. Many had no weapons and were armed with shovels. The forward air controller, a marine captain, had no choice but to call for a close quarter air strike from the four Corsairs flying directly over the troops. The Chinese, in places, were only ten yards from our troops. One of the pilots said later that this was the closest air support they had provided in the entire war. That he could actually see Chinese being clubbed off the sides of the trucks. The planes dropped napalm on the Chinese which caused many casualties and forced the enemy to withdraw. But the planes were flying very low, and one napalm canister landed short. The bouncing can exploded and killed twenty of our guys and injured many more.

"Ellis and Coley said the sight of men running around covered with gobs of flaming, jellied gasoline and rolling on the ground screaming for help was absolutely hell. This incident took the troops' remaining enthusiasm away. The column stopped. The officers had their hands full trying to get it moving again. The officer in command had to threaten the troops up front with his pistol to make them advance, for they were facing Chinese automatic weapons fire.

"The lead vehicle in the column was a M19 full track with twin 40-mm Bofors anti-aircraft guns mounted in a revolving turret. That armament was devastating and could blast away anything it faced.

"Behind it was a line of trucks. They were loaded with twenty wounded each, but there weren't enough trucks. Ellis, because of his size, carried the heavy Browning automatic rifle. His sergeant had placed him, six more BAR men, and the other M19 at the back of the column to provide additional firepower to cover the retreat. Ellis said while the column waited to start moving, the driver of the M19 decided to kill the motor to save precious fuel. As Ellis screamed, 'No!' at him, the motor went dead. When the column started moving, the M19 couldn't be cranked, and the rear was left unprotected. Because of the lack of radios and the urgency and chaos, the column commander didn't find out that the M19 had been left behind until hours later.

"The column was under constant Chinese fire. Fighting went on for hours. Realization set in that the task force was taking on too many casualties while trying to tend to the wounded. The law of diminishing returns was taking its toll. They started to abandon the wounded troops. Coley's legs were hit by shrapnel from a mortar round. Ellis put him on the front seat of a truck in place of a soldier who had been killed.

"Eventually, the command broke down, and leadership ceased to exist. The men were mostly on their own. All the trucks were either out of gas or immobilized by enemy fire. Because of the loss of the M19 that couldn't be cranked, the rear guard failed to check the advance of the Chinese. Ellis tried to get his platoon to stand and resist, which would buy precious time for the lead troops to fight through the enemy opposition.

"Finally, Ellis and the last troops started moving past the stalled vehicles. The wounded in the trucks, when they realized they were being abandoned, began to scream for someone to help them. Ellis said that every day of his life he could see the pleading eyes of wounded soldiers as he passed them by. He knew most of them. Several called him by name, begging for help. Every night of his life he would hear those desperate cries. And some nights, he would be visited by one of the soldiers who would accuse him of not stopping to assist. The ghost soldier would cry out, 'Why? Why did you leave me?' Ellis would wake up in a cold sweat, weak and trembling and afraid. And ashamed.

"As the Chinese troops closed in, he pulled Coley out of the truck cab and carried him on his back away from the road. Coley was the only person he was able to help. Ellis said that about six hundred wounded soldiers were left in the convoy when the Chinese captured it.

"The troops began to leave the road in small groups. The retreat became a rout with every man for himself. Some made it to the Chosin Reservoir where the ice was frozen deep enough to support the men. Others made their way overland back to our lines. The marines had patrols, other than mine, that were sent out on the ice of the lake to intercept the fleeing soldiers.

"The Chinese ransacked the trucks and took away all the prisoners who could walk. It was really weird out there. Sometimes prisoners would be mistreated. Other times, Chinese doctors would treat the wounded with morphine and release them in a few days.

"While I was recovering from my beating, I assessed the situation and decided that an immediate escape was necessary. The Chinese assault was unorganized, and the lines were still fluid. I decided the best opportunity for any escape was then. When night fell, Ellis, Coley, and I, along with six unwounded soldiers, slipped out of the building and made our way toward the Chosin, which was only a few miles away in a direct line. The weather was really cold, and the snow was deep. Our group stayed away from established trails in the snow for we feared they might be used by the Chinese. It's just natural for a human to take the easy route while moving in difficult terrain. We started out with Coley over Ellis's shoulder in a fireman's carry. I was breaking the trail. It took a lot of effort to push the snow away with my legs. Sometimes the drifts would be waist deep. Two of the men from my patrol were in this group. We were much more rested than the others who had been in the convoy. The lead would be swapped between us. When I wasn't breaking trail, I would carry Coley to rest Ellis. Some of the group had been opposed to bringing Coley along because of his wounds. But Ellis and I were not about to leave him. I mean, like, he was from home. And I didn't want to have to dodge his momma for the rest of my life. As we walked, two of the soldiers were continuously whining that Coley was slowing us. The first time we stopped to rest, I had a confrontation with the whiners. I preached a little sermon that the deal was all of us or none. That was after I grabbed the two by their collars and banged their heads together. That solved that problem. We made it to the reservoir at daylight and stopped to rest. Finally, we saw a force of marines on the ice with jeeps and sleds. They picked us up and took us back to their base.

"Two days later, a task force of marines in jeeps was sent to retrieve any wounded from the site where the truck convoy had been stopped by the Chinese fire block. Not a single vehicle had made it out. I had to go because I had some knowledge of the area. Thank goodness Ellis wasn't with us.

"It was a looted convoy. The silence was eerie. We began to open the canvas flaps at the back of the trucks. The sight was awful and was identical in each truck. All of the wounded were frozen to death. The bodies were lying there in grotesque positions. Frozen limbs sticking in all directions. Faces contorted. In excess of three hundred. The view was pitiful, more than a man could stand. By the time the command was given to start back, we were all numb. None of the dead could be taken with us."

"So that's why his life has been a wreck," Grady said.

"Yeah, you just don't know how many times over the years I've had to baby Ellis just to get him through the day. I kept telling Ellis that he could do only so much. He could have only carried one man away from the column, and that one man was Coley. I just couldn't get that explanation to register with him."

"What about Coley?"

"He had some of the same problems. He saw the burning soldiers, but he wasn't haunted by the begging, wounded troops that were left behind."

"A burden that ghastly is a lifetime curse."

Wade agreed. "The only release is when you die. Ellis is finally at peace. May God rest his soul."

CHAPTER 31
THE TRIAL

On the Friday afternoon before the trial was to begin on Monday, Josh called his colleague, Frank Poley in Tupelo. Josh began, "Hey, Frank. I thought I'd give you a last call. For some reason I'm uptight and worried about the trial. I've tried dozens in my career, but this one is different. I guess because so much is at stake."

Frank sympathized. "There can be a lot of humor in county courtrooms and as much drama as you could have at the Orpheum. And surprises too," he added.

"That's what I'm afraid of. Especially with that damn Archie involved. It's obvious that he can be dangerous."

"I warned you. He can be very bizarre. He works really hard at getting the edge."

"Yeah. I've already found out that he can do or say something to get everyone's attention. Then, it turns out that his stunt was completely orchestrated, but everybody was left hanging in the meantime."

Frank laughed. "An intentional, ulterior motive on his part."

"I can't imagine how he will approach this trial or even what he will wear to the courtroom."

"See. He is already getting under your skin. You need to shake this off. To be your best, you need to forget about Archie," Frank counseled.

The trial was to begin at 9:30 on Monday morning. Linda Nell entered her office by the back door at 8:00 o'clock. On her way over to the courtroom to open the front door, she saw that the parking lot was already full. Also, a crowd of people was meandering around and talking in groups, waiting to get inside. She unlocked the door and went back to her office to get the case files for the trial.

The courtroom quickly filled with spectators. Linda Nell called the sheriff's office and told the dispatcher that a couple of deputies might be needed to keep order in the courtroom. Even if all the people were well-behaved, there still would be noise and disorder. Grady said he would be there and would bring Jack and Wade.

Linda Nell and Crissy began to arrange the files in their area in the corner of the courtroom. The judge's bench was in the center against the back wall. Opposite the clerk's station was the jury box. Between the clerk's station and the bench, was a door that opened to the judge's chambers. On the other side of the bench another door went to the jury room.

The lawyers and their staffs began to drift into the courtroom. Linda Nell watched them roll in their briefcases from which they began to remove their files and place on the tables. Then an uproar began.

Judge Zack Dennis arrived and had just sat down at his desk in chambers when Linda Nell broke through the door. He was hoping this case would be tried and concluded within two days, maximum. Still, a jury had to be seated and any last-minute motions of the attorneys heard. And, he had no idea about how long the jury might deliberate.

He was startled when Linda Nell raced through the door and exclaimed, "Judge, we've got a problem in the courtroom!"

"Already?"

"Yes."

"What is it?"

"The lawyers are about to get into a fight."

"What?" asked the judge as he stood up with his hands placed on the desk for support.

"Yes. The Janes firm arrived first. They had put a lot of their files on the table next to my station. Then they all went into the jury room with their client and closed the door. That's when Archie walked in. He looked around a minute. Then he moved all the Janes files over to the table by the jury box. I had a third table brought in for Merci Hospital's lawyers. It sits in the middle toward the rail. When Stanley Robbs came out of the jury room, he noticed that his papers had been moved.

"Then he glared at Archie who was standing at the rail summing up the crowd. Every bench is filled. People are standing around the walls, and there are people in the hall wanting to get inside."

"What happened?"

"Stanley walked up to Archie, grabbed his shoulder and accused him of moving the papers. Archie told him to remove his hand. He refused, so Archie hooked a heel behind Stanley's leg and pushed him down on his back. Stanley jumped up and was trying to charge when Josh grabbed him. Wiley is out there holding Archie."

Linda Nell smiled. "And of course, there's Archie and his wardrobe."

The judge groaned, "Oh, no. I can't imagine."

"You should see him. He's outdone himself this time. Archie is dressed as an English barrister! He is wearing tight, tan britches, black shoes with huge shiny buckles, a white ruffled shirt, a red jacket, and a powered wig!"

The judge's blood pressure began to rise.

"I mean, Archie is the center of attention. Everyone in the room is hypnotized by his appearance. Even his own legal team. They are speechless, and Archie is strutting around the courtroom like a banty rooster."

The judge frowned. "What a way to get this trial started. Go tell all of them to get their tails in here."

The room was soon filled with lawyers who stood meekly against the walls. Linda Nell followed, closing the door.

"What seems to be the problem?" the judge addressed the lawyers who stood in silence.

Stanley was red-faced. He was glowering at Archie who wore an amused look. "I claimed the table to the right of the bench by putting our files upon it. We got here first, so we had the choice of tables."

"Local custom trumps first-grade manners," Archie smirked.

Stanley was about to reply when the judge spoke to him, "I'm going to clear up this matter right now. It is traditional in this courtroom for the petitioner to have the table that you chose. You and your colleagues, the respondents, will have the table by the jury box, and the Merci Hospital lawyers will sit at the table in the middle. Now y'all get out of here and see if you can't behave like adults. If any of you have motions, I will hear them when I come out on the bench."

Then he turned to Archie and lisped with a very phony British accent, "Me, Lord, Barrister Baker, get your tail in your horseless carriage, go home, and change into an American suit. I will not allow you to make a farce of this trial. Not in my courtroom. I've a good mind to find you in contempt."

At that, the lawyers meekly left.

Linda Nell said, "And we have another problem."

Judge Dennis winced. His day was going downhill fast. He asked, "What?"

"You can't get another camera into the courtroom. I'll bet every TV station within a hundred miles has set up equipment. There are sound trunks outside with satellites mounted on the tops. Also, there are plenty of reporters inside with cameras. They have been busy taking photos of Archie in his getup."

Judge Dennis scowled. He hated cameras, and he hated the State Supreme Court for ever allowing them to be present at a trial. Of course, their ruling left it up to a trial judge's discretion to allow them. He had already been into an argument the previous year in Marshall County with a smart aleck TV reporter from Memphis who thought he should be allowed to televise every single trial, regardless of sensitive issues concerning children.

"Just what I need. This puts me on the spot. I don't want media in the courtroom. They, for sure, are disruptive."

"The ladies on the jury panel got wind that cameras would be here. They are dressed to the nines," reported Linda Nell.

"That is the very reason I don't like cameras. Those ladies are here for themselves. They want to be celebrities. This trial could be sensational, and they want to get on the bandwagon about writing a book, afterwards, about what went on in the jury room."

Linda Nell admitted, "I'm wearing my best dress, and I had Norma Sue give me an after-hours appointment Saturday afternoon for my hair."

"Linda Nell! Of all people. How could you do this to me?" the judge protested.

Linda Nell smiled. "A girl has to do what a girl has to do! I won't ever have this opportunity again." She suggested, "Why don't you poll the lawyers to see what they wish about the cameras?"

"That's a great idea!"

Then Judge Dennis asked Linda Nell, "Is the bailiff ready to announce the opening of court?"

"Yes," she replied.

Scott Nail, the bailiff, was a former constable who now was eighty years old. He had been given this position in honor of his service to the county. It was only a part-time job, but the small check added to his meager retirement. The bailiff had been a tough constable and had been well respected. Mr. Nail was standing by the door to the chambers. When the judge came out ten minutes early, Mr. Nail was caught by surprise. He forgot his usual announcement about demanding all to rise. The bailiff stood there blankly, struggling to remember what he was supposed to say.

Scott blurted, to the amazement of all, "Git up! Git up! Git up!" Guess what! Everyone stood up. Then the bailiff compounded his problem. He stammered, "Cade County Chancery Court is now in session. The Honorable, the Honorable, the Honorable, uh....."

Judge Dennis was stepping up to his chair. He laughed and added, "Judge Dennis."

The bailiff whirled and pointed to him. "That's right. That's you."

The courtroom hooted. The judge gaveled for order.

The judge sat silently surveying the courtroom. Linda Nell had called the night before informing him about the diamond find in Texas. The young blonde who worked in the Texas bank had called her sister in Dallas on Saturday afternoon and told her about seeing thousands of diamonds at work the day before. She asked her sister not to tell anyone, but her sister had never kept a secret. She got on the Internet and posted the news. Before Monday morning everyone in the nation knew the identity of Mr. Joab's treasure.

Judge Dennis felt naked and exposed because Savannah wasn't here. Savannah was the pretty legal assistant for all the chancery judges in the district. She had practiced law for a while after her graduation from law school until she married. Faced with the task of raising her small children, she had accepted this research position. On the days when there were no trials, she could work from home. During a trial, she would sit by the clerk with her computer and instantly pull up whatever cases were cited by the lawyers. She would have an explanation of the cases ready for the judge when he retired to chambers to decide his verdict. The judges discovered her work was exceptional. But today, she was home with a sick child. Hopefully, Judge Dennis mused, no complicated motion would be argued during the course of this hearing.

The courtroom was alive with excitement. The buzz was as strong as extreme fear, but in a different way. You could see it, taste it, feel it.

The coffee crowd at Lola's had already speculated the worth of the diamonds. No one there knew the exact count; just that a couple of trays in the Muleshoe bank were slam full. The speculation had a range of values because the size of the trays was not known. All of a sudden, there were many diamond experts at Lola's, including those who had never bought even a chip for their wives, choosing to spend their spare money on guns and hunting equipment instead. Bobby Hubbard, an over-the-road truck driver with regular hauls to both coasts, had the most to add. He claimed he had a buddy who drove an armored car from the diamond district in Manhattan to large cities around the country. His buddy had told him the current market value of a carat and also cautioned about lots of fakes being around. That bit of news divided the coffee drinkers. There were those who, without having any evidence at all to support an opinion, declared the McMath diamonds to be fakes, making the upcoming trial an exercise in futility. This infuriated the other side, for they were predicting the value of the hoard to be from one hundred to two hundred million dollars. For anyone to say that the diamonds were fakes was an insult. An argument arose and became so fierce and loud that, for the first time in the history of the coffee shop, Lola warned if they didn't tone down, they would be banned from her establishment. That announcement hushed the noise.

Back in the courtroom, all eyes were on the judge. He coughed nervously and explained, "I see that the press, print and video, is well represented here today. It's up to my discretion whether or not to allow cameras in the courtroom. Before I rule on the matter, I will ask for input from the attorneys. As I see it, the issues in this matter are represented by three sets of counsel. So I will ask each of you whether or not you object to cameras being present. If any one of you three objects, then cameras will not be allowed. Mr. Nutt, what is your position?"

Josh conferred with his staff. He rose and said, "Your Honor, we don't object."

He couldn't if he wanted to, for one of the TV stations present was a client of his firm and was continually getting into legal trouble. The annual fees from this station paid the salaries of two lawyers and one paralegal.

Judge Dennis looked at Ken Arnoff and raised his eyebrows. Ken huddled with his staff. He rose and announced, "Your Honor, we don't object." Ken thought this a great opportunity to get free publicity for the hospital which was about to initiate a major drive for donations.

Judge Dennis told Wiley, "You're on."

Wiley and Archie put their heads together. Archie was now dressed in a nice suit that his secretary had rushed to him. Judge Dennis watched them. He felt that Archie would object in order to have better attention from the jury.

To his surprise, Archie rose and said, "We don't object either, Your Honor. But if cameras are allowed, we move that no pictures be published until after the trial is concluded."

The judge's heart sank. Now it was his call. He was about to rule against the press when he saw Linda Nell mouthing, "Election year." His campaign budget was tight, and he had decent opposition. Judge Dennis realized this would be good publicity, and it would be free. Also, the voters would see him in action as a tough judge. He could foresee having to call Archie and Stanley down frequently.

The judge ruled, "Okay. Cameras are allowed. The use of them cannot be disruptive. No flashes are allowed. If any picture, still or moving, hits the public before the trial is concluded, I will find those responsible to be in contempt of court, and that means jail time. Is that understood?"

He glanced toward the press as he spoke and noted that they all nodded in unison.

Then he said, "The jury has already been selected, but not yet identified. Linda Nell, would you seat the jury?"

Linda Nell walked to the rail where the twenty-five potential jurors were sitting and began to call the names of the fourteen people selected. As she called a name, that juror would rise and walk to a chair in the jury box. The cameras were rolling. Each person developed a swagger in their short walk along with a TV face.

The jury, when seated, consisted of seven women and five men. Those selected included Jon David Knox, a mail carrier's wife, a law student, a farmer, a bank teller, a schoolteacher, a pharmacist, a barber, a divorcee, a retired nurse, a pianist from the Baptist church in Baxter, and the owner of a menswear shop. The two alternates were office workers.

While the jury was being seated, Crissy noticed that one of the doors to the courtroom was cracked slightly open. She giggled; she could see a stack of single eyes in the crack, from down low to as high as a tall person could stretch. She knew that those people were waiting for the extra jurors to leave so they could get seats.

The judge spoke, "I want to thank all of you extra jurors for your patience and attendance here today. You all are excused and are free to leave and re-enter your normal, everyday lives." No one moved. The dismissed jurors weren't about to give up their seats. The judge asked, "Are there any motions for the court to consider?"

Stanley rose. "Yes, Your Honor. On behalf of my client here, Jeb Shaw...."

At that, Jeb, dressed in a clean pair of overalls and red undershirt, rose with his straw hat in his hand and beamed at the jury. "I'm Jeb Shaw from Arkansas, and I'm here to claim the belongings of my cousin, Joab McMath." With a sweeping wave of his hat to the entire jury, he sat down.

Archie chortled to Ken, "Look at that freak sitting in the middle of those high-dollar lawyers wearing tailored suits! Won't they look good on TV?"

Josh cringed. They had tried in vain to get Jeb to stay at home. No testimony was needed from him. But he insisted on coming because he wanted to get with Henry and go look at the fox hunting territory. They asked Jeb to wear sports clothes. He refused to do that, too, but he did agree to wash his overalls. To get him to wear his false teeth to look decent, a case of canned baby food had been sent to his wife so she wouldn't need to borrow them.

Jeb's outburst threw Stanley off stride. He began his motion anew, "Your Honor, we move that Archie Baker be excluded from representing Earl Ray Fowler in this will contest."

"On what grounds?" The judge appeared to be shocked. He noticed that all cameras were focused on him.

"Mr. Baker prepared the will. By local rules he can't be an advocate since he can be called to testify as to Mr. McMath's competence on the day the will was made."

Archie jumped up, "Your Honor, I object! I didn't make the will. I demand to know how my counsel opposite concludes that I did."

Judge Dennis ordered, "Mr. Robbs. State your grounds."

"Well, if you look at the pleadings in the case file, you can see that the font on them is the same as the font on the signed will."

The judge thumbed through the file jacket. He admitted, "I see your point. This is an uncommon font. The will was made in 2000, and the pleadings are recent. But the font on both is identical. What do you have to say, Mr. Baker?"

Stanley was gloating. He had the judge seeing his point. If the judge gave him his motion, the case would be won without a trial. Archie couldn't represent Earl Ray, and Ken Arnoff couldn't proceed with the hospital's claim. His firm was only allowed to be in court by their association of Archie.

Archie stood, gathering his wits. "Your Honor, that argument won't hold water. There are probably thousands of typewriters out there with the same font. I used my father's old portable Smith-Corona to type the pleadings because my computer was in the repair shop. My secretary was on vacation that week so I had to do my own typing. You can see where I used about fifty gallons of white-out." The jury laughed. Their vision of Archie typing his own papers was comical.

The judge said, as he glanced at the camera bank, "Before I was elected to the bench by the honest, hard-working people of this district, I used one of those typewriters myself. I was too broke to buy a better one. Mr. Robbs, unless you have any other proof, you're overruled."

Ken Arnoff noticed the law student on the jury nodding in agreement. Maybe one vote for us, he thought.

"Any other motions?" asked the judge.

The lawyers sat in silence.

The judge addressed the jury, "Ladies and Gentlemen of the jury, you are to hear the testimony of witnesses and to review evidence in this case. Mr. Baker is representing himself, as named Executor of the will, Wiley Downs the administrator still in place, and Earl Ray Fowler. The Arnoff Firm is representing the Merci Hospital of Memphis, Tennessee. Mr. Fowler and Merci Hospital inherit the bulk of the assets of the late Joab McMath as set forth in his Last Will and Testament. The will offered for probate is a copy of a signed will, not the original. Plainly speaking, the case is about the probate of a lost will. Jeb Shaw, who has already been declared by this court as the sole heir of Joab McMath, is contesting the will. He is being represented by the Janes Law Firm. Your job is to listen to the testimony of witnesses, and to consider any physical or written evidence admitted by the court, and to decide if this will is indeed the true last will of Joab McMath. The rule of law in Mississippi is will or no will. In other words, you must decide, since the original will hasn't been found, either that Mr. Joab destroyed his original will to allow his natural kin to inherit from him, or that it was his true intent for Mr. Fowler and the hospital and others to have his property."

He turned to the lawyers and asked, "Opening statements?"

They all declined, which mystified the judge. He couldn't believe these lawyers would pass on an opportunity to preen and posture before the cameras. He wondered what strategy underlay this declination.

"Call your first witness, Mr. Baker."

"I call Norma Sue Riley, the witness to the will."

The courtroom buzzed with anticipation. Wade Sumrall, being present in the courtroom, stepped in front of the bailiff in order to be the one to bring Norma Sue from the witness room down the hallway.

The side door opened and Norma Sue Riley entered.

Silence enveloped the courtroom. For a few seconds, everyone present was transformed into a gawker. Those who had never seen her before were awestricken. Unaware of the reaction caused by her presence, Norma Sue, all 36-23-36 of her, walked to the witness box. She was wearing a black beret at a slight angle atop her pretty brunette hair. She had on a long-sleeved white blouse with black polka-dots. It was open at the top, accenting a pearl necklace. She was wearing very tight jeans. She had on little make-up, and really, none was needed at all. Not only was Norma Sue beautiful, she carried herself in complete, unabashed confidence. No one there had ever seen a more beautiful woman, in person or on the movie screen.

Watching her caused Wiley to remember the time that Norma Sue and her mother had traveled with him to Holly Springs to testify in a divorce trial of a friend. At lunch, all three had walked down the sidewalk from the courthouse to a cafe. They met a man on the way. Wiley turned around and saw the man staring back at Norma Sue over his shoulder while he walked, causing him to slam into a utility pole! A friend of Wiley's told about riding to Southaven with Norma Sue to get hobby supplies. There was a crew of carpenters inside the store working on the floor. When Norma Sue walked by them, they all became so engrossed in her passing that one of them nailed his hand to the floor with the staple gun!

Norma Sue took her seat in the witness box totally unconcerned about the attention her entrance had attracted. Later, a cameraman for Memphis TV Channel One swore the lens on his camera fogged over when Norma Sue walked by. No one moved. What had been seen had not yet been completely absorbed. Finally, Judge Dennis, taking his eyes off Norma Sue, instructed Archie to proceed.

Archie asked her, "Would you state your name please?"

"Norma Sue Riley."

"Occupation?"

"I own my own beauty shop. It's on the square in Central City."

"How long have you had this business?"

"Since I graduated from college. I'll go ahead and tell so you won't have to ask. I'm thirty-four."

That answer satisfied several of the men in the courtroom who had always wondered her age.

Archie asked, "Did you know Joab McMath?"

"I did. I had cut his hair for the last twelve years."

"Did you have an occasion to be around him on March 13, 2000?"

"Yes."

"Explain."

"He came into my shop that day for a haircut. Kayla Weeks, my cousin, was working there that year. After I cut his hair, he asked if Kayla and I would witness him signing his will."

"And?"

"We did. He pulled papers out of his jacket pocket and told us it was his will, and that he had never made one before. Mr. Joab laid it down on the counter and signed the pages. Then he handed his pen to me and I signed as a witness. Kayla signed it too."

"Did he tell you what was in the will?"

"No. But he laughed and said after he died that it would really be talked about in the county. He hoped a lot of children would be helped with what he left."

"Who else, if anyone, was in the shop at this time?"

"No one."

"Tell the Court about Mr. Joab's physical and mental condition that day."

"Oh, he was his usual self. Witty. Talked about the weather. What he was going to plant in his garden that year. Carried on with Kayla. Asked about my mother."

"Would you say he was mentally alert?"

"Yes."

"How about his health?"

"Good. He was in good health, and he was about seventy-five. Still had a full head of white hair."

"I hand you a document that is marked Petitioner's Exhibit P-1. Would you tell us what it is?"

"It says Last Will and Testament of Joab McMath."

"Look at the last page and explain what you see."

"Sure. There is the signature of Mr. Joab that I saw him sign. And I see my signature and Kayla's."

"What did he do with the will?"

"He put it back into the pocket of his jacket."

"You said that Kayla Weeks was the other witness. Where is she today?"

"I heard from her a few months ago which was the first time in a year. She is moving about Southeast Asia doing mission work in areas that are still rebuilding from the tsunami. Kayla called from Singapore one night to catch up on the local news. When I told her Mr. Joab had died, she was really sad. We talked about him a while and about him coming in for haircuts. When I told her that his will had not been located, Kayla got excited. She said that one day when I wasn't at work, Mr. Joab brought a sealed envelope by for me. He said it was a copy of his will, and he wanted me to keep it. Kayla said she had forgotten to tell me about it. I asked her where the envelope was. She said she put it in the safe among my insurance papers, which I never go through. When I opened my shop the next morning, I went straight to the safe. The envelope was where Kayla had placed it."

"What did you do when you found it?"

"There was a penciled note on the outside to give it to you."

"Did you?"

"Yes."

"Do you know who made Mr. Joab's will?"

"No. It was typed, not handwritten."

"Did he mention who typed his will?"

"No."

"From March 13, 2000, until his death, did Mr. Joab ever tell you, in your shop or anywhere else, that he had destroyed his will?"

"No. But last year on the anniversary of his wife's death, he came in for a haircut. He was really in a pathetic mood. Just really down, still mourning. He let a lot of things pour out, and I patiently listened. When he was leaving, he gave me a hug and thanked me for being nice to him and for witnessing his will. That was the only time the will was mentioned."

"Your Honor, I tender the witness."

Stanley went to the lectern, "Miss Riley. It is Miss, isn't it?"

"Yes. I'm single."

"Any good reason why?"

Archie stood. "Your Honor, I object. That question is irrelevant."

The judge was caught by surprise. "Uh, I agree. Sustained."

Josh and Lillie Bess squirmed uneasily. They had agreed that Stanley would cross-examine Norma Sue and that Lillie Bess would cross-examine the doctor that the petitioner planned to call. Josh would monitor their questioning to make sure all points were covered. Josh had warned Stanley not to get cute. The original strategy had been to have Dudley cross Norma Sue, but he had to attend an emergency hearing in Mayfield, Kentucky.

Then Stanley asked, "Do you have an interest, direct or indirect, in Mr. Joab's wealth?"

"No. I didn't even know what his will said until Mr. Baker put it in the courthouse."

"What do you mean that you didn't know what was in the McMath will? Didn't you witness it?"

Again, Archie rose. "Objection, Your Honor. A testator doesn't have to disclose the content of the will to the witnesses. The witness is only required to watch the testator sign the pages of the will."

"Sustained. Mr. Robbs, try to keep your questions on point. Continue."

"Ms. Riley, have you ever had any connection to Merci Hospital?"

"No. I just know several children from here have been treated by that hospital."

"Do you know Earl Ray Fowler?"

"Yes. I cut his hair too."

"Have you ever dated him?"

Norma Sue smiled sweetly. "No. But that's because he's never asked me out. I'd crawl into his pickup with him anytime."

Everyone in the courtroom smiled and looked toward Earl Ray sitting at the petitioner's table. He blushed.

"Isn't he a lot older than you?"

"Yes, but that doesn't matter. Not with me. The older the violin, the sweeter the music."

Then Stanley changed tactics. "Do you enjoy being beautiful?"

"Beauty has its burdens."

He blurted, "Oh, whee-de-dee! Is that original? Or is that Keats, Bryon, or Tennyson? Or do you even know who they are? Ha! Ha!"

Norma Sue's expression hardened. "Yes, I know who they are. Look around the room, you jackass. Do you see them here? Since they're not, what I said is original."

Judge Dennis looked down and grinned. He wasn't about to get on to Norma Sue about her language. Not after the grand entrance she had made.

Taken aback Stanley stammered, "I'll move on."

She countered, "Why don't you? I have appointments at my shop."

Ken noticed the female jurors nodding in approval at that rebuke.

Then Stanley dropped a bombshell. He asked, "Do you suffer from Attention-Deficit Disorder?"

Archie jumped to his feet. "Your Honor, I object. That is irrelevant."

Stanley replied, "Oh, but it is not, Your Honor. In a will contest it has to be proven that the testator was of sound and disposing mind on the day he signed his will. Since Miss Riley is testifying to Mr. McMath's mental capacity, her own mental ability is also subject to scrutiny."

Judge Dennis stared at the ceiling and thoughtfully stroked his chin. He was thinking that never in any of the many will contests over which he had presided had an attorney pursued this point. But it made sense.

Judge Dennis agreed, "That's a valid point. Objection overruled. Continue."

Stanley repeated, "Do you suffer from ADD?"

Norma Sue sat there wondering how he had found out about that. She had been very careful to keep her ailment invisible.

Archie was stunned. He didn't know about this condition. He thought all along, as with the other men in Cade County, that Norma Sue was perfect. This could be a problem.

She admitted, "Yes."

"How long have you known that you have had this condition?"

"Since I was fifteen."

"Do you take medication for this condition?"

"Yes."

"How often do you take medication?"

"Daily."

"And on March 13, 2000, were you taking medication?"

"Yes."

"So on the day you witnessed Mr. Joab sign his will, you were a stark, raving lunatic, weren't you?"

Both Archie and Josh Nutt jumped up and screamed, "Objection!"

The judge stared at Josh as though he had taken leave of his senses. He couldn't believe what he had just heard.

"Mr. Nutt, you can't object to what your own co-counsel asked. My word, Mr. Robbs has the witness on cross. If he said something contrary to your trial strategy, you'll just have to live with it."

Mr. Nutt had told Lillie Bess to sit where she could observe the jury. She could see they had lost a few of them because of the remark, especially the women and the law student. And just when Stanley was beginning to destroy Norma Sue's credibility.

The Judge said, "Mr. Robbs, you need to rephrase the question. I'll direct the jury to disregard that last remark."

Archie gleefully thought, yeah, just like they have erasers in their minds. Stanley is my best ally at the moment.

Stanley asked, "Aren't symptoms of ADD the inability to focus normally and the inability to comprehend?"

"Yes."

"So on the day Mr. Joab signed his will, you were suffering from a condition of inability to focus and observe?"

"Yes, but I was taking my medication."

"Your Honor, I have no other questions for the witness."

"Mr. Baker, any re-direct?"

Archie said, "Yes, Your Honor. Miss Riley, do you attend counseling for your condition?"

"Yes."

"What does your counselor say about any progress?"

"He says I had my ADD under control while I was attending college to the extent that I can function normally."

"Was that the state of your condition in the year of 2000, and specifically on March 13, of that year?"

"Yes."

"I'm through your honor. And I request that the will be admitted into evidence."

"So admitted."

The judge looked at the clock on the wall. The trial had started late because of the presence of the TV camera crews. Time had been spent letting them get set up in locations that would cause the least disruption. Then the jury had been seated. A couple of recesses had taken up more time.

The judge said, "I think we will break for lunch. It's now 11:30. We will start back at 1:30. The sheriff will take the jury to Baxter where they will eat in a private room at the restaurant. Everybody stay seated until after the jury has left the courtroom."

Then he addressed the jurors, "Do not discuss this case with one another or anyone else. Is that understood?"

All the jurors nodded.

After they cleared the room, the bailiff correctly announced, "All rise."

The judge left the bench. Then he and all the attorneys left for lunch by the back door.

Judge Dennis came back to chambers at one o'clock. He was reading through the file of another case. As he read, he became aware of noise coming from the direction of the courtroom. It was distracting his reading. Then Linda Nell came through the door. She looked distraught and was shaking her head. The judge thought, what now?

Linda Nell said, "I need to call Grady. The courtroom is in complete turmoil."

"Tell me what's happening."

"At lunch after the jury left, the spectators cleared the courtroom. About the time the last one disappeared from sight, the courtroom was filled by all those who had been in the hall and on the outside who didn't get a seat this morning. The first set of spectators is arriving back from lunch and demanding their same seats. It's a ruckus out there. I'm afraid there is going to be violence. The cameras don't help. Everybody wants to be on TV. The cameramen were seen panning the room this morning."

"Tell the sheriff to get up here with his deputies and run everybody that is not seated out of the room."

By the time the lawyers returned and the judge went back out on the bench, Grady had the room under control.

"Call your next witness."

Then Ken Arnoff rose. "We call Dr. Guy Fancher."

The bailiff went for the doctor. Wade wasn't interested in going for him.

Dr. Fancher took the stand. Ken went through a series of questions establishing Dr. Fancher as an expert medical doctor. There were no objections. Then he asked, "Was Joab McMath a patient of yours?"

Dr. Fancher answered, "Yes. I've been practicing medicine in Central City for forty years. He and his wife were two of my first patients."

"What was the condition of his health during the time you treated him?"

"It was very good. I reviewed his card before I came to court. I treated him mostly for allergies in pollen season, upset stomach from time to time, some occasional cuts, flu shots, and in his later years, for high blood pressure and arthritis."

"What would you say was the state of his mental health?"

"Excellent."

"When was the last time you treated him?"

"He came to see me about a cold a week before he died."

"Did you have occasion to treat him around March 13, 2000?"

"Yes. It just happened that I saw him that same day."

"For what?"

"Routine blood work that he requested which, in my opinion, was overdue for it had been done about a year previously."

"Did you spend any time with him while he was in your office?"

"Yes. Quail season had just ended. We spent about twenty minutes discussing the season and how many birds I had killed out on his land."

"Did you notice anything unusual about his state of mind?"

"No. He was normal."

"One last question, Dr. Fancher. Over the many years that you have practiced medicine in Central City, how many patients have you treated?"

Dr. Fancher smiled wearily, "Tens of thousands! Currently, I'm seeing over a hundred a week."

"I tender the witness."

As Archie sat down he thought, "Here it comes. I've set a trap for the Shaw lawyers. I know which point of Dr. Fancher's testimony they are going to zero in on. They want to discredit Dr. Fancher, but this is going to blow back in their face. Big time." Archie wondered which lawyer for the defense had been assigned to cross Dr. Fancher. He noticed Lillie Bess getting out of her seat. Archie sighed. This was too bad. He liked her best of all that bunch of his opposition.

Lillie Bess began her cross examination. "Dr. Fancher, how is it that you remember so clearly the visit by Mr. McMath on March 13, 2000? Why, my goodness, that was ten years ago. Do you remember in such detail every conversation you've ever had with your every patient? You just testified that you have over a hundred patients visit each week. Come on now, explain to the jury why you recall that conversation with Mr. McMath so clearly."

"I will if you will shut up and let me get in a word edgewise," Dr. Fancher cut in.

That remark brought smiles to several of the jurors and from all of Dr. Fancher's patients who were in the courtroom watching the trial.

Dr. Fancher continued, "It's easy to explain. Mr. Joab and I were long-time quail hunters. We both loved the sport dearly. We each treated our dogs as pets, not just as an object to use to find coveys of quail. We loved the outdoors, the walking, the shooting. That day Mr. Joab brought his favorite shotgun, a Fox double-barrel, to my office and gave it to me. He said he was giving up bird hunting and had no heir to give the gun. I was overwhelmed. I had never owned a Fox. I was honored that he chose me to give the gun that he cherished most."

The jury was soaking up every word with approval. Archie sniggered. He could have asked the same question, but it would have been routine coming from him. Lillie Bess should have known not to ask any question to which she didn't know the answer. He had set her up! Now the jury has bought Dr. Fancher's testimony, lock, stock, and barrel.

Lillie Bess wilted but regained her composure and continued.

"Dr. Fancher, do you ever send patients to Merci Hospital?"

"Yes, I do."

"Explain."

"I'm a general practitioner. I'm always referring patients to specialists and to hospitals."

"What is your relationship with Merci?"

"Very good. Several of my medical school classmates are on its staff. It's a good hospital. It's small, but they have a research wing that's been successful. They've improved the quality of life for many children. Their advanced medicine has given long-term hope to their patients."

"Do you like to see the hospital do well?"

"Yes."

"To the extent that you want the will admitted so the hospital will greatly benefit?"

Ken Arnoff stood. "Objection! That question is inflammatory, irrelevant, uncalled for..."

The judge interrupted. "Ok. I get your point. Sustained."

Lillie Bess asked, "How long and often have you hunted on Mr. McMath's land?"

"Oh, I would say ten times a year for thirty years."

"Did he ever charge you for the privilege of hunting on his farm?"

"No."

"So you owe Mr. McMath a favor by testifying in a manner that his will be admitted so the hospital where you send patients will benefit?"

Ken screamed, "Objection. That's a leading question!"

"I agree. Sustained. Again the jury is to disregard," Judge Dennis said.

"I withdraw my question. No more questions," Lillie Bess said.

Archie rose. "The petitioner rests."

The judge looked at Nutt's table.

Josh, Lillie Bess, and Stanley put their heads together for a few minutes, whispering. They realized they had a weak case going into the trial. The clause in the will whereby all blood kin were disavowed was a problem. Jeb Shaw's redneck appearance wasn't an asset, either. The team had been unable to produce any evidence to show the jury why Mr. Joab would destroy his will so that Jeb would inherit. Before the lawyers left Memphis, Mr. Janes warned them not to put Jeb on the stand because he was so unpredictable. Josh whispered that Norma Sue's revelation about her health and that the jury makeup looked favorable enough to rest. He winked knowingly.

Then Stanley said, "Your Honor, we have a motion for the court to consider outside the presence of the jury."

Judge Dennis instructed the jury to retire to the jury room while he heard Stanley's motion.

Stanley stood and stated, "Your Honor, we may have a motion for a directed verdict in our favor. But first, I would like the court reporter to read back the testimony of Norma Sue Riley."

"Very well. Miss Anderson, please read back the testimony of Miss Riley."

As everyone listened, Ashley Anderson began to read what she had recorded. All of a sudden Stanley interrupted her. "That's not what that woman said."

Ashley's head jerked up. The phrase "that woman" burned her. She had been a court reporter at hundreds of trials and had been exposed to hundreds of lawyers. In her estimation, this lawyer was in the top tier of those she disliked. She had detested Stanley ever since an earlier run-in with him over the long transcript of a trial in Marshall County that she had provided his firm. He had berated her about something on every single page with a condescending attitude. Ashley put her pen down, stood up, looked Stanley in the eye, and fierily asked, "Are you calling me a damn lie?"

Stanley had not expected a reply of this nature. He thought they didn't warn us about this in law school! He could feel the heat from her eyeballs. He stammered, "No ma'am!"

Judge Dennis slammed the gavel on the bench with such force that the handle broke. The head bounced of the floor hitting the dozing bailiff in the chest. This rude remark was personal. He was not going to allow some jerk lawyer to talk that way to the reporter who had been with him ever since his election to the bench.

"Young man, you heard what Miss Anderson said. I remember Miss Riley testifying exactly as the record discloses. I soaked up every word she said. One more smart aleck remark out of you and your carcass will be in jail."

"I'm sorry, Your Honor. I was indeed brusque. In view of this disclosure, we rest."

Breathing heavily, Judge Dennis stated, "That's good young man. The motion that you didn't make is denied anyway!"

Archie stood and announced. "Your Honor, we move for a directed verdict. The testimony of our witnesses clearly shows the document offered for probate is the true Last Will and Testament of Joab McMath."

Judge Dennis took his time. Then he became political. He would have given Archie his request if there had been no jury. But there very well could be a difference of opinion in the community. The will contest had drawn a lot of national interest because of the value of the diamonds. He could foresee being invited to future TV talk shows and wanted his appearance to be commendatory. There also was some small doubt whether or not Norma Rae was stable the day she witnessed the will. And Archie's rehabilitation of Norma Sue had been sort of weak. So he took the easy way out. He would let the jury make the decision.

"Denied. The jury will deliberate on this matter and decide."

CHAPTER 32
THE UNFORESEEN VERDICT

The judge allowed the attorneys to make closing arguments to the jury. Of course, each side painted its own portrait of the decision the jury should decide. Then the judge gave only one instruction: the jury was to decide if the will offered for probate was the true Last Will and Testament of Joab McMath.

The jury retired for deliberation at three o'clock. The first thing the jurors did was to elect a foreman. No one wanted to hold that job, but before he knew what had hit him, law student Sean Murphy was elected. He had already participated in a moot court trial in law school, so he had more than a vague idea of how to manage a jury. Sean said they should have a vote right away to determine how everyone felt about the case. When he counted the ballots, the vote was eight to four for the will to be allowed. Sean opened the floor for discussion. Each juror expressed his or her view of what had been heard from the witnesses.

After they had been in the room for only thirty minutes with no apparent progress toward anyone changing their vote, Patricia, the pianist, complained, "I guess this is going to be another O. J. situation."

The schoolteacher laughed, thinking how that California trial had lasted nine months. "Surely we won't be here that long!" she whispered under her breath.

The deliberations continued.

Outside the jury room, the lawyers watched the clock tick. Five o'clock. Two hours in deliberations. Archie began to brood. He thought the jury would have already decided his way. This is not a good sign at all. He had wanted to scold Earl Ray for requesting a jury trial. But Earl Ray told him about a run-in his uncle had with Zack Dennis many years ago when Zack was practicing law. Earl Ray was afraid Zack might still be carrying the grudge.

Sean, the law student, was disgusted at what he was hearing from the jurors to the extent that he gave thought to changing his major. Jon David said he would vote for the hospital to get their share but not Earl Ray. Sean pointed out to him that, as the judge had said, it was will or no will, that you couldn't approve one part only. Jon David said he didn't care what the judge said. Rex, the men's store owner, spoke up and said that's how he felt too. Before he voted for Earl Ray to get his part, he wanted to know what he had done. Sean pointed out that had nothing at all to do with the will. Anyway, no one could make Earl Ray tell a secret. The farmer Leroy said he wasn't voting for the will because Earl Ray was included.

Patricia, the pianist, looked at him and asked, "Why? Because Norma Sue is sweet on Earl Ray and not you? Everybody knows that you got turned down by her and that the law had to scold you for stalking her."

Leroy looked down at his shoes, avoiding her sharp stare.

The barber spoke, "I don't like Norma Sue, and I think she had something going on with Mr. Joab."

The school teacher shouted, "You're just jealous because you lost a lot of business to her! Her being nice and good-looking and you being so obnoxious is a double-dip, isn't it?"

"It appears that all of the women on the jury and myself are the only ones for the will," Sean said.

The nurse remarked sweetly, "That's because we're the only ones in this room who have any common sense."

Then Jon David announced, "I think Mr. Joab tore up his real will. That means he didn't want this one."

Patricia objected, "You don't think he wanted that pig sitting outside to get his diamonds, do you?"

"Yes, that would somehow be against the Bible, wouldn't it?" the nurse chimed in.

"How do you figure that?" Jon David asked.

"That's too deep for you. You hang out at Sleazy's too much anyhow," the nurse scolded.

At six o'clock, Sean sent a note out to the judge by the bailiff that the jury was deadlocked. The judge had the jury come out to their seats in the box. He told them to go home and be back at eight o'clock the next morning and not to discuss the case with anyone. As the jury filed by the tables where the lawyers were seated, Patricia, the pianist, held her right arm against her side and discretely folded her right thumb under her palm wile looking directly at Archie. The judge left the bench and the courtroom buzzed with conversation.

Archie leaned over and told Ken, "My stooge on the jury signaled that four people are voting against us."

"That's not good. I thought we did a good job putting on our case. Do we have people on the jury that don't have common sense?"

Archie frowned. "I don't think that's it. I think that Jon David Knox is at work. When he heard about the value of those diamonds, I'm sure he decided to make a determined effort to see that Earl Ray won't get his share!"

"Why not?"

"Earl Ray brought a girl friend to Sleazy's one Saturday night. She was really good looking. Jon David was there and had drunk too much. He ambled over to where she and Earl Ray were sitting. He began to slobber over her and made some crude remarks. Jon David pushed it too far when he put his arm around her. Earl Ray hit him once breaking his nose and knocking out a couple of his teeth. The fight was over quickly, and Jon David has hated him ever since. It wasn't so much about getting hurt and humiliated in front of the bar crowd as it was having to spend money to pay the medical bills."

Ken had been bothered by something he had seen on the seat of Jon David's red pickup as he had walked past it going to lunch. A large brown envelope that had been opened was lying on the passenger seat. It was a business envelope with a return address of "Dodge and Trace, Bail Bonds, Memphis, TN." What business would Mr. Knox have with this company and at this particular time?

Then Ken began to fret. Archie had explained to him that they needed nine votes to win. If the jury stayed deadlocked, the will would not be admitted; and Jeb Shaw would inherit. Archie said either side could ask the judge to set aside a jury verdict as being against the weight of the evidence. But he probably wouldn't because of it being election year. Then they would have to appeal.

Archie announced smugly, "I think I may have an ace in the hole."

"What do you mean?"

"While you had Dr. Fancher on the stand, I received a call from my office. Someone in Memphis sent me a message." He told Ken the details.

———————————

Leah Fornet was in a dejected mood. She had called Josh on her cell phone while he was on the way to the trial in Poston. Leah needed to take off for a few days. Her ten-year old daughter had landed the top role in the school's play which started at one o'clock. She really wanted to attend; her daughter had begged her to come and watch. Leah also needed to visit her elderly grandparents who lived in Savannah, Tennessee. She needed to take them to their doctor in Nashville. If she couldn't be there for them, they would have to hire someone to drive their car.

She was caught up on her work. But when she asked Josh about taking off, he snarled, "No! I want everybody to be available in case something develops in this trial. I can't have you going to some child's stupid play. If I let this get started, every one of you women in the office will want off every time I turn around."

Leah had protested, pointing out that she had come in to work every weekend in the past when asked. She had put the job ahead of her weekend plans every time. Her loyalty should count for something. Josh snapped that she had been paid overtime, and he didn't owe her a thing.

She sat there for a while, depressed. Wearily, she went to Josh's office to get some files to store and accidentally knocked a stack of documents off the corner of his desk onto the floor. She almost cried. There was no way the papers could be placed back in order. Leah guessed that would cause another tirade from Mr. Nutt.

As she struggled to reorganize the papers, she couldn't help but notice that the death certificates of all those Shaw family members obtained from the Office of Vital Records in Little Rock were included. She looked at the names on the certificates as she gathered them together. Leah was about to add one to the stack when she froze. The name shocked her! She studied the information on the sheet. This had to be wrong. It was a death certificate for Jeb Shaw. That couldn't be! He had been in the office not long ago. She retrieved the Shaw family-tree book and turned to the page for Jeb Shaw. The birth date and the names of his parents matched the information on the death certificate. But the date of death on the certificate was two years ago. Wild thoughts raced through her mind. If Jeb is dead, who was this person claiming to be Jeb Shaw?

She went down the hall to the office of her best friend, Sara, and shut the door. Leah disclosed to Sara what she had found. Sara looked on in shock as the information on the death certificate was compared to the page in the family tree. Sara confirmed Leah's thoughts. They sat there awestruck. Sara, a seasoned paralegal, was already unhappy about how she had been treated around the office by the partners and that smart aleck, new lawyer, Stanley Robbs. Sara despised him. She had never seen such arrogant attitudes as these lawyers had. For the past few years, they had treated almost everyone in the office like dirt.

Leah said quietly, "This is not right. Mr. Nutt knew this man is not Jeb Shaw. Maybe not at first; but when the death certificate arrived, it was obvious. If he wins that trial, the hospital will be cheated."

"Yes. And that man, Mr. Joab, wanted to help the hospital, not some trashy relative. Mr. Nutt must have cut a deal with the imposter to share in the estate. Or, he is just so greedy that he wants the fee that will come from the case."

"What should we do?" Leah asked.

"What's right. I know how we can make sure that the scales of justice get balanced. After all, that's what they are always preaching in their staff meetings. Might as well give them a dose of their own medicine."

"How?"

"I'll make a phone call," Sara said.

"We could get fired."

"I don't give a rat's ass. I've had enough of this place. Anyway, this call will be anonymous. Give me that death certificate."

Sara left the building and went around the corner to a cell phone store. She bought a disposable phone and made the call. The person on the other end instructed her to send the death certificate from a commercial fax machine so the transmission couldn't be traced.

Ken got very excited about this development and what Archie proposed to do. He asked Archie if his office in Memphis could assist. Archie told him to relax. "I'm putting this into the capable hands of Sheriff Grady. He will get us some results."

The next morning the jury arrived to a packed courtroom. The first set of spectators who had lost their seats the afternoon before had all arrived very early to get their seats back. The second set, upon arriving later and discovering to their dismay that they were too late to get into the courtroom, took their place in the hall biding their time.

The jury went back to their deliberations. The clock ticked. Archie looked over at Wade, who winked. Archie needed some good news, and it would be better earlier than later. When the jury filed out at lunch, Patricia gave Archie the same hand signal. Still eight to four. Ken noticed and began to sweat.

The judge left the bench. The lawyers went to lunch. All the folks outside the courtroom charged through the doors expecting to get seats for the afternoon session. They stopped in their tracks. None of the spectators had left. They had brought their lunches with them! They weren't about to give up their places. Several had already pulled out bologna and onion sandwiches from paper bags and were munching on them. Others had opened Vienna sausage cans, spilling greasy juice on the courtroom floor in the process. Before the day was over, they would have stomped dropped soda crackers into the juice, making a slippery paste on the polished hardwood.

The jurors returned from lunch to continue deliberations. Sean, the foreman of the jury, was having trouble getting the jurors' attention. They had devoured a large meal at the county's expense, and some were nodding. It appeared they weren't interested in the case anymore. He sighed. If something didn't change, a deadlock was certain. What a shame. This was not how the matter should be left. Justice would be best served if this will was declared the true one.

Sean asked for comments. As it had been since the judge had put the case in their hands, the observation that came forth had nothing to do with the evidence. There was plenty of animosity in the room, and it was directed toward the lawyers and the witnesses. Tempers began to flare. Voices were raised.

Rufus said, "I'll bet Norma Sue never thought anyone would find out about her condition. Serves her right. Now everyone will be looking at her sideways."

Jon David quipped, "Is that disease contagious?" He laughed loudly at his own cleverness.

Patricia took up for Norma Sue and snapped, "I don't appreciate the way that smart lawyer got personal with her. There was no reason for him to ask her about her health. I've got a pink and green butterfly tattoo on my butt, but that's not none of his business! "

The other jurors looked at her in shock, more about the tattoo than the lawyer's remarks. The nurse wondered when she got it. Now watching her play the piano in church would never be the same. The school teacher puzzled over what caused her to choose that particular color combination. Was she a hippy in her youth? Patricia had lived in California when she first got out of college.

The deliberations were still going on in the middle of the afternoon when Sheriff Grady Powers arrived and motioned for Archie and Ken to step down the hall to an empty witness room. He had a printout from the National Crime Information Center, and he was smiling. Archie read the sheet with Ken looking over his shoulder. Their faces beamed.

Ken looked at Archie and said, "Go for it! I'm going to call Monsieur Paul and tell him what we've found."

They all went back into the courtroom. Judge Dennis was reading a newspaper when Linda Nell entered his chambers. "Judge, Archie has a motion for you to hear."

"What about?"

"I don't know, but his team looks very excited."

Puzzled, Judge Dennis put on his robe and went to the bench.

The Nutt team was in the clerk's break area drinking coffee when Crissy came in and announced that they were wanted in the courtroom.

"What about?" Stanley asked. "Has the jury reached a verdict?"

"No. Mr. Baker wants to argue a motion to dismiss your will contest."

"What?"

"Yes. All I know is I heard him tell Miss Linda Nell that they had discovered some credible new evidence of which the court needs to be aware."

The lawyers anxiously moved to the courtroom, trying to imagine what this was about. There was Ken Arnoff beaming from ear to ear. Josh could see that the jury was still out, so a verdict was still forthcoming.

Judge Dennis was already on the bench. The spectators were still and quiet, waiting to hear from Archie.

The judge said, "Proceed, Mr. Baker."

Archie took his time. It was obvious he was enjoying the scene. Archie was gloating inside. Arguing the upcoming motion was about to be the highlight of his career, and the TV cameras were here. After the rug was pulled out from under the defense, he would, no doubt, be the most celebrated lawyer in the state. And, maybe the nation. He paced back and forth. Archie would stop, as if about to speak. Everyone leaned forward with anticipation. Then he resumed his pacing. He straightened his tie and ran his fingers through his hair.

Judge Dennis looked at him crossly. "Mr. Baker, do you want me to set the clock on you?"

Archie smiled. "Oh, no, Your Honor. Not at all. I'm ready."

"Well, begin, and this motion had better not be a waste of my time."

"Your Honor, I have a motion joined by Mr. Arnoff and his firm."

Not to be outdone and to get his share of the public attention, Ken shot out of his chair and said, "That's me, Your Honor. Ken Arnoff of the Ricks, Tyson, Tinsley, and Arnoff Firm located in Memphis."

Judge Dennis glowered at him. "I know who you are. Sit." He did.

During this exchange, Archie had walked to the rail and moved along it from one side of the room to the other, smiling and waving at the spectators. With his back turned to the judge and using his body as a shield, he held up two fingers in the shape of a victory sign and pointed at himself with the other hand. Then he gestured in the direction of the Nutt team and made a slicing motion across his throat. The courtroom cackled. They couldn't wait to hear what he had to say.

Archie went to the lectern. Looking around, he observed that Jeb Shaw wasn't in his seat. "Your Honor, where is Mr. Shaw? He needs to hear what I have to say," he asked.

Stanley and the judge looked around for Jeb.

The bailiff spoke, "Judge, I heard him say he felt sick and had to go outside."

What they didn't know was that a few minutes earlier, Jeb had noticed the sheriff staring at him. He began to feel uneasy; and when the sheriff turned his back, he fled.

Judge Dennis said, "His presence is not necessary. Proceed, Mr. Baker. I, and everyone else in this courtroom, want to hear what *you* have to say."

Archie said, "Your Honor, late yesterday I received some startling news about a party in this case. Acting on the tip, I asked Sheriff Grady Powers to investigate. What he has to say will support my motion for the will contest filed by Mr. Nutt on behalf of his client, Jeb Shaw, to be dismissed."

He turned and looked directly at Josh Nutt who began to sink in his chair. Josh had a distressed look upon his face.

Archie continued, "I call Sheriff Powers to the stand."

When the Sheriff was seated holding some papers in his hand, Archie asked, "Sir, would you state your name and position?"

"My name is Grady Powers. I am the Sheriff of Cade County, Mississippi."

"Were you in the courtroom yesterday when this trial started?"

"Yes."

"Do you remember the man dressed in blue coveralls seated at the respondent's table?"

"Yes."

"Do you remember him standing and telling the jury who he was?"

"Yes."

"What did he say?"

"He said he was Jeb Shaw and he was claiming his cousin's estate."

"Sheriff, did you have a conversation with me yesterday?"

"Yes, I did."

"Did you react accordingly?"

"Yes."

"What did you do?"

"I lifted Jeb Shaw's fingerprints from a sheet of paper he had been holding and also from a soft drink bottle he had left on the table. I had observed him drinking from that same bottle."

"And?"

"I sent them to the NCIC. I received a printout from them a while ago."

"Who do the prints match?"

"A small-time crook with an extensive criminal record named Walt Mason. He has a record of insurance fraud, arson, and false claims. He has been in and out of prison often."

The courtroom went wild! Judge Dennis began banging on the bench with a carpenter's hammer that he had borrowed from the janitor to replace his broken gavel. "Order! Order!" he shouted.

Several minutes passed before the noise abated. Stanley and Lillie Bess looked as if they were about to faint. Josh Nutt was white as a sheet.

"Did you find out anything else?"

"Yes, I called a colleague of mine who is a sheriff in an Arkansas county. He said this guy, Mason, has a reputation of convincing lawyers to fall for his scams. Mason is really shrewd. He continually searches for financial opportunities. Walt Mason will always have a fake family or friend to participate and fit into his current scam."

Archie smiled. "So, the man who came here claiming he was Jeb Shaw is not the real Jeb Shaw?"

"No, he is not. I have here a death certificate from the State of Arkansas that certifies that the real Jeb Shaw died two years ago."

"Who does it say that he was survived by?"

"No one."

Archie spoke, "Your Honor, in light of the testimony of Sheriff Powers, I move that the will contest be dismissed. And in light of the revelation that the real Jeb Shaw had no heirs, I request that the court adjudicate that the will offered for probate is the true Last Will and Testament of Joab McMath."

The judge looked around. All eyes were upon him. He said, "It doesn't matter what that certificate says about no heirs. The time has passed for anyone to assert a claim as an heir. The only one who came forward was an imposter. I hereby grant your motion, Mr. Baker and the will contest is dismissed. The will is admitted for probate."

The courtroom erupted again. Ken Arnoff and his staff went wild with joy!

When order was restored, the judge said, "Bring the jury out."

The noise of the celebration had carried through the door of the jury room. The jury couldn't imagine what was happening. They had just taken their twelfth vote and were still deadlocked at eight to four. Sean, the foreman, was about to send word to the judge that it was certain that no one would change his or her position. The jurors filed to their seats. Jon David was happy. He and his cohorts had hung in there. But he couldn't believe his ears when the Judge simply thanked them for their service and informed them that something unusual had happened which caused him to rule for the will. Jon David couldn't wait to get to Lola's to learn what took the case from the jury's hands.

As the last of the crowd left the courthouse that day, Archie, Ken Arnoff, Wade, Earl Ray, and Henry, the Musician, lingered behind. They were overjoyed. Someone pulled out a calculator and began to estimate the value of what Earl Ray and the hospital had just inherited.

Henry said, "I'm going to take my share in four carat stones. Then I'm going back to Muleshoe and give each lady in the bank a nice diamond."

Wade agreed, "I'll match that offer. Each woman there should have two."

Ken said, "When the Dallas broker gets through appraising the diamonds, why don't we meet in Memphis at the hospital and divide them?"

"Does he have any idea what the total value will be?" Archie asked.

"I called him a while ago, and he thinks the value will be a minimum of one hundred, nine million dollars!" Henry said.

CHAPTER 33
A TRIP IN TIME

In late November, Wade and Archie were at the Merci Hospital for a meeting with Ken and Monsieur Paul. The day before, Wade and Grady had arrived back in Central City from Texas. They had the diamonds, which had been released by the Texas court. The stones had been appraised and bagged into two lots, one for the hospital and one for Earl Ray. After the diamonds were delivered, Archie could close Mr. Joab's estate. Archie had release documents to be signed by Monsieur Paul, and Wade had the hospital's share of the stones.

Wade had stopped in the lobby to make a call on his cell phone. After the call was over, Wade was walking down the hall when he heard a sweet, familiar voice, "Hey, big man. What are you doing here?"

He turned. There was Marla, dressed in her hospital uniform. He smiled. "Hello. How are you?"

She returned his smile and replied, "Fine!"

Wade could see that she was relaxed. He recognized that she was sending vibes of confidence that he wouldn't reveal her other side to anyone at the hospital. As Wade studied her, he began to think again that Toby might be right. Marla just might be prettier than Norma Sue.

She asked, "You didn't expect to see me here, did you?"

"I didn't, but I knew you worked at this hospital."

"Oh. I told you that already?"

"No, you didn't. You just said you worked at a hospital here in town. There are a half dozen in Memphis."

She looked at him quizzically. "Well then, how did you know it was this one?"

"A friend of your grandmother's in Muleshoe, Texas, told me."

Marla became very still. "Have you been to Muleshoe?"

"Yes."

"Why?"

"To pick up something very valuable that belongs to the hospital," Wade answered. Marla didn't reply. He said, "I have to go to a meeting. Could I have coffee with you afterwards? We need to talk."

"Sure. I would like that. Having coffee with you. Meet me at my work station and we'll go down the street." She told him where she could be found, turned, and walked back down the hall.

Wade went on to the meeting room where he found Archie, Ken, and Monsieur Paul gathered around a table. The hospital comptroller and several other employees were also there. Wade opened the soft, protective container of diamonds and pulled out the clear bags of stones which he laid on the table. Whistles erupted from those who had not already seen the diamonds. Archie and the comptroller checked off the individual bags against the master list. Archie had Ken and Monsieur Paul sign a receipt and a joinder to the court document that would permit the Joab McMath estate to be closed.

Sighs of relief were expelled. Archie said, "This is one for the books!"

Ken grinned. "You've got that right. My real joy will come when I'm sitting here tomorrow sticking a release in front of Josh Nutt's nose for their share of the contents of lockbox number thirteen!"

They all laughed.

Ken said, "When my tag comes due next month, I'm going to get a personalized plate, namely '13'! I'll drive downtown at noon as much as I can to be around the office building where the Janes Firm is located! I'll time it to be at the entrance when they all come out on the street for lunch."

Then he asked Archie, "Tell me, my friend, who did you get to serve the papers on Josh at the party? I had an anonymous call, the morning of the party, alerting me that I should be in the room when Nutt was to make his remarks and there would be much fun for my firm, at his expense."

"Who else but Henry, the Musician. He is a master at getting even!"

"I'll keep that in mind. There might be a use for him in the future," replied Ken.

Monsieur Paul invited them to the hospital's break room where a celebration for the hospital had been arranged. Wade excused himself. "I have an afternoon date with a pretty woman!"

When the others left the room for the party, Wade went to Marla's work area. She had finished her last task and was anxiously waiting. She said, "Come on, We'll go to one of my favorite places." She took him to a cozy little brasserie around the corner where they were seated at a booth in the back. When the waitress appeared, they ordered coffee.

Wade said, "I'll tell you in confidence why I'm here today. I delivered a large stash of diamonds to the hospital valued in the multi-millions. Let me explain."

Marla solemnly listened as Wade explained that Joab McMath had paid for her medical expenses when she was a baby. He said, "Mr. Joab knew your grandmother, who had befriended his brother in World War II. Mr. Joab found out that you were hospitalized for an extended time after you were born. He had been charged with a legacy from his brother but had never been acted upon it. When Mr. Joab became aware of your medical problems and where you were being treated, he felt your illness had happened for a reason. He sold enough diamonds to pay your bills and to make a substantial donation to Merci. Mr. Joab was so impressed with the hospital and its mission that he contributed every year at Christmas. Monsieur Paul said Mr. Joab requested you not be told who took care of your bills and for his future donations to be kept confidential."

Tears came to Marla's eyes.

Wade continued, "Look, baby, I wasn't acquainted with your grandmother, but Mr. Joab was. I met a wonderful lady in Muleshoe who grew up with your mother. This lady spoke so well of your grandmother that I feel like I knew her, too. Would you do something for me?"

"What?"

"I want you to drop your dance job. You owe your grandmother that. I understand why you dance, but it's time to quit. But don't move on to the next best thing. Just dig in and settle down. Your work here is helping a lot of children."

With that, Marla began to weep uncontrollably. She began to shake. The waitress glanced their way with concern. Wade moved in by Marla and put his arms around her. Between sobs, she let it all spill out: her whole life and all that had gone wrong; her mistakes; her disappointments; why she danced; what kept her going.

Wade offered sympathy. He kindly discussed some of his life's lessons with her for comparison. Finally, Marla regained her composure.

She left the booth and went to the restroom to redo her makeup. When she returned to the booth, she hugged Wade and smiled.

He asked, "Feel better?"

"Yes. I'm good to go now. Thank you so much."

He walked her back to work, holding her hand all the way. As they stood by the entrance, she turned to him and meekly asked, "Would you take me out sometime?"

Wade said, "I would like to. Christmas will be here soon. By then I will be able to bring you something really pretty."

————————

The next morning, Wade met with Earl Ray and Henry at Sleazy's to divide their share of the McMath diamonds. Darlene let them go into Zeke's office. They closed the door, pulled down the blinds on its window and emptied the diamonds from a green bank bag onto Zeke's desk. Wade and Earl Ray's share was tolled to assemble Archie's cut which was fifteen percent by their agreement. Henry offered to deliver Archie's stones to him. Wade, out of the corner of his eye, caught Earl Ray frowning. He replied, "That won't be necessary. I'll drop them by his office. I'm less apt than you to be robbed on the way back to town." Earl Ray relaxed. Henry placed his share in a leather briefcase, left the office, winked at Darlene, got into his pink Cadillac, and quickly disappeared. He said he didn't want to be caught in a beer joint by the feds because he was still on probation. Henry didn't want to be picked up before he had a chance to enjoy his windfall.

As they sat there reflecting on Jerry and Mr. Joab's legacy, Earl Ray spoke, "Okay, Wade. I made a call to the army a few days ago. I have clearance to tell something if you will keep it to yourself."

"Earl Ray, have you ever known me to be anything but confidential?"

Earl Ray laughed. "No."

Then he started. "Wade, I don't know how you found out. You discovered that I didn't come back home from basic training. You nailed down that the reason had something to do with my ability to speak Korean and that the capture of the *USS Pueblo* was part of the puzzle. But there's no way you could ever imagine what happened to me. You were right; the army did know that I could speak Korean. When that ship was captured, the country was in political turmoil about our involvement in Vietnam. President Johnson's popularity had tanked, and the elections were coming up. LBJ needed to commit more troops to Nam; but to do so would cause the riots and protests that were going on around the country to intensify. There was a belief that the military purposefully had the *Pueblo* go into North Korean waters so it would be captured. That way, Washington could use the incident as an excuse to call up National Guard and Army Reserve units to counter any North Korean aggression. If the confrontation cooled down, then the activated U. S. troops could be diverted to Nam. The military was aware that no sailor on the ship could speak Korean. How long the sailors would be in captivity was unknown. The North Koreans had the reputation of being the most brutal people in the world to their prisoners of war. So the military came up with the idea to plant servicemen in with the Pueblo crew to assist and support them. The plan was to send five servicemen ashore to North Korea under the ruse of a commando raid to rescue the *Pueblo* crew. They intended for the commandos to be captured. Our intelligence had a pretty good knowledge of where the sailors were being held.

"The CIA made a hasty search of the personnel records of every single man that was on duty world-wide. They found nineteen who could speak fluent Korean. The five of us chosen were in the best physical and mental condition of the nineteen. We had three weeks of intense training toward what we might face in captivity.

"I found out what my enlistment contract with the National Guard meant. I could be diverted to any other military need that would be in the best interest of my country. The army pulled me out of my training company under the pretense that I had the flu and out of commission long enough that I would have to start basic all over. My buddies in my training company were led to believe I had 'boloed.' Because of winter training in the extreme cold at Ft. Leonard Wood, a lot of trainees came down with flu and pneumonia. No one would give it a second thought that a soldier disappeared from the ranks.

"The plan worked well. One night in February, a submarine dropped us off near the coast, and we rowed ashore. I was the only army guy in the bunch and the only enlisted man. The others were three navy officers and one marine officer. We were hoping to be captured without any of us being shot or killed. Contact was soon made with a North Korean patrol. Gunfire ensued, and one Navy officer was shot in the leg. Fortunately, he did recover from the wound.

"For the first few weeks, we went through hell. The torture they put us through was inhumane. I didn't think I could survive. The funny thing about the situation was that we resisted their torture as long as we could. Then, one by one, we all 'confessed' that our purpose was to rescue the *Pueblo* crew. Our captors went for that, which was what our intelligence wanted. We all kept telling the same story, and finally the Koreans believed us. No one ever even hinted what our real reason was for being there.

"I took my resisting too far. I always did have a stubborn streak in me. I lasted longer than the officers. Then one day, the Koreans hauled me into a room that had an open fireplace. They took my shirt off and held me down on a table. This huge Korean pulled a red-hot branding iron out of the coals and plunged it into my back. The Korean symbol for 'Spy' was burned into my back muscles. That was a forever thing, which is what they intended."

Wade winced and asked, "Did you scream?"

"Yeah, Wade, I did. Real loud. I'm surprised you didn't hear me from Cade County! Then I passed out."

"Of course, there was a risk of being held somewhere away from the *Pueblo* crew. Then the Navy and CIA might not be able to locate where we were being kept. We got lucky, if you could call being held by the North Koreans as lucky. Our captors put us into the same prison with the *Pueblo* crew. Those guys sure were glad to see us! The commander of our patrol was able to have immediate contact with the captain of the *Pueblo*. He explained to the captain our mission and passed vital instructions to him.

"The five of us were valuable assets to the sailors, as the CIA had hoped. Our presence definitely made daily prison life more bearable for the Pueblo crew. We understood what the guards were discussing about upcoming treatment and could warn the sailors so they could get prepared. Most of the time, we were able to stay one step ahead of our captors. It was a tremendous boost for morale. Upon our release, every sailor expressed unbelievable gratitude to us five. Many said they would have gone insane if it hadn't been for our presence.

"The captivity lasted nearly a year. We expected that our release was being sought by our diplomats. Waiting was the down side of captivity.

Every single day we hoped we would get the news. When it didn't come, we would be depressed, which had to be fought off. It was like pacing ourselves to not let all hope drift away, but to hold on to at least a tiny bit for the next day.

"The guards were brutal. We figured out that they wouldn't take it too far, because if any of us was killed, the negotiations for our release would be strained. The North Koreans were seeking important concessions from the United States. About three weeks before our eventual release, the ship's captain was called to the prison headquarters for a meeting with a high-ranking North Korean military delegation. They gave him the news that all of us would soon be sent home. The place went wild. The food got better, and we received needed medical attention. Apparently, the Koreans wanted our physical appearance to improve.

"Then it happened. One morning the crew was ordered to formation in the prison yard. A general addressed us in English. He went on a tirade about how stupid we were, how we had insulted the sovereignty of North Korea, and how we were inferior to his people. He told us not to ever come back, as if we were going to book a vacation there soon! As he spoke, he became extremely angry. A long table had been placed in the front of the formation. Soldiers grabbed the five of us who came ashore from the sub. We were dragged to the table and held so tight we couldn't move. The little finger of the left hand of each of us was placed on the edge of the table. I figured what was coming up next when some mean looking soldiers with cleavers approached. The general held his hand up and screamed, 'Example!' When his hand came down, the cleavers did also, chopping our little fingers clean off. I thought the ship's crew was going to rush the butchers, but machine guns were trained on them. They backed down. When we were handed over to the Army at Pyongyang, protests were made about the finger-lopping, but the North Koreans just laughed. It was their Oriental way of sending a message.

"The others in my patrol were awarded the Navy Cross. I didn't get one because I was in the army and they couldn't figure out how to give me a medal and cover it in my personnel file. Typical military. And the North Koreans still have the boat, which really chaps me. I've been denied closure. When I dwell on that thought too long, I binge drink to forget."

Wade asked, "Is this what Mr. Joab was talking about in his will? About you giving part of your life to the service of your country?"

"Yes. Our mission has been kept secret by the navy all these years. Mr. Joab couldn't explain in his will why he provided for me because it was still classified."

"How did Mr. Joab find out about that?"

Earl Ray laughed. "The army told him. The weakest part of their plan to send five guys on that kind of mission was that their absence had to be explained to their family and community. That was not much of a problem for the other four guys since they were career men. The navy could say, if anyone was curious about their prolonged absence that they were on overseas assignments. But I was supposed to be gone only four months to basic training. Then I was to come home with James Henry. The military had to have me on the insertion team because, not only could I speak Korean the best, but I had also learned a lot of their customs from Mrs. Kak. Also, I was a qualified sniper. You know my parents were deceased; I had no siblings. So the CIA sent a couple of agents to Central City to find a dependable person who would keep his mouth shut and would cover my absence in the community. They contacted Mr. Joab, who I had recommended, and found the perfect cover. His character was impeccable. Before I left the country, I wrote a bunch of undated letters of how I had volunteered for the regular army, was stationed in Europe, and what was going on in my life. The CIA had a good paper hanger who could forge the appropriate date on them and make it look like my handwriting. The letters were mailed to Mr. Joab at intervals, and he would mention them around town."

Earl Ray laughed ruefully, "I found out later that hardly anyone missed me! When I came home, Mr. Joab and I joked about how he rarely had to tell about getting a letter. The two agents who came here to check him out met with me several times in my preparation. They would always laugh at what they heard the coffee crowd talk about at Lola's. Both had grown up in big cities and were amused at how country people lived."

Wade became pensive for a while. Finally, he asked, "What did that general, who had your finger cut off, look like?"

Earl Ray became curious about that question. He looked carefully at Wade and replied, "Well, he was short and heavy. He was an older guy, about your age. I won't forget him, though. He had a messed-up face. It looked like someone had broken his jaw years ago and it didn't heal very well."

Wade stood up, rubbed his forehead, and sighed, "You know, I feel like my whole life has passed in an unbroken circle. I think I'm gonna go to the coast for a few weeks and fish for some speckled trout." With that he turned and walked out of the room leaving Earl Ray staring at his back.

On his way back to Central City with Archie's share locked safely in his trunk, Wade was still thinking of Earl Ray's story. Being distracted he made a wrong turn and found himself going down the street on which Rita lived. As he passed her duplex he did a double-take. There, at her front door, was parked Sherman's vehicle. He grinned. "Well, well, well!"

A few minutes later he entered Archie's office. He handed Archie the container holding his diamonds. Archie nonchalantly placed it on the floor in a corner of the room.

Archie asked, "Where is Henry?"

Wade replied, "Headed to Memphis. He claimed he was going to have a huge gold and diamond ring made which he would wear everyday as a souvenir.

Archie laughed. "Well, he earned it!"

Wade asked, "Say, Archie, I've been wondering what happened to Mr. Joab's original will."

Archie chuckled slyly, "I've had that same thought. Do you reckon it's in a lockbox at a bank we don't know about?"

ABOUT THE AUTHOR

Sonny Clanton has practiced law for a number of years in Calhoun City, Mississippi, where he now lives. *Mr. Joab's Will* is his first novel. He is at work writing his next novel.

91283708R00162

Made in the USA
San Bernardino, CA
26 October 2018